W9-APW-101

Advance Praise

"A smart and funny novel about Hollywood, but where it truly shines is in Christopher Noxon's stunning and painfully accurate depiction of the complex rhythms and growing pains of a marriage."
— Jonathan Tropper, author of *This Is Where I Leave You* and *One Last Thing Before I Go*

"Behind every great man there's a great woman... and in Noxon's telling, behind every great woman there's a charming, deeply conflicted guy (sometimes holding a very expensive handbag). Hilarious and unflinching, *Plus One* is a funny, sharply observed, heartbreaking look at love, power, and happily-ever-after in Hollywood."
— Jennifer Weiner, author of *All Fall Down*, *The Next Best Thing*, and *Good in Bed*

"A funny, sharply observed novel about a guy with a first-world problem—a wife who's a hugely successful TV writer and producer—and the identity crisis that goes along with it. Noxon has reimagined the Hollywood novel from a whole new perspective."
— Tom Perrotta, author of *Election*, *Little Children*, and *The Leftovers*

"Well observed, honest, and laugh-out-loud funny, *Plus One* deftly tells a story from the inside of show business about being on the outside."
— Matthew Weiner, creator of *Mad Men*

"Hilarious and whip-smart, with a big beating heart at its center. I love this book, and so will you."
— Dana Reinhardt, author of *We Are the Goldens*

Plus One

a novel

CHRISTOPHER NOXON

PROSPECT
·PARK·
BOOKS

Published by Prospect Park Books

2359 Lincoln Avenue
Altadena, California 91001
www.prospectparkbooks.com

PROSPECT
· PARK ·
BOOKS

Distributed by Consortium Book Sales & Distribution
www.cbsd.com

Library of Congress Cataloging in Publication Data

Noxon, Christopher, author.
  Plus One : a novel / by Christopher Noxon.
    pages cm
  ISBN 978-1-938849-42-8 (hardback)
  1. Marriage--Fiction. 2. Marketing executives--Fiction. 3. Women television writers--Fiction. 4. Success--Fiction. 5. Hollywood (Los Angeles, Calif.)--Fiction. I. Title.
  PS3614.O97P58 2015
  813'.6--dc23
                              2014013282

Cover design by Robert Russell.
Illustrations by Christopher Noxon.
Book layout and design by Amy Inouye & Renee Nakagawa.
Printed in the United States of America.

For Jenji

One

Alex pulled the invitation out of his breast pocket and laid it on his lap, admiring once again how the lettering danced across the creamy cardstock, the gold metallic script bunched up tightly to fit in the allotted space: FIGGY SHERMAN-ZICKLIN. How the in-laws had harrumphed when he and Figgy had announced, way back when, their plans to hyphenate—and to further flout custom by putting her last name in the showy cleanup spot. Because who said they couldn't? Everything was up for grabs, and SHERMAN-ZICKLIN had a better ring to it than ZICKLIN-SHERMAN. Okay, it was a mouthful. And sure, it did kind of sound like a pharmaceutical conglomerate. But no, the kids would not get hand cramps every time they wrote their name on a school worksheet.

No one was harrumphing now, were they? Here she was, FIGGY SHERMAN-ZICKLIN, nominated for Best Comedy in the roman-numeral-whatever Primetime Emmy Awards. And here he was, the soft shaygetz SHERMAN at the center of all those hard, glottal, zingy, Semitic consonants, gliding along in a chauffeured Town Car through a camera-ready L.A. afternoon.

It was crazy, all of it, more than Alex could begin to get any sort of reasonable handle on. The Emmys weren't *real*; they came from inside the TV. He was pretty sure they were animated—they occurred in a make-believe world of fictional, distant-realm characters, ladies with shiny shoulders and men with faces three sizes too big for their heads. The Emmys may not have been quite as fictional as, say, the Oscars, but they were still plenty pretend, best viewed at home with wine and pizza and a gay or two for color commentary.

Barely fourteen months ago, Alex was the sensible one with a real job and Figgy was a fingernail-chewing, sporadically employed comedy writer who spent her days in a Cuban bakery drinking carrot juice until her teeth turned orange while banging out pilot scripts everyone liked but no one ever made. Until, miraculously, someone did. Her eleventh pilot, a dark and dirty dramedy about a housewife who runs a prostitution ring out of a scrapbooking shop, was picked up by a premium-cable network looking to "make some noise." Now she was in Valentino and he was arm candy.

"Have I got lipstick on my teeth?" Figgy said, peering into a compact. "Oh God—I'm terrifying. I'm a sea cow. Or a manatee. Whichever one. I'm a pre-op transsexual. I'm a fucking tranny sea cow. God!"

"Fig, stop," said Alex, scooting over and giving her thigh a squeeze, feeling the silver silk rub against her Spanx with a synthetic squeak. "You're gorgeous. Great looking. And you said it yourself—nobody looks at the writers anyway."

"True," she sighed, snapping the mirror shut. "We're the bathroom break. Fuck it. Why are we bothering with this at all? Why are we wasting the babysitter? Let's commandeer this bad boy and go for burritos!"

Was she serious? Would she really rather spackle the interior of a Town Car with carne asada than go to the actual Emmys? He wasn't entirely sure. She was wildly impulsive—she delighted in abandoning full shopping carts, dashing off on interstate road trips, and otherwise zigging off course at the last possible minute. It was Figgy who decided to call off the big formal wedding in favor of a civil ceremony that had all the pomp and romance of a driver's license renewal. Alex didn't regret it for a second—he'd had no desire to stand under a chuppah with three hundred of her family's temple friends and his crazy goy relatives—but for the Emmys, he wanted the full experience.

The truth was, Alex wouldn't miss this for anything. Figgy grew up on the funky, lower-rent peripheries of show business— her mom was a once-fabulous, now-cranky Hollywood party girl who'd married four times, twice to agents and currently to a Bronx-born hustler who made a mint in the seventies selling videotape supplies; Figgy had been to the Emmys herself when she was nine, famously falling asleep in Cloris Leachman's lap. But for Alex, all this was new. He'd grown up two hours and many worlds away in a mountain hippie hamlet near the Ojai Valley. He got comic mileage out of his upbringing now—people loved hearing about his Birkenstock lesbian mom, the llama who lived on their land, and the Indian shaman who shacked up on the back porch. But the reality was a lot lonelier and more chaotic than he let on. He didn't like to talk about it. Anyway, he'd gotten out, left all that behind, worked though his issues.

And now here he was, actual Alex in a real-life Town Car, with its impossibly immaculate exterior and musky oil smell and walnut inlays and immaculate black carpet so soft and lush that he wanted to rub his face in it. He pressed a button and the armrest slid back with a pleasing hiss. Beneath it he found a tin of candied almonds, a chilled bottle of Dom with a note from Figgy's agent, Jess, and the fall issue of *Elite Spirit*, a glossy brick of a magazine devoted to mini-jets and maxi-wristwatches.

The man at the wheel swiveled around and produced a card. Devon Winchester, Executive Transport.

"Well hello there, Devon Winchester," Alex said with a smile. "That's quite a name. You from Windsor Castle?"

"No sir," he said. "Inglewood."

Alex learned that Devon had two boys and a girl, but he and their mom weren't together, owing to some legal trouble Devon got into a few years ago, but he was dealing much better now and making some music and maybe he should put on his CD? Some serious jams. Gonna blow up. Maybe they could use a song on the show?

"Absolutely, put that on," Alex said, glad they were relating. Maybe they'd be friends.

"So you excited for tonight?" Devon asked. "I shouldn't be saying this, but I freaking *love* your show. Girlfriend and I binge-watched the whole season on demand in one night—up 'til 4 a.m. Could not even stop. Shit's crack."

Figgy leaned forward and craned her face over the seat. "Well thank you very much, Devon," she said. "So great you've actually seen it."

"Aw no way—it's the *lady's* show?" Devon put his face up to the mirror and smiled brightly. "I didn't realize. All my papers say is I'm driving the EP of *Tricks*—and it's you? No way! I like that *a lot.*"

"Well thank you very much," Figgy said, as Devon laughed and banged his fist on the steering wheel. "Not that I have a chance in hell of actually *winning.*"

"You never know," Devon said. "You watch. You could be going home with some metal tonight."

Alex sat up in his seat. "We're just happy for the party."

He'd been parroting the same line all week—it seemed like the thing to say. He'd checked the blogs and read the trades; the official line put the odds of a *Tricks* win at thirty to one. And that was factoring in the new voting rules and a palpable anti-network, anti-establishment mood among Academy membership. No comedy with women in lead roles had won since *Sex and the City*, and everyone knew that was really a show about gay men. It seemed to Alex that the whole enterprise was just another big corporate sham—deeply sexist, wildly political and not at all friendly to Figgy's frank, abrasive, lady-centric take on the world. *Tricks* was a token show, singled out as proof the industry valued women—even if it excluded them from the top jobs or overall deals or benefits that were the industry's genuine rewards.

But that didn't mean Alex couldn't hope. He knew how deeply uncool it was to give even half a shit about the Emmys, but the truth was he stupidly, desperately hoped for a win. It would mean so much. For Figgy and the show, obviously, but also for him. He couldn't help feeling like winning would validate their whole mismatched-but-mysteriously-right partnership. Him, the agreeable, even-keeled, happy-go-lucky husband; her, the opinionated, emotional, whip-smart, crazy-creative wife. He pictured her climbing up to the mic, clutching her chest and pouring her heart out to him, tearing up in a schmaltzy "you complete me" moment, like Oprah rhapsodizing about Stedman's "grace and dignity."

"You're sweet, Devon," Figgy cut in, fishing around for an Altoid. "But all I'm hoping for tonight is some nice shampoo in the swag bag."

Then she stretched out her arms, entwining her palms and twisting them around in a fancy yoga flex. Alex watched her stretch, unsure how to read the body language. He couldn't tell what she really thought. She'd been dismissive and super casual ever since the nominations were announced, rolling her eyes when he asked if she'd written a speech and making a *pew-pew* sound when his mom told her to make room on the mantle.

Alex, meanwhile, could barely contain his excitement. A few days before the awards, he paid a visit to Sergio's Formalwear, a storefront a few doors down from their vet. It was a musty, over-stocked shop, and Sergio turned out to be a pudgy Filipino guy who, after helping Alex up on a stool and going at him with his measuring tape, barely made a peep when informed that the tux wasn't for a quinceañera or a wedding or some other ceremony that marked the quaint rituals of mere mortals; this was for *the Emmys.*

"So you're on the TV?" Sergio asked, motioning to a wall of headshots picturing female wrestlers, seventies child actors, and puppets. "You have picture?"

"No, not me," Alex said. "My wife. She's up for best comedy. Very big."

"So *she's* on the TV?"

"Not her, no," he said. "She's a writer. It's her words—her whole *world.* She makes the show."

"So no picture," said Sergio, measuring his inseam with a little more roughness than Alex felt was entirely necessary.

The tux fit well enough, even if the first words to pop into Alex's mind when he put it on were: *dickhead maître d'.* Even so, with the dress shoes that Figgy picked up special for the occasion, Alex figured he looked decent enough—if not dapper, at least a passable partner to Figgy, who had secured the loaner Valentino through her costume department, with pleats and cinches and underwires and all sorts of enhancing lifts and supports.

"Be outside and ready to get us, okay—maybe circle around?" Figgy said, as the car funneled through traffic. "We may flee early, after we go down in flames to that ABC crap about the *lawyers.* I'd like to get home early and let the babysitter go."

And there it was again: the yoga flex. What was that?

Then the Town Car lurched to a stop and the door was flung open by a man with an earbud and a crewcut. Alex hopped out and looked up at the Shrine, a massive auditorium adorned with Moorish spires that extended upward like mounds of soft serve. Helicopters hovered above towering banks of bleachers. The entrance was flooded with a saturated glare that turned everyone into players on a soundstage. Everywhere there was lipstick and cleavage, tiny waists and gleaming dentistry. Welcome to Toontown. It really was a cartoon world.

Alex straightened up as the assembled fans and photographers zeroed in on them. He felt a sudden, palpable rush of longing and excitement. He adjusted his sunglasses and ducked his head down, prolonging the moment. For this brief second, he was someone they'd come to see—not a star, obviously, but maybe the sitcom best friend, or the host of a PBS wildlife series.

"Hey!" Figgy called. She was still in the car, reaching out and tugging at the tail of his jacket. "Little help?"

Alex swiveled and offered his hand. Figgy bounded up and plowed into the crowd, immediately falling into what appeared to be a strictly understood protocol. The actors and nominees flitted around the edges of the press lineup, pollinating at ripe spots along the way. Meanwhile the unfamous were funneled into the faster-moving current at the center.

"Come on," said Figgy over her shoulder, sticking her elbow back and guiding his hand around her inner arm. "Squire me."

Alex gave her a squeeze and started to join the procession, but within a few steps, Figgy was intercepted. In a flurry of squeals, a press agent from the network introduced herself as "one of the Melissas," issued a command on her walkie-talkie, uncoupled Figgy from Alex, and herded her away into the *Tricks* posse: five writers, two network executives, and Katherine Pool, the Ozarks-born, Yale-educated actress who played Toni, the housewife-turned-madam.

"Figgy honey—don't you clean up nice?" Katherine exclaimed, pulling her in for a stiff embrace. "Heels even! I don't think I've *ever* seen you out of those marvelous clogs!"

Figgy grimaced and poked out one foot. "I've already got blisters. But look at you! That dress? Gorgeous."

Katherine made a little curtsey, and the two of them headed toward the press line, all smiles, no visible sign whatsoever of the epic power plays they'd waged against each other over the past year. Katherine was an incredible actress—she had a wide-open, plate-shaped face that appeared to be constantly churning on some deep, mysterious thought—but she was famously difficult. Most of it was standard diva stuff—lateness, rudeness, a refusal to wear anything that didn't show off her yoga-toned arms—but her big problem revolved around the show itself. She spent much of the season complaining that her dialogue was substandard and out-of-character and, worst of all, there wasn't enough of it.

Alex made his way into the crowd, joining a lane of traffic just behind the press line. After a few steps, he realized he'd fallen in with the wife pack, a cluster of smooth-skinned, spooked-looking ladies from the leafier districts of the 310. He recognized a few as spouses of guys on Figgy's staff—they were stay-at-home moms, mostly; they met up for coffee or play dates when production kept their husbands at work until all hours. But just as he'd avoided them at work parties and ignored their occasional emails, he now took a few steps sideways out of their wake.

He didn't *dislike* them—not at all! They were all nice enough, and of course he had nothing but respect for their choices as women and mothers. But he wasn't one of them. His life maybe wasn't as over-the-top as all this, but it was at least vaguely creative. Alex was an account manager for BestSelf, a boutique ad shop that worked with nonprofits—or as described by his boss, the aggro-smarmy Jeff Kanter, BestSelf was "a values-driven agency." At the moment, Alex was working on testicular cancer, organic school lunches, and shaken babies. He took pride in finding clever ways to employ the dark arts of marketing for righteous causes. Nonprofits didn't bring in big money, but Alex did okay, well enough to have covered them through the lean years. He'd also taken full advantage of the agency's "family-friendly flex-time" policy and health insurance, working the system to get six months of paternity leave when the kids were born.

Close to the entrance to the hall, Alex stopped on the red carpet and stood on his tippy toes, peering over the coiffed heads. He spotted the *Tricks* crew at the end of the press line, Katherine huddled with Melissa Rivers and Figgy giving a thumbs-up to a reporter for Slavic TV. He caught up with Figgy at the towering front doors of the auditorium and led her inside.

Figgy leaned close. "Makeup check," she whispered. "Am I smudged? That guy from *Access Hollywood* was practically licking me. Have I got monster face?"

"No monster face," he said, looping a strand of her stiffly ironed hair over her ear. "You're perfect. Breathe. And breathe again."

Figgy smiled, the two of them having recently decided that a yoga studio near their house was obviously attempting to one-up and out-do mere breathers with a big sign out front that commanded: "Breathe. And Breathe Again."

"You know I love you, right?" she said.

"Right back at you."

Alex planted a kiss on her cheek and reached over Figgy's shoulder to flag down a tray of champagne. They downed their glasses in quick gulps and headed into the crowd, huddling close and submitting to the raw excitement of the spectacle. Alex was surprised at how pleasing it was, seeing so many heretofore fictional characters in person (Jon Stewart, futzing with his bow-tie! Rupert Murdoch at a urinal! Janeane Garofalo, smoking a Camel!). When they found their seats—center row, middle back, not far at all from the podium, a good sign—Alex was struck by a sweet, tingling, intoxicating feeling of... what was it?

Hopefulness? Hubris? Maybe it was just the proximity to so many fawned-over, sought-after powerful people. He got a chemical jolt of adrenaline just being in their air space, seeing them shift in their seats and scratch their marvelous faces and tug at their tailored collars—they were just people, after all, people not all that different from him. All the success in the room, all the fame, all the confidence and recognition and ego—for this moment, anyway, Alex felt like just being here was to be assimilated, incorporated, sucked into their force fields.

And the show itself—even that was more exciting than he'd thought possible for what was essentially a glorified TV taping, with an announcer breaking in during commercial breaks to remind everyone to keep smiling, keep clapping, keep up the *energy*. Ricky Gervais was a genius! And the interpretive dance tribute to the World War II miniseries: actually kind of moving! Alex felt irrationally happy for winners he deemed deserving, of whom there seemed to be a great many, more so than usual, which led to a faint hope that Figgy's dark-horse oddity might pull an upset.

Please, Alex thought, please let it happen. Just this once. Let her win.

The best comedy award came midway through the show, just after a commercial break. Alex knew it was imminent when an ox-shaped guy with a camera on his shoulder came loping up the aisle, crouched down and aimed his lens directly at them. Oh God, he thought: the reaction shot. He squeezed Figgy's arm. It suddenly occurred to him that his wife might actually flip off the camera when the award went to the lawyer show. "Don't even sweat this, 'k?" he whispered in her ear. "Just keep smiling."

And then it happened. Chris Rock opened the envelope, shook his head, grinned, and announced the winner. It took a second for Alex to realize what he'd said; by the time he rose to his feet, Figgy and the whole *Tricks* cast and crew were stampeding forward, down the row of seats and into the aisle. After climbing the steps to the stage, Figgy marched to the front of the crowd and exchanged a greeting with Rock (Alex couldn't believe it—did his wife just *fist bump* Chris Rock?).

"I want to thank the Academy and all the nominees—you guys are amazing, but sorry fellas!" she said. "This one's for the ladies!"

A great whoop went up from the crowd. Figgy held up the statue. She wasn't blinking or breathing hard or betraying any writerly anxiety at all. She beamed. Her skin looked luminous, dewy. It was as if she'd been buffed with the fame loofah.

"Oh gosh—I want to thank my killer agent Jess and my manager Jerry—you guys are *animals*," Figgy said. "And to Kate and all our fabulous actors. And to Neil at the network and Wanda at the studio and everyone on my crew and my whole darling family, you guys are amazing!"

Alex let out a sound: half-laugh, half-sob. He was suddenly aware of his fists, clenched tight and balled at his chest. Out of the corner of his eye he could see the blinking red light on the camera. He tried and failed to relax his hands. Breathe, he thought. Breathe again.

Figgy paused, nodded once, and seemed to reflect for a moment. "Most of all," she swallowed. "I want to thank... the Academy, for finally recognizing the oppressed minority of Jewish girls from Sherman Oaks. Rise up, my sisters!"

A huge round of applause sounded from the crowd, and Figgy raised the trophy in triumph. Alex clapped along as she was led away from the mic and into a darkened crowd off stage.

• • •

Figgy didn't come back after the next commercial break, or the one after that, leaving Alex to sit and stew, his fingertips tingling, a flutter in his throat, and a disbelieving grin locked on his face.

Her seat was soon snatched up by an older woman in a saggy, peach-colored gown. Alex gave her a confused greeting.

"Seat filler," she said, snapping her gum. He shook his head, not understanding. "We come out for the crowd shots. So it's always a full house? Don't worry—I'll skedaddle as soon as—"

"Oh, it's fine," Alex said, embarrassed that he needed the explanation.

"That was your wife, wasn't it?" she asked. "The *Tricks* lady?"

He nodded. "Right—Miss *Tricks*. Do you know if I can go backstage? For the press conference?"

"I wouldn't try that," she said, her breath sugary and hot. "You need a pass to get back there. Anyway, there's only enough seat fillers to cover the winners. You sit tight—she'll be back."

Then the stage lights brightened and the music swelled. Alex clapped and tried to feign interest in the other awards. Where was Figgy? In the moment after she won, he'd gone blank. It was as if he'd been concussed by the shock of it. Had he kissed her before she jumped up? One second Rock was ripping open the envelope... the next Figgy was up on stage, the speech spilling out, the joke, the thanks, all those names, the agent and manager and star....

Of course, he thought: *She'd had her remarks prepared all along.* He thought back to the limo and the way she'd stretched, that fancy yoga flex—it was a tell! Beneath all that never-gonna-happen bluster, she'd somehow known her name was in that envelope. Why *shouldn't* it be her? She was like this about much of her life—mysteriously certain. Whereas Alex was constantly plotting contingencies, drifting from one thing to another and clinging to vague notions of realistic expectations, Figgy plowed forward with the force of someone who absolutely deserved what it was they were as sure as hell about to get. To Alex, she seemed magic this way—"The force is strong in this one," he'd say, as she got the gig or the parking spot or the phone call she'd been counting on all along.

Not that she ever admitted such certainty out loud. That was part of her magic, the Evil Eye part, the part inherited from her gypsy-Ashkenazi ancestors: One never acknowledges or predicts good fortune, lest one incur fate's capricious wrath.

Figgy reappeared at last in the show's final few minutes, trophy clutched close like a football, the seat filler scurrying away at the sight of her. Alex leapt up in the narrow space between the seats, managing to get one arm around her in an awkward side-hug.

She pulled him close as they settled back into their seats.

"Oh God, honey—I am so, so sorry," she whispered. "I was a hot mess up there. I don't know what happened."

"Stop!" Alex said. "You were great."

"But the speech? I can't believe I pulled a Swank."

Alex narrowed his eyes, not getting it.

"You know—Hillary Swank? When she forgot Chad Lowe? That's all anyone remembers about her Oscar: forgot Chad. I'm so sorry—I meant to say something nice—I wanted to! But with those insane lights and the guy waving me offstage, all I could think of was my list of work people and my *darling* family. Darling? How lame is that? Like some basket of kitty cats?"

She let her weight fall against him, plopping the trophy into his lap. "I'm such a fucking idiot."

Alex shook his head and laughed. "It's fine. I'm fine. *Seriously*. You were incredible. Don't you dare get into a funk right now— this is nothing but good." He pinched one of the statue's wings and laughed. "How crazy is this?"

"The craziest," she said.

She gripped his hand tightly for the remainder of the show, and then pulled him, giggling, all the way up the aisle. They met up with Katherine and the rest of the *Tricks* contingent—more squeals, this time accompanied by big sloppy kisses—and headed into the crowd, which parted magically at the sight of the trophy.

Strangers smiled and flashed thumbs-ups. Alex began to feel that same loopy high he'd gotten in the auditorium, the same pang of confidence by osmosis. He clutched Figgy's hand and led her outside, across a concrete patio, and toward a press tent. Beyond two vinyl flaps, he could see a swath of red carpet and phalanx of waiting cameramen and correspondents.

Maybe it was all the time he'd spent stewing in his seat while Figgy was backstage, but looking inside, Alex felt a rush of take-charge urgency. He gave Figgy's hand a squeeze, sidestepped around Katherine, and led the way, waving in a half-salute like a candidate stepping onstage at a rally. As he moved forward, he felt something strange on his foot, like he'd stepped in gum. He looked down. Something was sticking out from underneath his right shoe, bending away from the sole.

Before he could investigate, Alex felt his face go hot. He was now alone at the entrance to the tent, lights flooding the space. He sucked in a breath and collected himself. He was, after all, the man behind the woman, the proudly feminist supporting spouse; this was his moment, too. He prepped himself for the questions from reporters preparing second-day think pieces about the significance of Figgy's win: *Mr. Sherman-Zicklin! Mr. Sherman-Zicklin! How does it feel? What are your thoughts on the evolving roles of women in Hollywood? How will this change things for you at home? For your kids? For your marriage?*

The gaze of the room zeroed in on him. Then silence. A cough. It was as if a thousand onlookers had simultaneously sucked in a breath, held it for a moment, and then exhaled in a single whisper: "noooooboooody."

Rushing forward on either side, Figgy and Katherine stepped around him. The energy of the room kicked back to life, flash-bulbs popping. "Over here!" "On your left!" "Over the shoulder!"

"Hold this a sec," Figgy said, passing her jeweled clutch with a deft backhand.

Alex took the purse and froze. The tent filled with the barks of photographers calling requests to Katherine, who ducked her chin coquettishly, one impossibly long leg peeking out from her high-slit gown.

"Excuse me—champ? Your shoes? What is *up* with the shoes?"

Alex turned. The voice was a lazy drawl. It was Huck somebody, Katherine's husband—he'd just come inside and was standing a few feet back. He had a shaved head, just-so stubble, and a fitted charcoal tux with a loosely knotted black silk tie. The Concierge. So named by the tabloids, which had feasted on his story a few years back: Nobody singer-songwriter working at Telluride hotel has whirlwind romance with TV star Katherine Pool, marries her in quickie Vegas ceremony, and becomes surrogate dad to her two kids, ten-year-old Penelope and an adopted Chinese baby named Bingwen. Now Huck motioned toward Alex's feet with a look of alarm. Alex followed his eyes down and saw that both soles of his shoes had peeled away from the undersides and were now flapping madly, like two long, moist tongues.

He hollered ahead to Figgy, his personal shopper. She was a few feet ahead and managed to cut away, mid sound bite.

"Fig, honey?" Alex said. "The shoes you got me? Where'd they come from?"

She smiled and flashed him a thumbs-up. "The County Morgue Thrift Store! Amazing, right? Fifteen bucks!"

Alex felt a knot bunch up in his gut. His Emmy shoes were never meant to hold the weight of a living man. They were made for a corpse. No wonder they were decomposing.

"Dude, you are *fucked*," laughed Huck, who shook his head and quickly ducked away, in a hurry to go God-knows-where. Alex stayed put. Any additional movement, he feared, would cause the shoes to come apart entirely. Figgy had gone back to her interview. As the procession flowed around him, he waved lamely toward the press lineup, as if, yes, he was thrilled to be here, the guy with the sudden paralysis, the jeweled clutch, and the crazy face.

Off to the side, a security guy muttered something into a mic on his lapel and took a few steps forward, intent on putting a stop to the spastic grandstanding of this mere civilian. Out of the corner of his eye, through the tent's entrance, Alex caught sight of someone clambering over a metal gate. It was Huck, head gleaming in the overhead kliegs. Just as the security guard reached Alex to physically shove him along, Huck burst through the entrance, proffered a role of duct tape, and ripped off two silver strips.

Huck knelt down on the red carpet and wrapped each of Alex's shoes in tape. "Got this from a gaffer," he said. "There you go, Cinderella—glass slipper fits. You're good to go."

"Thank you," Alex stammered, relief and gratefulness flooding over him. "Stupendous. Seriously—that's some MacGyver handiness right there."

"Just tape," Huck said, rising up and clapping him on the shoulder. "Shit seriously solves ninety percent of the world's problems. Come on—let's drink. Let the ladies do the dog and pony show. They'll catch up with us at the after party."

• • •

Tricks was assigned to table 852 on the far outer reaches of the tent, near the bathrooms. Somewhere near the center of the space, a football field away, a contortionist in a kelp-patterned unitard gyrated to the tune of plinky electronica, this year's party inexplicably done in an undersea/nautical theme. Swirly blue lights cast odd shadows over the thousand-plus tables below. Alex and Huck sat across from three wives huddled around an immaculately turned-out fellow called Dan who was describing his Hawaiian wedding to Phil the line producer, while the rest of the *Tricks* contingent mixed it up in the circulating mob.

"Would've been nice to be closer, wouldn't it?" Alex craned his head over the crowd, looking for their wives; the last time he'd spotted Figgy she'd been at the dessert table with Julia Louis-Dreyfus. "If this were a solar system, we'd be out near Pluto, on one of those icy planets that no one knows the names of."

"Dwarf planets," Huck said, the stem of a lollipop wagging in the corner of his broad grin. "Love those. Ceres, Makemake, Haumea—irregular orbits, all gaseous and icy. Total fucking mystery. Astronomers can't get a bead on where they are or even what they're made of. Dwarf planets *rule*, am I right?"

Alex shook his head and smiled. No dummy, this concierge. "Hey—thanks for the help with the shoes. That was incredible. I'm not sure electrical tape goes with my tie, but I'm just glad not to be barefoot."

Huck peered down at his handiwork and shook his head. "Nah—looks kind of slick, actually. Like it's a thing. Next thing you know taped-up shoes'll be going for $700 at Kitson. Dandy-pop?"

Huck reached into his breast pocket and offered Alex a green lollipop.

"No thanks." Alex shrugged.

"You sure? Government-strain medicine. Prime canabiotic. Takes a minute to kick in, but nice. Full-body high, no couch lock, like popping two Xanax. And it's *candy*. Greatest thing ever."

Alex took one. The two sat quietly for a while, sucking and slurping, Huck periodically shooting meaningful grins at Alex. As the lollipop took hold, Alex felt a cozy glaze settle over him. He felt a little bad he wasn't out there with Figgy, who might need him to disentangle her from an aggressive agent or refill her glass or do whatever it was spouses in these situations were supposed to do. But he didn't feel bad enough to move. She'd come get him if she needed him, and anyway, he was happy to kick back on the outskirts of the room with Huck, away from the roar of *you look so great* and *let's have lunch* and *I'm off gluten and I feel fantastic!*

Tonight, Huck said, was the fourth awards show in the last six weeks. "I don't mind this at all, but they're death for Kate." They got to chatting about music, Alex happily discovering that Huck knew enough about early eighties punk to keep up with his gushing fanboy rant about the Germs, the Adolescents, and Black Flag. Even better, he seemed to know a fair amount about food—he had his own sous vide machine and raved for a solid ten minutes about the smoker he'd just bought. More impressive than Huck's gastronomical cred was how genuinely happy he seemed. He loved his lady. He loved her kids. He seemed to especially love all the helpers who did their chores, freeing him up for writing songs, kickboxing, and sucking lollipops.

"I'm telling you, dude," he said. "The Plus One thing? It's the best."

"The what?"

"You know—what you are. And me. And—" Huck arched an eyebrow toward their tablemates, slugging back the last of the house wine. "The hot mommies getting shitfaced while all the power-partner spouses work the room? We're the Plus Ones."

Alex suddenly flashed again on the invite. He hadn't paid much attention to anything beyond the curlicue lettering. Now he plucked the card out of his coat pocket and inspected the small print at the bottom of the card. There it was, in small Helvetica type the same size as the instructions for parking: Plus One.

"You gotta claim that shit," Huck said, leaning back. "I say it loud and proud to anyone and everyone—that way no one can ever use it against me. I don't ever forget. Look—today at two in the afternoon I was sipping mint-cucumber water at a spa on Robertson getting my whole business..." Huck waved generally at his midsection, "waxed. A brozilla, they call it. I've done the trimming and clipping and manscaping—but this is a whole new level. I'm cleaner than I've ever been in my whole sorry life."

Alex choked on his lollipop. He knew women waxed, but he was opposed to such things on ideological grounds—as a scholarship undergrad at Hampshire, he'd even written a paper that concluded that the bare pubis "is for Barbie dolls and little girls, expressions of a pervy corporate patriarchy." Discovering that guys, or at least guys like Huck, were now shaving their pubes scrambled his ideological radar. Was it a sign of progress, of gender parity? Was the shorn male groin evidence of post-feminist liberation?

Alex's theorizing ended with a horrifying mental picture of his own hairless wang, freed from its fuzzy, protective nest of reddish fur, the fleshy bits dangling alone and fully exposed. A shudder rocked through him as he looked back over at Huck, who was now chomping meaningfully on his lollipop. "I'm telling you," Huck pronounced, "the second you lose sight of who you are, who you *really* are, you're dead. Wreckage on the roadside. Being a Plus One is like riding a motorcycle: crazy fun, but a ton of ways to die."

"Dying? Who's dying?" Alex crossed his arms. "I don't follow."

Huck motioned over Alex's shoulder. "Over there. Second table on the right? In that pathetic *fedora*?"

Alex turned and peered through the crowd. Standing behind a seat and brandishing a deck of playing cards was a guy in his early forties. Gray felt hat, tiny black eyes, micro-sculpted beard that extended across his jaw like a cut-here mark. "The magic guy?"

"That's Randall Watkins. He was some kind of radio producer—documentary stuff. Then his wife Sandra gets named VP of production at Fox. You know what they say, right? Behind every successful woman in Hollywood, there's a guy she's too resentful to fuck? That's Randall. Right after the wife hits it, he stops working, gets bored, takes a class in sleight of hand, cute, whatever—but then he starts dumping a ton of money into props and costumes, trying to get a whole stage show going. Just bleeding cash. Wife goes around saying she's a magic widow, complaining that her husband is turning into Doug fucking Henning."

Alex looked closer. Randall plucked a card from the floral centerpiece and handed it to one of the women at the table, who shrugged and handed it back apologetically. Wrong card. Alex winced. "How do you know all this?"

"Sandra has lunch at the Davies all the time," he said. "I'm kind of the mayor over there. At least on weekdays from one to four."

Alex had only seen pictures of the Davies, a members-only club atop a curvy glass office tower on the western edge of the Sunset Strip. It figured Huck was a regular—Alex had no trouble picturing him sprawled out on the low, modular seating with a mojito and a gang of screenwriters, producers, and other industry-associated loafers.

Huck motioned for Alex to come in close. "Poor fucker has no idea what's about to hit him."

Alex bent in. "What? What's hitting him?"

"Petition for dissolution—all drawn up. Sandra's got another guy in the wings. Trading up. She's been lining up the notification requirement for months. No therapy, no arbitration, nothing. And get this: They're two months shy of the magic ten."

Alex leaned back and nodded. He got the general sense of what Huck was saying—the studio lady was leaving the magician—but the stuff about the petition, the notification requirement.... "What," he finally asked, "is the magic ten?"

Huck reared back. "How does a fucking concierge from Colorado know about the magic ten and you don't? California statutory law—split up before your tenth anniversary and you get alimony for half the length of the marriage. Past ten, you get alimony for life. *Life*, son."

Alex took a swig of wine and tried to absorb this information. "So he's getting dumped because of... California statutory law?"

"That, and he's a shitty magician."

Alex looked up at the underside of the tent roof, lights dancing across the vinyl in a kaleidoscopic swirl. He wasn't sure if it was the effects of the lollipop, or Huck's story, or just the weirdness of the night catching up with him, but he felt an intense sadness spread out inside his chest. He craned his head around the table, looking for Figgy in the crowd. Was she ready to leave?

"So," Huck said after a long pause. "How long have you been married?"

Alex straightened up. "Last year was—eight? Nine? Yeah—ten is next March."

Two

Her foot was in his face again. At seven, Sylvie was far too old to be in their bed. But here she was, tangled up in the duvet between Alex and Figgy, a smug grin between her soft cheeks, one hammerlike heel lodged against Alex's throat.

It had been the same with Sam, who'd fall asleep in his own bed (after a long and ritualistic routine, the rigid complexities of which Alex never quite got right), only to appear at their bedside in the wee hours, pawing and pleading. Some nights Alex managed to turn the intruder away, but Figgy was a sucker, especially after production on the show began and she didn't get home until late. When she hadn't seen them all day, she was helpless against their dozy warm forms, their yeasty aroma, their sweet silence. It was true, about kids, or theirs anyway: they're most lovable when semi-conscious.

Sam mostly left Alex alone, wrapping himself like a kudzu around Figgy, until a moment of reckoning one day when she had been putting him down for a nap and asked him to please remove his hand from her boob. The feel of it made his limbs go slack and his eyelids flutter with narcotic satisfaction. "Okay, deal," he said drowsily. "Under the shirt, but over the bra."

Alex was fuzzy on specifics from the dozen half-read parenting manuals on his bedside, but he felt pretty sure the experts agreed that co-sleeping had officially become inappropriate when a child could negotiate for tit time. Their son's banishment, however, coincided with the arrival of Sylvie. Normally the nightly brawl with his daughter left Alex feeling cranky come morning, like he'd spent the night being mauled by a koala.

Today, however, the morning after the big award night, Sylvie's foot in his face was okay. Reassuring, even. He scooched into it. It meant normalcy had returned. The events of the night before had come and gone. The special was over, and we now rejoin our regularly scheduled program.

Alex let out a grunt and stumbled to the toilet, where he came face to face with the trophy itself, which Figgy had (ha fucking ha) set on the tank, shoving aside a stack of Sudoku books and *Sunset* magazines. He gave it a long look. Its golden wings zigzagged in a backward diagonal, sharp as switchblades. Its bust thrust forward in a stance of regal confidence. He picked it up; Jesus, it was the weight of a bowling ball. He looked at it square in the face. The swirling ball of atoms held high above the figure's head—what was that about? A goddess with a monumental bust and lightning bolts for wings, holding aloft the basic particle of all matter? How was that the symbol for excellence in TV comedy? Alex stared at the blank face, its features flat and revealing nothing. *You don't scare me,* he thought. *Half the d-bags cruising Sunset Boulevard have one of these things—they give 'em out like Chiclets at the Tijuana border.* Winning one didn't change anything.

Alex was still smarting a little about last night—it was as if the moment Figgy had accepted the award, he'd gone into freefall, as if everyone at the party had been staring out from the sides of a bottomless hole as he tumbled past. Or maybe that was just the lollipop? The business with the shoes—it wasn't as if Figgy had planned for them to fall apart, and it had worked out fine, but it still left a sting of resentment. Didn't he deserve better than a dead man's shoes? And then there'd been all that talk from Huck about the perils of Plus One-ness and the looming threat of the magic ten.

Stop it, he thought. He and Figgy were good. He shouldn't start doubting his whole marriage because of a single stoned conversation. Especially now, on the morning after Figgy's big win. She'd actually won! That was nothing but good. Of course it was.

"Daaaaad?" It was Sam, calling from down the hall. Alex followed the singsong down to the kids' room, where Sylvie's bottom bunk was empty and Sam was splayed on the floor in a pair of faded orange pajamas, shirt hiked up under his armpits, staring at a pile of Legos.

"Hey buddy." Alex lowered down, crossed his legs and grabbed a handful. He knew the drill. If Alex wasn't around, Sam would lie there raking his hand through the pile, scattering the clinking bits across the carpet. But as soon as Alex showed up, Sam would get to work, concentration locked.

Sam murmured a greeting as Alex handed over a roof shingle. Sam showed no interest in the spaceships and vehicles that seemed to excite other nine-year-olds; he preferred to build houses and shops and stables, all of them vaguely medieval.

Over the course of an hour, the two kept quiet, the only sounds murmured bits of dialogue from Sam, who kept his head down close to the carpet to get the proper cinematic angle. Cross-legged beside his busy little boy, Alex felt a familiar rush of feeling wash over him, at once tender and panicked. The boy's slim shoulders, narrow wrists, wispy bangs—he was so delicate, so fragile. Alex flashed to a scene of his son on a basketball court, their first and only attempt to get Sam involved in a team sport, his face tilted wistfully toward the silver glow from the frosted gymnasium windows—and then his head snapping sideways from the impact of a ball whose very existence apparently came as a total shock. They'd moved on to soccer (bad), judo (worse), and finally, fencing (tolerable—Sam liked the outfit).

So he wasn't a jock—Alex hadn't been, either. Alex's mother, Jane, never missed an opportunity to point out how similar they were. Same straw-colored hair, same pinkish skin tone, same dreamy green-gray eyes. And the similarities went so much deeper, she'd gush—Sam was so obviously an "old soul," mindful and sensitive and fully conscious, just like his dad.

She meant it as a compliment, but it never failed to get a rise from Alex. Not only because the observation came dressed in the softheaded hippie prattle he'd grown up with in Ojai. No, what really bothered Alex was his mom pretending to have an actual recollection of who he'd been as a kid—his mom being almost entirely checked out for the first twenty-odd years of his life. She was better now, sober and in a committed relationship, but the fact remained that she'd been barely present in Alex's life for much of his childhood, her energies consumed by booze, brief, tragic romances, and epic bouts of self-actualization.

"How'd you turn out so normal?" This was the inevitable question when Alex ran through the high points of his origin story: Midwestern mom moves to California, hooks up with proprietor of highway goat-milk stand. Shortly after Alex is born, marriage implodes—booze a factor, also money, also Jane's dawning awareness that she's gay. After dad splits, mom dives headlong into feminist-mystic-folksinger reinvention, dates biker chicks and massage therapists and energy healers. Memories from the period are fuzzy and charged with intense loneliness—he remembers her passed out on a rattan chair on the deck of their small aluminum-sided house, draped in a woolen poncho, her yellowed

fingers still clenched around a cup of chablis. He remembers playing parachute games in a scrubby dirt lot, going weeks without
bathing, and subsisting mostly on cans of chili and candy bought
with coins stolen from his mom's change bucket. He remembers
watching ungodly amounts of TV.

At fourteen, he discovered punk, decided hippies were the
Enemy, and managed to land a scholarship spot at a local boarding school. He packed a bag and never came back.

Not that Alex was resentful. He'd done his time in therapy,
dealt with his abandonment issues, sorted through his mother's
internalized messages about men (who were, she maintained,
power-tripping oppressors, with the possible exception of Phil
Donahue, Alan Alda, and the turtle-necked guy at the food co-
op). In some ways, he had come to believe that his upbringing
benefitted him as a man and a father. He'd had some rough years
after college, drifting from shitty relationship to dead-end job, but
as soon as he met Figgy, he'd resolved to get right what his own
parents had gotten so wrong. He'd pay attention, stay involved, be
the parent he'd never had. He'd even patched things up with his
mom, their relations much improved after she went through AA,
met Carol, and finally got with the standard lesbian program of
shacking up with cats and mystery novels and a matching wardrobe of Polarfleece.

The only real downside of the way he was raised, Alex
thought, was how it affected his relationship with Sam—he
couldn't seem to figure out how to handle him. Things with Sylvie were so much easier. Yes, she was demanding. True, she was
persnickety. She was self-possessed in a way many adults found
off-putting. Part of it was her voice, a whiskey-and-cigarettes rasp
that sounded like it should belong to a bridge-playing retiree in
Boca more than a seven-year-old girl from Southern California.
She was also, quite plainly, a pain in the ass, defiant and strong-
willed and willfully oblivious. But she was *his* pain in the ass. She

clung to Daddy and obeyed his commands to put on her shoes or get in the bath, even as she cheerfully ignored the same requests from Figgy. ("No thank you!" she'd sing-song over her shoulder, as if she'd been asked if she'd like a second piece of pie.)

Their deepest bond centered on food. Sylvie, Alex was delighted to discover, possessed an unusually sophisticated palate. Sam survived on a diet of quesadillas and applesauce, but Sylvie would eat pretty much anything you put in front of her, and Alex took this as license to expose her to the most exotic edibles he could rustle up, serving rare chunks of blue cheese, dried leaves of salted seaweed, and spicy dishes of kimchi. It was exhilarating, having a little sidekick for his continuing culinary adventures. He'd come to feel about food the same way he once felt about punk. He loved it irrationally, felt sorry for those who didn't, and instantly bonded with those who did. Was it weird that the only person who seemed to really *get* his obsessions was his seven-year-old daughter? Probably.

Then again, weirdness was kind of a fact of life for the Sherman-Zicklins. Sylvie was the only second grader whose lunchbox routinely included separate thermoses for soup and sauces. And he didn't know any other families who dealt with domestic chores the way they did. Their family rule was All Hands on Deck, which in the chaos of their domestic life was often shortened to "All Hands" or just "Hands" or even a flashed palm. The rule was this: Whoever was closest to something that needed tending, tended it. If you opened the bill, you paid it. If a kid had a meltdown and you were inside the blast zone, it was your job to blot the tears and offer the Popsicle. If you turned on the TV and woke up the baby, you cooed and soothed. Alex loved the raw physicality of the arrangement, the way it flew beneath all the explosive gender expectations that seemed to torment other, less practically minded couples. Let them confront and unpack notions of femininity and masculinity and duke it out with the ghosts of their mothers and fathers; he and Figgy would obey the god of *proximity*.

The major flaws in All Hands became apparent pretty quickly. For one thing, Figgy had a way of being either just out of range or totally absent when jobs needed doing. Alex wasn't sure whether she was simply better at anticipating problems and removing herself from domestic flashpoints, but it was Alex who, when Sylvie was little, always seemed to be with the baby when she erupted in a level-eleven doodie explosion, Alex who was in the kitchen cooking when the fridge broke and needed a new Dispenser Control Board.

Then there were all the All Hands exceptions, tasks that without question always fell to him. Like changing light bulbs. Or operating the barbecue. Or handling household finances. Or anything at all related to computers, cameras, or electronics. Figgy never said out loud that these jobs were, you know, man's work. She simply ignored them.

Like, for instance, playing Legos with the boy. Assembling tiny villages being one of the tasks exclusively for people with penises, apparently. Not that Alex minded this particular task—he actually felt a tinge of sadness when, after an hour or so of work, the phone rang and the ladies stirred and playtime was over.

Figgy answered from the bedroom, hollering for Alex to pick up the phone.

"...it was just marvelous! Empowering!" It was Alex's mom Jane, mid-gush. He hadn't known she'd been aware of the previous night—he doubted she'd changed the TV from the local PBS station since the Carter administration—but judging from her frantic, jubilant tone, she'd not only seen the Emmys but viewed it as a historic milestone, a crowning victory for The Movement. "That shout-out to the sisters!" she went on. "Needless to say, *tears*. The symbolic victories, Figgy—they're so meaningful. They matter. We marched for this. We did. I can't tell you how it feels to see all the hard work we've done over the years paying off. I could've done without the 'girl power'—really Figgy, you are so not a girl, so very much a woman."

"Hear me roar," Figgy croaked, still half asleep. Figgy adored Jane. Where Alex felt a mix of embarrassment and bitterness when it came to his mom, Figgy was amused.

Jane went on: "Oh! And that dress! Sumptuous."

"Mom, *gross*," Alex piped in. "I'd swear you're trying to pick up my... girl."

"Oh yes, Alex," she said, her voice darkening. "Did you see yourself? On the TV? Carol taped it and you come on right after Figgy does the power salute with her fist. We've been rewatching it all morning. Oh, Carol—freeze there! Right there—on Alex's face."

Jane quieted down. He pictured his mother at home on the couch, snug in her sweatpants and reading glasses pushed down her nose, a honeyed mug of chamomile in her lap. "That's *unfortunate*," she said, the receiver dropping away as she assessed the frozen image of Alex on TV. "Do you see? I can't tell if it's the camera angle, or what? It's only a second or two, but do you see how *sickly*? How *waxy*? Did you have some kind of makeup on? Some kind of... cakey base?"

"No, Mom—that's just my face," Alex said. "My waxy, cakey face."

"Oh sweetie," she said. "I'm just saying. With Figgy looking so splendid, it's just such a *contrast*. Did you have to *pee*, honey?"

A parental alert had gone out, apparently, because not twenty seconds after they got off the phone with Jane, Figgy's folks called to weigh in. Joanie Zicklin was an opinionated, anxious shut-in with a thicket of Clairol-red hair. She'd had troubles with pharmaceuticals in the eighties, which had led to a brief affair with Figgy's birth dad—a plastic surgeon she called "a putz with no business raising a child"—and then, when Figgy was eleven, a marriage to Clive. He'd been a stabilizing presence for Joan, but he and Figgy never quite connected—to this day, he seemed weirdly competitive with his stepdaughter.

As usual, Clive and Joan spoke at high volume and simultaneously, in only occasionally related monologues. Joan's revolved around a call that morning from her poker friend Audrey. "She was full of *mazel tovs* and *how wonderfuls*, but oh, how it was killing her," she said. "Do you know what her daughter the Ivy League lawyer is doing right this minute, while you're home with your Emmy and those gorgeous grandchildren? Divorced, thirty-seven, and in Zanzibar or Zaire—one of the Zas. Signed up with a Jewish legal charity something-or-another to examine ballots and get malaria."

"Ma, Pam's in Zambia," Figgy said. "We emailed last week. She's doing great. Met a pro surfer. Having the time of her life."

Joan barreled on. "And remember when she was at Northwestern and you were working at that yogurt shop? Passing out samples on La Cienega, wearing that horrible *visor*? Living with that Hispanic boy? Just a few years until Sylvie starts putting *you* through such worry—just wait, honeybee, your turn's coming."

Meanwhile, Clive's basso profundo boomed on a simultaneous track, reviewing the morning trades. "You see the Internet today? 'Academy Wowed by Zicklin's *Tricks!*' That is some nice coverage—whose palm did the network grease for that? Listen—I know you've got a lot on your plate, but when you talk to *Deadline*, see if you can work in a plug for *Top Dog*. You're talking to *Deadline*, aren't you? For their Emmy wrap-up?"

Clive was supposed to be retired—he'd sold his video distribution company to Paramount fifteen years ago. And while Figgy pointed out that his actual job had been about as glamorous as that of an auto parts distributor, he had somehow managed to exploit every industry perk and, to Alex anyway, pulled off a respectable version of the shaggy, glam, Robert Evans–era showbiz mogul: He drove a smoke-spewing Alfa Romeo, which he piloted to Fitzerman's Deli in Chatsworth three afternoons a week for cabbage soup and rice pudding, devouring his lunch while swiping his perpetually wet lips with a silk calico-print kerchief. For the past few years he'd been shopping around reality-show ideas, his latest about a family of dog trainers.

"We could really *leverage* this, honey," Clive said. "Build on your cable success? Help get *Top Dog* on track? These network guys just need a reminder—this could really get us some momentum."

A holler came from the front hall, and Alex took the excuse to say goodbye and get off the phone. Sam was standing at the front door, scratching his belly and squinting into the buttery light. On the front stoop stood... something. Sprouting up from an enormous wicker basket was a thicket of jungle flora, a chaotic web of tendrils splayed around a dome of tropical blossoms in full flower. It wasn't so much a bouquet as an ecosystem.

"Oh, it's the *big basket.*" Figgy had joined him on the porch. "It's gotta be from Jess. His assistant told me: Big clients get the big basket. There's gotta be a card—find it, will you?"

"No way," Alex said. "I think I saw a cheetah crawling around in there."

Figgy made a face and dug the card out. "'To the new Queen of the Jungle. From Jess and all your friends at Forefront,'" she read, flipping it over. "Oh my God. It's the Supreme Tropical Paradise."

She dropped the card and crumpled in laughter, picking up the arrangement with a grunt and hurrying inside. "Come on!" she called. "Let's look it up!"

They fired up the kitchen computer and checked the website of the florist: The Supreme Tropical Paradise retailed for $600.

The figure jumped out at Alex. "That's how much I paid for Doug." Doug was the name they had for the dented, mustard-colored Datsun B210 that had reliably if unfashionably transported him around L.A. in his temping days, when they first started dating.

"You overpaid for that car," Figgy said. "This is in another league entirely."

Alex took a second. Look at the two of them! Figgy, whose mom had grown up dirt poor in the Bronx, whose grandfather fled the Nazis for a factory job in the U.S., whose great grand-parents had been terrorized by Cossacks. Then he flashed on his own ancestors, Iowa farmers and Ontario Quakers who, from what Alex could tell, spent their entire lives catching infections in drafty meeting halls. Now here they were, staring down a flower arrangement that cost more than a car.

The florist's website showed the Supreme Tropical Paradise in a sleek, modern kitchen, a burst of lurid color in an otherwise placid expanse, like a sculptural piece of farm equipment on a pol-ished glass coffee table. It was what was called, Alex recalled from the home décor reality show he guilt-watched, a *contrast item*.

Not here it wasn't. He looked around at their cluttered coun-tertops and overflowing shelves. They owned nothing *but* con-trast items. Their plumbing was bad and the electrical system was fritzy, but they'd amassed a hive of tchotchkes, evidence of Figgy's extensive travels through the thrift shops and estate sales and dis-count emporiums of Southern California.

Once upon a time, back before kids in the days of $600 cars, Alex was an eager accomplice. She taught him which San Ga-briel Valley Sally Armies were off the radar and which ones were picked over by the Melrose Avenue scouts. She showed him where to find 1960s three-button suits and obscure punk rock LPs for a quarter a pop.

Alex had appreciated thrifting in the abstract, as an act of re-bellion against disposable retail culture. He liked Figgy's name for it: urban archeology. The actual experience of thrifting, however, made him sad. He always seemed to bump into a lady reading a Robert Ludlum paperback to an invisible best friend, or trip over a kid cradling a moldy stuffed animal. Even the stuff itself freaked him out: the amateur oil painting of the big-eyed poodle, the Dollywood ashtray, the picture frame with the photo of the cross-eyed kid *still in it*. Each item had a person attached to it, and a lot of these people, he knew, were diseased, demented, or just plain dead.

Alex finally had enough during a thrifting holiday in Vegas. Figgy had heard the shops near the strip were packed with the treasures of transients and gamblers. One afternoon Alex was looking through an assorted bin near the register of a shop near Fremont when he saw it. On top of the pile, marked with a price tag reading ONE DOLLAR, was an old jock strap. He picked it up. The front section, the little beige pouch where you put your business, was splattered with blood.

Alex stood at the register, the item dangling limply from his pinched thumb and forefinger. He couldn't even begin to comprehend the back story. It was all too horrifying... someone had a jock strap, somehow got blood on it, and now it was in his hand, for sale... for a dollar.

And that was it: the end of Alex's career as Figgy's thrifting wingman. From then on, when asked if he'd accompany her, he need only utter those three words: bloody jock strap.

Figgy kept right on, of course. The arrival of the kids may have cut down on her shopping time, but it gave her expeditions a new urgency. Now, along with the glass grape centerpieces and Franciscan dishware, she began amassing vast numbers of Little Golden Books, Fisher-Price toys, and View-Master slides.

All of which contributed to an atmosphere of barely controlled chaos at home. Their house was nice enough, a compact Craftsman in Atwater Village, what real estate people hopefully called "a transitional neighborhood." The house had good bones, actual character, and, if you stood on tippy toes from the patio, a view across the concrete drainage ditch of the L.A. River to Griffith Park. But what had seemed funkily adventurous when they were cohabitating singles now felt shabby and inadequate.

Clearing away a pile of crap in the entry hall to make room for the flowers, Alex felt breathless and jumpy. There was no way he could spend the whole day here, with Figgy holed up in the bathroom with her winged lady and the Supreme Tropical Paradise lording over him as he navigated through goat trails of clutter.

So in a rush, he got the kids dressed and announced the commencement of a Sherman-Zicklin Family Adventure Day. Figgy agreed, quickly rallying and calling up a page on her iPhone listing ethnic festivals within a fifty-mile radius. (Lithuanians! Koreans! Greeks! Alex was pretty sure that since the advent of Family Adventure Day, he'd consumed every global variation of fried dough and barbecued meat.) As they hustled out the door, Figgy leading the pack, Alex smiled. Figgy was his playmate, his co-conspirator; whatever happened with her work, she was still the girl who'd drop everything and get up and go. She was game— always had been.

Today's Sherman-Zicklin Family Adventure Day began as it always did, strapping the kids into Alex's trusty green Subaru. As he buckled Sylvie in, Alex felt a wave of calm descend over him. They were contained. Their range of wrongdoing had been reduced.

"You're a girl," Sylvie announced to Sam as they pulled out into traffic, apropos of nothing. Second only to her love of food was her enthusiasm for bugging the living shit out of her brother.

Figgy looked up from her iPhone. "Honey, don't. Please."

"It's true," she said. "You're a girl."

"Stop!" shrieked Sam.

"You're *so* a girl."

"Cut it out!"

Alex peered through his rearview mirror at Sylvie, who was

now gazing calmly at the passing traffic. How did a second grader who still seemed baffled by the mechanics of wiping her own ass know so well how to engineer a full meltdown in her older brother?

"Girl," Sylvie said, economizing.

"Sylvie, what's the first family rule?" asked Figgy.

A bright smile lit up her face as she spat out the oft-repeated line: "Don't be a dick."

"That's right," Figgy nodded. Alex cringed. He'd never liked Figgy's habit of addressing the kids like college roommates, even as he marveled at how the kids' use of what Figgy called "strong words" ("Because there are no 'bad' words," she'd say) would often distract them from whatever nonsense had caused a fight in the first place.

This time, however, Sylvie was too far gone to pull back. After a momentary pause, she took a deep breath and started singing, the words linking together into a lilting Broadway show tune: "Girl, girl, girl, girl, girl, girl, girl, girl, girl—"

Sam began to screech.

Alex swiveled his head back. "Order in the court, the monkey's going to speak," he said. Sylvie took the bait and got quiet. She loved this game. "Speak monkey speak!"

Silence followed. By the rules of the game, after someone called out the opening line, everyone got quiet. It would last a minute, maybe two, before one of the kids either spaced out and forgot about the game or blurted out something, thereby prompting the rest of the family to call out, in a precise descending melody, "Mon-key!"

Mom was first to speak: "I'm hungry."

"Mon-key!" came the reply, Alex reflexively joining the kids.

"Okay, I'm a monkey," said Figgy. "But I'm a hungry monkey. So let's vote. What do you want for lunch?"

Alex held his breath, the choice of where to eat being for the

Sherman-Zicklins a notoriously agonizing negotiation. Fast food was obviously out of the question, the children having accepted Alex's explanation that all chains save In-N-Out belonged in the same general forbidden zone that encompassed tattoo parlors, gun shops, and North Korea. Which left mostly small, loud, shabby, ethnic restaurants whose first-generation immigrant proprietors, Alex maintained, were simply more comfortable with families. Figgy wasn't so sure; she'd seen plenty of annoyed Thai waiters and peeved Chinese hostesses. Maybe, she suggested, Alex simply didn't mind bothering foreigners as much as he did white people.

Sam and his sister hollered out, in unison, their choices: "Tapas!" "Hamburgers!"

"Christ," said Alex. "Fig, you choose. Second family rule—this is not a democracy."

"We know," Sam said, clumsily mouthing the line: "It's a benevolent dictatorship."

"That's right," Figgy said. "Okay, Sam, fine. Shake N' Burger's right off the freeway. They've got those amazing curly fries."

"Tapas!" Sylvie screamed.

"It's Shake N' Burger, honey," Alex said. "The decision's been made. You *like* Shake N' Burger."

"I *hate* hamburgers!" Sylvie hollered, her voice ascending to a shriek. Tears began welling up on her lashes.

"Come on honey—relax," Figgy said. "It's just lunch."

"But I'm *starving*!" Sylvie sputtered.

"Black dot!" said Sam. In one of his fitful efforts at actual proactive parenting, Alex had tacked up a poster board where the kids were rewarded with gold stars for acts of generosity, civility, or kindness and given black dots for acts of disobedience, vandalism, or general douchebaggery. Poking your brother in the eye was a three-dot offense. Saying you were "starving" when your lunchbox overflowed with food and other children not so far away were actually starving, earned you a dot. Ten stars equaled a toy or trip for gelato. Dots negated stars. Sylvie was currently at negative sixteen stars.

"I hate you!" Sylvie said.

"Please, guys, cut it out," Alex said. "Sylvie, remember what we talked about—about your blood sugar? Hate is too strong a word. So is starving."

"I know an even stronger word," said Sam.

"Sam, honey, stay out of this," said Figgy.

"I do!" Sam said proudly.

Sylvie continued the caterwaul. Alex steadied himself and tried to focus on the road. "Please, please calm down, Sylvie honey," he begged.

Figgy switched off her phone and swiveled around to the kids. "Look: stop," she said. "If you can get control of yourself right now, we'll go for tapas. Just calm down."

Sylvie instantly quieted. The echo of her cry hung in the air.

Alex directed a pleading look at his wife. "Wow, thanks," he said. "Negotiating with terrorists. Great."

"Cock!" blurted Sam. "That's a much stronger word."

• • •

Figgy's agent, Jess, called just as they sat down to eat. It was, in keeping with Jess's special knack for interruption, terrible timing. Sam was in a deep sulk over his hamburger defeat, head plopped on the tabletop. Sylvie, meanwhile, was in a snit over a proposed substitute for her favorite chorizo appetizer. Figgy put the cell phone on the table and turned on the speakerphone, just in time to capture Sylvie's tantrum revving up anew: "No chorizo blanco!" she hollered, fresh tears bursting from her face. "Nooooo chorizo blanco!"

"Fig, honey—get that girl whatever she wants," came the voice of Jess. "Get her some caviar! Pop that girlie some champagne!"

Fig leaned forward, pulling her hair forward over her face. "She's seven, Jess. It's bad enough she knows from Spanish sausage."

"You get the flowers?" he asked.

"I did. Gorgeous. Nowhere to go but down from here. Now it'll be all the more devastating when you send supermarket carnations after the backlash next year."

"Oh please," Jess said. "The approval cycle's not *that* short. You've got at least two seasons before the honeymoon ends. Do you have any idea what we're gonna *do* with this? As far as your deal? Serves the studio right for being so cheap last go-around. They got their three-year commitments from the cast, but your contract is wide open. You see the TV today? All the morning shows are running that 'girl power' clip. You're the *face* of the show!"

"No thank you," Figgy said. "That's Kate's job. I'm strictly behind the camera."

"Speaking of, tiny talent issue," he said. "Got a message from the studio this morning. They want to see outlines for the first three episodes ASAP. Herb's taking a personal interest. Wants to have lunch next week. I'll run interference, but they're talking about pushing production up three weeks. Your star has a commitment. Something about a graduation?"

Katherine Pool's children had become a constantly evolving X-factor in production, every play date and pediatrician appointment throwing a wrench into the show's schedule.

"For Christsakes, the kid's graduating *preschool*," Figgy said. "We are not holding up production for Bingwen Pool's glorious entry into kindergarten."

"We'll work it out," Jess said. "I'm hearing they're about to up their order from thirteen to twenty-three! No hiatus, but you'll bang 'em out. You're a superstar!"

Figgy went quiet. For a second the only sound was the slurp of Sylvie devouring slices of Serrano ham like so many strips of fruit roll-ups.

"Twenty-three episodes?" Figgy said. "Am I finally gonna get paid?"

After a pause, Jess filled the silence with a sound: *beep, beep, beep.*

"Hear that?" he said. Then he did it again, with a fidelity that Alex found surprising, mimicked sound effects not being a talent Alex would expect to find in an Armani-clad TV agent: *beep, beep, beep.*

"Hear that? That's the money truck, Figgy, backin' on up."

• • •

Alex knew enough not to believe anything that came out of the mouth of an agent. All that crazy *beep-beep-beeping*—that was just theatrics. Alex wasn't even sure what it meant, precisely— tens of thousands of dollars? Hundreds? Millions? How much went to agents, lawyers, and taxes? Figgy certainly didn't seem all that fazed, getting off the phone with a raised eyebrow and a shrug before returning to her ceviche.

It was only later, while the kids worked off lunch inside the humid innards of an enormous indoor play structure, that Alex looked over and found Figgy crying. She was slumped over on a bench beside the snack bar, her shoulders rocking. Alex reached over and pulled her into a hug. She'd been so composed the night before, which Alex chalked up to the fact that big shows of emotion were rare in Figgy. (At the movies when everyone else was doubled over in hysterics, she'd stab out a finger and declare, "That's funny.") But now, eighteen hours later on a moist vinyl cushion at the Little Critters Indoor Playground, it was all crashing down.

"I'm so fucked," she said, going limp in his embrace. "I'm utterly and completely fucked."

Alex held her tight and stroked her hair. They sat like that for a while, until the sobs subsided and she looked up, her face splotchy and wide open.

"That call?" she said. "The network and the pickup and the notes? *Twenty-three* episodes? In six months? There's no way. I'll die. I'll never make it. I'll strangle Kate by her skinny long swan neck. Or she'll kill me first. Last year was bad enough, and no one was paying any attention. We were just this weird cable show. Now everyone is expecting it to be, like, *great*. And not just great in the same way—better."

Her eyes went glassy again.

"Aw Fig." Alex ran his hand down her back. "This is nothing but good. Forget all that agent business. Just make your show."

"This isn't like before. I'm looking at twenty-three episodes in six months with the network up my ass and a star who hates my guts. It's the real fucking thing. I'm not gonna have time for you or the kids or days like this or *anything* but... feeding the beast. I'm about to get swallowed up whole."

"Stop. You've got this. You've done it before—this is just a slightly higher level. How different could it be, really?"

The question hung there. The truth was, Alex had no idea how different it would be—for the show, for her, for him. Could she keep it together? He'd help, of course. But what did that mean, exactly?

"It's like the trophy—the Emmy," he said. "You're the atom. I'll hold you up. You do the wild spinning thing. I'll keep you steady."

Figgy wiped her nose and smiled. "So you're what? The lady holding the atom? With the tits?"

"I guess so—yeah," he said. "Don't forget, though—I've got those lightning bolts. So don't even fuck with me."

A long moment passed. He bumped her with his shoulder.

"And what about that money truck? We can start looking for a house, maybe a nanny? And maybe you should buy something, just for yourself. Anything. What do want?"

Figgy wiped her nose and thought it over. "A castle," she finally said. "David Chase got a castle in France for *The Sopranos*. I want a castle."

Three

BestSelf operated out of an unglamorous Culver City office suite with four full-time staffers: Erin the receptionist, Linda the business manager, Alex the account exec, and BestSelf's president and creative director, Jeff Kanter. As usual on Monday mornings, Alex was first to arrive; alone at his desk, he sat with a giant chai and a stack of cookbook proofs, soaking up the sweet silence. After the excitement of the awards and a weekend of family adventuring, a couple of hours alone in the empty office felt positively luxurious. By the time Kanter came in, Alex felt restored and energized, like a grownup again.

"Hey!" Kanter said, hustling past Alex's desk. "Saw you on the tee-vee Saturday! Ready for your close-up? Everything set for later?"

"Almost," Alex said. "We can prep whenever you're ready."

"Two clicks," Kanter said, snapping his fingers and clapping his fist against his palm. Kanter was a snapper. Also a back slapper.

And a hugger—he was famous for never ending a meeting without a full, wraparound embrace. Alex had long ago made peace with his boss's deep and profound cheesiness.

That was the Jeff Kanter mystique—how much he cared. About his business, his clients, his causes, and the fact that everyone *knew* that he cared. He was known to weep in pitch meetings. He was positively Clintonian in the way he could bring calm and confidence to a room with one soulful frown. It was a different story in the office, away from clients. One on one, he was often moody and blunt and hypercritical. He was also, Alex learned, strangely indifferent about his actual family. One day Alex asked his boss about the photos on the credenza behind his desk—they were blurry shots of small children scrambling around an inflatable raft, their faces turned away from the camera.

"Family whitewater raft trip," Kanter said. "Grand Canyon."

"When was that?" Alex asked.

"Ninety-two? Three? I don't know. Brenna said I needed to get some family photos in here, so I gave the interior designer a roll of film that I had in the glove compartment."

Alex figured that the kids in the photos were now—teenagers? Or all grown? "Wow, Jeff—that's super depressing."

Kanter waved him off. "Not as depressing as being stuck on a whitewater raft with three kids for ten days."

Kanter hadn't gotten to be successful by being Super Dad. Over the course of his career he'd won six CLIOs, a dozen Ogilvys, and a reputation as a rock star of food marketing. He made almond butter sexy. He was the top creative on Burger Stop's "Feed your monster" campaign. He was singlehandedly responsible for the entire category of toddler sports drinks.

Then came the unfortunate business with the carrot. Working with the California Carrot Council, Kanter came up with the idea of sculpting roots and scraps into bullet shapes, then packaging the pieces in clear plastic magazines. VeggieBullets! Boys gobbled 'em up. VeggieBullets were so successful that growers went to twenty-four-hour shifts to meet demand. In the rapid ramp-up, growers apparently skimped on sanitary provisions for the farm workers. A precise cause was never identified, but an E. coli outbreak in Tampa left two kids dead and one on dialysis. "Carrot contamination kills two: VeggieBullets blamed" read the headline in the *Herald-Tribune*. While neither Kanter nor his agency was named in the $32 million class-action suit that followed, he had been so front and center during the rollout that his client list had shrunk to zero overnight.

After laying low for a year, he opened BestSelf, a "boutique brand innovation and consultancy focusing on social purpose"—i.e., a tiny shop catering to nonprofits that were treated as pro-bono pissants at the big agencies. Alex was four years into a midlevel copywriting gig at Feinstein Pierce when he met Kanter at a demographic conference in Huntington Beach. At the time, Alex was getting increasingly sick of his job and harboring doubts about the whole profession. Jeff convinced him to join BestSelf "to do something unprecedented."

Alex's own mother was appalled when he told her he'd accepted a job with Kanter.

"The carrot killer?" she asked. "I understand advertising is just a... stepping stone for you into other creative work. I've made peace with that. But I just don't know how you can you live with yourself, working for a man like that."

"Ma, *he* didn't kill anyone," he said. "It's not his fault that growers were too cheap to provide portapotties. All Kanter did was get kids to eat more vegetables. And look what he's done since then. Nothing but good."

That much was true, kind of. They'd done a decent campaign on behalf of a state recycling initiative and produced a series of PSAs to promote spaying and neutering of pets. Mostly, however, Kanter specialized in nonprofits of dubious worth backed by bloated foundations. Today, for instance, Alex was doing final revisions on a promotional cookbook for TestiCure, a testicular cancer charity run by real estate developer Simon Russo Jr., a cancer survivor who claimed he "owed his life to brussels sprouts." (Alex thought radiation therapy, hormone treatments, and the radical inguinal orchiectomy might deserve some credit, too, but never mind.)

Alex was nearly done making corrections when Kanter emerged from his office and headed over with Erin and Linda in tow, the three of them grinning and big eyed. "So?" Kanter said. "Tell us!"

He put down his chai and tapped the pile of proofs with a blue pencil. "Layout looks great. Should be good to go."

"No, silly!" Linda said. "No one cares about *that*! Tell us about the big night!"

Linda wanted to know whether he'd seen Julianna Margulies in person and what he thought of her scoop-neck dress and whether he agreed that the two of them looked alike, twins maybe, fraternal at least. Erin wanted to know why he wasn't home wrapped in one of the gorgeous cashmere throws they gave out at the after-party, given his obviously weakened state. ("Poor dear," she croaked. "All flustered like that on national TV.") Kanter played it cooler, hanging back and saying only that Figgy's speech was "masterful—totally on point."

"So, presentation's at two, yes?" Alex said after ten minutes of Emmy chat. "Should we go over the cookbook? Run over main points?"

With that, Linda and Erin rolled their eyes and scurried back to their desks.

"If we *must*," Kanter said, hopping up on the edge of Alex's desk. Alex had spent the last six weeks collecting the recipes (Chili con Tempeh, Seaweed Caesar Salad, Tofu Sloppy Joes), arranging the photo shoot, and doing pagination and proofreading. Kanter peered down at the pages, shoulders bunched and a faint twitch around his mouth. Alex pulled out a recipe for the Soystrami Reuben. The photograph pictured a dollop of mustard sliding silkily down a shred of pinkish protein.

"Start with this," Alex said. "Russo'll wet himself. You should've heard him on the conference call—couldn't shut up about that marble rye."

"What the hell is 'soystrami'?" Jeff said. "I don't even want to *think* what that tastes like."

"I had a bite at the shoot," Alex said. "All the flavor of packing peanuts. But look at that picture! We make soystrami look *good*."

"That you do," Kanter said, popping off the desk. "I'll read it through on the way over. Nice work."

Alex bunched together the pages and gathered them into a leather binder. Just as he was about to hand it over, he stopped. He'd done this same transaction dozens of times before—the hand-off. He'd done the brainstorming, the prep, the research, the production. Now Kanter would take what Alex had prepared and waltz into the client meeting in his sleek gray suit and berry-colored shirt, radiating golden-boy confidence. He imagined him opening with a riff on the Australian Open or the Tour de France or whatever high-end gentleman's sport was in season. Then he'd get down to business, underscoring how excited they all were, what an *impact* this was going to have. Then he'd present the work—Alex's work. If the mood was right and approval was in the air, he'd flash the cover art like a magician showing the card picked at the end of a trick and get the sign-off right there.

Not that Alex had seen all that much of Kanter in action. He wasn't invited to client meetings. That was Kanter's domain. Kanter was the public face, the show pony, the salesman.

"Kiddo?" Kanter said, giving the binder a quick tug. Alex was still holding it, his grip locked.

He blinked. "I was just thinking," he heard himself say.

"Maybe I should come along? You know, as backup?"

"Backup? What for?"

"You know—in case they have questions? I know this backwards and forward—I could be an asset."

Kanter gave his shoulder a squeeze. "Alex, this is a bullshit promo piece—you know that. It's strictly donor fulfillment. It's nothing. Stay here, get started on the PSA for the shaken babies. I'll go, keep Russo happy, be back by three."

Alex tightened his grip on the folder. "I'd really like to come along."

Kanter gave him a sidelong look. "What's up with you, Sherman?"

"Maybe I'm a little proud how this turned out."

Kanter smirked and raised an eyebrow. "Soystrami? Seriously?"

Alex face went hot. "Okay, maybe it pisses me off that you don't want anyone in the room who knows more about the material than you do. Maybe—"

Kanter pulled the binder away and stepped back. "Whoa, kiddo. You want to meet with clients, fine, we'll talk about it. But not today—not for this. I promise you—you're not missing anything."

And with that, Kanter swiveled away and retreated to his office. Alex sat down and took a swig of his chai, agitation swirling in his chest. Of course, Jeff was right—it was just a bullshit promo piece. But for some reason he couldn't quite explain, he felt an overwhelming desire to deliver the cookbook himself, to see the clients' reaction when they saw that glorious sandwich.

Alex was still stewing, staring off into the middle distance when his phone buzzed. It was Figgy—she'd been conked out that morning when he'd gotten the kids ready for school.

"Ach," she said roughly. "I think I'm allergic to our house. I feel like my head's going to explode."

"There's some grapeseed extract in the cabinet—mix it up with some warm water and honey. Don't sneer at the holistic juju—just do it."

"Ach," she said again, dubiously. "You'll get the kids at one?"

Alex swallowed. "One? What's at one?"

"The kids—they're out today at one, remember? The flyer in Sam's backpack?"

"Shit," Alex said. Teachers at the kids' school insisted on communicating vital information via flyers that invariably came home smudged with banana or lost amid a jumble of worksheets. Figgy made it a habit to go through their backpacks when she got home and the kids were asleep. "Why can't they email like regular people?"

"Public school—hello?" she said. "I'm not even sure they have computers. Anyway, they've got some 'staff development' thing this afternoon and the kids are out at one."

Alex sighed. The TestiCure presentation was at two. Kanter wanted him to get started on materials for the shaken-baby spot, but right now he felt no particular desire to do Kanter's bidding. "I could cut out early," he said. "What've you got today?"

"Lunch with Herb, the studio guy? With the crazy eyebrows and the teeny-tiny Korean wife? I'm supposed to go and make nice—Jess says they're about to sign off on the deal."

Alex coughed. "That was fast. How's it looking?"

"Who knows? The schedule's crazy—we're looking at no hiatus and six-day shoots and the network wants outlines in a week. I'm already having panic attacks. And today I'm supposed to be at Mr. Woo at noon to eat lettuce cups with a guy with a private plane."

Alex leaned back in his chair and tried to imagine what sort of deal they were talking about. The metrics were mysterious, but Alex knew the proportions were outsized; he understood Figgy stood to earn more in her signing bonus than Alex made in an entire year. "All right—fuck the grapeseed. Take two Benadryl and go make nice. I'll get the kids and see you at home."

"Thanks," she said. "Wish me luck."

"Luck," he said. Alex put down the receiver and gathered up his things. If he ducked out now, Kanter might worry Alex planned to ambush him at the TestiCure meeting. Let him sweat it a little. He'd hit a taco truck in Echo Park and make the carpool line at school by one. At least he was needed somewhere.

• • •

Over the next few weeks, Alex felt himself disengage from work, the commitment and interest he always took for granted suddenly gone. Maybe it was the way Kanter had shut him out of the cookbook pitch, or maybe it was the fact that Figgy's deal had closed; whatever the reason, his own work now felt like a hobby he'd outgrown long ago and had somehow forgotten to give up.

Alex was fiddling with his phone one morning in line at Interlingua, the fair-trade coffee joint on Sunset staffed by baristas who approached the preparation of a latte with the precision of Swiss watchmakers. Dressed in tweed waistcoats and newsie caps, the staff looked like officers in a steampunk army, even as they spoke to the customers like Malibu surfers. No one said, "Here or to go?" Instead, they asked, "Hanging out or taking off?"

Alex looked up and saw a familiar figure crossing the courtyard, dressed in a fuzzy plaid shirt and skinny jeans that gave his legs the silhouette of a seabird. It was Huck, Katherine Pool's Plus One.

"Well, well, well," Huck said, gently punching Alex's shoulder. "If it isn't Dead Shoe Walking. Come sit—me and my boy Brandon got the hookup, get you a soy cap before this line moves a step. Come."

Alex followed Huck back to a table in the corner, where his

friend Brandon was deep into what sounded like a well-rehearsed rant about oil reserves and the International Monetary Fund. With his shaved head, aviator sunglasses, and a multi-pocketed jacket, he looked ready either for a runway in Milan or a military operation in Croatia. "You shoot?" he asked.

"Sorry, what? Shoot, like guns?"

"Yes, shoot like guns. Bang bang," Brandon ran a hand across his stubbly head and turned to Huck. "Don't tell me you've brought another hippie to the man table. Haven't we had enough patchouli up in here?"

Huck rolled his eyes and gave Alex a smile. Brandon, Alex learned, spent most mornings here holding forth on his theories of imminent social collapse and personal development, typically ending his monologues with a pitch for Operation: You, a paramilitary training seminar he ran out of a luxury hunting lodge in Colorado.

"Shooting practice and deep-dive seminars by day, wine pairings and spa treatments by night," Brandon said. "Do you some good, boyo. Identify obstacles blocking your path, take 'em out. Therapy with firepower. You're looking at the Tony Robbins of paramilitary personal development."

"Wow," Alex said, forcing a smile. "Send me a link."

Alex finished his cappuccino and ordered another. Minutes stretched by. Alex was dimly aware that he was well on his way to being very late for work. Still, he made no move to go. The busboy brought over a plate of cinnamon sticky buns. Alex looked around at the patio. Every table was filled with bearded guys with band stickers on their laptops and ladies with tasseled boots and filmy peasant blouses. Who were these people? Didn't they have anywhere to be? They nodded meaningfully and spoke slowly, in no particular hurry. All over the city, Alex could sense computers booting up, conference calls starting, emails flying. Not here. Alex broke off a piece of sticky bun and popped it in his mouth.

"Dude, you ever been to a Korean spa?" Huck leaned back and crossed his arms over his chest. "It's an experience. Let's go hang some dong."

• • •

Climbing into Huck's Audi, Alex slid his seat forward and did a drum roll on his thighs. "How long does this dong-hanging typically take? I probably should get to work at some point."

"Seriously?" Huck said, swiveling his steering wheel with the heel of his palm. "We can't put a clock on this. Take a personal day."

Alex settled back into his seat. "So what might that involve, generally?"

"Hit the Gem Spa, get a massage, then I dunno. I gotta cook tonight—maybe we hit Malcolm's for some protein."

Alex frowned and nodded. He considered putting a call into the office, and then stopped himself. He'd play hooky, full on—no need to spoil it with a tense exchange about a fictional childcare crisis or trumped-up tummy trouble. He left a message for Figgy that something had come up and she should pick up the kids.

Gem Spa was a four-story co-ed spa in a downtown building once occupied by a department store. Thankfully, the dong-hanging portion of the experience was brief, limited to the few minutes it took for Alex and Huck to stash their clothes in a locker and change into the Gem Spa shorts and T-shirt and head up to the *jimjilbang*, a windowless floor where napping housewives were splayed out on slabs of heated jade. Along two walls were doors leading to specialty saunas, one lined with salt crystals, another coated with ice, another containing an enormous pit of chalky, orange clay balls. Alex noted that he and Huck were the only Caucasians in the place.

"This is amazing," he said, wiggling into the ball pit. "I feel like I'm in some sort of seventies future. But Communist. Like a

North Korean *Logan's Run*."

"I know, right?" Huck said. He motioned to a flat screen mounted on the wall of the sauna, tuned to a subtitled Korean soap opera. "Awesome, it's *Honor Bride*. Guy in the silk poofy hat is a ghost. Super intense."

Alex squinted in the heat and tried to make sense of the show, which from what he could tell revolved around a princess, an opera singer, and a magical cantaloupe. They watched until droplets of sweat began leaking into Alex's eyes.

"Huck—can I ask you something?" He jiggled back and forth on the top layer of balls, dry heat radiating across his back. "How do you have *time* for this? With me, anyway? Don't you have a whole crew...."

Huck turned toward him. "Most of the guys in our position are too busy with their..." he rolled his eyes and spoke in a self-important bluster "...*projects*—photo exhibits and screenplays and artisanal, organic whatever-the-fuck," he said. "You give a guy a little room to breathe and they trip out, I'm telling you. I wish *I'd* had someone show me the ropes."

Alex nodded and shifted his weight, clay balls rattling under his back. "So what're Bing and Penelope doing while we're here in this...ball pit?"

"They're with their lovely and devoted nanny," Huck said. "Today is dance class. Or sign language. Maybe percussion. I forget. Anyway, they much prefer the nanny to me or Kate. Mama Bear gets weird about it sometimes, but I keep telling her: Everyone's happy, why stress? Hakuna matata, right?"

• • •

Malcolm's Meat and Fish was a narrow storefront beside a nail salon on Virgil, the Edwardian script of the logo a clear signal to the local fooderati that this was not just a run-of-the mill butcher shop. "You're going to freak," Huck said, leading the way through the glass door. "Malcolm's a genius. Dude's not a butcher. He's a *consigliere* of meat."

Alex stepped inside, a rich mineral tang heavy in the air. The boxcar-size store was immaculate and spare, the floors honed concrete and the walls chalkboard black. The glass case was a quarter filled, each item individually spotlit, the beef marbled and precisely trimmed, the poultry pink and succulent, the salmon fillets jewel-toned. Handwritten tags identified the farm, feeding, and preparation of each cut, along with the price, which Alex calculated as roughly 120 percent higher than anything he'd ever paid at his regular Armenian grocery.

"Huck! Homey!" came the call from Malcolm, bushy eyebrows darting in their direction. "How'd it go with the kalbi?"

"Amazing." Huck pressed down on the gleaming glass case. "I did it with that rice wine marinade, like you said. Best ever."

Malcolm seemed to know everything Huck had ever purchased here, referencing scallops and sausages like they were children dropped off in daycare. Alex hung back a few steps as the two traded firm and irrefutable opinions on spice rubs and wood chips.

Over Malcolm's shoulder, Alex caught sight of a young woman in chef's whites. She ducked behind the display case and slid a tray of hanger steaks through the sliding cabinet door. He watched her face through droplets of condensation. Pointy chin, blond eyelashes, red bandana knotted above her forehead, wheaty hair tied back in a complicated knot, a finely crosshatched tattoo of a cleaver on her forearm. There was something extra-terrestrial about her, something extreme-Nordic. Alex got a sudden picture of her on a rocky plain, in a knit sweater with a wolfhound at her side, the wind in her face and a dagger strapped to her thigh.

Alex took a step forward and tapped the glass, hoping to get her attention. She looked up and registered his interest, then motioned to Malcolm. "*He* can help you," she said.

She ducked toward the walk-in freezer, the bow of her apron strings dangling over a ridiculously high twentysomething rump. As he watched her recede into the chilly dark, he was suddenly aware of what she saw when she looked back at him. It registered in a flash: rumpled shirt, clumpy hair, baggy khakis. Not old, but not young. A cross between Bob Saget and a dollop of sour cream. Unthreatening, uninteresting, uncool, entirely *un*.

Outside, carrying a black cellophane bag heavy with $75 worth of rib-eye, Alex agreed that Malcolm's was indeed amazing. Then he asked about the woman stocking the case.

"That's Miranda," Huck said. "She's got some kind of Tumblr feed or blog? Meatchick or Meatgirl, some shit like that. Why?"

"I just don't think I've ever seen a lady butcher." Alex lowered himself into Huck's Audi and watched as Huck deposited their purchases into an icebox built into the dash. As he popped on his sunglasses and started up the car, Alex looked him over. Huck was about Alex's age, maybe a few years younger, but next to him, Huck seemed like a college kid.

"Can I ask you something lame? Where do you get your— clothes? For instance, those *trousers*?"

Huck laughed. "Why? You wanna do something about the daddy pants?"

"Kinda, yeah."

"Hold on." Huck pulled a quick U-turn, gunned the accelerator, and drove to a tiny sign-less storefront on 3rd Street with blacked-out windows. It could've been an auto showroom if not for the booming funk on the sound system and the steel racks of menswear. Alex wandered around, checking the tags on the sleeves of button-snap shirts and velour V-necks. Huck chatted up the shop assistant, a drowsy-eyed girl with tousled red hair. She sized Alex up, summed up what he needed—"French denim, stovepipe cut, distressed not wrecked"—and flashed Alex a wide smile. He knew she was only being pleasant because she knew Huck. But niceness by proxy was still nice. Alex lapped it up.

In the dressing room Alex discovered he'd been given a size twenty-eight. Not a chance. He passed the pants over the door. "How about a thirty-four?"

"Just put on the pants," Huck said. "It's how they're made."

Alex pulled the pair back over the top of the door. The fabric was the color of deep space and springy to the touch. He stepped into one leg and then the other and tugged, yanking the pants over his knees, where they stopped mid-thigh, budged tight. He stretched out and leaned against the wall, elongating his torso. The jeans moved up a few inches, but to get them on he'd need to get down on the floor and transfer his weight from his midsection upward in a yogic exercise of breath control. Fabric squeezing his legs like the sleeve of a blood-pressure cuff, Alex held his breath, wiggled spastically, and tugged on the belt loops. This, he thought, is how it must feel to have an epileptic seizure.

After a few minutes, the jeans settled into what he guessed was their proper place. He stepped out, and the swinging doors of the changing room flapped shut behind him, a gunslinger stepping in from the range. The salesgirl stepped forward with an approving nod, then reached down and brushed his hip with her finger.

"Good line," she purred.

His internal organs had realigned, and he'd lost feeling in his toes, but he couldn't argue with the view in the mirror. He had legs! A whole lower body, with a not-so-bad curve of the calves and a pleasing divot near his hip. To think he'd spent his entire manhood in sensible Levis and baggy khakis, when there was always this underneath—an actual form!

He wasn't sure what was more outrageous—the price or the instructions for care. (Washing machines and dry cleaners were out. The best way to clean them was in the ocean, "like every month or two." Alex knew his life was changing, but he didn't imagine those changes would involve periodic trips to Malibu to frolic in the surf in his new French jeans.)

Before today, it never would have occurred to Alex to wear a pair of pants like this. He was *not* a skinny jeans guy. But he was equally certain he was getting these pants. Things were different now. Normal was over. He'd had his fill of normal. He was ready for the skinny jeans.

Back in the changing room, before he could get the pants off, his gaze settled on the wall, which was decorated with old punk rock handbills, stickers, and ticket stubs. A familiar checkerboard pattern appeared on one of the shellacked pages, below a magic-marker cartoon of a kid with a Mohawk. Alex looked closer.

He knew that shaky lettering anywhere. It was the third issue of *R.I.P.*, the short-lived punk rock 'zine sold on consignment at a record shop on Melrose Avenue in the early eighties. This particular issue contained an interview with the band Minor Threat, a review of the latest Buzzcocks LP, and an energetic if not quite lucid screed against Reaganomics. The whole 'zine was written, published, and distributed by an enterprising and stupidly confident boarding school kid from Ojai named Alex Sherman.

He quickly did the math. Twenty-two years had passed since the afternoon Alex had put out issue #3 of *R.I.P.* Twenty-two fucking years. He clicked a picture of the wall.

Then he slipped his khakis into a shopping bag and strutted out, heading home to show his wife of nine-and-one-half years his new pair of skinny French jeans.

Four

On the drive home, Alex fast-forwarded through the 'zine's lifespan; he saw it flopping out of the innards of a refrigerator-size photocopier in the office at the Crestwood School, stuffed in Alex's backpack on a trip to the city, dropped off at Vinyl Fetish on Melrose, added to a confetti of flyers and stickers beside a cash register, tossed into an orange plastic bag, stashed in a basement, stuffed in a box and forgotten for years, then finally unearthed—and here its trip took its weirdest turn—by a decorator tasked with adding some authentic street-creddy ambiance to a pricey new boutique, a shop that Alex would never have even *thought* to enter before today.

But there he was. And there it was, so suddenly, so miraculously, at such a weird, vulnerable moment—it felt supernatural. It had to be a sign.

But of what? His first response was to cringe at the awful socio-cultural irony—like hearing Iggy Pop's "Lust for Life" on a

Holiday Cruise Line TV commercial. Here his crude, homemade, DIY tribute to punk rock protest was now literally the wallpaper of upscale consumerism.

Without even meaning to, without even knowing it, he'd sold out—and worst of all, without making a single cent.

Then again, the sight of *R.I.P.*—his scrawl, his words, his twitchy little middle finger raised high to the world—in that sleek, sexy context, repurposed as edgy modern décor... it was... kind of amazing. It meant that his misspent youth had maybe not been so misspent.

Which was terribly important to Alex, because even though he'd never admit such a thing out loud, he looked back on his stint as a teen publisher as one of the high points of his life. He had discovered punk at fourteen during one of his mom's periodic absences—she was always skipping off on road trips to Santa Fe or Big Sur. With her gone, Alex skipped school, slept in, and earned the top score on Missile Command at the local bowling alley. Every couple of days he'd get a visit from an older teenager named Dotti, whom his mom had tasked with checking in on Alex. Why his mother left her pubescent son in the care of a teenage girl with peroxide hair, raccoon eyeliner, and a magnificently mature physique never made a whole lot of sense to Alex—but in those days, not much did.

Dotti's developed, overt sexuality was a constant source of wonder and terror for Alex. For her part, the only thing she seemed interested in sharing with Alex was her love of glam rock. Until that point, all Alex had ever really heard was his mom's Joan Baez and Carole King. Dotti introduced him to Queen, the Runaways, and Alice Cooper. He liked glam fine, but all bets were off the moment she dropped the needle on the Stooges' "Funhouse." Even as Dotti pushed him back in the direction of Bowie or T Rex, all he wanted was the harder, louder, more aggressive stuff.

One night they took a trip to Oxnard for a Circle Jerks show in the back of a bowling alley. Alex remembered driving back up the hill drenched in sweat, ears ringing, revved up and excited for the future in a way he'd never felt before. Punk might have driven other kids to cynicism and rebellion, but to him it represented something else. It meant energy, discipline, take-charge initiative—in short, everything missing in Ojai. Overnight, he couldn't abide by his caring-sharing Freeschool and the calico-clad teachers playing mandolin under oak trees.

A few weeks after the Circle Jerks show, Alex got a buzzcut, put on a good shirt, and hitched a ride to the front gates of the Crestwood School, a live-in academy a few miles down the highway from home. Apparently, he was the first reasonably put-together townie to show up at the school, and as luck would have it, Crestwood had a scholarship program aimed at students in the surrounding community. Impressed with his relatively clean-cut appearance and earnest appeal, the admissions committee offered him a full ride. After a wan attempt to change his mind—"You know they make you wear shoes, right? And do *math*?"—Jane agreed to let him go. In short order he went from running wild with the feral kids of the Ojai Freeschool to living in a dorm with the sons of doctors and lawyers.

On weekends, when the other boys went home to Montecito or Laguna Beach, Alex would hitch rides to L.A. with Dotti for shows at the Starwood, Madame Wong's, and various foreign legions. He'd stay up late pounding out articles for his 'zine on a IBM Selectric and picking the lock of the staff office to run off copies on the school machine.

Alex liked to say he folded *R.I.P.* when the Scene Got Shitty. Jocks and surfers and swastikas started turning up at shows—the Orange County hardcore kids had taken over. For issue #23, he ran a front-page headline declaring "Nazi Frat Scum Kill Punk" and declared *R.I.P.* dead. He was a jaded purist at sixteen.

It took Alex many years to put together that the demise of

the 'zine had less to do with the dilution of the scene than the astounding arrival into Alex's life of a force even more powerful than punk. One night in his senior year, he got a call from Dotti, who'd quit babysitting to manage an apartment building in Ventura. She greeted him at the front door of a vacant unit with her top off and those magnificent babysitter breasts gloriously bare. She proceeded to take Alex on as her protégé yet again. She fucked him with a lazy nonchalance that astounded him just a little less than the sex itself. He still carried around with him a vivid, oft-replayed image of the white-haired, dark-eyed Dotti splayed out below him, back bent and ass up, face mashed into a pillow and head tilted to the side so she could carry on her phone conversation about a faulty air conditioner.

At some point in the years since, he'd read a magazine article about "Determining Your Mental Age"—it was hardly the deepest thought, but he couldn't shake the notion that while basic functions of personality grow and change and mature, the raw essence of identity is flash-frozen at a certain set point. If that was true, Figgy was eight, bright and imaginative but given to deep sulks and explosive bouts of insecurity. His mom was forever nineteen, endlessly a college freshman in the throes of self-discovery.

Alex's mental age was no great mystery: He'd locked in at seventeen.

He wasn't entirely stunted, of course—not like the middle-aged guys he saw cruising around L.A. in bill-sideways baseball caps, men with paintball guns and futons and dirty toilets. Alex passed as an adult. He had a 401K and a Subaru. Seeing the 'zine today, though, at the end of his hooky day with Huck—it had dislodged something, some deep reserve of DIY, burn it down, fuck-it-let's-do-itness. The jolt of desire looking at the girl at the butcher shop, the woozy feeling he'd gotten plopping down his credit card to pay for those jeans—for the first time in a long time, he remembered what it felt like to be old enough to move in the world but young enough not to have a place in it. That unsettled, jittery, excited feeling had been missing for years, smothered by the job and the wife and the kids.

Now he wanted it back. Or at least part of him did—a small but insistent part with a voice like Iggy, circa *Raw Power*. Another part knew he was being stupid, that he was too old for all that now, that however great and even meaningful it had felt to skip work and cut loose a little, he'd had his fun.

• • •

Arriving home after his day out with Huck, Alex marched through the kitchen door, dumped his keys and phone on a countertop, and scanned the room. Figgy wasn't around, but Sam was camped out on the floor, busy measuring homemade lotions into an assortment of vials and beakers. Sylvie was wrangling the dog, wedging her paws into what looked like a tennis outfit.

After unpacking the bags and planting kisses on the kids' heads, Alex got busy with the rib-eye from Malcolm's, coating the meat in sea salt, garlic, and rosemary and then tossing together some cherry tomatoes, red onion, and basil. As always, cooking was weirdly meditative for Alex, even as he banged saucepans and butcher knives in an impulsive, chaotic rush.

As he was finishing up the meal, he called for the kids. "Honey, please stop torturing the dog."

The dog lifted her head up balefully, shaking off a floppy pink visor. He'd found her ten years earlier wandering the streets in such a haggard, mangy, and swollen state that he'd mistaken her girl parts for male ones and given her a boy's name that never unstuck: Albert. For a while, in those carefree pre-kid days, Albert was lavished with stupid luxuries and sloppy, unbridled affection. The moment the first kid arrived, however, Albert went from spoiled alpha to neglected afterthought, her only treats coming when Sylvie slipped her bits of Korean takeout under the dinner table. By now she had eaten more bulgogi than most Koreans.

"Daddy!" Sylvie locked eyes with Alex and flashed a giant toothy grin. "Mommy took us for noodles after school and now she's taking a nap and Sam's making another batch of Sammy's Salves!"

Alex sighed and turned toward Sam. "More creams?" he said. "Didn't we agree we wouldn't make any more creams until the old creams were gone?"

Sam kept his head down as he poured a dollop of bright purple fluid into a vial of viscous goo. "I keep telling you, Dad—they're not creams. They're lotions. Herbal lotions. I need new product—Mrs. Ramirez told me today she wants bath balm."

Mrs. Ramirez was Sam's fourth grade teacher and, bless her heart, a loyal repeat customer of Sammy's Salves. Alex knew he should be nothing but thankful to Mrs. Ramirez and proud of Sam's industriousness. But looking now at his bottles, lined up in a row with filmy ribbons tied around their caps, Alex did not feel proud. He felt panicky.

He swiveled around to the cabinet and fished around for a drink, filling one of the kids' juice cups with Trader Joes' two-dollar cab. Then he headed over to the computer on the kitchen counter. He scanned through his music files for just the thing, a sonic response to this particular moment. He found what he was looking for in a playlist titled "Iggy": the Stooges' *Fun House* album. He clicked on a track and filled the kitchen with a squall of feedback. Tapping out the bass drum part with a spatula, he moved over to the corner where Sam was bent down with his concoction. It was suddenly crucial that Sam appreciate the Stooges' anarchic brilliance.

But the boy wasn't having it. Sam stayed planted on the floor, beakers and vials arranged like a tiny defending army. Sylvie scurried up from behind, calling "Up! Up! Up!" until Alex turned and lifted her by the armpits, her feet flailing against the counters with percussive plunks. After a few revolutions he lowered her down. Sylvie immediately crouched, bent her elbows out, and made a big cartoon frown.

"Slam dance!" she hollered, barreling toward Alex.

Alex pivoted to the side in time to offset the blow, sending her careening directly into the path of Sam and his many bottles. Seven or eight containers went down, skittering across the linoleum and releasing a pungent slick of oil, cream, and powder. Albert barked happily and immediately set to work lapping up the spill.

"Not the jojoba!" Sam cried. "No, Al! Not the jojoba!"

Alex went over and shooed away the dog. "My fault, Sam," he said. "But no biggie! I'll clean it up. It's not a party 'til someone spills the bath balm!"

Sam stayed mum, hands wedged over his eyes, as if the scene before him was too awful to look upon.

"What... for goddsakes... is going on down here?"

Alex turned. He wasn't sure when she'd come in, but now here was Figgy, wobbling against the doorframe, eyes half open, hair wild and arms crossed over her chest. She squinted into the light of the kitchen, crossed over to the computer, and punched off the music.

"Hey, honey!" Alex said. "We're slam dancing here! Come on—join the mosh pit!"

Figgy leaned against the counter and sighed. Alex held his breath and took a quick inventory. The phone message this morning, the music interrupting her nap, the mess, the tears beginning to spurt from behind Sam's fists... there was just so much for her to react to, so many avenues of disapproval she might charge down.

Figgy rubbed her eyes and finally spoke up. "Are those *jeggings*?" she said. "Is my husband wearing jeggings?"

"They're jeans," Alex said, rising up. "They're French. Are they ridiculous? I'm ridiculous, right?"

In one quick move, Figgy swiped a washcloth off a counter, tossed it to Sam, and motioned for Alex to turn around. Apparently, the array of unguents dripping across the hardwood was nothing serious; Alex's jeans were the thing. "Gimme the 360," she said.

Alex pivoted around. "The lady at the store said they gave me a nice line," he said. "Why didn't you ever tell me I have a *line*?"

Figgy grimaced. "*Panty line* is all I'm getting," she said, nose wrinkling. "If you're serious about those pants, you're gonna have to lose the boxers. You're bunchy."

Alex peered down. "Am I?"

Figgy sidled up behind him as he reached under the sink for a sponge and bucket. "Just saying, if you wanna pull those off you better go commando," she said. "Fly free, sweetie. Either that or you're into thong territory."

"Oh God, no." He moved over to Sam, who was standing helplessly over the mess. "I'll deal with this, buddy. You go play with the Xbox. Thirty minutes."

It never ceased to amaze Alex how fast his son could snap out of the most serious sulk when offered thirty minutes of sanctioned videogame time. As Sam bolted toward the living room, Alex lowered down to his knees and began sponging up the mess. Sylvie went back to the dog, taking advantage of Albert's interest in the spill to go after her hind quarters with a frilly white tennis skirt.

Figgy stayed at the counter and gave Alex a long look. "So I did carpool today so you could dip yourself in French denim? What *happened* to you?"

"What happened was the most amazing day in I-don't-even-know-how-long," he said. "I met up with Katherine's husband—Huck, remember? Turns out he's a super nice guy and he took me to this insane Korean sauna and then we went to this incredible butcher and went to get pants—and there was my 'zine, plastered on the wall of the changing room! *R.I.P.*! How crazy is that?"

"So you just ditched work? Went totally AWOL?"

"Oh." Alex stopped swabbing. He hadn't thought about work since getting into Huck's car ten hours earlier. He hadn't checked his voicemail or email. His phone was probably clogged with messages. A wave of nausea passed through him.

"Yeah, well, I don't think I'm going back there," he heard himself say.

"Sorry?"

Alex took a long breath and rocked back on his heels. "I think I'm quitting that job," he said. "I'm done. It just doesn't make sense any more."

"Look, Daddy, she's *beautiful*!" Sylvie was now standing behind Albert, holding her upright. Albert whimpered, her snout smudged with violet-colored cream.

Figgy gave him a pointed look over her glasses. "Listen to you now. You're just *leaving*?"

Alex leaned down to uncouple the dog from Sylvie's grasp. "We can talk about it, but yeah—it's time, isn't it? I mean, you're busy. And getting busier. And I just can't really see the point in me going in every day to slave away on whatever bullshit campaign Kanter thinks will make clients forget about the goddamn carrots. And with the deal you're getting, we've got some room to breathe a little."

"It's just kind... not really like you. You sure you're not getting... midlife crisis-y?"

Was that what this was—a midlife crisis? He hooked a thumb through the belt loop of his jeans and rotated his hips around. "Whatever gave you that idea?" he said.

Figgy smiled and put out her arms. "Come here."

He stepped forward, tipping his head up as she pressed her face into his neck.

"*Am* I being crazy?" he said. "I just think, with all that's happening right now, one of us should be home. There's stuff I'd like to pursue on my own, plus I really think I can help get a handle on the home front."

She looked up at him, her expression intent. "You want this? You won't go batshit?"

"I'm the stable one, remember?"

Figgy gave him a squeeze. Alex felt certain, for this second anyway. This was a good and sensible decision. He'd leave an old job for a better one; he'd keep the family intact, protect his kids from the bullshit of Hollywood, be the sort of man that Figgy could depend on.

Figgy took a long breath and pressed herself up against him. "I'm about to spend the next six months locked in a conference room with the smell of dry-erase markers and half-eaten takeout. So I'm a little jealous is all. But if I'm stuck at work, why shouldn't you be at home in your French jeans, slam dancing with the kiddies?"

"So you're okay with this? Really?"

"I am. You're such a great dad. If you're gonna be home, maybe… you know, we could try for another."

Alex frowned. "Another what?"

"You know. Another squishy."

Figgy had been making noises about having a third kid for a while now, but he'd so far managed to avoid any real negotiation. "I dunno, hon," he said. "That's a lot all at once. Maybe we take this one step at a time."

She pulled him in. "You're such a great dad. You'll be the most awesome househusband in Atwater Village."

Alex frowned. "Please don't ever call me that."

Under their chair, he felt the dog brush up against his leg. Her whimpering had taken on a low, throaty rumble.

"Why not?"

"Maybe because the most awesome househusband in Atwater Village never gets laid, ever."

She pulled him close. "I wouldn't be so sure about that," she said. "Caretaking is *hot*."

"Just don't call me a househusband. I'm thinking something more along the lines of... domestic first responder."

Figgy cocked an eyebrow. And then the bejeweled dog coughed up the contents of Sammy's Salves all over the leg of Alex's new $350 jeans.

• • •

Alex wrote a resignation letter that night, heaping praise on Kanter and BestSelf but saying he'd "reached a crossroads," that he "wanted to spend more time with family," and that he'd decided to "pursue other projects."

It sounded grandiose, like the parting missive of a CEO resigning under suspicious circumstances. But it was true—he *had* reached a crossroads. He *did* want to spend more time with his family. Notwithstanding the occasional toxic spill, he was good with the kids (or with Sylvie anyway). He was at least better than his own parents had been with him—which was, he thought, the bottom-line goal of all parents. But he wanted to do better than that, to "parent" as a verb. When Sam and Sylvie were little, he reveled in the extra credit he got for mundane chores that mothers did routinely (he'd learned to turn a diaper change into an elaborate performance piece). Now he got a quick vision of himself wearing a BabyBjorn and sitting beside that redheaded mother of twins at the playground. She'd never given him the time of day before, but now he'd be a regular. She'd share her park bench, let him sample from her sack of healthy snacks and thermos of good coffee. In soft-focus slow motion, he saw her lean over, lay a hand on his leg, and confide how she wished her own husband was half as attentive and involved as Alex was.

Of course, there was another, more pertinent truth about quitting his job that he didn't bother mentioning in the letter: His wife was about to make more in a single deal than either one of them had made in their entire careers, enough to make his own $85K annual salary seem irrelevant. He no longer had to work up a lather of temporary enthusiasm about this or that campaign, to scrape and hustle and pitch, hoping this cookbook or pamphlet or TV spot or direct mailing piece would turn into a huge deal and make some actual difference in the world. Let Kanter hype his millionaire friends' pet charities. Alex would do something creative, something entrepreneurial, the exact nature of which he wasn't entirely sure about but which had something to do with the feeling that life was getting bigger and he needed to stop being the same smallish guy.

As he drove to work the next morning with the resignation letter stashed in his bag, he felt an intense, whole-body certainty that the time had come to get what he'd always wanted.

Alex planned to drop the letter off in Kanter's office before the boss arrived. He knew he really should sit down for a face-to-face, but an official exit interview with Jeff Kanter was more than he could stomach. What could Alex possibly say? And why bother saying it? He'd leave his letter, get out, and move on.

After packing a box with his things, he folded his letter into a BestSelf envelope, padded into Kanter's office, and propped it up on his burnished, steel-topped desk. He lingered a moment, plopping down in Kanter's mesh-topped chair and looking around the room.

"Hey." Kanter was in the doorway, slinging his messenger bag off his shoulder. "What's happening in here?"

Alex jolted up. "I was just dropping something off—"

"What?" Kanter said, crossing the room and eyeing the envelope.

Alex coughed. "It's a letter."

"I see that. What kind of letter?"

"You don't have to read it now—"

Kanter picked it up and tapped it against his palm. "So you'd rather I wait until you're in the elevator on the way out? I saw the box on your desk."

"I didn't know when you'd be in—"

"Chickenshit move, kiddo." Kanter stayed standing in front of his desk, jaw set, shoulders squared, not an ounce of that famed gooey Jeff Kanter empathy in evidence.

Alex said nothing, embarrassment and confusion pounding in his chest. Chickenshit? How could Kanter not recognize that quitting this job was the exact opposite of chickenshit—it was quite possibly the bravest thing he'd ever done?

"So where to? Back to Feinstein Pierce?"

"No." Alex's shoulders tightened up.

"Rainman-Kott?"

"No—nowhere. No other job. I'm out. Done."

Jeff frowned and dropped down into his chair. "So what—you're off-ramping?" He let out a hissing half-laugh. "Okay then. Just gonna let the wife carry the load while you—what? Kick back, hang out?"

"No—not at all. I've got kids, Jeff. They're little. I'd like to be around for them. Plus I've got... other projects. Some really exciting projects. I've got this amazing punk rock publication—there's talk of a relaunch. Also some exciting things happening with sustainable meats. Plus there's some writing I'd like to do."

The room fell silent. Alex shifted uncomfortably.

Kanter leaned back and laced his fingers around the back of his head. "Look, if this is about the cookbook thing—I could've spun that better. But you've gotta understand—clients expect me to present the work. I'm the *brand* here. TestiCure hired Jeff Kanter. Jeff Kanter delivers. And I can't afford to dilute the Jeff

Kanter brand."

Alex stiffened. "So that makes me, what? A *brand diluter*?"

"No, no, you're more of... a brand *enhancer*."

Disgust roiled up in Alex's chest. He needed to make a quick exit. He rapped his knuckles on the desk. "I wish you all the best. Really I do. But I can't stay on now—it wouldn't be fair to either of us. There's just a lot going on for me right now. I can't ignore these opportunities."

He was two steps from the door when Kanter called after him.

"I like the confidence, kiddo," Kanter said. "But a word of advice—don't be an idiot. What's happened for your wife is great, the show's terrific, all that—but you, you don't get it. Your wife's success didn't somehow magically transfer to you. Her hitting it didn't give you superpowers."

Alex paused at the door, suddenly dizzy. He swiveled around, his gaze spinning around the room before landing on the credenza beside the desk: the CLIOs, the Ogilvys, those creepy framed photos of his kids. "Okay—a little advice for *you*," he said. "Maybe get some different pictures in here? Something that's not—twenty years old? These aren't so good... for the *brand*."

Five

Did Katherine Pool count as a celebrity? Did a Paperless Post invite count as an email? Alex surveyed his inbox and chewed on a fingernail, finally deciding that yes, Katherine Pool's starring role in *Tricks* and occasional appearance in the tabloids qualified her as a celebrity, and that yes, a Paperless Post message, having traveled through the tubes and slots of the Internet, did indeed count as an email. All of which meant that yes, he'd just received an actual email from a real celebrity.

As he clicked on the link on the message, he cringed at the subject line—"A sip and a dip with Kate & Huck"—quickly concluding this was probably just an invite to a cutesy charity event, the kind of thing where you pay $1,000 for the privilege of milling around in the backyard of a fancy house. (*Please use the Honey Wagons by the guesthouse! Thanks so much!*) But as the invitation loaded into his browser, he saw that he and Figgy were the only recipients. And while the message had come from Katherine

Pool's account, it had clearly been prepared by the man of the house. "I'm doing dry-rub short ribs," Huck wrote. "Get your skinny-jeans-ass over here. Bring the kiddies."

"Might be fun?" Alex wrote, forwarding the invite to Figgy. She and Katherine Pool weren't on the best terms—they communicated mostly through agents and intermediaries and had started the second season in a cordial but simmering stand-off. Alex figured he'd have to employ some major diplomacy to convince Figgy to go.

It turned out, however, that Figgy needed no convincing. She'd been dying, in fact, to get inside Katherine Pool's house, a six-bedroom Hancock Park spread that had been lavishly covered in the StarHomes.com celebrity real estate blog. "I heard they did an *insane* remodel," she said.

As they walked up the curved flagstone path on the appointed morning, lugging a sack of bathing suits and a box of pastries, Alex shook his head at the sight of the Sherman-Zicklin clan. Somehow, the kids had gotten the message they were going somewhere *fancy*. While this wasn't enough to get Sylvie to comb her hair, which was its usual chaotic tangle, she'd insisted on wearing a frilly yellow party dress, which was already smudged with chocolate croissant. Sam was in a button-down shirt two sizes too big and a paisley patterned vest, his hair slicked back with homemade Sammy's Salves Styling Mousse. He stood primly on the stoop with hands folded at his chest, radiating a look Alex scanned as Seedy Mormon.

"Figgy, sweetie!" The door had swung open and there was Katherine. She looked just like she did on TV but more so, with the big moony face, long tapering neck, and huge hazel eyes unblinking over a fluorescent stroke of coral lipstick. She pulled Figgy into a tight embrace and held it for a good five or six seconds, emitting a long *mmmm*. "Soooo glad you could make it."

Katherine showed them through the door. "Kids—we'll all

jump in the pool later," she said. "For now we've got a trampoline and art stuff outside. And Alex, I think Huck needs you."

She trailed off on the introduction once they'd arrived in the kitchen. Alex stopped cold. The room was the size of a gymnasium and had the spare, strictly accessorized feel of a Nancy Meyers movie set. The whiteness was overwhelming—white glass-front cabinets, white leather barstools, a white honed-marble island so large it qualified as a continent. Every visible surface was smooth, stainless, gleaming.

"Oh my," Alex said, suddenly picturing his own kitchen piled high with mismatched kitchenware, banged-up appliances, and unopened mail. "So this is what they call a great room."

"We redid everything last year before moving in," Katherine said, twirling around near the sink. "Or rather, Huck redid everything. He was here with the contractor every single day. He hammered. He plastered. He caulked!"

"I'm known for my huge caulk," Huck called from the cutting board, his voice echoing off the cathedral ceiling. Alex went over and gave him a one-armed embrace. He wore a short-sleeved polo underneath some sort of black nylon cover that snapped at the back. It took Alex a second to realize what it was.

"Dude, is that a *man apron*?"

"Got it at Malcolm's," Huck said, giving himself a quick brush-off. "Separate pockets for utensils. Keep my best ceramic carving knife right here," he said, reaching down and then twirling a white blade around like a pistol.

"Your place," Alex said. "It's incredible. You did the remodel?"

Huck motioned toward a cutting board near Alex. "Ton of work, but we got there. You can't let those contractors get comfortable. Dudes will rob you blind."

Alex picked up a mound of scallions and got to chopping. As they worked, Huck monologued about the awesomeness of his tube-amp record player setup, the awesomeness of his jujitsu trainer Sensei Rick, and the awesomeness of his urologist, Dr. Finkelstein. "I went in for the ol' snip-snip last month," he said proudly, thrusting his hips forward. "Changed my life. Finkelstein's a total rock star. You barely feel it—then you get two days watching TV with some Vicodin and a bag of frozen peas."

Alex offered an appreciative murmur here and there, but it was clear his participation in the conversation was not required. His only job was to bear witness to the utter excellence of Huck's life.

Out the sliding glass doors, Alex watched the kids frolicking across a rolling green lawn. Sylvie and the raven-haired Penelope were running circles around a pair of easels while Sam and Bingwen attempted somersaults on a trampoline sunk to grass-level. The ladies had pulled up seats at the island and were halfway into a pitcher of Bloody Marys. From his station near the stove, Huck motioned majestically at the scene and touched Alex on the shoulder.

"It just gets better, am I right?"

Alex swallowed hard, stifling a gag. He wanted so much to like Huck, but declarations like this made it hard. Huck seemed blissfully unaware of Katherine's contribution, or for that matter any of the nannies, nutritionists, contractors, beauticians, trainers, life coaches, and metaphysical therapists that kept the show going. It seemed to Alex that Huck had made a deal with himself. If househusbandry made him a pussy, then he'd be the most capable and involved and commanding pussy ever to don a man apron: the alpha pussy.

Huck turned to get a tray from the stove, and Alex headed over to the ladies, who were deep into a conversation about schools (this, along with vacation plans and dietary regimens, seemed to be the sole topics up for discussion in their social circles of late). Figgy was halfway into a complaint about the neighborhood elementary school where the kids had been enrolled since kindergarten. "We've *got* to get out of there," she said, shaking her head. "Seriously, you can bake all the vegan muffins you like, but when you've got thirty-five kids in a trailer they call a classroom, you're pretty much screwed. Her teacher can't even spell the signs on the reading wall. I had to rip down a sign that said A-M-I-N-A-L."

Alex nodded and made a sympathetic grunt. He'd given up defending their local public school. He loved how close it was and how they could, in theory anyway, walk the four blocks from their house. He loved the school's squat, solid, geometric architecture, the comforting beige of the walls, and the heavy metal desks. He even kind of liked the crazy mix of Spanish, Farsi, and Armenian on the schoolyard. But Figgy was right: The overcrowding was ridiculous, and the teaching was uninspired. The whole place was, when he thought about it now, downright *raunchy*. He could feel his staunch commitment to public education wilting by the second.

"Oh, you've *got* to come look at the Pines," Katherine said.

So they were Pines people—of course. The Pines was a progressive private school that would, for $32K a year, teach your kids calculus and Mandarin without ever forcing them to wear a collared shirt. It was something like the K-12, co-op Freeschool he'd attended in Ojai, except with an endowment and actual academic standards. Pines people were famously loyal. Cultish even.

"Penelope is *thriving* in the music program—you should hear her on the trombone!" Katherine said. "You know, trombone is basically a free pass into the Ivies. It's crazy, I know—but you've *got* to keep these things in mind. Saves a whole lot of worry down the line." Alex looked out the window at the girls. Penelope was peering at a half-complete pointillist landscape, while his own daughter was slumped on the grass, one hand busy adjusting her underpants and the other lodged up a nostril.

Alex sucked in a breath, suddenly registering a delicious odor, a mix of warm dough and melting cheese. Huck came over with a basket of cheddar muffins. The four of them lurched forward and began stuffing themselves. He watched Katherine tip her face back in orgasmic pleasure. "Oh hon," she said. "You are a god. A cheese-muffin god. Never leave me and never stop making these."

Alex took a big bite and looked out at the kids. "The Pines?" he said. "Definitely on our list."

• • •

Figgy had a conference call with the network when they got home—episode two needed a stronger third act or ramped-up stakes or smash-cut or blow-out, Alex couldn't keep the lingo straight—so he was put in charge of the nightly ritual of bath, books, and bed. He hustled Sam in and out of the shower and got him settled without much fuss, but he ran into trouble with Sylvie and her bath.

Sylvie had been fighting a mysterious, stubborn urinary infection for the past month. Alex had finally broken down and taken her to the pediatrician the day she woke up shrieking and scratching. Thankfully, it seemed to be clearing up after a dose of antibiotics, a talk about the importance of wiping correctly, and the regular use of a special soap Sylvie called her "gi-gi soap."

All things gi-gi-related were usually Figgy's department, but she was on her call, so Alex was left to handle it. He knelt next to the tub and shampooed her hair, wiping streaks of paint off her face and arms and then picking up the medicated soap.

"You okay, hon?" Alex said, rubbing up a lather in the washcloth and lowering it into the steaming water.

Sylvie was busy with a rubber duck with devil horns and sunglasses. "I'm fine."

Alex soaped up her stomach first, and then, as gently as he could, worked his way down. Sylvie released the duck and appeared to tense up.

"Oh honey, does that hurt? Does that feel okay?"

Sylvie closed her eyes.

"No, Daddy," she said, her voice husky. "That feels *fantastic*."

Alex pulled the washcloth out of the bathwater and placed it in her hand. "Here, honey. You finish up."

• • •

"I think it's probably a good idea for you to do Sylvie's bath from now on, okay?"

The notes call was done, the kids were down, and the two of them were plopped back on the sofa, Figgy with a Sudoku book and Alex half watching the Nature Channel.

Figgy snapped her puzzle book closed. "You can't give her a simple bath? I had to take that call—"

"No, Fig—not that. I'm just saying… it got weird with the washing up."

"Weird how?"

Alex paused, unsure how to put it. "Girl loves her gi-gi soap."

"Oh." Figgy smiled, going back to her puzzle. "Can't blame her for that."

Alex settled back and tried to concentrate on the screen. A dull throb pulsed from his neck; he'd tweaked it in the pool that afternoon. Huck had been excited to show him the zip line he'd strung up in the backyard—it extended from the upper branches of a cypress, over the patio, and to the pool. Huck had rigged it up so you could let go from the halfway point and splash down in the deep end. It was a good fifteen-foot drop. When Alex went to join the guys, Figgy had grabbed him by the wrist. "Don't you dare," she said. "What happens if your timing is off?"

Alex shook her off and headed for the ladder. "I got this," he said. He wasn't entirely convinced he did, but Huck had made the leap three times, and there was no way Alex was going to sit back with Sam and the ladies while watching one magnificent synchronized drop after another.

And it *was* fun, at least the part where he scaled the tree trunk in his bare feet, grabbed onto the bar, and hoisted himself into position. Then he stepped off the branch and accelerated through the air, high over the women and children and letting out a squealing whoop as he released his grasp and fell, arms flapping, a safe distance away from the concrete lip of the pool. No problem. Perfecto. It would have been a complete success if Alex hadn't bent back *just* before touching down, bringing the flatness of his back level with the surface and producing a thunderous clap that echoed across the backyard.

"Oooooooo."

When he surfaced, Huck and Sam and the ladies and kids were focused on him, fists balled in empathetic anguish.

"I'm okay," he gargled, his back a mottled red under the surface. "Fine! Fine!"

Now he reached back and pressed down on a hard knot in the crux between his neck and back. The spot had the firmness of a baseball.

"I think I might have whiplash."

"Oh, honey," Figgy said. "That was quite the flop."

She moved over and began rubbing. She immediately honed in on the spot. Alex closed his eyes and let out a moan. "God bless you."

"You stupid, stupid man."

"That would be me."

Figgy kept working. He sighed and tried to isolate the tension and let it go. He reached over and gave her leg a tug. They were good, like this, alone together. Always were. It was when they separated and went out on their own—that's when he couldn't be sure.

He slouched forward and moaned. "Let's never leave this couch, okay?"

She patted his shoulder. "Could you believe that house? It was *so* done. Every inch. Done."

Alex kept quiet, opening his eyes and focusing on the TV. The Australian star of *Wildman* was fashioning a fishhook and spear out of a piece of bamboo. It looked easy enough, but it was one of those things Alex knew he himself could never pull off. He could barely clear a clogged toilet. He felt a sudden wave of resentment for his mom. Weren't lesbians supposed to be good with tools and home maintenance? How come he got all the self-righteous touchy-feely baggage of a dyke mom and none of the *handiness*?

Figgy whispered in his ear. "Huck did an amazing job, didn't he?" Then, when he didn't respond: "Would you ever want to take on a big remodel like that?"

The house was amazing, obviously. And Huck was clearly impressive in the domestic department. But for reasons Alex couldn't quite explain, there was no way in hell he could acknowledge that out loud. "It was all just a little Pottery Barn for me."

"Did you get a look inside that fridge?" Figgy continued. "Did you see the perfect symmetrical rows of Oranginas and Perriers? It was like the best minibar ever."

"Exactly," Alex said. "Like a hotel. You want to live in a hotel?"

"Did you see the icemaker?" she went on. "It made those little square cubes—just like a hotel. And that sauna? Katherine was going on and on about their *house manager*. Everything is handled by this lady in the guesthouse out back. Ukrainian. Klara someone. I'm supposed to email her about setting up a play date for Sam."

"Their house manager handles play dates? When is Sam going over?"

"He's not," Figgy said. "They're meeting up online. In that game that Sam plays with the igloos and penguins and whatever."

"So Klara the Ukrainian house manager... is arranging a play date for our boys... on Club Penguin?"

"Yup."

"Fuck me."

Alex rubbed his eyes and felt a shudder roll through him, simultaneously overcome by a sludgy mix of revulsion and envy. All that *giving over*—to house managers and private schools and nannies... he knew on one hand that Katherine and Huck's life was objectively nice. More than nice: It was spacious and easy and cushioned in a way he'd never ever felt. At the same time, the way Huck and Katherine lived felt offensive—nauseating even. The punk in him felt sure that they were to be if not reviled, definitely belittled.

"We could get some help, too, you know," Figgy said. "Someone to help with the kids and the house. Could be nice, right?"

Alex sat up and rubbed his face. He pictured himself interviewing applicants with a notepad and a jug of iced tea, holding court at the kitchen table with a procession of bright, attentive, eager young women. One might be Catholic, the eldest from a huge, happy family from the Midwest, looking for work while she pursued a teaching credential. Another might be grandmotherly and Jamaican, a career caretaker with references from here to Kingston. One might even be a guy. Alex was cool with a manny—he pictured a cheerful jock, a Kyle or a Tony, tossing perfect spiral football passes to Sam in the backyard as Sylvie looked on adoringly. Man, woman, old, young, white, black, brown—he was open! The point was, their nanny would be fully vetted, fairly compensated, and not in any way representative of the L.A. underclass that well-to-do families hired to do the work they were too lazy or spoiled to do themselves.

"Yeah, maybe," he said. "I could call some agencies."

"What about Rosa?" Figgy said. Rosa was the nice lady from El Salvador who came in once a week to clean the bathrooms and do laundry.

Alex made a face. "Actually, I was thinking more in terms of a professional."

"A professional? Fancy."

"Come on," he said. "With everything going on right now, shouldn't we do this right? On the up and up? Rosa barely speaks English. The only time she ever babysat, she just turned on the TV and fed the kids crap. Do you know what I found in the trash? A container from Yoshinoya Beef Bowl. Do you have any idea what they put in Yoshinoya Beef Bowl?"

"Meat?"

"Hooves, maybe, but definitely no actual meat."

"The kids *adore* Rosa," Figgy said. "She's comforting. She's got those big, soft El Salvadoran arms. Don't you want to crawl up in those arms? Take a nap in them? Let them *enfold* you?"

"Not really, no."

"She's perfect, then. Because no way am I going to leave you at home with some hot Australian with those ropy yoga arms. Besides, production is starting and I do *not* have time to find and train and get comfortable with a whole new person. I know Rosa. The kids know Rosa. Done."

Alex started to protest, then stopped. Figgy had clearly made up her mind—she wanted Rosa, and he was in no real position to object. Not with production starting and his position at home still tenuous. She tapped him on the shoulder with her pen. "Besides, have you seen Rosa chop an onion? Senora has some serious knife skills. She can be your sous! Now that you're done with the day job, aren't you getting busy in the kitchen?"

Alex felt himself smile. He flashed on the look of ecstasy on Kate's upturned face as she chewed that cheese muffin. "Could be okay," he said. "Anything to save the kids from more beef hooves."

• • •

Rosa happily accepted the offer and started the following Monday, arriving early to pack the kids' lunches and get scrambled eggs and toast on the table. Over the next few weeks, they fell into an uneasy new routine. The kids were, just as Figgy had said they would be, thrilled to have Rosa around. She snuck them candy and cleared their plates and made them pupusas. Alex, meanwhile, struggled to get the arrangement worked out. When he wasn't apologizing for dishes in the sink, he was hiding in the bathroom to stay out of her way. And as nice as it was having someone else around to pick up the laundry, it also made him nervous, having household tasks outsourced so early in his career as a domestic first responder.

More profoundly, having Rosa around meant they'd officially gone *bougie*, which for most of Alex's existence was one of the worst things you could say about anyone. Alex had thrown that word around a lot when he'd met Figgy, back when he was driving his $600 car and working as a legal temp and living with four housemates. On the weekends they'd walk around one of the nicer neighborhoods nearby, looking at all the big houses filled with families and flower arrangements and people whose lives seemed entirely alien.

At some point they started playing a game they called Come the Revolution. The L.A. riots were still fresh in everyone's minds, and Alex and his friends began fabricating detailed scenarios of exactly what they would do in the event of another one. Most of the neighbors, they agreed, would flee at the first sign of trouble. That would leave them the pick of whatever home struck their fancy.

One day Alex and two housemates hopped the wall of a Mediterranean mansion on the southern slopes of Griffith Park. It was gigantic and crumbling and apparently abandoned, one of the few properties owned by old-guard families who hadn't made deals with speculators flipping every halfway decent property in the neighborhood. This one was definitely decent—beneath the weather damage and creeping vines, the house had tall arched windows, intricate iron grilles, and hand-painted tiles. The pool was halfway filled with rank yellow rainwater, and the yard was teeming with scrubby lavender bushes and towering eucalyptus trees.

He remembered smearing dirt from a window and peering into the living room, squinting at a darkened expanse of oak paneled walls. "Come the revolution," he'd said, "this shit is *mine*."

It was right around the time that he was breaking into neighbors' houses that he met Figgy. They hooked up at a softball game. Alex had never played sports as a kid, his teachers in Ojai discouraging games they viewed as warlike and adversarial. A few weeks after learning about a friendly Sunday softball game, he signed up. He loved how the outfielders would chant lines from *The Bad News Bears*: *We wanna kicker, not a sock-knitter. We wanna kicker, not a belly-itcher.*

In his first time at the plate, Alex managed to hit a grounder through the cargo-shorted legs of an animator at short. He took off, huffing and puffing and failing to suppress a girly squeal. Meanwhile the ball, which had been headed into a gap in center left, was stopped short by a bull terrier. Alex charged forward in a sweaty blur, his head swollen with visions of Davey Lopes charging around first. He sprinted toward second, and without any thought to the distance he needed to cover or the tenderness of his ankles or his utter inexperience in any team sport, he leaped forward and slid.

Which is where he met Figgy.

She was standing over him when the dirt plume settled, a sturdy girl with big boobs, hip cocked, wearing baggy shorts and a purple bowling shirt. A heavy tangle of curly hair was tied back with a pair of red lacquer chopsticks. She held the ball in one hand and looked down at him with a wry smile. Only then did he realize that he'd come to rest a good three feet away from the base, his left cleat bent inward at an unnatural angle.

"Ow," she said.

"The dog! Interference!" he said. "Interference!"

"Infield dog rule," she said, tapping the ball on his hip. "Ball is in play. You're out."

"Uncool." He scrunched his eyes shut, took a breath, and became aware of a sharp burst of pain radiating up from his ankle. "Oh shit. Ow!"

"Like I said—ow," she said. "Your foot?"

Alex's ankle, it turned out, was sprained and maybe worse. He got up and hobbled off the field.

After two tumblers of Pabst and a muscle relaxant fetched from Figgy's glove compartment, Alex was convinced to head to the ER. She insisted on taking him, loading him into her Honda and heading across town to Cedars, because, "I don't care if it's not in your HMO, there's no way in *hell* I'm taking you to County and letting some comatose resident saw off your foot or bleed you with leeches or whatever it is they do there."

As they made the long drive west, he distracted himself from the pain by quizzing her on her background. She'd grown up in Sherman Oaks, studied theater at NYU, and was now working retail while writing plays and spec TV pilots. She'd had a show produced at a black box in Echo Park, *Mork & Masha*, which she described as "a theatrical collage of Chekhov, hip hop, and *Mork & Mindy*."

She'd landed a TV agent but had flamed out while on the staff of a WB sitcom about a hipster bowling league. She'd been the lone "girl hire" who her boss, a cocky schlub called Josh, could point to as proof his staff could sympathetically portray female characters. Not that any of the guys on staff had any real interest in sympathetically portraying female characters—the writers' room was too busy inventing detailed bondage scenarios involving the evangelical former beauty queen who starred in the show. Figgy was fired after four episodes and hadn't had a staff job since.

Alex learned all this before being called back into an exam room, where he was told his foot was fractured in two places and he was fitted with a protective orthopedic boot. And so it was that he was hobbled from the start of what turned out to be a fast and furious courtship; they moved in together six weeks after the trip to the ER.

Not all their friends and family understood them as a couple—his mom, for one, excused herself from the table of their introductory brunch when she deciphered the tiny alphabet beads on Figgy's barrette, which spelled out the word CUNT. Meanwhile, Joan had complained loudly about Figgy's cohabitation with "that weak-chinned *goy*" whose biggest professional achievement since graduating Hampshire had been a regional print campaign for a fried chicken and waffle franchise.

But he and Figgy made sense to Alex. She was solid where he was flexible, prickly where he was soft, certain where he was open to considering all viewpoints. And most significantly, he thought, the two of them shared an uncanny sense of timing. They were synced. Eating, sleeping, browsing a store, leaving a party—they were always, it seemed, miraculously ready at the same time, as if they had the same internal clock. It was clear neither one of them had quite figured out just who they were, but as a couple, they fit.

Besides, Alex was naturally attracted to funny, tough, intense women. That was kind of his thing. The women other men went for—the glam ones, the beauty queens, the nurturing earth mothers—they glanced right past him, registering their disinterest even before bothering to properly snub him. But the weird girls, the pudgy poetesses and tiny spitfires and socially awkward shut-ins—he was all over them.

And with her collection of Shriner fezzes and her obscene barrettes and her apartment packed with bric-a-brac, Figgy was the team captain of the weird girls. She lit him up from the word go.

Figgy's attraction to Alex, meanwhile, was at first not much more than a pleasant surprise. Her previous boyfriends had been nothing at all like him—she'd spent two years with a tattooed Mexican playwright before dating a Sephardic engineer with anger-management issues. So Alex was positively exotic in his tall, agreeable goyishness. She joked that he was her white-boy prize, her trophy boyfriend. But despite the surface differences, there was something primal, even animal about the way she loved him. She'd bury her face in his chest and inhale, murmuring about marzipan and cinnamon and the tiniest hint of jalapeño. He made her feel safe, she told him—secure, tethered. With Alex in her corner, Figgy was free to flail and wander and indulge. He was always there when she wore out, steady and supportive and with that same irresistible smell.

Nine years into their marriage, they'd settled into their respective roles. He was the steady one, the realist, the rudder that kept the ship upright. And she was the bright light, the instigator who provided spark and magic and the occasional upheaval to keep things interesting.

Things were definitely interesting now. Maybe too interesting. Lately he'd begun to worry that the secret something he'd recognized in Figgy was no longer a secret. Everyone now knew how amazing she was. And his kind of stability didn't feel like such a virtue anymore. How hot, really, was caretaking? Maybe now, Alex felt, it was *his* turn to do some upheaving.

• • •

"Alex! Alex!"

Alex was dozing off on the couch when Figgy started yelping and scrambling backward. It took a few seconds for him to wake up and see what she was hollering about.

Right there, not more than six feet away, holding court on a wide expanse of the living room carpet, was a rat.

It stood upright, grasping a nugget of dog food in one paw, as if balancing an hors d'oeuvre. For a moment, the room was silent. The rat stood its ground, head cocked and whiskers twitching. He thought he saw actual musculature rippling beneath its fur. It was, he knew, the kind of rat that male rats wanted to be and female rats wanted to mate.

And it was in their house. Snacking on their dog food. Staring him down.

Alex reached over and hurled a pillow. The rat regarded the passing cushion, lowered to the floor, and backed away. It took its time, slipping underneath a door that led to the cellar.

What followed were two solid hours of frantic scrambling. Alex put on dish gloves and tied a bandana around his face before going down to inspect the cellar and finding, illuminated in the glare of his flashlight, a gruesome array of telltale droppings. He got a stack of towels and jammed them into the inch-high space between the door and the floor, cutting off the rat's one obvious point of entry.

Meanwhile Figgy fired up the computer. As soon as she typed the words "rat removal" into Google, the screen lit up with gruesome images of slick-coated vermin scurrying through kitchen pantries, teeth bared and eyes beady. She lingered on a page that claimed a single rat indicated "a full blown infestation." Rats leave toxic droppings, gnaw through wood and wire, and have been known to bite children. And they carry disease: typhus, rabies, bubonic plague.

"Bubonic plague?" Alex said out loud. "Christ."

Figgy punched in "extermination." Apparently, the search engine algorithm had a mistaken impression of people in their zip code, because the top results were all "environmentally friendly" and "cruelty free" pest-removal services that used "nontoxic baits" and "comfortable cages" to release animals back into their native habitats.

"Fuck this," Figgy said, fiercely clicking ahead to a site for a Simi Valley exterminator called, simply, Annihilate. Its home page included a flashlit gallery of "kill zones" picturing vermin crushed by the rusty arms of medieval snap traps, bloated with toxic poisons, and smeared with sickly yellow glue.

"Now we're talking," she said, clicking on the "About Us" page, which featured a headshot of general manager Andre Wallace, a greasy adolescent with rheumy eyes, a wide, moist grin, and stringy hair pulled back in a ponytail. He was proudly holding a trap from which dangled a full-grown trophy kill.

"Can Andre come over right now?" Figgy said.

"Let's go to bed," Alex said. "Shut it down. We'll deal in the morning."

Figgy moaned apprehensively but followed Alex into the bedroom. There was some panic around the fetching of pajamas from the closet and the brushing of teeth, but at last, they settled into bed. Figgy sat bolt upright with the covers pulled up to her armpits and a police Maglight between her knees.

"I hear scurrying," she said. "It's in the walls. Go check."

"It's nothing," he said, rolling over. "Little fucker is probably in some corner of the cellar right now, traumatized. I almost got him, you know."

"That pillow attack was vicious."

Alex let that go and shut his eyes. He'd call Andre first thing in the morning. He drifted into sleep, shaken but resigned to handling it all tomorrow....

"Sylvie, stop it."

It was Figgy. It was sometime later; Alex had no idea how much time had passed.

"Sylvie honey," she said again. "Cut it out!"

Alex opened his eyes enough to make out the digital clock next to his bed: 5:43. Sylvie had obviously gotten into bed with them at some point; he could feel her warm little form on his left. But now he was confused. She wasn't anywhere near Figgy. "Hon, Sylvie's over here," he said.

Suddenly the covers whipped up and Figgy was out of bed, hopping up and down, clutching at her NYU T-shirt with one hand and pointing to the headboard with the other.

"Rat!" she yelled, flipping on the overhead light. "It's the rat! It's in the bed!"

Alex took a deep breath and flopped over. There was no way the rat had gotten upstairs. Figgy was having night terrors. He'd stay calm, stay in bed, model the sane and mature response.

"Hon, I jammed towels under the door, remember?" he croaked. "We're safe and sound. Come back to bed."

"It's *in* the fucking bed!"

Alex propped up on his elbows and cracked open his eyes. And there was the rat, dropping off the duvet and onto the floor, making a lazy diagonal path over the ridges of a thrift-store throw rug and under the door to the bathroom.

"It was *on* me!" Figgy shouted, hands flailing around her head. "It crawled across my back and into my hair! My *hair*!"

Alex got out of bed. Sylvie scampered into the room, rubbing her eyes with balled-up fists. She clung on to Figgy's leg. "It's okay, Momma. Daddy will get the rat. Won't you, Daddy?"

"Sure, pudding." He grabbed a magazine off his bedside table and headed toward the bathroom.

"Hold it," Figgy said. "That's your weapon? *Harper's*?"

Alex banged his hand with the magazine, which he'd twisted into a tight roll. "I'm *improvising*."

"I'll be right back," she said, rushing into the hall to the pantry and returning with three items, which she presented as if he'd know exactly what to do with them: a broom, a can of Lysol, and a cardboard box. "Go on," she said, pointing a chin at the closed bathroom door. "I'll cover the door."

Alex took the stuff. As he took hold of the doorknob, he hesitated.

Figgy gave him a shove. "One of you is coming out of there."

He flipped on the light and went in. He spotted the rat right away, munching on a pink tampon wrapper beside the toilet. He hopped up onto the rim of the clawfoot tub, balancing high above bite range. He wished he had some clothes on—he doubted his droopy boxers provided any real protection. He felt hollow, emptied out, like a shore sucked dry before a mounting wave.

"Get out where I can see you," he pleaded, poking his broom in its direction. The broom connected with the rat's side and it scampered into the open. Alex saw his chance, and while maintaining his balance atop the tub, he tossed the box forward. His aim was right, but the rat seemed to anticipate the throw and darted sideways, onto the base of a standup makeup mirror.

Looking for an escape route, the rat climbed up the steel pole, scampered around the fixed bracket, and stopped briefly on the face of the glass. It was now level with Alex's face, a foot or two away, its small, hot eyes and wiry whiskers in crisp focus. It kept scurrying, the mirror whirring around beneath it.

Alex smacked the mirror with a broom and it fell to the floor. The rat barely flinched before darting into an open cabinet, behind a thicket of bottles.

He hopped along the bathtub rim to get a better look inside. The rat was back in there somewhere, nestled deep in the protective cover of Sammy's Salves.

"You get him?" Sylvie called through the door.

"Working on it," Alex said, crouching down.

Heart pounding, he extended one foot and then another clear across the bathroom to the sink counter and shifted over to a perch above the cabinet. Then he retrieved the cardboard box and picked up the Lysol. A tense moment passed. He reached down and began spraying through the open cabinet door. A cloud of chemical mist wafted up his arm.

It did the trick. A moment later, in a quick gray blur, the rat leapt out. Alex dropped the box.

"Gotcha!" he hollered. The rat tumbled around inside, colliding off the walls.

Alex let out a triumphant cry and Figgy and Sylvie rushed in. Figgy was sent off to fetch something flat to slide below the box, returning with a piece of foam board from the craft drawer. Alex carefully pushed the board under the box, lifted it up and then headed down the stairs.

"Okay buddy—out you go," he said, stepping out onto the front stoop. The dawn was just breaking and the sky was a dull orange. His prey captured, his bare chest heaving and his daughter and wife trailing behind him, Alex felt an unfamiliar rush of pride.

"Oh no," Figgy said, gripping his arm. "You're not just letting him go. He'll come right back. Didn't you see what the website said? They leave trails of hormones. Trails! He'll come back. He'll bring friends."

"Aw Fig, come on," Alex said, putting the box down. "We got him, let's just open the box and be done with it."

"Honey—he was *on me.*"

Alex paused. She wasn't wrong. If he let the rat go and it came back, he'd have to go through all this again. He quickly ran through all the ways he could dispatch the thing bumping around in the box. He could crush it. A big coffee-table book—one of those giant Taschen art books? Run it over with his car? Poison it? Stuff it in the garbage disposal?

Each idea was too horrific, too messy, too awful to contemplate. Suddenly, it came to him. Bloodless, passive, silent. He put the box down and headed for the laundry room.

On a high shelf he found a big Tupperware storage bin they used to store holiday décor. He dumped the contents into a pile, a scattering of menorahs, pilgrim candles, and pumpkin-shaped trick-or-treat buckets.

"Sylvie, go inside and shut the door," he said, returning to the stoop and heading toward the bushes.

She didn't move. She hopped up and down just behind Figgy, sucking on a balled-up bit of her nightgown. "No way," she said firmly. "I wanna see."

Alex exchanged a look with Figgy, who narrowed her eyes and made no move to take Sylvie inside.

"Go on," Figgy said.

And so he did, dropping the end of the garden hose in the bin and then standing back as it filled, splattering the sides and making a low gurgle. When the water was close to the top, Alex turned off the hose and deposited the rat into the water.

Alex would think later how gracefully it all happened, how weirdly but perfectly timed it was for the sun to pick that precise moment to break over the neighbor's rooftop. The clear plastic bin lit up like a jewelry box, all golden and pink. The rat sank, and then began paddling around at the surface, making slow clockwise circles, its coat darkening and becoming sleek and aquatic. It seemed to swim forever, circling round and round. Alex, Figgy, and Sylvie moved closer. At some point Sylvie sat down beside the box, cupping her chin in her palms and watching intently.

After what could have been five minutes or an hour, the rat slowed and then stopped, seizing up once and then again, its tail slackening and the glow of dawn delineating the threadlike veins in its ears. Sylvie began to cry. Figgy bent down and wrapped her up in her arms.

Alex crossed his arms over his chest and shuddered.

"*Now* we move," Figgy said, getting up and guiding Sylvie back inside. "We've got to get out of this house."

Six

The hunt for a new house began in earnest the next week. As he scoured the MLS and made his first calls to agents, Alex felt an unfamiliar rush of urgency. The exterminator had plugged up holes around the foundation and stashed containers of poison in the bushes, but the house had been breached. Invisible trails of pheromones! And while he'd never admit it out loud, he was emboldened by what had become—at least in his retelling of the tale—an epic battle of father versus intruder, man versus wild. The rat, which was maybe six inches long from nose to tail, had become a feral beast. And he'd captured it, killed it! He'd repelled the threat, defended his family. Maybe he wasn't such a softie after all. Now he'd lead the charge once again, bringing his family out of the thicket and into a new and better place.

Clive had recommended a real estate agent whose name Alex vaguely recognized. It was only after hopping into the agent's pearlescent Mercedes one Tuesday morning that he realized he'd been set up with none other than Colby McNamara. McNamara had been a fixture on local bus bench ads since the eighties. In the ads, he held a brick-size phone to a great crown of feathered auburn hair. A cartoon bubble rose over his head: "ON IT! Colby McNamara: Your Dream House Deliveryman!"

"Hello there, Mr. Sherman," Colby said, leaning over to shake Alex's hand. Incredibly, the hair was intact; only his skin, which had the synthetic, high-gloss sheen of vinyl, gave away the twenty-plus-years between the picture and the present. "Let's go nab you that dream house!"

Alex gave a wary thumbs-up and settled in for the ride. Colby's plan for the first day was to hit three listings in the Hollywood Hills, then make a quick pass through Coldwater Canyon. As they crested Mulholland, Alex recalled heading out on similar scouting missions with his father, in the first few years after his parents' divorce. He never understood why at the time, but his dad, Barry, had used his weekend visitation days to hit every open house in the San Fernando Valley. At the time Barry was sporting a thick, blondish mustache and renting a gloomy, mustard-colored studio apartment in Van Nuys. After spending the night on a trundle bed in the living room, Alex would get into his dad's silver Lincoln and they'd head out on the hunt, Alex bitter and cross-armed in the passenger seat, Barry chasing curb signs and lawn flags to tiny Chatsworth bungalows and vast Encino estates. Nominally, Barry was looking for a good step-up from his current digs. But as the weeks spread into months, it seemed clear that Barry was content to search indefinitely, chomping on a toothpick and cranking the steering wheel, craning his head out the window and lecturing Alex on the importance of curb appeal.

It wasn't lost on Alex that Barry seemed inordinately interested in sales resulting from divorce—he'd look over every square inch of those properties, inspecting the contents of medicine cabinets and spice racks like a crime scene investigator.

"Well, now, what have we here," he'd say, nosing around an empty closet. "All the lady's things—gone! Obviously a runner. Judging from the color of that powder room, a real *tramp*, too. Ten bucks she's down in Baja with a señor ten years her junior."

"Come on, Rockford," Alex would whine, hanging back. "This place reeks of cabbage. Can we please go?"

It was so pathetic, so obvious, he thought, the way his dad was working through the mental wreckage of his marriage. It was all just a sad demonstration of the deep superficiality of his father and the whole adult world.

Now he was the one looking for a house, and he wished he'd paid a little more attention when he'd had the chance.

"I think you're really going to love this property," Colby said now, peeking out from the top of his mirrored aviators as he maneuvered the car along a narrow hill road. "Modern jewel. Real man-cave situation downstairs—you look like a guy who enjoys his poker and cigars."

"Sure," Alex said, grinning weakly. They'd pulled up to the entrance to what looked like a regional banking office.

"Hey, Colby, mind if I make a call?"

Colby gave him a thumbs-up. "Join me when you're ready— I'll just go inside."

Barry was in Tucson now, recently divorced from his third wife, a high-energy, bird-faced socialite whom he was still entirely attached to. The last time they'd spoken, Barry had spent the entire conversation talking about his two step-granddaughters' ballet recital and the wonders of testosterone therapy. ("The engine's humming again!") While Alex had zero interest in getting the update on adorable Eva or Caitlin or his dad's virility, he hoped Barry could offer some advice on the house hunt, or at least some general sense of whether Alex was foolish to be entering the market at a moment when the economy was in freefall.

"Are you crazy?" his dad hollered. A monstrous backyard

water feature thrummed in the background. "It's the best time to buy since ninety-two! Half the houses out here are in foreclosure. I'm safe, thank God, but with Lehman kaput and AIG crashed and Fannie Mae taking such a high holy dump, it's mayhem. And now's the moment you hit the jackpot? Honestly, your timing could *not* be better."

"It's actually *Figgy* who got the deal," Alex felt compelled to point out. "But you know—all boats rise, right?"

He'd made the same point to their accountant the day before, after she'd said they'd be safe looking "in the high twos or low threes." He kept playing that phrase back: high twos or low threes. He was amazed at the ease with which the words rolled off the tongue, how they so spunkily described more money than he'd imagined spending on anything, ever.

The truth was that Alex felt queasy whenever he considered numbers like the high twos or low threes. None of these sorts of calculations made any sense. How could it be good, for instance, that they were making the biggest financial bet of their lives in the midst of what his dad called Total Fucking Mayhem? Banks were toppling, industries collapsing, loans imploding—all of which meant, at least theoretically, that actual people were scrambling, suffering, and being evicted, foreclosed, and laid off. And yet here his dad and bookkeeper and everyone else he knew was claiming it was *great* news. It seemed to Alex that the whole system was built on wreckage, that for every big, celebrated success there were several thousand anonymous losses, that the whole enterprise ran on the fossil fuel of failure.

"The only upside I can make out is how bad it makes Bush look," Alex said, knee-jerk liberalism coming easily when talking to his fiercely libertarian dad. "It's all comeuppance for the red hot pigs in charge."

"Red. Hot. Pigs." Barry repeated. "Well then: Welcome to the pigsty, son. Jump in! The mud's fine!"

"Come on," Alex said, getting out of Colby's car and approaching the front door. "Just because I'm looking for a bigger house doesn't make me a *pig*. I'm still me. I just have a hard time getting all excited about the fact that everyone's money is on fire."

"You always were too sensitive," Barry said. "But listen, if it'll make you feel any better, I could help out with the down payment. I haven't always been there for you—and it might help on the marriage front, adding some family money to the pot. Just so it doesn't feel so... one-sided."

Alex wasn't sure whether to be touched or offended. "Thanks. Don't worry about it, though. We're fine. Figgy doesn't worry about that stuff—we're in this together."

"Sure you are," he said. "Just thank the Lord you found such a ball-buster for a wife. Hang on tight to that one, Alex boy."

Then, trying to sound jokey and light but with more seriousness than Alex felt was at all humorous, Barry added, "I never have understood it, though: What is that woman doing with you, anyway?"

Oh yeah, Alex thought as he hung up and walked inside, Barry signing off with a cheerful "oink!": *That's why I never call my dad.*

• • •

Alex walked in to find Colby waiting in the entryway, his well-coiffed head lowered and hands spread out beside him as if mid-bow. "Welcome," he purred, "to a true show house."

Alex squinted upward. Sunlight flooded in from a pyramid-shaped skylight three or four floors above. As a guy who delivered dream houses, Colby apparently believed Alex fantasized about acres of multicolored marble and furnishings that had all the coziness of medical equipment.

"Isn't it sumptuous?" Colby said, eyes bulging.

Alex followed him upstairs, cataloging the multitude of pointy edges and sudden drop-offs and imagining all the ways Sam and Sylvie would be impaled or concussed if set loose here for five unmonitored minutes. He made a few displeased sighs, and Colby must have gotten the message because he abruptly cut off the tour and hurried them along to the next property, a newly completed spec house that he was happy to report had been built on parkland the developer managed to scoop up in a "sweet under-the-table deal with the Nature Conservancy."

"It's nothing like the other one," Colby said, all his enthusiasm for the modern jewel now forgotten. "This is truly the essence of elegance."

Colby was right: It was nothing like the last place. The entry contained a chandelier the size of a satellite, a stained glass window that gave off a Jolly Rancher–green glow, and an iron railing fashioned into a tangle of grapevines.

Alex thought he'd been clear about what they were looking for—three bedrooms on one floor, pool, good flow—but he'd apparently failed on the aesthetic front. The problem, he realized now, was that Colby simply had no experience dealing with a customer like him. For that matter, Alex had little experience dealing with someone like Colby, with his crisp shirts and precise haircut and pleated slacks. Alex would've guessed he was a department store menswear salesman. The only personal detail Colby had offered at all was his devotion to a three-year-old Weimaraner named Hannah, whom he "spoiled like a baby girl."

"This is super impressive, Colby—really," Alex said. "And don't get me wrong—I've got nothing against impressive. But I wonder if we might see something a little older? Something with a little more… character?"

"Right! Got it! Character!" Colby said, his fingers suddenly breaking into a little hand jive. "You guys are *funky*."

They headed back early, Colby promising to recheck the inventories, Alex brooding over what to do now that the house hunt had been called off for the day. He sat down on the front steps, suddenly terrified by the to-do list that awaited him inside. There was so much to get done—or at least so many lists to make of things to get done. Lately he'd been spending an inordinate amount of time wandering around the house with a Wonder Woman notebook bought at Rite Aid, noting all the tasks that needed doing. Then he'd sit down at the dining room table and rearrange and reprioritize and incorporate previous lists into a single master list. Only then would he try to tackle an actual task. On good days he'd tick off one or two items—sort the board games in the closet, get dog license, research summer camps. Then it was time for carpool.

Meanwhile Figgy had been swallowed up by the new season of *Tricks*. The timing had been, at least on paper, perfect—Alex had quit his job just as she was getting sucked into the vortex of production. He knew the drill: Figgy would be either absent or effectively brain-dead for the next six months. She'd win the bread and he'd hold the fort. And somewhere in there, he'd carve out time to work on his own as-yet-undefined-but-nonetheless-crucial Creative Project.

"Free at last," Huck announced the day he strolled onto the patio at Interlingua that first free week. "You, daddy-o, are one lucky fuck."

Alex responded with a laugh and a nod before heading home to the Wonder Woman notebook, declining Huck's invitation to join him at the 11 a.m. spinning class with Annabelle, storied possessor of the Greatest Ass in All the Land. Alex could've used the workout if he ever hoped to get into those new jeans without prompting an actual aneurysm, but something told him he shouldn't be making plans that revolved around other women's asses.

Other women's asses—and their necks, arms, breasts, and really all the lady parts—seemed to be everywhere lately. The lady butcher at Malcolm's Meat and Fish, Miranda with the blond eye-lashes and the chef's whites—she was becoming a problem. Alex had been stopping by Malcolm's once or twice a week. Their product was ridiculously good, and it didn't hurt that a visit to Malcolm's also included a few minutes peering over the case watching Miranda feeding chuck into the sausage maker or thumbing out the ribs for a short loin. She had long, shapely calves and the sweetest little boobs he'd ever seen.

The last time he'd stopped by, they'd had an actual conversation. Miranda usually kept busy in the back of the shop, leaving Alex to crane his head over the case and observe her from afar. But today she marched right over while he was shooting the shit with Malcolm about the parsley–celery root slaw he'd served with halves of roasted bone marrow.

"So *you're* the guy who keeps buying up all our marrow?" she said, her cheeks flushed and eyes bright, wiping her blade on a rag tucked into a belt loop. "You back for more?"

"Maybe," Alex said. "Pretty tempting."

"Maybe time to cut you off."

"What? How do you mean?"

"You've been on kind of a bender."

She went up on tiptoes and looked over the counter, giving Alex the once-over. "You're fine for now, but keep going at this rate and say goodbye to that girlish figure."

Alex stepped back, protectively cupping his gut. Was she razzing him, or flirting? He had gotten a little thicker around the middle—was it that obvious?

"All right then—no marrow today." He started to turn away but stopped. "So… you cook, too?"

"Sure. It's bad. I pretty much blog every meal I make—God help me." She pulled a pen from a can on the counter, ripped off a page of butcher paper, and scribbled something on the corner. "Check it out. Total food porn. You'll dig."

"Thanks." Alex took his bag back and backed away, suddenly in a hurry to get out of there. The next day, he made a point of telling Figgy about the lady butcher.

"I'm off to ogle the woman who cuts our meat!" he said as he was headed out the door. "You can't even believe it—our butcher's a babe."

"Oh, so you're a *dirtbag* now? You gonna ditch me for some *butcher*?"

"Oh God, no," he said. "It's nothing. It's all about the fact that she brings me meat. It's Pavlovian."

"Good thing you're so evolved."

They kissed and off he went, free to ogle to his heart's content. Figgy was great that way, proudly loosey-goosey. That was one of the tradeoffs for having such an independent spouse—she might not be home packing the kids' lunches, but she didn't care about the sort of marital rules and regulations that seemed so important to other wives. They Went to Bed Angry. They held grudges and slammed doors. They said "you always" and "you never" when discussing her purchase of that horrid orange couch or his daily dusting of whiskers in the bathroom sink.

The big vows were still observed—partially because Alex suspected having a real life affair would be more exhausting than exciting, but also because the only actual opportunity he'd ever recognized was at a bar where he was propositioned by a not-unhot redhead who fixed Air Force jet fighters. The whole thing was so perfectly *Top Gun* that all he could think to do was run home to tell Figgy all about it. After he'd finished describing the girl's greasy fingers and boot-camp physique, she'd said something surprising.

"You'd never tell me if you *did* cheat, would you? Don't you *ever* dare cheat. But if you do, don't be an idiot and come confessing—I do *not* want to know."

He couldn't tell if she was affecting an air of sophistication or if she really did believe in a marital version of Don't Ask, Don't

Tell. In any case, it was all theoretical—he had never really been tempted, and he'd never worried about Figgy. She was too busy, too insecure, too manically consumed by her own life to start living a secret one.

Now, though, he'd begun to worry. When had that started? Since she'd gone back into production? Her days were so long now, and late at night he'd find himself fixating on all the attractive and attentive men surrounding her at work. He'd seen them, scruffy Yale-grad baby writers and ruggedly handsome actors, all of them fawning and flirtatious in the presence of the lady boss. Alex had identified one guy in particular, Zev someone—he was their house DP, and like most directors of photography, he was arty and masculine and foreign, with wiry black hair, green eyes, and a deep, glottal accent. (He was Israeli, wasn't he? Figgy would love that.) Alex imagined her huddling with Zev over shot lists late into the night, then coming home to her newly unemployed husband at the kitchen counter stressing over the new carpool schedule. How could she not stray? Or at least be tempted to? And how would he ever know? She'd made it clear she'd never tell.

Or maybe Alex just wasn't used to spending so much time alone. Wherever its source, the thought quickly replicated and got caught in a feedback loop, repeating over and over as he went about his day: *While you knock around the house by your lonesome, Figgy is moving on, moving up, at the show with all the fancy people... If you fail to Hold Up Your End she'll be gone gone gone....*

The voice only amplified when he visited Figgy at work. She'd asked that he bring the kids by the studio a few times a week, "so they remember who their mom is." He didn't mind. It was a thrill to get waved through the guard gate and find his assigned spot in the crew lot and then venture into the vast, cavernous stages, where burly Teamsters hauled around lighting rigs and flats of scenery. Inevitably some young woman from props would swoop up one of the kids for a raid on the catering truck for gelato or hot chocolate. Unlimited free Red Vines? As far as the kids were concerned, their mom was the overlord of a magical realm of helpful attendants and unlimited sweets.

It seemed pretty great to Alex, too. Just before production began, on a whim, Figgy had the art department do up her office to resemble the inside of the *I Dream of Jeannie* bottle, with a round, silk-covered queen-size bed in place of a desk. Alex and the kids would barge into her office and find her propped up against a pile of fluffy cushions, her laptop balanced on a breakfast tray and her assistant, Anne-Marie, a Korean USC grad with bleached teeth, running in and out with fresh batches of tea and sunflower seeds. If Figgy wasn't in bed, she'd be in the writer's room stationed at the end of a long conference table, surrounded by dry-erase boards and a staff of wisecracking young writers who always appeared to be dressed for a backyard barbecue.

Alex knew the work could be ridiculously hard and the politics and hierarchies were brutal, but sampled periodically, from the safe distance of a visiting spouse, Figgy's workplace looked like the best clubhouse ever.

If you don't hold up your end... she'll be gone gone gone.

And then a month after production began, the money arrived. There was no beeping truck, no giant check, no crash of cymbals, no clinking of champagne flutes. The only way Alex knew they had it was a call from Valerie, an associate in the Encino accounting firm they'd hired last year when Figgy's show was picked up.

"FYI—the first studio payment just cleared," she said cheerfully. "I can stick it in a cash account or money market but wanted to check with you first. Where do you stand on munis?"

"I'm pro-munis, absolutely," he said, knowing nothing whatsoever about munis. "Let me talk to Figgy and get her to weigh in. We'll talk things over."

But of course there was no talking things over with Figgy, who greeted news of the payment that night in bed with a weary,

"It's about fucking time," before vanishing behind a cushioned sleep mask and passing out. Alex knew better than to think Figgy would care one way or another about municipal bonds; she was even fuzzier on finances than Alex. In annual meetings with the bookkeeper, she'd squint during the discussion of tax brackets and deductions and then come out with the only economic question that seemed to make any sense to her:

"How long can we survive if I have a nervous breakdown tomorrow and no one ever hires me again?"

Which left Alex as family CFO as well as domestic first responder. In this capacity, he let a few days pass before getting back to the accountant. He knew they needed to make a decision, but it somehow cheered him that the new infusion was only temporarily contained. It wasn't locked down. It was liquid. It didn't belong in municipals. It belonged in a house.

• • •

And so Alex kept up the house hunt. He checked in with Colby each morning and did a tour of open houses on Tuesdays and Saturdays. Still, every time he got in Colby's car, he was struck by the wrongness of it all—the forced friendship between them, the peppery whiff of Colby's cologne, the smooth jazz on his car radio. The houses weren't much better. Colby had learned to steer away from the crazy moderns and grand McMansions, which left the deeply creepy, the highly impractical, or the offensively tacky. Great recession or not, it turned out that high-twos-low-threes was not exactly the ticket to easy street he'd imagined it would be.

And then, two weeks into the hunt, Colby called about a pocket listing a few blocks down from Griffith Park. The house was on Sumter Court, a looping side street a few blocks away from the duplex Alex had lived in during his temping days. As they pulled up to the address in Colby's Mercedes, Alex's heart began to race. He leapt out of the car and hurried to the tall iron gate, peering down a leafy path at a pink Mediterranean centered in the middle of a flat acre. The gate buzzed and Alex took three steps into the garden and stopped.

The last time he'd been here, the lawn was overgrown, the pool was halfway drained, and Alex was a trespasser. But there was no mistaking it. It was his Come the Revolution House, restored and repainted and up for grabs to the highest bidder.

• • •

He wandered from room to room, his mouth slack and head spinning, pausing in the same cavernous, wood-paneled room he'd peered into twenty-odd years before. Could you even call it a *house*? Or was it a compound? An estate? It was enormous, with a drawing room (a drawing room!), a solarium (solarium!), and actual provenance—the architect had what Colby had called "A-list credits."

What really got Alex was the yard—one lawn spilled into another, with park benches and gurgling fountains peeking out from leafy corners, all of it shaded by fragrant eucalyptus and old-growth redwoods. He surveyed the scene and pictured Sylvie frolicking across the grass, twirling a white parasol. He wanted this yard with an unadulterated ache. The feeling was only slightly undercut by a nagging picture of the gardeners he knew maintained all this water-chugging, non-native flora, who he knew in an instant were Latino, underpaid, and armed with squealing, smoke-belching leaf blowers.

In any case, it was beyond them—way too expensive, too grand, too old. Even with the recent influx of money, Alex was sure there wasn't a jumbo loan jumbo enough to swing it. Besides, their new money was just that: new. This place reeked of Old.

Besides, in the fantasy of his youth, he'd taken possession of this house after the actual owners fled. He hadn't bought it; he'd *reclaimed* it. He'd strung up hammocks in the ballroom, burned antiques in the fireplace. He didn't want to buy it; he wanted to invade it.

Now he was really here, in the role of a potential buyer. It was all wrong. There had been no revolution, no urban uprising. He wasn't the proletariat. He was the oppressor.

He caught up with Colby on the back patio, where he was talking to the seller's agent, an elegant Persian woman in a nubby-fabric cardigan. Colby broke off a conversation about "the list price, vis-à-vis the neighborhood specs," raised his eyebrows at Alex, and quickly sized him up. He laughed and clapped him on the back. "I've seen that look before my friend. You're in love. Don't deny it. It's incredible. Nice? Nice!"

"It's definitely nice," Alex said. He had to give it to him: Somehow, Colby had succeeded in delivering his literal dream house.

Colby took him by the elbow and turned them away. "The agent says she's got multiple offers coming in tomorrow. If you want to make a move, we should be first."

Alex coughed and shook his head. "I don't think so," he said. "It's pretty out of our range, pricewise."

Colby frowned. "Oh, you'd be amazed what a good mortgage broker can make happen," he said, pulling out his cell phone. "Let's just get Figgy down here. See if she can swing by? Get her feeling on it. This house is gonna go fast—I don't want you two missing out."

Colby punched in her number—Alex registering that Colby had her work number on speed-dial, which meant the two of them had been talking a lot more than he realized—and in a few short sentences, he got across the message that she needed to get over here. Fast. Then Colby hurried out to his car to "get some papers together."

Fifteen minutes later, Figgy was walking down the flagstone path with Colby at her side, a bulging manila folder under his arm. Alex trailed behind as they made a brisk tour through the property. This wasn't the nervous, nail-chewing Figgy at all. This was the other Figgy, the hard-charging dynamo, the ass-kicker who picked up her Emmy with a fist bump. Alex flashed back to the delivery room at Cedars-Sinai hospital when Sam was born. She'd spent much of the pregnancy a nauseous wreck, hobbled and terrified about the violence that was about to break out in her holiest of holies. But when the day arrived and it turned out the baby was positioned badly and labor would be worse even than she had feared, a steely calm fell over her. Alex nearly fainted when the doctor wiped away a miasma of fluids and advanced on her with a glinting pair of metal salad tongs. But Figgy kept calm, receding somewhere deep inside herself. He could still see her staring up at him, stroking his splotchy cheek with the back of her middle finger and saying, simply, "I got this."

And she did. All ten pounds, nine ounces of it.

Now that same preternatural calm was back.

After the tour, she plopped into a wicker lounge chair by the pool. The last glimmer of sun was disappearing below the hills of Griffith Park, lighting up the yard with a thin violet glow.

"So," he said.

"So," she agreed.

"You love it?"

"What's not to love?" she said. "What about you?"

"I'm terrified," he said with a laugh. "Isn't a little out of our league?"

A sly grin crept across Figgy's face. "Out of *your* league maybe."

He winced and looked out over the swimming pool. Little candles on floating cups made golden flecks on the surface. This was entirely too pleasant a place to stage a protest, but he needed to talk some sense. "Remember what you always say about studio executives? What they crave more than anything else in the world?"

"A reason for living?"

"Besides that," Alex said. "They want a writer with a mortgage. One they can push around. And who's to say Katherine doesn't storm off tomorrow or the writers' strike doesn't happen again or you show up and find your office occupied by some hack the network has decided is the next Chuck Lorre? What then?"

Figgy looked away and sucked in a deep breath. "We'll be fine—we just will. If we close escrow soon, we can use the house for shooting. Wouldn't this be perfect for the commissioner's house?"

Angela Bassett was in talks to play the local police commissioner in a six-episode arc of the new season. As Figgy had scripted the part, the commissioner becomes obsessed with the madam played by Katherine Pool during a surveillance operation. Episode eight ended at a fundraiser at the commissioner's house with the madam and the commissioner engaged in some hot girl-on-girl action (known in the writers' room as "goga").

"Standard fee for that kind of shoot is eight thousand a day," Figgy said, the calculations ticking across her face. "We could do five or six days before we move in, pay for most of the remodel. If we move a few scenes inside, I could do a few product placements and get us a new fridge, at least a dishwasher."

She hopped up and went toward the French doors leading to the kitchen. "What have they got in there now?"

Alex trailed after her. Eight thousand? For a single day? Maybe she was right. Maybe they *could* pull this off. What was he so opposed to anyway? Maybe the fact that he'd been here before was a *good* omen—like the discovery of the 'zine, a sign that he was on the right path. Besides, all that space, that land—how could that *not* be good for the kids, the dog, everyone? It obviously made

Figgy happy. Her happiness made everyone happier. All boats rose. Did he really think buying a house like this would somehow *corrupt* them? Maybe it was a win-win world after all. Maybe it was like he'd told his dad—just a house.

He followed her through the French doors, resolute now. Cheerful even. Figgy wanted it—and Alex wanted it for her. Was he really going to let some crazy apocalyptic fantasy get in the way of their happiness? Figgy marched through the back door into the kitchen, Alex close on her heels.

• • •

In the kitchen they found a woman with a severe black bob and a drapey, scoop-neck top, furiously pumping the valves of a gigantic countertop stainless steel cappuccino maker embedded with the word MAGNIFICA. Next to her, an older man emerged from a cloud of hissing steam, revealing a full head of silver hair and a pair of reading glasses dangling on a gold chain.

"The open house ended a half hour ago," the man said, mashing his hands in a damp rag.

Alex shrugged and advanced into the room. "Oh, sorry, we won't be a minute," he said, the words scrambling together. "I'm Alex Sherman-Zicklin. This is my wife Figgy. Also Sherman-Zicklin. Hyphenates—we went that route. Beautiful home!"

"Rex Benjamin." He looked them over, and then nodded slowly. "Lots to see here, obviously. People have been in and out all day—but I've gotta get out into the yard before we lose the light. Finish with the compost."

"Sorry?"

"Truckload of compost in the driveway," he said, moving past them. "Spreading it around the azaleas. Once a year—they'll die without it."

The door shut hard behind him as he tromped out. Figgy and

Alex watched him go.

"Espresso?" The woman was collecting cups from the cabinet. The skin on her arms and neck was an unnatural shade of orange; Alex guessed she'd had some assistance in the tanning department. "Don't mind Rex. He's not himself. Don't mind either one of us. I'm Judy—the wife. Everything's pretty scattered, as you can imagine. Him with his compost. Me with my estate sale. Everything's available, you know. The light fixtures, the plants, the furniture. Everything must go!"

"Okay then," Alex said. "We'll keep that in mind."

Judy yanked a lever on the machine and a squealing hiss filled the room. Alex admired the coffee machine's coiled tubes and gleaming metal finish. While rotating a cup under the spout, Judy nodded toward Figgy. "Did you get up to the shoe closet? I must have three hundred pairs up there. A little Imelda Marcos, I know—but what can I say? Women and their shoes, right? You're what? About a nine? Nine and a half? Same as me. I've barely worn half of them. I'll do twenty-five a pair, Ferragamos, too."

Figgy leaned over. "I'll have a look."

There was another awkward pause as Judy poured foam over their coffees, her jaw set.

Alex coughed and offered, "Are you moving far? Out of state?"

"We're not sure *where* we're going," she said. "But we're not going anywhere 'til we get rid of everything. We can't just sit around ignoring the phone, talking to lawyers, spreading compost. Compost, can you believe it?"

"I'm sorry—I don't understand," Alex said. "What happened? Did something happen?"

"Oh, I thought you knew—I thought *everyone* knew," she cried. She laid a coffee cup down on the tile countertop with a definitive clink. "We've had some bad luck. That's what Rex calls it: 'a rather epic turn of bad luck'. But you ask me, luck has nothing to do with it. The lawyers are calling it 'misappropriation'. But come on—it's *thievery*. That's why we're selling. The things you see, the little bit of equity in the house—that's it. That's all we've got."

"What? How?"

Her face scrunched up, a fluttering in her upper lip. "It was a trust," she said. "Isn't that rich? *Trust*? All our money, all my family money. Rex turned it *all* over to this money manager— Greg Helman? The Whiz of WeHo? It was in all the papers— took a plea for fraud, looking at twenty years. Lot of good it'll do us. We're wiped out."

"Oh, God," Alex said. "I'm so sorry."

Judy looked down into her cup, examining the pattern of the foam. "What can you do?"

She set her cup down on the granite countertop and shrugged, the silence stretching out far past Alex's comfort. He opened his mouth to say something, anything, but stopped short—*at least you have your health? Sorry your family lost everything, thanks for letting us pick through the ruins?* He looked over beseechingly at Figgy, who shot him a look and stepped forward. "Well, I guess we better take a look at those Ferragamos of yours."

Seven

News of the Benjamins' misfortune sent Colby into a frenzy; they needed to act fast, he said, go in big, make a bold first move. "I love a distress sale!" he said, hyperventilating. Figgy was in the front seat, and Colby was behind the wheel; they'd been parked on the curb of Sumter Court strategizing for the past half hour, the offer propped up on the parking brake of Colby's Mercedes. Alex kept quiet in back, slumped in his seat, a light year away. The two of them up front were like teenagers warming up for a makeout sesh, each palpably aroused by the pile of documents between them and the obscene financial risk it described.

Colby was adamant about the correct way to proceed (speaking, Alex noticed, entirely to Figgy). They shouldn't lowball. This offer said they were serious. And in the grand scheme of things, considering the current inventory and the swing in the market and the neighborhood specs, the house was actually *cheap*.

"Cheap?" Alex lobbed from the back seat. "In what reverse-reality world is this *cheap*?"

"Sweetie, I have clients who spend this kind of money on their kids' bar mitzvahs," Colby said, flashing Figgy a you-get-it grin.

Figgy leaned over and plucked a pen from Colby's breast pocket. Then she started laying down initials. "We're getting this house," Figgy said, her pen making a series of piercing, definitive pops. "Alex, honey—take this home with Colby and go over it. And make sure there's nothing we shouldn't be signing."

Alex looked out the window at the wall surrounding the house. Painted the same shade of dusty pink, the wall ran along the sidewalk's edge. It really was nine feet tall—grandfathered in, Colby had said. The city wouldn't let you build a wall over six feet anymore. Alex objected to it on principle. Driving around certain precincts of Brentwood or Cheviot Hills, all you saw were walls like that, or else gates, hedges, blackout fences, security cameras, or those elephant-size trash barrels. L.A. was becoming a South American bunker town, the haves barricaded from the have-nots by pink stucco and topiary.

When he looked back, Figgy was out of the car, standing outside his window and passing him the stack of documents. "I gotta get back to work," she said. "We'll be shooting late—I may need to stay over tonight. Kiss the kids. Talk me up—tell them how much I love them."

She reached in for a one-armed embrace through the car window. Alex swallowed hard, wishing she'd blow off work and help him deal. He needed her certainty, her decisiveness, the cushion against harm he felt when they were together. Left alone, he feared he might throw up all over Colby's papers.

Figgy looked at him with concern. "You know you're amazing, right?" she said. "You found this place, and now you just gotta go *get* it. I'm sorry I'm dumping this on you and disappearing."

Alex nodded uncertainly, panic darting across his face. Figgy gave his shoulder a squeeze before jumping in her car and heading to work. "Just pretend to know what you're doing," she called out the window. "Fake it! It's gonna work out fine. I promise."

• • •

Alex led Colby through the front door to find the kids sprawled in front of the TV and Rosa hovering nearby with a stack of laundry. He waved and dumped the documents on the kitchen counter.

"Hola, Rosa! Buenos días!" he said, thus exhausting his supply of Spanish.

"Hola, Mr. Alex," Rosa smiled and stuffed a pile of Sylvie's dresses into a basket.

"Say hi to Mr. Dreamhouse everyone! This is Mr. McNamara. Kids?"

Sylvie grunted, her mouth moving the minimum required to produce sound while her eyes stayed locked on the TV. Sam popped up from the couch and followed the adults into the kitchen, where Colby was clearing a spot on the counter amid a scattering of newspapers and an assortment of vintage fondue skewers that Figgy had bought at the Rose Bowl flea market.

"How soon do you think you could get some bank statements together?" Colby asked, picking up a shellacked plaque printed with an image of praying hands and the insignia: "God Bless Our Mobile Home." He frowned, setting the plaque down. "Best thing would be a pre-approval letter from your mortgage guy. Have you got someone?"

"Shouldn't be a problem," Alex said, not having any idea if it would be a problem. The amount of Figgy's bonus seemed inconceivable a month ago, but now there were even more inconceivable numbers to reckon with. Alex figured the bonus would cover the twenty-five percent down, but what about after? With taxes, insurance, maintenance, their monthly nut would be... what? His stomach churned. Figgy was so confident they'd swing it, but how did she really know? This next week she was editing episode five, shooting episode seven, and writing nine. He was on his own.

Colby tapped on Alex's shoulder and motioned toward the papers. "Don't mean to rush, but we want to get this into the office before they close," he said. "Just put your initials where you see a green tab."

"Green tabs—okay," Alex said, rising up and returning to the stack.

Sam made a small whining sound and turned his attention to the dog, holding her by the collar and rubbing the bushy part of her neck. "You don't want to move, do you Albert?" he said. "You're just fine right here, aren't you, girl?"

• • •

Colby said they could expect a counter offer within a day or two. Which would give Alex time to shop for a loan, line up inspectors, and dig into the ever-deepening cavity of anxiety that had opened up the moment he'd signed the offer. Was he actually the co-signatory on a multi-million-dollar real estate deal? How did he become *that* guy?

But the counteroffer didn't come the next day, or the day after. Alex stayed busy with phone calls to accountants and brokers, assembling the ins and outs of what would be, far and away, the riskiest purchase of their lives. Valerie the accountant tried to talk them out of it: "Do you have any idea the kind of mortgage shitshows I'm dealing with over here? You've had a good year, but you're not network rich—you're cable rich. Big difference." She finally gave her blessing with the proviso that Figgy stay on *Tricks* for at least two more seasons. "You'll be hyper-extended," she said. "It's a house of cards, but if you can string together another couple of good years, you'll be fine—just like Lehman! Too big to fail!"

"I feel awful," Alex said, cracking a triangle of herbed pita. He was out for lunch with Huck at the Davies Club. Alex had been wanting to check out the Davies for a while; he'd heard stories about Huck drinking Red Bulls with Tom Cruise in the rooftop lounge high above the Sunset Strip. But now that he was actually here, in a crowd of agents and Beverly Hills housewives, he wished they'd just gone to his neighborhood Thai place. Surrounded by all the fanciness, he felt panicky and extra awkward; he'd spent the last half hour describing how on his last visit to the house, he'd run into Mr. Benjamin shoveling hot clumps of manure. "He looked like one of those automatronic ghosts in the Haunted Mansion," Alex said. "Just talking to him feels like bad luck, you know? He's at the center of this unbelievable havoc and we're just waltzing right into it. How crazy is that? *Is* it crazy? What do you think—do you think bad luck is contagious?"

"Seriously, hombre?" Huck said, picking at his beet salad. "Detachment. You can't let this get to you. You're bidding on a house. That's all. It's a fucking sport out here, okay? A game. You're like some meth-head over there, mashing your little mitts together and gnashing your pretty white teeth."

Alex's TMJ *had* been acting up—he didn't know anyone could tell. The muscles beneath his earlobes felt sore and balled up; he imagined his molars were grinding down to dusty little stumps.

He took a deep breath and picked up his phone, looking for the one thing that had reliably relaxed him over the last few days: meatgirl.com. He'd had to dig through the trash container to retrieve the butcher paper on which she'd written the name of her Tumblr. Thankfully, he found the scrap and was able to decipher the name beneath a smear of grease. Miranda, it turned out, was a serious obsessive. She updated the site daily with lavishly photographed accounts of her cooking and dining. There was an account of her first-ever pig roast, a rumination on the glory of organ meat—"the pure inner essence of the animal"—and a series of dispatches from her field trips to East L.A. carnicerias. Today there was a snapshot of mason jars filled with duck confit alongside a dish of pickled onions on the counter of her Koreatown kitchen.

Alex sighed and handed his phone to Huck. "Check out this duck—how delicious does that look?"

Huck glanced at the picture and gave Alex a dubious look. "I'm *so* over mason jars," he said. "Can we please go back to using actual plates and stop pretending like we're frontier people? Anyhow, I've got something so much better—check this out."

Alex took Huck's phone.

"Look—that's Bing doing a full *head spin*," Huck said. "Unassisted! What a little badass, am I right? Preschool showcase yesterday. Seriously—kid's got some *mad* moves."

On the screen, Katherine's adopted son Bingwen was furiously twirling at the center of a crowd of kids, arms stuck out straight and his legs scissor-kicking as he spun. When Huck told Alex about enrolling Bingwen at the new Blue Man Preschool a month or two before, he'd framed it as a crazy lark, another hilarious example of their over-the-top Hollywood lifestyle. The irony, apparently, had faded.

"Wow," Alex said. "Is that, like, part of the standard Blue Man curriculum?"

"Sure—head spinning, puppetry, trash-can percussion," Huck said. "*Shitload* of mime. Kid drives me crazy with all the windstorms he gets caught in. But beats macaroni crafts and circle time, am I right? Skinny dude in the back is Bing's head-spin mentor. Or maybe it's the short one."

"That's great, Huck—but seriously?" Alex cut in. "Can we get back to the house?"

"What about it?"

"We were supposed to get an answer day before yesterday. But now they've gone silent. Radio silence. I'm going bananas.

Worst thing, it feels wrong to even be angry, you know? That poor family. What they're going through? Can you even *imagine*?"

Alex filled Huck in on the back story of the house, which they'd pieced together through friends-of-friends and realtor gossip. It seemed that the Benjamins had moved into the house a few years back after Judy's father had a stroke. She was named executor of his estate; she pooled her family money with Mr. Benjamin's savings, funneling all the accounts into a single fund operated by the money manager Greg Helman. A year later, the SEC busted Helman for raiding clients' accounts to cover a series of disastrous foreign investments.

It wasn't clear precisely how much the Benjamins had lost, but their plan now was to take the equity they had in Sumter Court and move all of them—Mr. Benjamin, Judy, her elderly father, the nurse, and a load of rattling oxygen tanks—into a rental unit they could afford, which Alex immediately pictured as a wobbly tenement wrapped in rusting fire escapes and stinking of medical waste and cat pee.

"That *is* some bad mojo," Huck agreed. "But guys like that manage just fine. Don't forget—with the money they make on this deal, they'll be able to pay rent for the rest of their natural lives."

"I just feel like we have no business getting anywhere near this place. I literally have *no idea* what I'm doing—and somehow I'm in charge of the whole fucking negotiation. I'm gonna screw it up."

"Seriously, Alex—you need to relax," Huck said. "Figgy's right—you guys deserve this house. And the guy you're getting it from, you're not taking advantage. He's *drowning*—and you're pulling up beside him in big cruise ship."

Alex straightened up, flashing on an image of himself at the wheel of a luxury ocean liner, in one of those ridiculous Captain Stubing beanies.

Huck leaned in and made a little hooking motion with his finger. "And don't forget, this house—it's nothing but good for you. Big asset, whole new bracket. Big reset on the marital standard of living—very good for you down the line. Don't forget that anniversary of yours. You keep your head down, take care of the kids, feather that nest—it's all good."

Alex scratched the back of his head and looked at his lap. "You're disgusting, you know that?"

"What?" Huck put his palms up and shrugged. "Be smart is all I'm saying. You start flipping out now and you lose the house *and* your lady. Don't give her any reason to bail. You don't think she's checking her watch, figuring the odds?"

Alex looked out the window and tried to wrap his head around what Huck was suggesting. Figgy had seemed distant lately, but that was just because she was busy. The other day she'd brought up the third kid discussion again—that wasn't the talk of a wife planning an exit.

"You're wrong. We're good. And I am not gonna start cataloging everything in my life in terms of 'marital assets'."

Huck interlaced his fingers and leaned back. "Would it be wrong if you were the woman married to a guy making bank? No way. You'd do what you do to take care of yourself. And no one would think the less of you for it."

Huck's Blackberry vibrated on the glass table, and he snatched it up. "It's my boy Les," he said, eyes rolling. "Kid texts me like twenty times a day. Girlfriend troubles. 'Lindsay won't call me back!' Pathetic."

"Is this *the* Les? Lester Price Les?"

Huck gave a slight shrug, happy to slag the likes of Lester Price, a movie actor known for playing snarky-sweet, overconfident hipsters in A-list studio projects. He was also, if the tabloids were to be believed, a raging pill popper and a class-A prick, given to ugly romantic entanglements and crazed explosions of temper. Last year he did thirty-five hours of community service after an altercation with a fan who'd dared address him by his given name, Leslie Sychak.

"'Getting a crash pad in the city,'" Huck read. "'Big pimping. Pink palace.'"

"*Pink* palace? No way. Can't be."

"Hold on," Huck said, furiously thumbing out a response. "Where's the house again?"

"Street is Sumter Court," Alex said. "Sumter—like the fort."

Huck kept on thumbing, and then paused. He set his phone on the table and rubbed his forehead. "Yup," he said. "Same. He put in a bid last night."

"How can that even be?" Alex said. "That's insanity."

"Not really—inventory is zero right now. For rollers like you and Les, there are maybe three or four halfway decent houses on the market. That's how it goes."

Alex took a swig of iced tea and thought this over. "So *that's* why we're still waiting for our answer?" Alex said. "We're in a bidding war—with Les Price?"

"Appears so, yeah."

"That's it then," Alex said. "We're done."

Huck shrugged. "He *does* need a place in the city. You'll find something else."

Alex felt his stomach turn over. A long moment passed.

"I'm sorry, but screw Lester Price," he heard himself say. "This house is not a crash pad. And I am not going to spend another day playing lookie-loo with Mr. Dreamhouse. We are getting this house. Lester Price has got to get out of the way."

• • •

A call to Benjamin's agent confirmed it: They were now considering multiple offers. Given "certain pressures from creditors," the seller was seeking to avoid a protracted negotiation. They would therefore accept "best and final" offers and make their decision within the week.

Figgy's disappointment that the house was being "poached by a goddamn *actor*" quickly shrank into shrugging acceptance. On the phone from the writers' room, where she was in hour six of an all-nighter addressing notes from the network on episode four, Alex heard her sigh heavily, the fight draining out of her. "It was a nice dream while it lasted. Oh well."

"So we drop out?" Alex said.

"Honey, do you have any idea how much movie actors make? This house is *chickenshit* to Lester Price. He spends more on scotch and pinball machines."

Alex knocked the receiver on his forehead and grimaced. A small part of him knew he should be relieved. The pressure was off. After all, the house was still outrageous, irrational, ridiculous, way beyond anything they needed or could afford. But he couldn't just let it go—not like this.

"I'm sorry, we can't let Les Price win this," he finally said. "This house is everything he isn't—it's gracious. It's domestic. We'll fill it up, make it happy. It should belong to us."

"Sweetie, talent always gets the goodies."

"This isn't a gifting suite," Alex said, remembering Huck's story about the hotel rooms where Emmy nominees had their pick of luxury goods. "He can't just waltz in and scoop it up."

Figgy sighed again, her breath making a distorted hiss on the phone. "I can't do this now," she said. "See what Colby says. If you guys really think it's worth trying, take a shot."

And so, after a few frantic phone calls, the offer was upped to over asking. *Same difference*, Alex thought, the figures spinning in his brain like lotto balls. *They were only upping the amount by, what, point-two? Point-three?* They were all just digits now, swirling symbols that had some distant relationship to real money but that seemed now more like little blunt instruments to beat back an encroaching threat.

Money, Alex knew, wouldn't be enough to beat Lester Price. Extra steps were required.

Over two feverish, teeth-grinding nights, he devised a black-ops campaign. Huck had said Price was unusually concerned with security—he'd amassed an impressive arsenal of spy gear, including motion sensors, an electrical fence, and a koi-pond moat around his Malibu compound. The nine-foot wall at Sumter Court was clearly a plus. But perhaps, Alex thought, Price was unaware of other potential vulnerabilities? Perhaps a few looming breaches in privacy might be brought to his attention?

"Huck, just text him," Alex said into the phone, trying not to plead. "He has a right to know that TMZ Tours has a fleet of double-decker buses that stand roughly twelve and a half feet above street level. He *deserves* to know that while the current TMZ route does not include Sumter Court, their routes change frequently... based on tips from any schmo with a cell phone!"

"I am *so* not getting involved," Huck said. "A guy's house is like his girlfriend—they may be bitchy or fugly or prone to drink six margaritas and pin you to a wall and try to grab your balls— but you *don't* bring that shit up. Ever."

Alex soldiered on. "Do you really want Scandinavian tourists with black socks peering into your boy's cabaña? Tourists with telephoto lenses and spec scripts? Isn't this a *security* issue?"

"Listen, Alex, I'm rooting for you. I am. I like an underdog. But I'm not getting involved."

Fine—he didn't need Huck's help. Alex had already brain-stormed other ways to break through the protective scrim sur-rounding Lester Price. His first move was the simplest: a single email to the tip account of StarHomes-dot-com, the dishy and heavily trafficked blog that covered open houses in prime L.A. neighborhoods with the sort of intensity and attention to detail that Alex noted had entirely disappeared from coverage of things like public schools and local government.

Apparently, the people behind StarHomes.com didn't even live in L.A.—Alex heard it was compiled by interns at a startup in Tempe, Arizona. You'd never know it from "Price Eyeballing Park-Adjacent Crash Pad," a three-paragraph item that appeared the day after Alex's tip. The blog duly reported that Lester Price was bidding on a three-bedroom house with sumptuous interiors and lush grounds at such-and-such address, alongside a complete floor plan and a street-view photograph. All that was missing was a Google map.

It was almost too easy.

On the Wednesday before the Benjamins were to make their final decision, Colby learned that Lester Price had arranged for a final visit, to show the house to his girlfriend. As it happened, Colby had a listing for a split-level modern just up the hill—the two houses were so close, in fact, that you could see the balcony of the empty house from the backyard. Alex got busy with the kids' art supplies and a sheet of butcher paper. He took no small measure of pleasure picturing Lester Price stepping out onto the patio of the home he felt sure would soon be his and spotting, not one hundred yards away, a ten-foot banner printed with the cheerful greeting:

"WELCOME TO THE NEIGHBORHOOD LESLIE SYCHAK!"

• • •

Les Price dropped out the next day. Apparently, he'd decided his place in Malibu was fine. "Too many freaks east of Fairfax," he told the agent.

"What'd I tell you?" Colby said when he called with the news. "You didn't think I'd pull this off, did you? Going toe to toe with high-profile Hollywood competition—it's what I do. It takes some pretty crafty maneuvering, let me tell you. The Mr. Dreamhouse thing—corny, right? But I hope you can see now Alex, where the title originates, right? Right?"

Alex thought for a second about pointing out that all his "crafty maneuvering" consisted of lending Alex a spare key to a vacant house so he could hang a banner. He didn't even know about the blog. For that matter, neither did Figgy. She was so busy, and anyway Alex thought it best to spare her the details—especially his agreement to finalize financing and inspections in just ten days.

A thirty-day inspection period was quick. Ten days was insane. But Colby had urged Alex to go forward—he'd heard Zooey Deschanel and the director McG had both called his office to get a showing of that fabulous house they'd seen on Starhomes-dot-com. "Get the accepted offer on paper," he said. "The terms are tight, but we'll get it done. I can hustle the mortgage guys. And you know how inspections go—they'll clomp around, poke their flashlights all over, and be on their merry way. Don't worry: It'll go fine!"

Alex tried to wait up for Figgy to come home from the set so he could catch her up on the news. When she finally arrived, the clock radio read two a.m., and Alex was passed out with the light on.

"Huge fight over wardrobe," Figgy said, collapsing into bed. Apparently, Katherine was feeling "unsafe on set" and had demanded that five members of the crew be replaced for "looking at her in a predatory, offensive way." Today she'd gone to the network with complaints about the latest script, which she found "sitcommy and hammy and nothing I want my name associated with."

"So today the network decides we need to handle our quote-unquote 'talent issues' and in waltzes Dani Dooling. Non-writing producer, total glad-hander, lasted seven or eight seasons on that NBC show about the trampy pharmaceutical reps?

She launches into this whole spiel about 'process' and 'inclusion'. The Diva Whisperer, they call her. She's only supposed to handle Kate, but I've seen this act before. The network brought her in to take over, give them a show runner who'll roll over, take every one of their notes."

"Honey, stop," Alex said. "It's your show, remember? They can't replace you. Not so soon after the Emmys, right? You're the show runner. The *creator*."

"Apparently, *creator* counts for jack. I'm so depressed. I ate an entire tub of Red Vines today."

Alex reached over and put his hand on her arm. "It's not *all* bad," he said. "I have some good news. Our offer was accepted today. Formally. On the house."

Figgy's eyes got wide. "What about Les Price? He didn't outbid us?"

"I guess our offer was just more attractive," Alex said.

Figgy wiggled up close. "We *beat* Les Price?" she said, grinning. "How the hell did we *do* that?"

"I dunno," he smiled, loving the mysterious aura he'd cast around himself. "Just a little crafty maneuvering."

Figgy let out a big breath and turned onto her back. "I am so turned on right now."

• • •

Alex met up with Colby at the house the next day to sign the offer and do a walk-around with Rex Benjamin. Alex wandered around the front yard for close to an hour while Mr. Benjamin was upstairs on the phone. When he finally appeared, he shoved a handful of papers toward Colby and took Alex's hand in a ridiculously tight grip. "Back again," he said. "Wanna see what you're getting into? You'll want to see the sprinkler timers before anything. Trust me."

Alex raised an eyebrow to Colby and followed Mr. Benjamin out the back door into the garden. Colby flashed a thumbs up. That was it? He'd expected some sort of ceremony—if not bugle calls or an exchange of family crests, maybe a nice WASPY gin and tonic on the patio. Instead, it seemed Mr. Benjamin intended to seal the deal with a tutorial on sprinkler timers.

"The raccoons ate all my koi," Mr. Benjamin said, pointing to a fountain on the patio. He stopped at a patch of overgrown rose bushes. "Judy was supposed to prune these. She's let them go. She's either upstairs getting crispy in that goddamned tanning contraption or running around *labeling* everything. For the auction people—she's putting prices on every doily and serving spoon."

"Those label makers *are* pretty addictive," Alex offered. "I love the way you can change the font—"

"*Women*, you know?" he said, ignoring him. "She's not taking any of this very well. I keep telling her: Yes, we had expectations. But whatever happens, *we're* the same—they can't change that. They can't get you in *here*," he said, tapping his temple with a muscular index finger. "Judy seems to think we're finished now, that all bets are off. All bets are *not* off."

"Oh no—not off at all," Alex said, leaning in toward the sprinkler box. He felt something on his face. It made a horrible crinkling sound and seemed to wrap around his cheek. He reared back.

"Shit—spider!" he yelped.

"Hold still," Mr. Benjamin said, stepping forward and plucking a tangle of filmy web from his face. "It's just a goddamn *web*."

His voice rang with authority. He had the sort of voice that belonged in a boardroom or a court chamber. Alex slid down that voice, into the upstairs bedroom in better times, where Mr. Benjamin was undoing his cufflinks after a night out, kicking off his wingtips and running a hand through his thick head of silver hair. Over at the vanity, Judy perched in a slip, dabbing off her foundation and readying herself for the heaving, one-sided bout of lovemaking that Mr. Benjamin would soon initiate. She'd yield, lay open for him, do what was necessary. She was his bottom, his base, his support. She took care of her man; he expected it, deserved it.

Alex brushed off his shirt and picked a strand of web from his cheek. "Sorry—just surprised."

Mr. Benjamin turned his attention on Alex. He seemed to take him in for the first time. "So I understand your wife is in television—what line of work are you in?"

Alex swallowed. "Advertising—but I recently left a job," he said. "I was working on a big testicular cancer campaign. Not pro-testicular cancer, of course. Anti. It's a charity!"

The tendons on Mr. Benjamin's neck twitched. "And now? What are you doing now?"

"Looking after the wife and kids," Alex said. "Also early stages on a new project. Still working out the nuts and bolts. Centered on punk rock, if you know anything about that. Early eighties L.A. hardcore, the Misfits, Circle Jerks, *that* whole milieu, seminal stuff, really under-appreciated."

Had Alex really just managed to group together testicular cancer, the Circle Jerks, and the word "seminal" in his career re-cap? He wouldn't blame Mr. Benjamin for thinking Alex made his living in gay porn.

"I see," was all he said.

• • •

Alex couldn't help wondering if things would've gone differently if he and Mr. Benjamin *hadn't* had that exchange in the bushes. If he hadn't left Mr. Benjamin with the impression that he was leaving his family estate in the hands of a flinchy punk who used words like "milieu" and complained of a weak stomach when taken to the spare refrigerator to view the bags of venison Mr.

Benjamin brought home from Wyoming.

In any case, after their little man-to-man, Rex Benjamin seemed to go into a full adversarial crouch, doing everything in his power to undermine the transaction. The first troubles centered on inspections. According to the official report, the chimney's firebox was damaged, roots had broken through the sewer line, and three types of toxic mold spores had been detected in the basement.

Colby swore the report was standard, routine for a house of that size and age. They'd know more once they brought in the chimney, sewer, and mold specialists.

The Benjamins, however, were having none of it. After complaining that the general inspection was "intrusive," they dropped all pretenses of civility, cursing and slamming down the phone when Colby called and telling their agent they refused to speak to "that hustler with the haircut." The sewer technician arrived at the arranged time to find the gates locked; inside, his calls were apparently unheard by Judy, who he spotted in the driveway chatting with a car detailer scrubbing the tires of her SUV.

Two days later, the mold man found Mr. Benjamin wiping down the basement with a bucket of dishwashing detergent. After "inadvertently" locking the mold guy in the basement for ninety minutes and then ordering him to leave their property immediately, Mr. Benjamin told his agents his house was available as-is, with no credits for repair or remediation of any kind.

Colby said they should lodge a formal complaint. But somehow Alex couldn't muster much anger. For one thing, he couldn't help feeling sympathetic toward Mr. Benjamin. *Of course* he was upset. And anyway, the chimney was probably fine; according to Huck, inspectors were always finding problems they could charge you thousands of dollars to correct; similarly, Huck told him he shouldn't get too worked up over the mold, which he called "a pretend poison hyped by fake specialists for paranoid housewives trying to explain why their kids can't do math—what do you think *cheese* is made of?"

Still, as the deadline approached, Alex began to panic. Maybe Colby's theory was right and Lester Price had circled back with a bigger offer. Maybe Mr. Benjamin wasn't wounded and irrational but devious and manipulative? Maybe bad things happen to bad people, too?

Or maybe Alex was just over-thinking. This was business. However grievous the injury Mr. Benjamin had sustained, Alex was pretty sure *he* hadn't had anything to do with it. Fair was fair. An agreement was an agreement. He wouldn't be bullied out of a deal so Mr. Benjamin could get a better price from Mr. Movie Star. Not only would he not drop out, he would add up the total estimated repairs and throw around a few decimals of his own.

Thirty-six-thousand-nine-hundred-and-two. Alex's request for credits was eminently reasonable, nothing like the hideous digits associated with the purchase itself. He itemized the repairs in a packet that also included a stack of bank statements and in what Alex believed would be the clincher, a snapshot of Sam and Sylvie.

"It's like *Silence of the Lambs*," he told Huck over coffee. "Psychos have a harder time killing their victims when they know details about their lives. Just look at that picture."

"Cute," Huck agreed.

"No—adorable," Alex said. The picture had been taken on a crisp fall afternoon in Echo Park, the kids rosy-cheeked and wind-swept, as sweet and presentable as catalog models. "Now check the back. I've been poking around online. Read my little note."

Huck turned over the photo. "Children's exposure to airborne toxic mold can lead to bronchitis, chronic diarrhea, bleeding in the lungs, and even death,'" he read. "Jesus, dude—you are not kidding around."

"You think it's too much?" Alex asked.

• • •

Ordinarily, as far as Alex understood the process, the rest was up to the agents. But apparently his letter had upset the normal order. "He's lost faith in his representation," said Colby. Mr. Benjamin would only discuss credits with Alex face to face. And the soonest he could do it was Friday morning, the last day of their ten-day accelerated escrow.

"Is that even *legal*?" Alex said. "I can't just go in there and *hash* something out. He'll eat me alive."

"Just go in there and hold your ground," Colby said. "Time to *nut up*, Alex!"

As he walked up the long front pathway Friday morning, his heart started to race. It was a fine day, crisp and bright. The front yard looked vast and lush. By the time he reached the front door and gave it a few tentative taps, his hands were shaking.

Mr. Benjamin was waiting in a room overlooking the garden, with tall arched windows and Persian rugs. He was in a tweed jacket and chinos, an empty cappuccino cup and Alex's packet arranged before him on a spindly antique table. His reading glasses were propped on the end of his nose.

"Take a seat," he said, motioning to an overstuffed chair. Alex clasped his hands together and sat. He should've guessed Rexford Benjamin would go for this sort of formality. Here *he* was in his ratty cargo shorts and vintage Dead Kennedys shirt; he'd made a conscious choice not to dress any differently than he normally would on a Saturday morning.

"So," Alex said, then stopped. Silence. He'd rehearsed how to start, but now that he was here, "so" was all he had. He felt himself sinking into the armchair.

Mr. Benjamin tapped on the folder of bank statements. "Let's start with this, shall we? I don't really watch TV, but from the looks of it, your *wife* has done quite nicely. At least lately. Must be nice."

"The show business dollar is a very nice dollar," Alex said.

"But if you'll allow me," he said. "You're all over the place here. You've got stock reports, pension plans, bank records, some sort of promissory note here from someone at a studio. Why aren't you better consolidated?"

Alex had only a vague understanding of "consolidated," but he was pretty sure that a guy who'd just had his entire family fortune embezzled by a single crooked money manager was telling him to put all his money in one pot.

Heart racing, Alex racked his brain for a halfway-informed response, mentioning a "portfolio manager's asset allocation." Across the table, Mr. Benjamin looked pained. Alex got quiet and tried to straighten his back against the quicksand of upholstery.

"Let's move on to the inspections," Mr. Benjamin said, holding up the chimney report with a thumb and index finger. "This," he said, "*is horseshit.*"

Then, with a dramatic flourish, he held up the sewer inspection. "*Bullcrap.*"

Finally, he held up the mold report. "Absolute one-hundred-percent *mooseturd.*" He waved a pencil in front of him like a baton. "This home has been *scrupulously* maintained. Any suggestion otherwise is unconscionable."

Alex crossed one leg over the other and nodded, he hoped thoughtfully. He chose his words carefully.

"I want you to know, Mr. Benjamin, that I appreciate, given all you've been through, that you may have some difficulties with *trust*," he said. "But I also hope you can appreciate that I'm not trying to cheat you out of anything."

Mr. Benjamin took off his reading glasses and drummed his fingers on the pile of papers.

"Please," Alex went on. "Big picture here. Our agreement is more than fair. And these credits are such a tiny piece of this, comparatively."

The old man narrowed his eyes. "I'll do half."

"Half?" Alex said. "I was thinking more like the full thirty-six."

Mr. Benjamin scratched his chin. "Let's put a pin in that for the moment. Have you had a chance to look over the sale list?"

Colby had passed along a list of sale items—Alex had stopped reading after two pages of French antiques, Persian rugs, and ornamental fixtures. "We're not really chandelier people."

"There's one item in particular that didn't go on that list—and I really think you should take it."

"What's that?"

"Judy's tanning bed. It's in the guest room upstairs? Big bronze monster, with the fluorescent lights? Judy *adores* it, but no way can we fit it in the new place."

Alex nodded, not quite getting where this was going.

"She got it for eight thousand a year ago. I'll give it to you for three. Take it and we've got a deal."

"So—what are you saying? I buy the tanning bed... you take the credits? We're done here?"

Mr. Benjamin leaned forward. "It would mean a lot to me," he said.

Alex scratched the back of his head. No way this wasn't a win. But from the look on Mr. Benjamin's face, this wasn't about the money—to him, it was a fuck-you. To him, to his wife, to this whole situation. But so what if unloading his wife's tanning bed on Alex let Mr. Benjamin feel like he was the real man? Let him have the bullshit symbolic victory. The only thing it said about Alex was that he could pull himself out of this horrible armchair, close the deal, and never see Mr. Benjamin again.

"Deal," he said.

Eight

Somehow, in a blur of conference calls and signatures and notary stamps, it was official: Alex and Figgy were the legal owners of the house on Sumter Court. Or to be precise, the house was owned by a blind trust with Alex listed as sole officer—Figgy's lawyers had arranged it that way to keep her name off public records. It seemed overly secretive—who did they think they were, Brangelina?—but he began to see the sense in it when Figgy brought home a stack of letters she'd received at the studio from a fan with an obsessive, tiny-print scrawl ruminating about her inspiration, her children, her underwear.

"I'm the sole officer of a blind trust—can you believe that?" said Alex, leaning back in the orange vinyl booth of Hop Ming, the Zicklin's favorite Chinese place. The table was crowded with platters of glazed pork, hunks of spicy eggplant, and mounds of egg foo young. The kids were squirmy and restless, but Alex couldn't have been happier.

Alex had been riding the same weird high since the heavy cluster of keys dropped into his hand that afternoon, signaling they'd officially "taken possession"—how he loved that phrase, almost as much as he hated the phrase "jumbo loan." To mark the occasion, Clive had invited them out for a celebratory dinner. Figgy was still at work, but Alex cleaned up the kids and made the trek over the hill to Encino for the five-thirty reservation.

"Mazel tov, Alex," Clive said. "It's quite a house. Home for Hollywood royalty."

Beside him, Figgy's mom, Joan, murmured through teeth clenched on a rubber band. She'd been attempting to get a braid into Sylvie's hair since the hot and sour soup. "I'm just not sure I like this trust of yours," she said. "What's to stop you from—"

"From what?" Alex said. "What am I going to do? Kick everyone out and force my family to move in with *you*? I'd never do that to my children."

"Thanks, Dad," called Sam from the corner, slumped, bored, done with his dinner and ripping up a napkin. "I'm not moving to Bubbie's house—it smells like armpits."

Joan ignored the remark and kept on braiding, motioning at Alex with her elbow. "I'm just saying—I don't like it. It's dangerous. A husband shouldn't have so much power."

"God knows I don't," intoned Clive, dipping a shred of duck into a dish of hoisin. "I can barely sign a check without an okay from the boss. Anyway, Joannie—your daughter's got nothing to worry about. Mr. A here is doing right by Figgy."

"Thank you, Clive," Alex said.

"And for a goy, I understand you're quite the dealmaker. I hear you drove a real bargain on credits."

Alex was pleased at the thought that Figgy had bragged about his negotiating. "You should have heard him at the end," he said, launching into the *Frost vs. Nixon* version of the story he'd told ten or fifteen times over the past three days. "At the front door, on my way out, he grabs my elbow and says"—here Alex lowered his voice into an old-fogey croak— " 'Go ahead and dig up the sewer system, bring in hazmat crews, rip off the roof, and start all over again for all I care.' "

"What a piece of work," Clive said.

"Oh, he was just getting started. Then he goes..." and here Alex's voice dropped back down... " 'Fair warning, young man. *Everyone* who comes into this house is going to look around and say to themselves, *I'm gonna make my* nut *right here.*' "

"Some people," Clive said. "They're just not happy unless everyone else is as miserable as they are."

Alex swirled around the contents of his glass. "I honestly feel bad for the guy. What he's been through?"

"This man was trying to take advantage—and you wouldn't let him," Clive said. "Good for you."

"That's right," Joan said. "Don't let *anyone* spit in your kasha. Ever. Oh! I almost forgot—a little housewarming present."

Joan leaned over with a grunt and pulled out her purse, a bulging leather sack with copper clasps that shook the tabletop as she laid it down. "Here we are." She pulled out a paper bag. "I wasn't sure how many to get—maybe I overdid."

"What's in there?"

"Mezuzahs," she said, spilling out a pile of intricately carved metal cylinders. "Tiny Torah scroll inside each one. You post one on every doorpost—how many do you think you have?"

Alex ran his hand through the pile. There was no way they were putting up these things all over their house. He'd bring the bag home, stash it in a drawer with the shabbos candles they never lit and the yarmulkes they brought home from bar mitzvahs. Figgy went to temple with her mom for high holidays and had firm and deeply held opinions about the best pastrami in town, but that was pretty much the extent of her Jewishness. But Joan was just trying to be nice. "Including the dog door, we've got... twenty doorways? Thirty maybe?"

"Oh mazel tov, honey—mazel tov," Joan said, squeezing his wrist.

Clive made a motion toward the waiter and turned back to Alex. "I got some great news today about *Top Dog*. Our family just found a location. We're full speed ahead."

Alex settled in for an update in the continuing saga of Clive's post-retirement campaign to produce his own reality show. Last fall he'd taken his beloved corgi to a groomer in Glendale and got to talking with the owners. The dad was a round, gruff Armenian widower in a blue track suit, "a cross between Tony Soprano and Cesar Milan." His daughter was brash and fast-talking—"a super extrovert and a real looker," Clive said. The father-daughter team had recently won a regional kennel club show with a purebred Pekingese and had started a sideline training pets for show competitions. Encouraged by friends in the business (which Alex took to mean the *alter kakers* at Fitzerman's Deli), Clive had been developing a reality show around the family ever since. His only real holdup had been the actual family—the daughter had loved the idea immediately, but the dad was unmoved by Clive's repeated attempts to get them officially on board. "TV only brings trouble," Mr. Barsaghian had said. "And all those cords and cameras and lights? The dogs lose focus. We're fine as we are."

Today, though, Clive had a breakthrough. "I finally got 'em! The dad tipped when I offered to get them set up in a brand-new shop—we found this amazing spot right over on La Brea! They need some startup cash, and we've got a ton of particulars to nail down, but I've got interest from the Nature Channel, and I'm looking to get cameras in the new space from the get-go. I'm telling you, Alex, this thing is gold. Huge aftermarket."

Joan shot Alex a dubious look. "Tell him he's crazy, will you?" She pointed a chopstick at her husband. "Who wants to see a bunch of silly dogs prancing around?"

Clive smiled knowingly. "I keep telling you, hon—it's not about the dogs. The characters—that's what all these competition shows forget. And my stars, Al and Gina, they're screaming at each other one minute, weeping and falling into each other's arms the next. They're the next *Duck Dynasty* people, I'm telling you."

"That's great, Mr. C," Alex said, uncertainly. He had a hard time picturing old-school Clive as a reality show producer, but unlike ideas he'd floated in the past (last year he'd tried selling a variety show hosted by a hotel piano bar singer), this one sounded halfway plausible.

"Sylvie, sweetie, pass me those pot stickers," Clive said, lurching forward. "I'm stuffed but I can't help it—we're celebrating over here!"

• • •

Over the next few days, as the reality of the house sunk in, Alex began to think harder about whose house it was anyway. Of course it was *theirs*, at least on paper. Still, he couldn't help notice Figgy falling into weirdly possessive language: In *her* version of the New House Story, *she'd* known the second she walked in that she'd get it. *She'd* never spent so much money on anything. She had no idea how she'd pay for it, but sometimes a girl's just got to leap and hope for the best, right?

Alex had to stop himself from reminding her of all *he'd* done to acquire the property. But that would have meant sharing with her the particulars of his black-ops campaign, which he'd decided to keep to himself. And while Figgy might appreciate his underhandedness, it seemed important to Alex that she believe he'd prevailed through nothing more than confrontational, upfront, manly negotiation. And anyway, he didn't want to start a fight over—what? Semantics? Let it be *her* house if it made her happy. It was, after all, a basic and unavoidable fact: She made the money. And with production now in full swing and work as awful and dispiriting as ever, she needed all the ego biscuits she could gobble up, however empty-calorie they happened to be.

And work, she told him, was truly at its worst—while tensions with the cast had eased, and the network was celebrating huge ratings in the all-important eighteen-to-forty-nine demo, she'd entered that middle portion of the season where she was on three separate tracks, writing episodes, overseeing production, and, whenever she could, dropping into editing. By the time she got home, typically past eleven but as late as two in the morning or sometimes not at all, any semblance of good cheer had been wrung clean out of her. She'd come tumbling through the front door, eyes glazed, stumbling into the kids' room for a quick smooch and sniff before collapsing into bed with her laptop for a bout of Bejeweled or Words with Friends or some other mystifying IQ-amplifying computer game. She was done, cooked.

Alex knew better than to tell her about his morning with the boys at Interlingua or the afternoon spent on the phone negotiating with movers and contractors. And he definitely knew better than to press her for details about her day. He wouldn't try to solve her problems. He knew how to *empathize*.

Or at least he could make a good show of it. Still, some nights when she'd come home groaning and anxious, he simply couldn't work up the energy to play the caring-sharing househusband. He wanted to take her by the shoulders and plead: Why do I get the worst of you? Aren't I your favorite person in the world? Isn't that what you say? And what is so *bad,* really? Isn't this everything you'd always hoped for? The hit show, the healthy, intact family— and now, the dream house? What part of *getting everything you've ever worked for* is so terrible exactly?

It was as if Figgy had made a bargain with the Evil Eye that as long as she stayed outwardly unhappy and apparently untouched by her success, she'd get to keep on having it. All of which meant her moods seemed to rise and fall in an inverse relationship to how much there was to be happy about.

If that was true, then the show's new ad campaign was cause for deep despair. The network had pulled out the big guns for the new season, plastering every other billboard and bus bench with a super-saturated image of Katherine Pool's raven-haired, yoga-toned form emerging from an enormous velvet top hat. *TRICKS*: THE MADAM WILL SEE YOU NOW. Alex snapped pictures every time he saw one, giddy at the sight of that purple top hat. The ads made it official, apparently in a way the Emmys had not: The little show Figgy dreamed up over guava empanadas two years ago had become a piece of pop-culture currency. People who'd missed it the first year were scrambling to get caught up. One night a stranger at a neighborhood wine bar approached the table and asked if it was really her, the real Figgy Sherman-Zicklin.

The week before, her agent had even gotten an out-of-the-blue phone call from Brad Goodson, the inscrutable media mogul. He'd just watched the entire first season while yachting in the Caribbean and wondered if Figgy had any interest in spending a weekend on his boat off Cabo San Lucas around Christmastime with Diane Sawyer and Lady Gaga.

Naturally, Figgy had never felt worse.

Alex had hoped the new house would brighten her mood, but so far it seemed only to add to her agitation. Mostly she was annoyed that they had to wait six to eight weeks to move in. That was the minimum time required to do the repairs Alex had fought so hard for; as an added bonus, it meant they wouldn't be in the house while Figgy's crew was there shooting. The timing had worked out perfectly—the show had just entered the arc of the season that centered on the crime boss and her deluxe Mediterranean mansion. Alex decided not to be bothered by the fact that the show's production designer agreed that the house where they'd raise their children needed hardly any set dressing to stand in for the headquarters of a criminal kingpin.

• • •

Alex made disgruntled noises about *Tricks* filming at the new house, but the truth was he was weirdly excited to watch production up close. While Figgy said the show's production manager would handle the particulars, he insisted he should be around to ensure the house didn't get trashed. He'd gotten the house, and now he'd oversee the filming, get the repairs done, and move them all in. Figgy would take care of her business. He'd take care of everything else. Before they knew it, he'd be making frittatas on the Viking range.

And for a week anyway, he had a semiofficial connection to the show. It would give him and Figgy something to talk about. It would also, he thought, give him a chance to keep an eye on her—not that he put any stock in Huck's advice, but it wouldn't hurt to let everyone on set know that the woman in charge had an actual husband.

Alex made it a point to arrive a half-hour before the trucks rolled up, armed with a clipboard, a pair of leather gloves, and a bullhorn. Today his to-do list included making sure craft services stayed out of the neighbor's driveway and talking with the transpo chief about trucks blocking the alley. But first he needed to drop gift baskets on the doorsteps of all the houses along Sumter Court, a small gesture he hoped would smooth neighborhood relations and prevent complaints to the city.

The door of the big colonial a few doors down was ajar as he approached, revealing a woman in dangly earrings, a Juicy Couture sweatshirt, and sheepskin slippers.

"Can I help you?" The woman gripped a glass tumbler at her chest protectively.

"Oh hi—sorry. I'm Alex—I'm moving into the house across the street. The big pink one?"

The woman kept quiet and took a long draw on her straw.

"Just wanted to swing by and introduce myself and apologize—you know, for the filming?" He gestured across the street, at the two semis, three flatbeds, five trailers, and two generators rumbling along the curb, watched over by a beefy retired cop on a motorcycle. "And ask if I can help in any way."

"My husband told me if I played the radio full blast and opened the windows someone would come over and offer me money," the woman said. "Is that the kind of help you mean?"

Alex laughed. "How about a nice basket of jams and jellies?"

"I like a nice marmalade."

Alex fished around in the basket, pointed out a jar, and then handed the whole thing over.

"Nice to meet you," she said, squinting down and examining the contents. "You're getting *some* house over there. I've only been here six years, and I swear there's been a parade of people in and outta there. I'm sure you know about all that, though."

Alex frowned. "You mean besides the Benjamins?"

"Let's see—few years ago it was the Braggs? Nice family—at least I thought so. Three daughters. Wife did a *giant* renovation, redid the kitchen, added that solarium, took eight months and at least three or four hundred thou. Craziness! When it was all done, she marches into the gorgeous new bedroom and tells her husband she wants a divorce. Fallen in love with the contractor, Grant. Moving out with the girls. To Grant's tract house. In Valencia."

"Seriously?" he said. "Valencia?"

"I *know*," she grinned. "Have you ever heard anything more terrifying? You wanna come in? I just made smoothies."

Alex held up his clipboard and shrugged. "I wish I could," he said. "I've gotta get back to the crew. But thanks for the intel—"

"Oh there's *much* more," she said. "The people after the

Braggs? Southern couple—he was a hedge-fund guy? Here less than a year, moved in after adopting one of those babies from Russia. Apparently the mom had some sort of *mental* issue— she thought everyone who stepped on the property was trying to kidnap her little precious. Had a total conniption one day right here on the sidewalk, hollering and screaming, accusing the mailman of trying to snatch away little Caitlin. Next thing you know they're moving out. Nasty custody battle. You sure you won't come in?"

Alex took a step back and shook his head. "I'd really like to," he said. "But I'd better get back—gotta keep a close eye on these guys! Enjoy the marmalade!"

• • •

Heading back into the yard, Alex's first instinct was to find Figgy to share the news from the gossipy neighbor. The story about the housewife and the contractor? And the imaginary plot to kidnap Caitlin the Russian toddler? Alex could only guess what other horror stories awaited him if he'd gone inside for smoothies.

He walked past a group of grips as they unspooled tangles of cord, the crackle of their walkie-talkies buzzing from their utility belts. Beyond them, Alex saw a bank of scaffolds rising over Mr. Benjamin's prized azaleas. Alex barely recognized his own back-yard. The garden of tranquility was now a battlefield.

Alex finally spotted Figgy on the patio, perched on a canvas director's chair wearing a pair of headphones. She sat with her chin in her hands, face lit up by a monitor. She seemed to like what she saw, her mouth bent into a wry little smile. Alex craned his head to the side and saw that she wasn't smiling at the screen at all—she was looking down to her side, where, kneeling down with a stack of camera equipment, was none other than Zev the Israeli DP. The two of them exploded in laughter.

Alex took a few steps toward them and stopped. Zev's hand was on the lower part of Figgy's leg, held there not in greeting or for balance. Just planted. Alex felt his face go hot.

"Okay—moving on!" Figgy bounded up from her chair and signaled to the crew. At once, Zev hoisted a camera, and the tech guys who'd been loitering on the fringes popped up and sprang into action, hauling in fresh banks of lights, tangles of cable, and carts of equipment.

Alex kept his focus on Zev as he walked over to the Jacuzzi. Dressed in a snug leather jacket with the hood of a sweatshirt poking out from under the collar, he spoke briefly with an assistant and checked a light meter attached to a belt loop. As the two talked, Zev kept one hand on the assistant's shoulder. Okay, Alex thought—he's a toucher. Maybe it's an Israeli thing.

On the other side of the lawn, Alex caught sight of Katherine Pool, cross-legged in a high director's chair and fussed over by two assistants and Dani Dooling, the Diva Whisperer. Katherine's performances had been flat the past few episodes, which Figgy attributed to cosmetic surgery or a new med combo. Her face had always had a vaguely sock puppet–like quality, all wiggly and expressive. But now it was as flat and hard as a dinner plate. At the moment she stared impassively into the middle distance. Beside her, one assistant dabbed her forehead and a second held a tray of freshly cut pineapple spears. Katherine's neck was long and luxuriously curved. Dani wedged herself into the scrum, whispering notes for the upcoming scene.

Despite Figgy's initial worries, Dani was turning out to be a godsend. Where Figgy approached her star like a toddler whose tantrums would only be encouraged if indulged, Dani was only too happy to sit for hours as Katherine recited her grievances. Eventually she'd run out of steam and they'd move on to the only subject that seemed to bring Katherine any real happiness: Dani as a makeover model.

"Just let me get my hands on you," she'd say, stroking Dani's chin. Katherine had taken her on as a sort of top-to-tail makeover project. Dani now showed up to work each day in one of Katherine's castoff outfits and a new Kate-approved hairstyle. It seemed creepy to Alex, this grown woman submitting so completely to a celebrity's control, but the results were undeniable—Dani looked terrific.

• • •

The crew was setting up by the Jacuzzi, and Alex went over to check on the water. There had been a whole rigmarole over the Jacuzzi after the mother of the brooding, blond-haired Cliff Clampert, who played Toni the madam's teenage son, complained he was "uncomfortable" with standard chlorination. He wouldn't agree to do the Jacuzzi scene unless they equipped the pool with reverse-osmosis filtration. The production refused, so Mrs. Clampert threatened to lodge a grievance with SAG. So now, seven grand later, the Jacuzzi had been drained, retrofitted, and refilled with water as clear and chemical-free as Evian.

Alex turned around at the percussive slap of flip-flops on the granite pavers. Coming around the corner from the trailers were nine women in cotton bathrobes. They'd just come out of hair and makeup, and their eyes were huge and raccoon-like beneath thick streaks of kohl. Alex hopped up and made way for today's crop of hookers.

It was a running bit on *Tricks* that the stable of prostitutes changed from week to week. Hardly an episode went by when Toni wasn't breaking in a new hire or headhunting new girls to meet her clients' ever-enlarging list of specialty kinks. This week's crop included a heavily tattooed Indian girl, a couple of Kardashian lookalikes, and a freckled redhead who Alex guessed was about seven months pregnant.

One by one, the women dropped their robes and took up positions in and around the water. Just like that, there were breasts everywhere. Big, bulbous, tiny, pointy, natural, fabricated—he'd never seen so many boobs in one place. Alex's mouth went dry.

"Oh Alex! There you are!"

He turned, quickly scanning the crowd to confirm that the voice booming across the patio indeed belonged to his mother. She hustled through the crowd, charging ahead of a flustered production assistant.

How had he forgotten? His mother. Coming today from Ojai. 10:30. To see the house.

She crossed the patio and enfolded him in a big hug. Alex grinned weakly.

"Cashmere?" she said, smoothing his sleeve as she pulled away, oblivious to the scene behind them. "My sweater, on the other hand," she motioned to the nubby purple pullover she had on. "*Acrylic*. Sums it up, doesn't it?"

"Oh stop it—you look great," he said, taking a quick sideways step in an attempt to block her view. She'd dressed up for the occasion, in spangly slippers and some sort of beaded hair band.

"Alex, do you know there are *police* outside? They wouldn't let me in. They *questioned* me."

"That's just the detail guys—they're retired cops," Alex said. "That's their job—security for the shoot."

She shook her head furiously, jostling the brown-frosted sunglasses propped on her forehead. "Well if they're *retired* I don't see why they're allowed to wear those awful costumes."

"They're *uniforms*, ma. You made it here, so I guess—"

Alex stopped short as his mother looked past him and registered the scene around the Jacuzzi. Figgy was checking in with each of the day players, who'd arranged themselves in a stunning tableau of extended limbs, splayed pelvises, and oiled rumps. Two of the Latino girls—twins?—had taken up positions on either side of Cliff, whose expression, Alex noticed, had gotten noticeably less relaxed.

"Oh hi, Jane!" Figgy called from across the water. "Good to see you!"

Jane brought a quivering hand to her chest. "Good to see *you*," she said.

Alex was frozen, unsure whether to stay put or grab his mom and flee. Figgy flashed another smile and got back to work, kneeling beside the Indian woman, who was tossing a great bundle of dark hair over her headrest. "Nice vejazzling!" Figgy cooed, nodding down at the woman's midsection, where a glittering constellation of rhinestones burst forth in the place of pubic hair. "Let's get that in the shot. Don't hurt yourself, but really stretch out—arch that back!"

Figgy reached under the woman's back and tilted her pelvis a few inches forward. Then she turned and called out to the rest of the set: "Don't be shy, ladies! Absolutely no crossing of legs! Remember: premium cable!"

Alex took a quick, sharp breath and looked over at his mom. She was rigid in the same stricken pose, her breath sucked in and one hand clenched over her chest.

"Are you... okay, Ma?" he asked. "I probably should've warned you."

"Don't be silly," she finally said, blowing out a long hot breath. "I'm just *fine*."

• • •

She *was* fine, too, a lot finer than Alex. When the makeup artist appeared to administer spritzes of moisture to the women's cheeks and shoulders, he looked away, crossing his arms tightly and trying desperately to think of a single thing more uncomfortable than admiring naked women with his mother.

"I'm *so* glad you invited me over," she finally said. "Why didn't you do it sooner?"

"I have no idea," he said.

The fact was, he'd been trying to get her to visit for weeks. She'd just been so busy, she said. A couple of years ago she'd secured a state grant for a program devoted to introducing fourth graders to the protest songs of Appalachia. It was great on paper— "Grant-makers go absolutely ga-ga for Appalachia," she said— but Alex could only wonder what sort of response this hefty white lady got from crammed classrooms to the same loud, throaty, super-enunciated rendition of "If I Had a Hammer" that had pretty much been the soundtrack to his childhood.

"How about that tour?" he asked.

Jane kept her eyes locked forward, her only response a long, low moan.

"Can you *try* to contain yourself?" he said.

She turned toward him, annoyed. "What?"

"Maybe dial down the ogling?" he whispered.

"Oh Alex. You're missing the point entirely."

She motioned toward the pregnant woman, who was now splayed across a lounge chair, her great swollen belly huge and glistening.

"She's *obviously* doing a statement about fertility," she said, her eyes locked forward. "That lone boy, so isolated and ignored, amidst all that female power. It's a Sapphic fantasia."

"Pretty sure it's just a Jacuzzi full of hookers."

"Whatever it is," she said, "it's marvelous."

Zev called "action," and two of the women closest to the camera began an animated exchange about the environmental impact of petroleum-based rubber sex toys. "Oh, Tammy," one said, "you lube up a daikon radish and it's just as good as a dildo." The other women giggled and arched, the lot of them completely ignoring Cliff in the back of the shot, whose expression turned progressively more intense. Alex noticed a handheld camera positioned off to the side to get a close-up of the water near Cliff's foot, which was pressed up against a jet. As Cliff began to thrash around in the water, Alex felt his face go hot.

"Okay—time to go," he said.

"But it's just getting good," his mom whispered as he hustled her away. "That boy? Can't you see? No one's even touching him! And he's about to...."

"I know what he's about to do," Alex said. "Let's go inside. Please. Please, Mom."

He led her away from the cameras and toward a pair of French doors leading to the house. Swap the naked day players for his grandmother and the scene was a faithful reenactment of what was quite possibly the most humiliating episode of Alex's adolescence. It was the footgasm story. *His* footgasm story. Figgy often used material from her own life for the show, but she hadn't warned him about this. It was especially bad because of the presence of his mom, who he blamed for the whole thing. When he was ten or eleven, she'd sat him down with a stack of richly illustrated books and magazines to give him a complete rundown on "the many beautiful varieties of sexual expression." Intercourse, cunnilingus, fellatio, sadomasochism, group sex, transgender issues—she'd covered it all. He seemed to remember a detour into the topic of *fisting*.

This graphic crash course on the subject of sex did not have the liberating effect his mother had intended. After the talk, Alex knew abstractly that boys played with their penises and that was okay; that knowledge was filed alongside the fact that some men took drugs that allowed them to grow breasts and that some cut off their penises and that these brave and oppressed people were called transgendered. Stunned by all the new information, Alex steered well clear of his own equipment long after other boys his age had become self-taught experts in the operation of theirs. He finally got some direct experience at the age of fifteen while visiting his grandparent's condo in Palm Springs and resting his foot against the jet of a Jacuzzi. In an instant his legs straightened out, his belly got quivery, and he exploded right there, a few feet away from his grandma.

Jacuzzis had never been the same for Alex after that.

• • •

He could still hear the teenage actor making exaggerated whoops of pleasure as he and Jane made their way up the main stairwell. In Sylvie's bathroom, he pointed out the pink-and-black checkerboard tile, determined to change the subject from the scene downstairs. After leading her into the hall and pointing out the carved walnut moldings, he noticed his mother's expression turn, her eyebrows arch and mouth set.

"Amazing, right?" he asked, standing on the balcony of the master bedroom, looking out over the front lawn. "I'd like to get some solar panels in here, maybe a cistern to help with the water."

Jane made a noncommittal murmur, then turned away and kept walking. He followed her to a pair of pocket doors that led to a spare bedroom that Judy Benjamin had lined with floor-to-ceiling shoe racks. Oh God, Alex thought: not the shoe closet. For all her sex-positive, "Free to Be You and Me" tolerance, he knew his mother to be a woman of scorchingly severe opinions about certain things. SUVs. Golf. Obscenely large shoe closets.

Alex knew he shouldn't care what she thought—what did he expect from a mountain mystic with a LIVE SIMPLY SO OTHERS MAY SIMPLY LIVE bumper sticker on her guitar case and defiantly hairy legs and armpits (Jane apparently being the last lesbian alive still waging war against the hypocrisy of gender-based personal grooming)? He was a grown man with a life of his own—why did he physically flinch at the thought of her disapproval?

Jane ran a finger down the metal rack, and then swiveled around to face him. "All this space!"

Alex leaned up against the doorframe and hung his head.

"Every mother hopes her children find some security," she said, sweeping her hand out with a regal wave. "But this—this is something else."

"I know—it's way more than we need. But do you, you know... like it?"

She dropped her arms to her sides and released a big laugh. "What's not to like? It's a dream!"

"I thought you'd be, I don't know, *offended*. By the excess. I'm still kind of shocked I get to live here. I mean, this couldn't possibly be *my* house, right?"

"Oh sweetie," she said. "Of course it's your house—yours and that marvelous woman of yours. Just look at her down there at the center of all that action."

Alex went over to the window. The lighting guys were inflating a huge, white hot-air balloon that mimicked the effulgence of moonlight. He spotted Figgy back on her canvas chair, huddled with a costume guy.

His mom came over and stood beside him, her fingers cradling a turquoise amulet strung around her neck with a leather cord. "And just think how great this house is going to feel after a good cleansing."

"We already had a service come in and do the floors—"

"No sweetie," she said. "A *spiritual* cleansing. Deny it all you want, but Alex—you're sensitive to these things. You feel all the bottled-up energy in here, all that residual juju."

"Oh, Ma." There was no way he was going to pay some Ojai crackpot to come wave feathers around.

"I put together a bag of goodies—it's in my car," she said, practically levitating with excitement. "Wild sage from the mountain. Vials of spring water blessed by a nephew of the Krishnamurti.

It'll be fun! The kids will love it—did you know that it's an ancient Native American rite to urinate on the perimeter of a new homestead?"

Alex smiled and agreed that yes, his kids would undoubtedly love that particular ritual. But he knew what he'd do with his mother's bag of mystical do-dads—the same thing he'd done with Joan's assortment of mezuzahs. Show it to Figgy for laughs, then stash it away in a junk drawer and forget about it.

Jane touched his shoulder. "It's a beautiful house, honey. It's even more beautiful because you and Figgy are in it. You have to understand, Alex, honey—never in my lifetime did I think that we'd make such tremendous gains so fast, that our daughters would achieve so much. We thought the movement would be a long, slow, gradual struggle. But look around—right here! We won!"

She smiled triumphantly, and then stepped around Alex toward the door. "The age of testosterone is over," she said. "Now show me this solarium of yours."

• • •

At the end of the tour, Jane went out to her car to fetch her bag of magical do-dads, and Alex marched over to the half-circle of canvas folding chairs where Figgy and Dani were huddled around a monitor playing back the Jacuzzi scene.

Alex was relieved to discover that Zev was nowhere to be seen. He watched a few seconds of Cliff's contorted face on the monitor and then hooked a finger under one of Figgy's headphones and popped them off.

"Footgasm? Really?"

"Oh, honey!" Figgy made a half-grimace, half-laugh. "I know—I forgot to tell you! It's just that I mentioned it in the room and everyone agreed it's the best first orgasm story ever."

Alex didn't return the smile. "You might have checked. You know—before using the unbelievably embarrassing thing I told you privately… in your *TV show*!"

Figgy started to respond, but Dani came to her aid. "Oh, Alex, we *absolutely* had to use it. Obviously, we added the naked girls—no one would ever believe how it really happened, would they? Seriously, did you actually—*splooge*? Next to your grandmother?"

Alex coughed. "She was a very youthful eighty-year-old. And water pressure in the seventies was *entirely* different."

Dani hopped up and down and clapped. "Oh, you are hi-larious," she said. "He is, Figgy. Just like you're always saying. You really *are* the man behind the woman."

Alex kept an accusing stare focused on Figgy.

She got up from her chair and wrapped her arms around him. "Oh shit honey," she said. Alex could hear the concern in her voice—it hadn't occurred to her before this moment what a betrayal this was. "I'm sorry for not talking to you about it beforehand. But I've been so crazy. I haven't seen the kids in a week. I'm so exhausted I can barely walk. I just forgot. Don't be mad."

Alex softened, his complaint now dwarfed by her upset. He knew the drill. They were back in the misery marathon—whoever had it worse earned the credit and forgiveness. And according to those rules, she'd just inched ahead. "It's okay," he said. "I guess no one but us knows it's… true, right?"

Figgy made a quick—Alex thought a little too quick—pulling-it-together snuffle and then collected herself, looking up at the house. "So how was the tour? Jane give you grief?"

"No—not really," he said. "Apparently she made it all possible."

"What? How's that?"

"You know, by singlehandedly forging the way for you—and women everywhere? Kind of like how she invented lesbianism."

"Oh right," Figgy said. "Well, she *was* a dyke way before it was cool."

Dani motioned to the yard, where Jane was barreling onto the grass, her battered guitar swinging at her side. She quickly surveyed the scene, fixing herself on a spot a few feet down a hill from where Zev was about to start the next scene. Jane made a theatrical toss of her pullover and then knelt down and unpacked her instrument.

Dani arched an eyebrow and smiled warily. "She's not going to—"

Alex felt his stomach turn.

Within a minute, Jane was crouched into a cross-legged position in the grass. She closed her eyes and locked her face in a beatific, rapt expression Alex recognized from a picture on her bathroom wall of Joan Baez at the Newport Folk Festival in 1966. And then she broke into the first chords of "If I Had a Hammer."

Nine

I'm out of my gourd on cough syrup and malt liquor the night I catch the Germs at the Starwood. I'm too young and fucked up to be out on my own, but so's everyone. We're all crazy, no-clue, wayward juvie punks, latchkey kids getting our ears blasted and our minds exploded. And for a glorious nanosecond, the sorry horde of us gets just what we're after: oblivion.

Alex punched the return key and looked out the window. He'd set up his office in a corner of the solarium when they'd moved in two months ago. Every day after dropping the kids at school, he'd head home, march to his desk, and plop down under an arched window with a panoramic view of the backyard. Framed by clumps of pink rhododendron, the scene was ridiculously pretty. A flagstone path rolled across the lawn to the guest cottage, nestled in a thicket of trees like something out of a Thomas Kinkade painting. Looking over the scene now, he felt a knot of anxiety coil up in his throat.

What was his problem? Was it the work, the house? It couldn't be the writing. He'd started working on his book the day after they moved in. Coming across his fanzine, he'd decided, had been a *sign*. He needed to write a balls-out account of the birth of SoCal punk, a hard-nosed, knockabout tour through the clubs and halls and garages where the scene took root. That's how he'd pitched it to Figgy: *Almost Famous* without the muttonchops or shitty classic rock.

Partly to compensate for the wrongness of writing his paean to punk in a fucking *solarium*, he'd decided to work on the same model typewriter he'd used to produce his 'zine way back when. It had been easy enough to locate an IBM Selectric on Craigslist. It came with three fresh, still-in-the-box ribbons and had the same chipped avocado-green frame as the typewriter he'd used to write *R.I.P.* It emitted a deep hum when switched on, vibrating the desktop. Unfortunately, the punk rock choice was turning out to be kind of a hassle. The keys were constantly getting jammed, and he kept smearing globs of Wite-Out on the plastic window that flattened the paper against the roller. Still, he soldiered on.

With my notebook tucked in the back pocket of my Dickies and my bodacious eighteen-year-old babysitter Dotti as a ride, I'm a wide-eyed waif among hardcore diehards from OC and the South Bay. Those fuckers will pound your face or unleash globs of mucus in your eye just for shits and giggles. I keep my back to the wall and stay busy noting detailed set lists. The music is sloppy and disgusting and unhealthy, like a chili dog dripping down your shirt. I gorge myself on the greasy mess of it.

Alex stopped typing and looked up, a mysterious thud emanating from upstairs. He felt like he spent half the day wandering from room to room, staring at the bare walls, trying to decipher the groans, creaks, and thuds that constituted the house's secret vocabulary. He kept waiting for the tranquility of new ownership to kick in, the satisfaction he'd expected to take over once the initial shock of the move wore off. But so far, being here just made him feel like he was squatting while the real owners were away. Hoo boy, were they gonna be *pissed* when they got home.

Yesterday he'd barely written a word, getting up every five minutes to let Albert outside to pee or help Rosa with the washing machine or sign for FedEx. At a certain point he gave up entirely and decided what he really needed was a long soak in the big whirlpool tub upstairs. Because why not? He could do that. He'd while away an hour scrubbing and dozing and maybe even cracking one of Sammy's scented bath oils. He needed to enjoy the spoils a little, soak it up, stop worrying so much.

But of course, not three minutes after stripping down, pouring a half bottle of hibiscus-scented oil and lowering himself into the water—and feeling in a delicious rush how incredible it was that he was *here* and not, say, slaving in his old cubicle at BestSelf—right then, a metallic clank thudded down over his head. Just above the windowsill, not three feet away, appeared the ruddy, mustachioed face of Rudolfo the gardener. He scrambled out of the bath, bubbles flying, his penis flapping around in a horrific soapy scramble.

He wasn't sure how much Rudolfo had actually seen—he'd been busy trimming the ivy, and Alex had retrieved a towel with bionic quickness. But even if the particulars had been fuzzy, there was no mistaking the overall gestalt, which was that the new boss, the man of the house, El Jefe, was having a big frothy pink-hued bubble bath at eleven in the morning.

Why was it so difficult to get comfortable in a house built for comfort? Figgy still basically lived at work, and Alex, the kids, and the dog found themselves moving in a tight herd from room to room, still not quite knowing what to do with all the new space. Getting home from carpool each afternoon, the kids would turn on the TV on the kitchen counter, and Alex would stand by their side chopping and slow roasting and arranging intricate bento boxes for the next day's lunches.

"You don't value what comes easy to you," Figgy had said recently, home at midnight and biting into a corn fritter. "Maybe you're a cook, honey. Why don't you take some classes?"

Alex knew she was trying to be encouraging, but the suggestion landed with a sting. She obviously didn't appreciate how busy his days were, with the book and the kids' new school schedule and all the house repairs and the rest of it. She seemed to think he had vast, open chunks of the day free to formulate sauces. It also suggested Figgy wasn't really on board with his book project. He bore down on the typewriter.

I pay insane money for Cramps vinyl, get a pair of Creepers, shout and stomp and pogo in dark halls that reek of teen flop sweat. I'm caught up in the scrum, colliding and smashing and heaving. The pain is half the fun. I'm on the receiving end of an elbow to the ribs that leaves a fist-size purple welt. Think of all the chiropractors punk rock made rich! To say nothing of the manufacturers of hearing aids. I ask you: How many of my skinhead brothers are cuddled up on Tempurpedic pillows today?

Hearing loss? Chiropractor bills? Shit. Alex reached for the Wite-Out. He'd set out to write about teen angst and go-for-broke, free-for-all fanaticism. But he kept getting sidetracked on cranky asides about torn ACLs, overcrowded venues, and the shocking amount of secondhand smoke.

He ripped out the paper. Maybe he should ditch the memoir idea altogether. Who the hell was he to write a memoir anyhow? He felt like he'd spent his whole work life thinking: *if only*. If only I had time and freedom to do my own thing. Now *if only* was here. For at least these few hours a day, he could now do whatever he wanted. And right now what he wanted was to erase all traces of the nervous, equivocating, whiny, injured, *virginal* boarding school kid he'd been and reinvent his hero as a scrappy, snarling tough. A kid who'd bust his lip fighting neo-Nazi dirtbags. Who'd do lines of crank in bathroom stalls. Who'd get crabs from girls in ripped fishnets.

That was it: He'd rewrite the whole thing in the third person, put some distance between himself and his lead guy. His own story, after all, wasn't that interesting—the mountain hippie stuff had no place in a book on the L.A. hardcore scene, plus no self-respecting punk would ever trust a story from a scholarship kid at the Crestwood Academy. He could create an alter ego who'd be free to do all the stupid, risky, impulsive things Alex himself never did. But that would mean he'd be writing—what? A novel? And who read *novels* anymore?

Alex got up from his desk and headed out to the kitchen. Pickup at the Pines was an hour away. And he'd promised Figgy he'd call the decorator about the backsplash tile.

• • •

Alex eased into his still-shiny Toyota Sienna—he'd just unloaded his old Subaru, which despite its outdoorsy cred didn't have the Sienna's computerized nav system or twenty-seven cup holders. While backing out into traffic, he called Dana the decorator. They'd hired Dana when house repairs escalated into something approaching a full redecoration—the contractors were already there, Figgy reasoned, so why not swap out the kitchen counters and fixtures, redo the master bath, and knock out all the little fix-its they'd never get to later? Alex took charge, pushing hard to finish everything before they moved in, but they'd been in the house for eight weeks now and there were still unpainted walls and unfurnished rooms and endless decisions to be made. It was true: Everything took twice as long and cost twice as much as you thought. Also true: Remodeling was hell on a marriage. Every chair, every fabric, every handle, every hinge, every little goddamned screw—everything was a negotiation, a cost comparison, a referendum on their taste, their sensibilities, their budget, their confidence in themselves, and their trust in one another.

"So sweetie—are we all good with the backsplash tile?" asked Dana, a pleasant hint of her native Tennessee in her voice. She was a slim, red-haired former set designer with a flirty, unfailingly upbeat manner that put Alex on edge. He didn't think he'd ever get used to being called "sweetie" by someone who got a twenty percent commission.

"We are good—absolutely," he said, turning into traffic. He'd sent Dana an email the day before about tiles for the kitchen walls. He'd selected a plain, matte-finish subway tile the color of milky tea. Like most of his choices for the house, it was mid-priced, produced by an eco-friendly manufacturer, and passably grownup. "Let's carry that right over the stove, across the counter. I think that cream color will be really nice—wouldn't you say it's more mocha?"

There was a pause on the line. "So this is *instead* of the French ones? The hexagons?" asked Dana.

"Hexagons? What hexagons?"

"Figgy sent me a link yesterday. Said it was urgent? You know, the picture from *Elle Decor*. Looks like some sort of hacienda? Moroccan maybe? Hand painted, with the little goblin faces? Whimsical, for sure. My guy in Culver City said he could knock them off. Twenty-two bucks."

Alex took this in. "I know nothing of hexagons. Or goblins. But... the fee sounds okay, I guess."

"Oh, sweetie, it's not a *fee*," Dana laughed. "That's cost-per-unit. Twenty-two a *tile*. We'll need eight hundred—maybe a thousand."

Alex felt his pulse quicken as he tried to do the math and then flashed to a picture of their sun-dappled great room encircled by a thousand hand-painted goblin faces.

"Let me have a conversation with Fig," he finally said, knowing instantly how that conversation would go. It would go like the one about the color of the living room ceiling ("Metallic gold! How great is that?"), the dining room curtains ("Crushed purple velvet! Like Grauman's Chinese!"), and the light fixture in the master bath ("Salvaged from the Googie coffee shop in El Monte! One of a kind!"). Somehow in the process of this renovation he'd been revealed as the moderate, penny-pinching superego to Figgy's voracious, extravagant id.

"I put in the order yesterday," Dana said. "So I just need a check from you and we're good to go."

Alex bumped his head back into the headrest, his mouth wide open in a silent wail. After his little private freakout was done, he rolled down the window and took a big breath. "Do me a favor, Dana, and just send me a picture of these goblin heads? I'll get back to you."

• • •

Alex drove in silence, fuming. After a few blocks, a text arrived from Dana with a snapshot of the backsplash tiles. Alex pulled over, picked up his phone, and enlarged the image with a quick reverse pinch. He was already composing his speech about the latest silly extravagance, how irony had no place in interior design... but as he looked at the backsplash tile, his fury broke apart at once. The goblin motif was more like a fleur de lis or a sunburst, and the tiles fit together in a repeating, Escher-like puzzle pattern. The design was odd, intricate, and undeniably wonderful. He'd just have to get over the fact that he'd spent the last two days comparing the subtle differences between various shades of cream only to have Figgy rip out a page of *Elle Decor*, which she probably did in about two seconds while sitting on the toilet.

Alex merged back into traffic and hopped on the 101, feeding the address of the school into the minivan's nav system. He knew the route fine. But in moments like these, with his jaw locked and his fingers clenched on the steering wheel, he liked the GPS on. There was something about the voice—he loved its calm assurance, its soothing authority.

"Turn left in one hundred yards," the GPS purred.

And so he did, joining the long line of Volvos, Siennas, and Pri-i (that being the proper plural, he'd decided, for Prius) along the sidewalk beside the east gate of the Pines School. He pulled up behind Angela, the squat, square-jawed Honduran woman who looked after Huck and Kate's kids. Angela was out of the car and standing at the ready clutching a foil juice pouch and a Ziploc of apple wedges. He scanned the sidewalk and saw a line of other nannies and mommies, out of their cars and ready for a little meet-and-greet, most of them ready with beverages and a nibble.

As the kids began to dribble out, Alex bent over the passenger seat to look for Sam and Sylvie amid the crowd of kids. Pines boys generally wore fitted jeans, aviator shades, shaggy hair, and reproduction rock T-shirts (what eleven-year-old, Alex wanted to know, had ever actually *heard* Peter Frampton?). The girls were similarly disheveled but more artfully so, draped in diaphanous scarves and bangly beads and giant bulging leather bags.

Alex caught sight of Sam and Sylvie. Sylvie had retired the orange backpack with her name stitched on the flap in favor of a new suede messenger bag. She was dressed in a ratty blue cardigan and brown cords. Just behind her, Sam lumbered along in some kind of newsie cap and checkered button-down. It felt like a month ago that they were still in Target basics and mini-mall haircuts: now they'd clearly joined the mid-seventies Topanga Canyon revival.

Sylvie shuffled toward the car behind a teacher's assistant. She was sturdy—Alex would say stocky, Figgy would say plump. Alex kept telling her they shouldn't worry, shouldn't discourage Sylvie's adventurous diet, shouldn't risk getting a seven-year-old girl started on body issues. Figgy countered that seven years old was maybe too young to tutor a girl on the varieties of Spanish ham.

As they were led to the van, Alex saw the teacher squeeze Sylvie's shoulder and release a big honking laugh. Alex was wary about the Pines kids, but the teachers were a huge improvement over the irritable civil servants they'd encountered at their old public school. So far anyway, it looked to be true, what they said in the sales pitch: The Pines was indeed a school where "kids are pushed to greater levels of creativity and achievement in a warm and nurturing environment."

For $32,000 a year, Alex thought, it better be true.

"Hey kiddos!" Alex said as the door heaved open and the two piled in. "All good?"

Sam murmured an assent while Sylvie vaulted over the second row of seats and popped up in the far corner, a distant and mysterious region of the vehicle that Alex visited every few weeks to clear out the pistachio shells, seaweed scraps, cheese rinds, and other bits of castoff foodstuffs that Sylvie left in her wake.

Ahead of the van, Alex noticed Huck and Kate's daughter Penelope standing on the sidewalk beside her waiting car. Hip cocked as she sipped a juice pocket, she watched impassively as Angela loaded her knapsack into the trunk. Penelope looked as dazed and disinterested as a socialite emerging from a long night at a downtown club.

"Everyone buckled?" Alex hollered, not waiting for a response. He put his foot down on the gas pedal, more forcefully than he'd intended, a squeal of rubber sounding out behind them. Indignant stares flashed from the sidewalk.

"What the *heck*, Dad!" Sam called. "Slow down!"

"Woo-hoo!" Sylvie said. "Allll-right!"

"Sorry," Alex looked in the rearview mirror at the kids. "Foot slipped. Not used to this baby's horsepower. You okay?"

"I guess," Sam murmured. "Just don't *peel out* anymore. Rodney and Jake were right there. They totally saw."

"Okay," Alex said, wondering how peeling out with your dad could be construed as embarrassing. Wasn't that cooler than nibbling Teddy Grahams while your nanny hauled your backpack? Then again, a lot of what Sam did at school seemed mortifying to Alex—like setting up a Sammy's Salves booth on the quad and appearing in a red unitard in the school production of *Alice in Wonderland*. Alex had urged Sam to maybe hold off launching the skin cream line and go out for another part besides the mincing, cuckolded King of Hearts in the school musical, but Sam did what he pleased.

"How was school today? Do anything cool?"

"Not really," he said. "Drama in woodworking. None of the kids would line up! What kind of school doesn't make the kids line up? Took us like an hour before we got to whittling."

Woodworking was big at the Pines—along with sewing, gardening, and pottery. It was all part of a "hands-on, experiential" curriculum that distinguished the Pines from other, more "achievement-oriented" private schools. Sylvie had come home last week with a clay pot filled with butter she'd churned herself. Alex wasn't totally sold on the program—he was particularly ambivalent about the school's discouragement of electronic media—but he loved the idea of his kids becoming skilled artisans in pioneer-era crafts. Someone needed to know how to rebuild Come the Revolution.

"What'd you whittle?"

"'A natural form'—whatever *that* means," he said. "The art teacher Sonya said we should 'listen to the wood.' This kid Jason said mine looked like boobs. His thing was supposed to be like a

wave, but Sonya could tell it wasn't that at all. It was totally a bazooka."

"Jason whittled a bazooka?"

"It had a little shoulder holder and everything. Sonya got
all mad and started talking about the non-violence dialogue we
had at assembly. But Jason swore she was misinterpreting it. The
whole thing took forever and I didn't even get to finish my form."

"Come on, Sammy," Alex said. "Just a few more days—school's
out next Friday. That's good, right? Then we're off to Maui! You
excited?"

"Sure," he said, sounding not the least bit excited.

They'd just booked ten days in Maui after an agonizing negotiation; Figgy was still sulking about the crazy Caribbean invitation from Brad Goodson, which Alex discovered didn't extend to
the entire family. ("We're just not set up for *chil*-dren," Goodson's
aide said, pronouncing the last word as if it were the name of a
communicable disease.) Alex suggested they stick close to home,
maybe even head up to Ojai to spend the holiday with his mom
and Carol, but Figgy said she'd lose her mind if forced to spend her
first break in six months rattling rain sticks and chanting seasonal
incantations as part of a winter solstice ritual. Besides, a bunch of
Pines families were meeting up at the Rutlidge Wailea, including
the Bampers. Figgy had recently gotten friendly with Cary Bamper, creator of *The Ambassadors*, a classy, much-admired hour-
long set at the American embassy in London. Wouldn't it be fun
to get their whole families together? And hadn't Alex hit it off
with Helen Bamper at that dinner party last week? And how was
it they'd never been to Maui anyway?

• • •

Figgy had promised to be home by seven, which meant Alex
had a menu to put together. So on the way home from school, he

stopped by Malcolm's and told the kids to hang out in the car so he could quickly run inside and pick up a roast.

"Alex! Bro!" Malcolm called from behind the counter. "How'd it go with the pig ears for shabbat? Work out?"

Alex grinned. "Crispy like onion rings—just like you said," he said. "Best trayf ever. I did the marrow like you said, too. Unbelievable. You were so right."

Malcolm gave him an approving nod. "It's just true: Fat is where the flavor is."

"Amen," Alex said.

Alex peered into the case and surveyed the day's selection. The scallops looked gorgeous, the lamb perfect. He pinched his chin studiously, taking his time. Malcolm wouldn't mind. Alex would often spend a half hour or more shooting the shit about the provenance of balsamic vinegars before getting around to his actual order. Malcolm's was not a high-volume business.

"Hey—show this week was great," Malcolm said, wiping his hands with a rag. "The thing with the kid in the Jacuzzi? Hilarious."

Alex nodded in agreement and shrugged. The episode they'd shot at the house back in August had just aired, and the response had been huge; fans had already started swapping "footgasm" T-shirts online. He hadn't realized Malcolm knew about Figgy or his connection to the show, but lately it seemed everyone knew who he was. He was husband-of.

A few friends had also picked up the resemblance to a new character on the show, the commissioner's househusband. The character was a middle-aged fragile flower who bragged about his wild rock and roll youth and who remained entirely ignorant about his wife's nefarious business. Figgy insisted the character was pure fiction, but Alex wasn't so sure. He couldn't help but wonder how much Figgy kept from him now, how much of her life she didn't share. They were both just so busy. He flashed on a memory from when Sylvie was in preschool. Alex used to wait for her in the hall, watching through the doorway as she moved around the classroom, a feather boa around her neck, a little plastic mallet in her fist, intense and busy and utterly oblivious to everyone around her. Parallel play, the teachers called it. That's what he and Figgy were doing now.

"This season is just full-on," Malcolm said. "So great."

"Thanks," Alex said, not sure why he was accepting the compliment. "I'll tell the wife you said so."

Just then another customer stepped up to the counter and Miranda appeared. "Hey Sher," she said. "Back for more bone marrow?"

Sher? He had a nickname now? He'd been keeping an eye on her blog for weeks, but he had no idea that she had any idea who he was. But maybe this was just part of the shop's full-service customer relations.

"Nope—looking for something a little lighter," Alex said, his mouth going dry. "How's the seafood today? Anything nice back there?"

She smiled and motioned to a cutting board nearby. "We got a section of bluefin in this morning. Straight off the plane from Tokyo. If you're nice I could cut you off some."

Alex looked back and spotted a section of the silvery fish, its scales phosphorescent in the light. He could do a poke; Sylvie would love that. "Sounds good," he said. "You mind cleaning it up?"

"One sec," she smiled, pivoting back to the center-island chopping block. With a few strokes the fish fell apart into perfect fillets, coming undone like a knot she'd loosened a hundred times before. She folded some paper around it, wrapped it all up and laid it next to the register. Alex felt woozy.

"Nice knife work," he said, pulling out his wallet. "You been doing this a while?"

"Not really," she said, swiping his card. "Eight or nine months. Malcolm says I'm a natural. Which is bizarre, since I was a hardcore vegan until like a year ago."

Alex cocked an eyebrow. "Really? How does *that* happen?"

She put his bag down and leaned up against the counter. "I dunno. Bunch of stuff happened all at once. Job ended, big breakup, and at some point I sort of realized I'd been this staunch vegan for the worst reasons. When I was really truthful with myself, I loved how it made me feel special, how *accommodations* had to be made for me. And that's kind of bullshit, right? A week later, I answered an ad for Malcolm, and every since it's been all meat, all the time."

"Huh," Alex said, signing his credit card slip. "No evangelist like the convert, right?"

"Tell me about it," she said, handing over the bag. She smiled.

Alex started to turn away but stopped. "Love the blog, by the way," he said. "Great stuff."

She brightened and looked away shyly. "Thanks," she said. "Shoot me an email some time. Fun to swap recipes or whatever."

Or whatever? What did that mean? Alex took his bag back and headed out the door, suddenly in a hurry to get back to the van.

• • •

Alex herded the kids inside when he got home, plopping them in front of the kitchen TV and then getting to work on the fish. He set the brown paper package on the counter and filled an aluminum mixing bowl with chopped scallions, soy sauce, red pepper flakes, black sesame, and crushed macadamias. Heaving open the door of the fridge—an industrial-grade Sub-Zero that Figgy had insisted they get after seeing the same model in the commissioner's kitchen set—he marveled at how packed it was, how a double-wide monstrosity that he'd protested was completely excessive was now jammed with yogurts and salads, takeout containers and leftovers, jugs of juice blends and gifted bottles of champagne. How could it be that they'd graduated to a refrigerator the size of a walk-in meat locker and they were still overflowing? How *was* it that whatever space they had was constantly filled to bursting?

That was Figgy's influence—even in absentia, she always ensured they had more than enough. Her maximalism would not be contained.

Alex retrieved his favorite knife, gave it a swipe with a sharpening steel and unfolded the package of fish. Peeling back the tissue, he stooped down and sniffed. It had the tang of deep ocean. It glowed ruby red, as if lit from inside. He made careful work of it, making inch-long strips and then rotating the cutting board to crisscross the wedges into symmetrical pink cubes.

This was Miranda's reserve stuff, and it was magnificent. He pictured her face now, glimpsed through the cold glass of the display cabinet. That story about becoming a butcher—she'd tossed it off like it was just idle chitchat. He got the impression she offered up confessions like that all the time, to anyone and everyone. He was nothing special, he thought; she was just an over-sharer, someone who treated her own failings as shtick to be performed for perfect strangers.

Alex dumped the cubed fish into the bowl and walked over to the computer to call up the Meatgirl website. He looked over at the kids—they were slack-jawed and splayed out before the TV, not paying him the least attention. He was free to browse.

He clicked through until he found what he was looking for: a photo of Miranda in the kitchen, dressed in a loose tank top and snug jeans, her mouth open in a half-smile as she gripped a roast with a pair of tongs. He enlarged the picture, zooming in on the hand (strong, impossibly long fingers, unpainted nails) and felt his heart begin to pound. Jesus—what was his problem? If this was infidelity, he sucked at it.

A minute or two passed. Alex bent forward, looking intently at the view down Miranda's unbuttoned chef's coat as she leaned over: that long, slender throat, the scattering of tiny brown freckles. The spastic soundtrack of the kids' cartoon echoed dimly in the distance. He thought of his book and his idea this morning to rewrite it as fiction, to break from what actually happened and embrace what *might be*.

Alex clicked on the window and closed it. He needed to get back to dinner, but first he needed to find that magic command he knew from the occasional trip to XTube or UPorn. This hadn't been anything close to illicit—it was just food, and hadn't Figgy said he should take cooking more seriously?—but sitting here now, Alex felt an intense desire to erase these particular steps. After futzing around on the nav bar for a few minutes, he finally found it, that magic command, the one he wished he could apply to whole stretches of his life: CLEAR HISTORY.

• • •

Figgy wasn't picking up her phone. It was after eleven, and Alex knew from the *Tricks* call sheet that shooting was scheduled to wrap at nine. Where was she? Alex had fed and showered the kids and was back in the kitchen, the countertop TV casting a flickering bluish light on Alex's wine glass. Production often went late, and she'd probably turned off her phone while cameras were rolling. She'd come home when she came home. Like she always did.

Alex leaned down and gave the scruff around Albert's neck a rub. Something told him Figgy hadn't turned off her phone; something told him she just wasn't answering. He needed to know. Wait—he *could* know. He switched on the computer, signed into their family cell phone account, and called up ZeroIn, which allowed you to track your phone's location. He'd used the app a few times before when he'd misplaced his phone; tonight he'd misplaced his wife.

The streets of L.A. materialized in chunks across the screen. Two green dots popped up. The first hovered above their house on Sumter Court (that would be his phone) and the second dot, the one indicating Figgy's phone... where was that? It wasn't at the studio. Alex magnified the view and scrolled northward, five or so miles away, deep in the chaotic tangle of side streets above Sunset Boulevard. Figgy—or at least her phone—was somewhere in the Hollywood Hills.

Alex dialed her number. Voicemail. Again. What the hell? Where was she?

Alex rose from his seat and did a circuit around the kitchen, then sat back down at the computer and pressed refresh. The green dot stayed put. He got up again, refilled his wine glass, and backed himself up against the pantry, his eyes fixed on the computer. From this distance across the room, the green dot pulsed in place, brightening and dimming, as if tracking Figgy's circulation system, her every breath.

Hadn't she mentioned that Zev the DP had just rented a place in West Hollywood? A crazy modern with a kickboxing gym? And an infinity pool?

He flashed again on that pathetic magician at the Emmys, that Randall guy in the fedora. What was it Huck had said? Poor fucker had no clue what was about to hit him?

Five miles—he could be there and back in less than twenty minutes. The kids were fast asleep. They were fine. As he grabbed his keys, jotted down the address on a Post-it, and headed out the back door, he heard a voice shrieking somewhere in the back of his head: *Stop! You don't leave your kids home alone! Ever! Breathe! Breathe again!*

Alex jumped into the minivan and backed out of the driveway, knocking into a trash barrel before accelerating westward. Fucking Zev. Of course it was Zev—he was everything Alex wasn't. He was successful, decisive, confident. Jewish. He wouldn't have any issue with Figgy's success. He was into mindfulness. He did yoga. He had those big round shoulders and a dark thicket of chest hair. The sex was probably amazing.

By the time Alex was in West Hollywood, gunning his minivan up a steep slope toward the address on the Post-it, he'd worked up a full steam of panic. He sucked in a breath as he pulled up to Zev's house. *I won't go in*, he thought. *I'll just creep around and peek inside, get a look at what's happening.*

Behind a row of scrubby hedges was a low-slung seventies ranch house with a lava rock chimney and a wood-shingled roof. As he got closer, brake lights flashed ahead of him—a pair of cars were pulling out. He slowed down and peered closer. Lit up in the glare of a porch light was a shortish, roundish figure—wait, was that Dani? Dani the Diva Whisperer?—chatting with a couple who exchanged quick hugs and headed out to the street.

Okay. So maybe this wasn't Zev's house. Maybe this was a work party. An after-work gathering at the line producer's house.

Alex reared back in his seat and drove on, shielding his face as he passed a guy he recognized from the set returning to his car. A wave of relief and embarrassment washed over him. His wife hadn't left work to go skinny dip in Zev's infinity pool. She'd stopped off at a co-worker's wrap party.

So where was her car? He scanned the street for Figgy's Volvo. No sign of it. He turned around and did another pass. No Volvo.

Alex did another fast U-turn and gunned it down the hill, scenarios spinning out in quick succession. Figgy had left the party and went... somewhere more private? A hotel? Zev's place? The ZeroIn app—he didn't have it on his phone, so Alex would hurry home and check her location on the home computer....

Outside their house, sitting in the driveway, was Figgy's Volvo.

They'd probably passed each other coming and going. He quickly passed a hand over the hood of her car—it was still warm, making a little ticking sound—then rushed inside.

"Fig?" Around the corner from the entry, he could see light from the living room.

"There you are."

The TV was on, and Figgy was seated in the center of the couch, a wine glass balanced on her knee. She pressed a button on the remote, and Alex looked up at the screen, registering in a glance Albert Finney in a bubble bath, before looking back and seeing Sylvie curled up in Figgy's lap. Behind them, on the far side of the sofa, elbows on his knees and a big smile cutting across his square-jawed face, was Zev.

"Great to meet you!" Zev popped up from the couch. Before Alex knew what was happening, Zev had moved in for a man hug. "Sorry to bust in like this—school night, isn't it?"

Alex patted Zev a few times on the shoulder, then reared back. "Zev, right?"

"Yeah—hey, grab a glass from the kitchen and join us. We're just—"

Figgy called out from her spot on the couch. "Where've you been?" she asked. Her eyes were glassy and her voice was giddy. Was she drunk? "When I got home I went up to check on the kids and I woke up Sylvie so—"

"You weren't picking up your phone." Alex said. "And Sylvie was coughing in her sleep—did you hear her *coughing*? I couldn't find the... cough stuff. So I just made a super-quick run to the CVS."

Zev frowned and reached over the couch, giving Sylvie's back a quick rub. "She sounded fine when we carried her down from bed," he said. "She's probably got a little bug, though. You poor sweetie."

Sylvie opened one eye and grunted.

Figgy hooked a strand of Sylvie's hair over her ear and shot Alex a look. "We've got a ton of medicine." Figgy said. "In the kids' bathroom, under the—"

Alex took a step forward into the room, suddenly unsure how to respond to his wife and the large Israeli man soothing his daughter's fictitious cough. What was he even doing here? She never would've brought him home if she was fucking him, would she?

Figgy was telling Alex where to find the measuring caps when he cut in. "So you guys are just—what? Having a little movie party?"

Figgy swirled her glass and smiled. "Oh yeah—I was just telling Zev about the bathtub scene in *Two for the Road*—can you believe he's never seen it? We're doing something similar and I wanted to show him—"

Alex crossed his arms. "So this was over at Dani's?"

"Yeah, she had a bunch of us..." she said, then cocked her head curiously. "How'd you know I was at Dani's?"

Alex paused, then reached in his pants and pulled out his phone. "You weren't picking up—so I did that ZeroIn thing."

Figgy narrowed her eyes, releasing a small exasperated cough. "What, you... *tracked* me?"

Next to her, Zev clapped his hands together. "I better get going. It's late and—"

Figgy motioned for Zev to stay and looked at Alex. "Why would you—"

"I was worried," he said.

Figgy took a breath and paused, Alex waiting for a tirade about the pharmacy run or the secret surveillance. But she just shook her head and took a long draw on her wine glass. "Oh sweetie, I'm fine," she said. "I just left my phone in the car and didn't check it… were you really that worried?"

Alex shrugged. "You could've been anywhere and—"

"I so get it," Zev said, crossing around the couch to sit. "One hundred percent. You've gotta keep a close eye on each other these days, don't you? The city's a scary place."

Figgy giggled again and clapped Zev on the knee. She smiled and motioned to Alex. "So hey, how about you go into the kitchen and maybe find us another bottle. Have we got any cheese? I'm super hungry."

Alex shook his head. "I'm going to bed," he said, waiting a beat before turning to head up to their room, their laughter following him up the stairs.

Ten

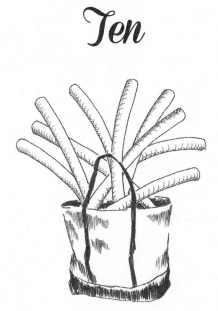

Alex raised his lounge chair a notch, stretched out his legs, and crossed one foot over the other. He tucked his hands in his armpits, wishing he'd brought something more substantial than a beach towel to keep warm. He'd been sitting here, *stationed* here really, since just after six. Three hours camped out by the pool at the Rutlidge Wailea, one of a scattering of nannies and personal assistants, the lot of them twitchy and territorial and ever watchful of one another; no way was Alex getting up now. He'd just watched a pool attendant swoop in, scoop up an unattended tote bag, and hand over a prime poolside cabana to a waiting nanny.

Lounge wars. That's what they called it yesterday, when Alex wandered out from the buffet at 10:30, looking for a place to plop and not finding a single available chaise within one hundred feet of the pool. Turns out the week around Christmas was the busiest week of the year at the Rutlidge, the enormous, objectively gorgeous, but aggressively beige hotel where half of Hollywood was spending the holiday break. Demand for prime pool space was so intense that the hotel had implemented a strict occupancy policy, the specifics of which were explained to Alex by a buff Polynesian woman in a Santa hat and an orange polo shirt whose nametag read GLADYS.

"Guests must be physically present at all times," said Gladys. "Unattended personal belongings will be collected and held at the concierge desk."

Alex had laughed at her spiel, proudly declaring himself a conscientious objector in lounge wars and laying out four towels on a far-off stretch of sand by the Aloha Snack Stand. "It's *better* over here!" he said when Figgy came down from breakfast. "We can spread out and relax, nobody up in our business. I think I saw David Spade by the pool yesterday—you really think we're gonna be able to relax next to *Spade*? Besides—how great is this view?"

"Great," she said, pulling out the bag of pineapple spears she'd smuggled from the buffet. She'd completed production the night before their flight from LAX, skipping the wrap party and leaving behind a clusterfuck of unresolved issues. Standing in the sand in a pair of linen shorts and an Indian-print top, shoulders slumped and eyes bloodshot, she looked like a person who'd witnessed a violent crime, the insanity of production intensified by the prospect of her fortieth birthday, which was just three weeks away. She was weirdly testy when he brought it up on the plane ride over, saying only that she felt like it was "an expiration date."

"You know I've got my laptop, right?" she said now. "I've got notes due on the last two episodes. I'm not even sure I can get a WiFi signal out here. And all this sand? How am I going to keep it off the keyboard?"

Alex scanned the beach. "I'll find a table," he said. "I'll borrow one from over by the snack stand—they've gotta have a little table over there. And I'll bring you mai tais and those amazing taro chips and it'll be great, I promise—"

He stopped short. No way was he going to talk Figgy into being okay with this spot. Sticking up for it would only reinforce her sense that three days in, the Sherman-Zicklin holiday vacation, their first big fancy family trip, was not going well at all. The rental van stunk of cigarette smoke. They got stuck behind a bulldozer on the drive from the airport. Their room looked over a parking lot, and when they'd checked in, Alex didn't have cash to tip the bellboy. Then there'd been some pointed discussion of Alex's packing and the fact that he'd brought a single bathing suit for each kid. "Who packs *one* bathing suit for a week on the beach?" she asked. "Not a Jew—that's who."

This morning, Alex had set the alarm for 6:30 and headed down to the pool, determined to claim the primest cabaña he could find. It was ludicrous, sure, but if waging lounge wars meant making Figgy happy—or at least a little less miserable—it was worth it. It was like his book—he needed to start *pretending*. He'd pretend to be a man who took care of business, one of those guys he saw in the hotel lobby with the barrel chests and commanding baritones, men who knew how to arrange for a suite upgrade and an 8 p.m. dinner reservation for twelve. Alex wasn't that guy, but he sure as hell could fake it.

He was rolling his head around trying to work out a kink when a familiar voice sounded out.

"Hey," said Sam, plopping down in the lounger next to him and madly strumming the screen on Alex's iPhone. "Mom's sleeping in. Getting room service. Said she'd meet us later. Sylvie's in the Jacuzzi with that girl from Tucson."

Sam gave him an appraising look. "Aren't you freezing?"

"I am, but I can't go get my sweatshirt," said Alex. "Hotel policy—super strict. One guest can reserve a maximum of three loungers. Minute you step away, you're out. Doesn't matter who you are. Kind of democratic, really. And would you look at the spot I got for us? Best seat in the house."

"It's okay," Sam sighed. "The ones by the grotto are shadier. Closer to the Jacuzzi, too."

"Those don't count," Alex said, squinting across the pool at the row of cabañas roped off for guests staying in the so-called supersuites. "Do you have any idea what those cost? They're like a grand a day. How crazy is that?"

"I heard the supersuites have a private buffet open all day on their floor. Eugene Bamper had like twenty-seven mango slushies yesterday."

"Good for Eugene," Alex said. He regarded his boy. Sam's hair was poofy and uncombed. His left knee bounced lazily up and down, two enormous warts clinging tenaciously to the kneecap. Something about the way his mouth hung open, the way his fingers twitched frantically against the iPhone—Alex suddenly felt an incredible urge to swat his son upside the head.

"Gimme my phone," Alex said. "I didn't haul myself out here this morning so you could waste my battery on Pastry King. Go jump in the pool."

Sam sighed. "Let me finish this profiterole first."

"Come on, Sam—go swim. Now."

"There's nothing to *do* in the pool."

"Get wet. Splash around. *Go.*"

He sighed heavily and handed over the phone. "*God*, Dad—would you relax? We're on vacation."

"I am completely relaxed," he said, a little louder than he meant to. "I am *Mister* Vacation. Go on."

Sam stood his ground and tugged at his swim trunks, his posture a full-body gesture of disgust.

Alex sat up and stabbed his finger forward. "You wanna know where *I* went on Christmas vacation when I was eleven years old? Iowa. To visit my grandpa in a nursing home. Big highlight of that trip was a visit to the John Deere factory—dirty snow and tractors behind glass. So, just do me a favor, okay? Look around and try to at least pretend to enjoy yourself."

"So we're not in Iowa," Sam said. "Hoo-ray."

Sam turned and took two steps toward the lip of the pool, then dropped into the water and began dog paddling into the deep end. Craning his neck to keep his head dry—he'd complained yesterday about what the saline was doing to his hair—he was cut off midway by a giant splash and a hysterical boyish whoop.

The three sons of Cary and Helen Bamper had a thing for entrances—last night out on the beach, they'd charged into the surf in a great bellowing herd, on their way demolishing a drip castle Alex and Sylvie had built. Today the first Bamper to hit the water was Eugene, a broad-shouldered thirteen-year-old, followed closely by the twins, black haired, squinty eyed, and vaguely vulpine. The three of them were constantly punching, swatting, and otherwise assaulting each other; they fascinated Alex as much as they terrified Sam, who now madly paddled back toward the shallow end.

"Leo!" called Helen, crouching down on the lip of the pool. "Constantine! Eugene! Here! Sunscreen!"

Helen dabbed sunscreen on Constantine's face while Cary paced the concrete behind her. Really, Alex thought: Who names their kids after Roman emperors? Even from this distance, he could see Helen's amused frown as she wrangled her squirming child. Her expression never wavered; she seemed endlessly entertained by the mini riots her boys were constantly initiating. Cary, meanwhile, hung back, oblivious, his attention focused on his Blackberry, which he held out in front of him like a dictaphone. With his Bermuda shorts, Hawaiian shirt, and broad, thick shoulders, Cary looked every bit like the nickname Figgy had for him: Big Daddy. It fit—besides his three boys, Big Daddy Bamper oversaw two crazy-successful network shows and was possibly the most confident human Alex had ever encountered.

"Boys, come!" Helen called, holding up a big canvas bag of

Styrofoam flotation noodles. "I've got the noodle bag!" Alex propped himself up and watched as she tossed the toys one by one, her boys barking like seals.

"Leo—grab the orange one!" Helen called. "That's right—whack your brother! Not on the face—back of the head! Nice one!"

Sam climbed up the ladder and began waddling back over to Alex, hands crossed over his chest. "Where'd they get the noodles?"

"I have no idea," Alex said. He'd checked the hotel shop the day before; it was all hideous pastel-y crafts and rayon resort wear. The most fun thing they sold was a stuffed sea turtle. "She must've brought 'em from home."

Sam eased back into his lounger. "Bet they have more than one bathing suit, too."

Alex sat forward. "May I remind you who's got it going on right now? Check out Big Daddy Bamper over there. Stuck in the sun, nowhere to sit, pacing back and forth on the hot concrete... and look at us, kiddo. Sitting pretty."

Sam nodded across the pool. "I wouldn't worry about Mr. Bamper."

Alex looked over—the boys were still whooping it up in the water, but Cary and Helen had left the pool area. He spotted them following an attendant with long black hair—it was the same attendant he'd met yesterday, Gladys!—down a winding path that led to... the grotto. The supersuite cabañas—of course. Still talking on the phone, Cary casually stretched out and wrapped his neck in a towel. As Alex watched, the attendant spritzed his face with a canister of scented mist, squirted her hands from a bottle, and began kneading one of his feet with her long, muscular hands. Cabaña-side food massage? Evian spritzers?

"Face it, Dad," Sam finally said. "The Bampers do everything we do but better."

• • •

Alex sat there for a good half hour, watching the Bampers get spritzed and rubbed and fussed over. He wanted to *be* the Bampers and he *hated* the Bampers, all at once. Huck had a name for it—the approach/avoidance conflict. Coveting something you can't stand. Under-examined source of male anxiety, Huck said.

A wet hand flopped down on Alex's knee. Sylvie was back from the Jacuzzi; she took a big mouthful of virgin piña colada and gargled: "Goggles?"

She had figured out how to charge drinks to the room within twenty minutes of check-in and was now on a first-name basis with the entire waitstaff. Her eyes were bright red.

"Everything's up in the room," Alex said.

Sylvie sat down on his lounger and laid a wet hand on his knee. "Please?"

"Fine—stay here." Alex got up and exhaled swiftly. "I'll be right back."

The walk from the pool to the room was ridiculously long, across the pink marble courtyard, up the elevator, and down a long wainscoted hallway broken up with vast, empty chambers containing tables set with tropical flowers. Alex swiped his key card and tiptoed inside.

Figgy was propped up in bed, sipping from a bowl of miso soup and tapping on her laptop. She looked up, her eyes big and glassy. "Where've *you* been?"

"Down at the pool," he said. "I got us a really nice spot—"

"The kids woke up two minutes after you left and jumped all over me. We *so* should've gotten two adjoining rooms."

"Oh hon." Alex sat down on the side of the bed. He nodded at her laptop. "Work stuff?"

"New ads started airing last night. Disaster. Dipshits in publicity completely spoiled the finale."

Alex made a disapproving cluck and took hold of her foot through the bedspread. "Can't Jess handle it? Isn't that his job?"

"It's *supposed* to be," she said, snapping shut the laptop. "You coming back to bed?"

"I gotta grab some stuff and get back to the kids before Sylvie drains the entire island of mai tais."

"If we'd brought Rosa—"

Alex made a face. He'd been adamant that the Sherman-Zicklins would not be the sort of family who lugged a domestic servant along on holiday. While it was true that Figgy had work and wouldn't be much use with the kids, and also true that Rosa would hardly object to an all-expenses-paid workweek in Maui, Alex held firm. No way would he be the white-skinned privileged doofus roasting in the sun while plump-armed, brown-skinned Rosa played paddy-cake with the kids. He was entirely capable of monitoring the children while Figgy recuperated.

Figgy laid her head down on his lap. "So the kids are in the cabaña? Is Helen watching them?"

"She's nearby, yeah," he said.

"The cabaña's near the pool?"

"Kissing it."

She made a purring sound and threw open the covers of the bed. "Get in here."

Alex did as he was told. Apparently, setting down stakes at the pool had been impressive, maybe even a little sexy. She opened her robe and he pressed up against her. God, he thought as he tugged off his pajama bottoms, they needed this. Things had been so chilly between them, even before they left—really, it had been weird since that night at the house with Zev, the Israeli DP. He'd been so paranoid, so stupid—and in the end, there wasn't anything to indicate that Figgy had been anything but faithful. But still. He didn't like that guy. And clearly some trust issue had been stirred up for Figgy. Alex went on ZeroIn a few days later and discovered she'd changed her password.

He kissed her on the neck and chest and let out a long sigh. He needed this. He needed to reconnect, to feel the warmth of her, to get out of his head. He tried to remember the last time they'd done it—two weeks? Three? He worked his way around each breast and settled between her legs. Figgy tensed and arched her back, pushing her hips forward into him. After all these years together, Alex still enjoyed going down on his wife, feeling her tense and shudder at his touch. But it was also, he thought now, an obligation. He had to do it—it was a matter of principle that she reach a satisfying climax. Which sometimes took awhile, time that often resulted in neck cramps or sudden uncomfortable flashes of self-consciousness. Like now, as he tried to vary his movement and time his pace to her breathing, he was buffeted by questions that were not particularly helpful, performance-wise: What part of the marital bargain am I fulfilling right now? Is this how I pay my fare? If I was the one stressing over work and signing the bill at checkout, would I be getting my dick sucked right now instead of laboring on an equal-work, equal-pay orgasm?

He must've lost his concentration, or maybe Figgy was dealing with distractions of her own, because before he'd finished the task at hand, she reached down, gave Alex a nice tug, and whispered, "I want you inside."

It wasn't his finest performance—it took him a few thrusts to get hard—but it was still good. Of course it was. Why did he always forget that it was never *not* good? Even a quickie like this was better than nothing at all. It was like when they were first together—they'd do it on the fly, scratch the itch, then hurriedly get their clothes back on and go back to their day. Nowadays a month would go by with nothing and then there'd be this incredible pressure to make it special, and they were just so wiped out. Who had the energy? But here she was, below him, yielding. And all the usual stuff of their marriage—the logistics, the petty resentments, the scorekeeping, the second-guessing—melted away.

"Whew," he said afterward, rolling off her and reaching for something to clean them up.

Alex felt the mattress sink.

He looked at the ceiling and mulled, "Hotel sex—objectively better than bedroom sex. Why is that, do you think?"

Figgy didn't respond. He turned to face her. Her legs were curled up over her head, knees against the headboard, hands on the inside of her legs, pelvis held up high.

"Fig, honey?" he said. "What're you doing?"

"Yoga," she grunted. "Modified plow."

• • •

"Isn't this fun?" Figgy hollered across the table. She'd been in a terrific mood all day. It was heightened now by her closeness to Cary Bamper, who'd scored a reservation for fifteen at Onofisk, the hotel restaurant run by the Norwegian celebrity chef Gunda Gunderson. Alex was excited for the food but frustrated by the seating; their table was high and narrow, and he kept having to yell at the kids to stop rocking on the barstools. On his right, the Bamper boys had demolished a basket of taro crisps and were now blindfolding Sam with a napkin. On his left, Helen Bamper and a Pines dad whose name Alex couldn't remember were locked in an intense discussion of the banking bailout. Beyond them, a mile or two down the table, Figgy and Cary were huddled close, all nods and smiles and periodic explosions of laughter.

Alex's phone buzzed in his pocket and he pulled it out. Miranda had texted him another photo—for the last month or so, they'd been trading food pictures with short, suggestive captions. This time she'd sent a close-up of a caramelized cube of foie gras sprinkled with shredded herbs and mustard seeds. Her caption: "Just whipped this up, Sher. Foraged the greens from the side of the 101 Freeway. When do we cook something up together?"

Best ignore that, he thought. It was one thing trading food porn—quite another "cooking something up." He put the phone down and craned his head down the table. "Who's got the wine?"

The dad whose name Alex now guessed was Alan handed over a bottle of Sancerre. He was a baby-faced guy with pink cheeks, wiry eyebrows, and a gleaming bald head (Alex suddenly flashed on something he'd read about the link between testosterone and baldness—the balder the man, the higher the T-count. Could that be?). Alex seemed to remember him saying he worked in finance—portfolio management maybe? Alex felt Alan's gaze from across the table. To him, Alex must seem like an unmade bed or a sweet farm animal. They'd met once or twice, but like most Pines dads they didn't take much interest in each other. The moms at the school often met up for book club or trips to Target, but the dads barely knew each other. The line from the ladies at school was that all their husbands were dull and unsociable compared to the dynamic and energetic women, an impression this dad was doing nothing to contradict.

"So really, the best thing we can do now for Obama is keep spending!" he said. "Keep capital flowing! It's our patriotic duty to splurge. The Hawaiian-in-chief is counting on us!"

Helen Bamper laughed and raised her glass. "Hear, hear!" She was dressed in a sleeveless silk top, frosted curls falling loosely across her bare shoulders. Her skin gave off a glow of rare oils. Her muscles had been finely sculpted on Pilates tables. All traces of excess body hair had been vaporized. She'd had liposuction, hormone replacement therapy, Botox. Her face radiated a placid calm. Alex hadn't realized it before, but looking at Helen now, he decided it was true: The rich didn't just have fancier clothes and cars and houses and stuff. Their *bodies* had been improved, perhaps cellularly.

On Alex's right, Sylvie tossed down her fork and wrinkled

her nose.

He leaned down. "Don't you like your dinner? That's mahi mahi with lingonberries!"

Sylvie looked skeptically at her plate. "I thought we were getting *real* Hawaiian food."

"It's *fusion*, honey," Alex said. "Meeting of two cuisines, remember how I told you? You want to try mine? Pickled spam. Yum."

She wrinkled her nose. "There's no good food in this whole hotel. Why couldn't we just go to the parking lot place?"

"We'll go the parking lot place tomorrow."

She crossed her arms and frowned. "I don't see why we can't eat real Hawaiian."

It was his own fault, he thought; he'd been the one who'd made the speech about *real* Hawaiian on the drive from the airport. They'd driven past a roadside barbecue, and Sylvie had fixated on the scene around the smoky grill, kids underfoot holding plastic plates piled high with cabbage and caramelized pork, served up by a big lump of a guy with steel tongs and wrap-around shades. Then yesterday at lunch she must have overheard Alex's gripes about the poolside dining menu; when a waiter asked if she'd rather have mac and cheese or chicken fingers, she shook her head and said, wearily, "L.C.D., L.C.D."

"What?" the waiter had replied, confused.

"Lowest. Common. Denominator."

"Just eat," Alex said now, turning back to the grownups. The Pines dad had finished explaining the economy to Helen. Now he turned to Alex.

"So... Alex"—damn, he knew *his* name—"What is it you do?"

Alex sucked in a breath. Sometimes it felt like his whole life revolved around this one goddamn question.

"About what?" he said, he hoped not too snarkily.

"For work," he said.

"I used to be in advertising, but now I'm working on a book. A novel, actually. Been cooking a lot. Mostly try to keep up with Figgy and the kids, you know...."

"That's great—so great," he said, nodding emphatically. "That must be so hard, though—you work out of the house? You've got to be so *disciplined*. I swear I'd go crazy. Seriously nuts. Me on my own, I'd be swimming in Cheetos and soap operas by noon every day."

Alex took another big pull off his glass and tried to smile. Why was he getting this speech? Why not Helen? He knew immediately: Women married to successful men have a place. But guys in the same position? No one knows what to do with them. He could hear the interior dialogue: boy scored; must be hard on him; must make up for it in other ways.

"It's not so bad," he said. "I was never really an office guy—"

"Sure, the whole cubicle farm—all penned in, believe me I know," he said. "But I need my team around me to keep me sharp. Without nine-to-five, I'd fall apart...."

"Huh," Alex said, looking across the table at Helen. "What about you? Can't imagine you home balls-deep in Cheetos...."

"I wish," she said. "Between the foundation, the boards, and the kids' athletics, I'm *never* home."

Helen proceeded to describe a domestic routine the likes of which Alex could hardly comprehend. She sat on the boards of three nonprofits, organized the annual Pines fundraiser, chauffeured her boys to football and lacrosse practices, and ladled goulash at a soup kitchen on the weekends. So in addition to being the most preternaturally calm mother he'd ever seen up close, she also seemed to be a good and decent person.

"So—what about this supersuite?" Alex blurted out. "The private cabaña? Your own floor at the hotel? How much is that running you?"

Helen shrugged, unshaken by the abrupt change of topic.

"Three? Six?" she said, touching the tips of her fingers and then dismissing the calculation with a languid wave. "The whole thing is ridiculous. But I'd go crazy if I thought for a second about all *that*. Cary gets this one week between shows—and he's got such unbelievable stress at work. This one week I just want things to be *easy* for him."

A commotion sounded out from the crowd of kids. Alex looked over and saw Eugene standing behind the blindfolded Sam, tying his hands behind his back with a napkin. The other boys were at his side, tugging at his arm to follow them away from the table.

"Guys," Helen called after them. "Stop torturing poor Sam—"

"It's okay, Mom," Eugene said, smiling. "We're *play* torturing."

"Yeah—I like it," Sam said.

Alex could see from the grin under Sam's blindfold that he meant it, either because he enjoyed the attention the Bamper boys were finally paying him or, more distressingly, because of an eagerness to play bottom to the boys' top. Alex drained his wine glass and gave the thumbs up.

"Go ahead," Alex said. "Just be safe! No water boarding!"

• • •

Alex awoke the next morning before dawn, head pounding. He'd had too much to drink, that much was clear. The rest was fuzzy. Had there been yelling? He had a vague recollection of yelling something late in the evening after the Pines dad—whose name, it turned out, was Bill—puffed his chest and bared his teeth and said that the chair of the Pines parent association needed to "man up" with the board of directors. Which for some reason had prompted Alex to uncork a monologue about the etymology of the phrase, pointing out that "man up" had no female equivalent—and wasn't it sexist to equate bravery and aggression with masculinity? *Oh God.*

The night ended when Sylvie fell off her barstool and Sam came back to the table crying, the blindfold game having taken an unpleasant turn.

Alex hauled himself out of bed, cracked open a bottle of water, and downed it in one long pull. All night he'd been dipping in and out of intense, overly literal stress dreams. Just before waking he'd had a doozy. He and Figgy had scored a reservation to a pop-up restaurant run by a molecular gastronomist who was doing amazing work "on the boundary between food and non-food." He lifted a forkful of saffron-glazed something to his mouth. Next to him, Figgy tilted her head back and groaned something about the succulent flavors. He bit down and chewed. He chewed and chewed. He realized with a start what was in his mouth: rubber. He looked back at Figgy, whose face was flushed with satisfaction. "Maybe you just don't have the *palate*?" she laughed. He stood up from the table and turned away; was this supposed to be funny? How come you got dinner and I got *sneaker*?

He woke from the dream shaking with anger. He pulled the mouth guard from his bottom teeth with a pop and turned to Figgy, who was splayed beside him still asleep, her mouth half open. He wanted to shake her awake, demand an explanation, slap her in the face.

Then it occurred to him: Oh right, none of that actually *happened.* Figgy didn't say those things. That was me, wearing her face. And that wasn't sneaker. It was my motherfucking mouth guard.

• • •

The next day by the pool, Alex decided, would be different—today, he knew the drill. He'd do what was required. He arrived at the pool at 7 a.m. with an empty bladder, a fresh coffee, and a wad of reading material to keep him occupied until the family arrived. Staking his claim on the cabaña closest to the grotto, he settled in.

He picked up a photocopied "news digest" printed for those guests who found ordinary newspapers too cumbersome or complicated for their holiday on the beach. Printed in two stapled pages with no pictures, no jumps, and a crossword puzzle on the back, the digest had a way of sanitizing even the most distressing news. One item grabbed Alex's attention—lawmakers in Colorado were fighting the spread of so-called Coitus Co-Ops after the passage of a controversial ballot measure in the fall. The measure, modeled after initiatives already passed in Florida, Nevada, and Vermont, legalized so-called peer-to-peer prostitution. Hundreds of unregulated clubs had opened in those states in the past year, prompting outrage from social conservatives.

Alex reminded himself to show the story to Figgy. Politics and public policy had been the last thing on her mind when she created *Tricks*, but the legalization effort that had sprung up in the last few years was obviously good for the show. It tickled Alex to think that Figgy's dirty little cable show was having real-world impact. The fact that social conservatives were outraged only confirmed that the impact was for the best.

His phone emitted a little cartoon *ploop*. It was a text from Huck, in a small green bubble: "What up homosapien? You in HI?"

He thumbed back a response: "Yup. All good. U?"

"Crashing at the Oakwood. Drama on homefront. Epic."

Alex stared at the phone for a second, then switched over to the phone and punched in Huck's cell.

Huck answered on the first ring, his voice raw and laboring to maintain its usual confident nonchalance. His marriage, he said flatly, was cooked. Things had been rocky for a while; they'd finally blown up over his plans to launch a line of Katherine Pool–endorsed sex toys.

"Think of it—celebrities have their own fragrances, their own fashion lines. Why not vibrators?" he said. "How great would that be, butt plugs from the star of TV's *Tricks*? Come on, right? She just can't *stand* the idea I might have some success on my own."

"You think?" Alex said. "I mean, the sex toy thing—isn't that just a little... *foul*?"

"No, it wouldn't be sleazy at all—we'd go upscale with nice packaging, super designy—"

"That's not what I mean," Alex interrupted. "It just kind of sounds like—a betrayal? Using her fame to get your thing out there? If you want to start a line of vibrators, go ahead and sell vibrators—why do you need to use—"

"Look, Kate hates all the attention she gets. All I'm saying is why not see some actual benefit? I was just *updrafting*, you know, getting my thing off the ground. The products are amazing—I'm telling you, Alex, once they were out there, people would've gone crazy."

Alex made a noncommittal murmur.

"Look, I love her and all that," Huck said. "But I don't know. I'm just not sure I can stand living in Pool world anymore."

Alex thought back to the brunch at their house. The gleaming white kitchen. The basil frittata. The zip line. "So that's it? What about the kids? The house?"

"I don't know—I'm renting this horrible apartment 'til we figure it out. It's gonna get ugly. Her people are already on the warpath, but I've got this kick-ass lady from Century City—she's got actual *fangs*. Drives a red Audi with a vanity plate that says lit-i-gate, with a number 8? She says as long as I stay single, I'm set for at least a few years. Won't prevent me from hooking up, maybe even get good ol' Dr. Finkelstein to unclip the tubes. Start over with someone who knows how to *appreciate* a man."

"I don't know, Huck. You sure this isn't something you can work through? What about counseling?"

"No—we're done. I'm ninety percent sure she's fucking her faith healer anyway. No way am I letting her get away with *that* while I sit on some shrink's sofa rehashing ground rules and boundaries and *bottom lines*."

Huck got an incoming call from his lawyer, promised to call back, and hung up. Resting the phone on the frosted glass table beside the chaise, Alex sat up straight. A dull ache rippled though him. No sooner had it passed than he was struck by the urgent need to tell Figgy all about the call. It wasn't nice, but he knew from the last few years of marriage that nothing made you feel better about your own relationship like recounting the details of another couple's meltdown.

When she finally came down to the pool an hour or so later, he launched into a breathless recap, clucking and frowning, shaking his head at the Katherine Pool–branded dildos and Huck's plan to undo his vasectomy.

"He sounded wrecked," Alex said. "What's he going to do now? He's pushing forty with no job and no marketable skills. Now he's gonna go out and score a hot young cocktail waitress and start all over again?"

"Sure," she said. "Happens all the time. You know how many single forty-year-old men are out there—who can cook? And redecorate a kitchen? He'll have no trouble at all."

Alex got quiet and looked out at the ocean. Maalaea Bay was chopped with whitecaps and striped in a dozen shades of blue.

"You think? Really?"

"Oh yeah."

Figgy pushed her sunglasses up and peered over at a patch of lawn near the grotto. Helen, dressed in a sleek, black one-piece bathing suit and floppy straw hat, had all the Bamper boys crouched in a line in front of her.

"What're they up to now?" Figgy said.

"Something amazing, undoubtedly."

As they watched, Helen helped each boy make a tripod with their forearms and extend their bodies up until their legs were sticking straight up. Helen clapped and laughed as the boys flailed and kicked, moving from one kid to the next, gently repositioning their hips or adjusting their weight.

Figgy leaned forward and propped her chin on her knees, eyes fixed on the scene. Helen was leading a game, challenging the boys to get into a handstand at the same time. As soon as one tumbled over, she helped him pop back up into position, moving among their upturned legs, a graceful ringleader among wild animals.

"She's such a great mom," Figgy said flatly.

"So are you," Alex said. "Really, hon. So you're not a gym coach. You get more points for doing what you do—your degree of difficulty is higher. A lot higher."

Figgy grinned and popped her elbow into Alex's side. "Thank you." She paused for a second and took a deep breath. "How many years have they got, do you know?"

"Huck and Kate? Four, I think. Maybe five."

"You sure?"

Alex felt an alarm bell go off in his head. "I think so—why?"

"Difference in the payout, obviously. She probably had him sign a pre-nup, but if not, he's due alimony for half the length of the marriage. Given that she joined the show a year and a half ago, he might make a case for a bigger piece... Hope she's got good representation."

Alex nodded and said nothing, glad his sunglasses were on to obscure his bug-eyed expression. He had no idea Figgy was so conversant in divorce law. Had she always been?

"Don't go getting any ideas," she said after a long pause. "But absolutely—Huck's gonna do *just fine.*"

• • •

Figgy had dozed off soon after their little talk, leaving Alex to stew on her analysis of California divorce law. Maybe Huck was right—maybe she'd decided to get informed. She'd be stupid not to, right?

He was fighting off a full panic attack when he heard a cry ring out from the beach. He hopped up at the sound of it. It was Sam, who he saw scampering up from the surf, clutching his side and yowling, eyes clamped tight and mouth locked in a wide O. Cary had been on the beach playing football with his boys, so he was first to reach him. Alex hurried over.

"Ow!" Sam sputtered, motioning to his side. "Stings!"

Cary leaned down and lifted the fabric of Sam's swim shirt. Bulbous white welts wrapped around his side, tracing an angry trail from the small of his back to his belly button.

"Jellyfish," said Cary. "Got you good."

Sam let out a yelp and started to hyperventilate.

Alex took hold of Sam's arm and led him up onto the dry sand. "Easy now. Just breathe."

The Bamper boys crowded close as Cary helped Sam down into a sitting position. Alex moved in and pulled the swim shirt over Sam's head—the full view of Sam's rash, mottled and white, sending the Bamper boys into a paroxysm of "ewwwwws." Sam's shoulders began to rock with sobs, and Alex racked his brain: Was Sam allergic? Was he going into anaphylactic shock? Why couldn't he recall a single bit of first aid from his three years as camp counselor? Heart racing, he looked around the beach, scanning the crowd for... a beach medic? Someone in a uniform?

"Help?" he called miserably.

"Boys—look away," announced Cary, feet planted far apart and motioning for room. "Sam, in a second it's gonna feel much better. Just hold still."

Before Alex could register what was happening, Cary reached down, untied his swim trunks and pulled out his penis, a small pink slug. Then he pivoted around and aimed his hips at Sam's midsection. "Just one second—"

Alex froze, confronted with the full view of Cary's genitals. "What the hell—"

"Old lifeguard trick," Cary said. "Enzymes. Reduces swelling."

Cary hovered there, knees bent and hips rocking. After a few tense seconds, he turned to Alex and snapped, "Could you maybe stop staring?"

Alex reflexively moved forward and reached down and started undoing the Velcro strip on his own shorts.

"Put that away, Bamper," he said. "I got this. No one pees on my son but me."

Sam looked up and registered the sight of his father and Mr. Bamper now fully unsheathed and jockeying for position over him.

"Stop—no!" Sam called, scrambling backward. "Get away, both of you!"

From behind Sam, streaking forward in her black one-piece at an athletic clip, came Helen Bamper. She waved Alex and Cary off, took Sam by the shoulder and sat him down on a fresh towel. Then she reached into her tote and pulled out a box of Benadryl soft-melts and a bottle of apple cider vinegar. "There, there, honey," she said, wiping a stray tear from Sam's chin and dabbing his rash with a vinegar-soaked tissue. "Good thing I brought this, right? Doesn't that feel better?"

"Thank you, Mrs. Bamper—thank you thank you," Sam said, relief spreading across his face. "It was horrible. The jellyfish... all those penises... Oh God."

• • •

The rash remained, but the pain was relieved instantly—though Sam seemed so grateful to be out of shooting range of the two dads that Alex suspected a slab of pickled spam would have provided equally miraculous relief. Alex thanked Helen again and again, gushing over her magic bag of supplies.

"What else have you got in there?" he said. "Xanax?"

Helen considered it. "I've got Ambien back at the room. Cary snores."

Cary gave Sam a thumbs up and Alex a firm clap on the back. "I usually have to buy a guy dinner to get his dick out."

Alex grinned sheepishly, wary of this new bond between them. "Thank God for Helen here is all I'm saying. Neither one of us was exactly gushing—"

"Whoa, buddy," Cary said, rearing back in mock offense. "I was about to give your boy a full and proper baptism!"

Alex helped Sam to his feet, and the group began trudging back toward the hotel. As they got closer, Alex saw Figgy heading down the steps toward the sand. Something in her hunched shoulders, the way her hand was held stiffly over her brow as she looked up and down the beach... something was wrong. He hurried over.

"Have you got Sylvie?" she said.

"What?" Alex said. "No. I've been dealing with Sam—"

"She's not by the pool or in the room," she said. "I thought she was with you."

"She was with me by the Jacuzzi a few minutes ago—did you check the bar?" he said. "She's probably downing piña coladas with that girl from Tucson. Don't worry."

Figgy shook her head definitively. "The Tucson girl hasn't seen her. I checked everywhere. She's gone."

Alex puffed out his cheeks. "Fuck. Okay. I'll go look."

Alex took off in the direction of the hotel, jogging past other guests and peering into bunches of children for Sylvie's yellow polka-dot bathing suit. He checked the cabaña, the pool, the Jacuzzi, the croquet field, the indoor and outdoor bars, the store, the teen lounge. No Sylvie. At the counter of the spa, he asked a curly-haired, middle-age desk clerk to check the women's locker area—maybe she'd hit the sauna? That would be like her.

"Sorry," the clerk said. "No one in there."

Breathing hard, Alex put his hands on his knees, trying to tamp down the scenarios now blasting in his head. Sylvie was awfully cute. And she had no trouble talking to adults. He could see her wandering away on the beach with a childless Hawaiian woman. Or innocently following a pockmark-cheeked Slavic guy through the lobby to the driveway, where she'd be tossed through the side doors of a black van.

Heart racing, he put his hands on his knees and shook his head. "Call security. We can't find my daughter. We've checked everywhere. Please."

The clerk picked up the phone and punched a button. "It's Tara at the spa. We have a gentleman here who seems to have lost his daughter. Seven years old. One-piece bathing suit, yellow polka dots. Okay, sure. I'll send him down."

The clerk held up a finger to Alex and frowned, waiting. Alex closed his eyes tight and tried to think.

A terrible thought flashed across his mind; it sent him spinning around and through the glass doors, across the courtyard, and toward the beach. Now at full sprint, he reached the sand in a few seconds and continued to the water's edge. The waves were ragged and formless, kicked up by the afternoon breeze. Alex squinted into the warm glare, looking past the snorkelers and men on paddleboards. If Sylvie was out there, could he see her? Would she be floating? Or would she have been pulled too far out by now?

A minute passed, maybe five. Figgy and the Bampers divided up into groups of two and began double-checking the hotel. Walkie-talkies crackled as hotel staff joined the hunt. Alex stayed on the shore, marching back and forth in the surf and squinting into the distance, looking for a speck of bathing suit or a flash of skin, his stomach turning circles.

"Alex! Alex!"

It was Cary, waving him over to a beach attendant with a walkie-talkie. He raised a fist into the air and smiled. "We've got her! She's fine."

Alex let out a heavy sigh. "What? Where?"

The attendant lowered his walkie-talkie. "Off campus," he said. "Shuttle bus driver spotted her at the supermarket over in town. He's bringing her back now. She was at some barbecue place? Says she couldn't stand another chicken finger."

• • •

The whole group waited for Sylvie at the front desk, rushing toward the orange hotel bus when it pulled up to the curb. She popped out with a big smile, emerging like a returning dignitary, cheeks smeared in sauce. Alex took her by the shoulders, hugged her tight. Then he put his face up to hers and demanded: How could she just wander off like that? Why didn't she tell someone? And where did she even get the money?

"From your schmearing wad," she whimpered. "You left it on the dresser. Real Hawaiian food, remember? I was bringing you some!"

Figgy shot Alex a look. "So you left the hotel and went running into town by yourself—for Daddy?"

Sylvie stepped toward Alex and held up a foil to-go bag. "Here," she said. "This pork? It's crazy good, Dad. It was going to be a surprise."

Alex took the bag and brought it to his face, sniffing it. Figgy raised a hand up and turned away, a percussive "bah" sound exploding from her mouth.

"What?" Alex said.

Helen moved in and cupped Sylvie on the shoulder. "We're just all glad you're safe," she said. "Why don't I take you to the bathroom and get you cleaned up. Your dad and mom have been so worried—they should have some time to relax."

Alex started to object, but Figgy was already nodding in agreement and sending Helen and Sylvie on their way. Alex watched as Sylvie happily skipped alongside Helen and her boys, down the wide marble stairs and out of sight. He didn't move. He felt woozy and lightheaded, like he'd been punched in the gut.

"You realize that she'll literally do *anything* to please you," she said, pivoting toward the elevators.

Alex tailed behind her. "Honey, she's *seven!*" he called after her. "I didn't ask her to go anywhere! This is so not my fault."

"You were supposed to have her. You know I've got work to do. And if you hadn't gotten her so worked up about *authentic* Hawaiian food—"

Alex turned her around. "So I'm to blame—because I made her hate chicken fingers? I don't even know what to say. I was with Sam on the beach—and where were you? Napping?"

The elevator doors slid open. They got in, taking a moment while the doors closed and they were alone.

"You knew the deal with this trip," she said. "I'm wiped out. I need rest. I've been carrying the load all year long—I just need a break. Why can't you give that to me?"

The elevator jolted upward. So this is what Helen Bamper meant the night before, about making things *easy*. Was that really his job now? He crossed his arms. "Look—I thought this was a family vacation. I didn't realize I'm just here as help."

They rode in silence for a floor before she exhaled and turned to him. "Of course you're not *help*." She slouched against the wall, the fight draining out of her. "I'm not saying this was your fault. I was just so scared. I'm crazy when I'm ovulating."

Alex sucked in a breath.

"Wait—you're what?"

"All the hormones," she said. "I get nuts."

He blinked, the obvious finally hitting him. This afternoon in the hotel room, when he'd headed out the door, Figgy was still balled up in bed, rocking back and forth like an automatic paint mixer. *Modified plow my ass.*

"Wait—so you're... off the pill?"

She said nothing, her shoulder rising in a small shrug. Alex felt his head throb as what she was saying sank in.

"You... pulled the goalie? Without any discussion—"

"We've talked about it," she said.

"Barely!" Alex blinked hard, his chest swelling. "This isn't a good time, Fig—how could you think it is? It's not like before with Sam and Sylvie—you were home, remember?"

"And *you're* home now," she said. "Look, I'm going to be forty in a few weeks—I can't wait for a good time. There's never a good time. Didn't you see Helen and her kids today on the lawn? I want that—don't you want that? A whole crew? I'll put in a nursery at the studio. I'll get a work nanny, breastfeed in the room—it'll be fine."

So this is how it was, Alex thought—she'd gone into steamroller mode. This is how she was with her career, with the house, with everything she wanted—singular, unwavering. She wanted a third kid and she was going to get it—no matter how he felt about it. "You're kidding, right?" Alex was hollering now. "Do you realize we almost *lost* one today? Two, if you count the thing with the jellyfish?"

Figgy started to respond, then stopped short. She reared back, eyes glassy with tears. "Sam looks pretty rough," she said. "Oh God. I'm so sorry—I'm just so *tired.*"

She collapsed into his chest, arms slack at her side, sobbing. "I'm failing everyone. I'm exhausted at work. The kids barely know me and now *you* hate me. I'm doing everything wrong. The only thing I do well is get pregnant. And I guess I figure getting knocked up will force me to slow down at work—I'll finally have an excuse to take some time."

Alex shook his head. He lifted a hand and stroked her hair. "Oh, stop," he said softly, following the script he knew would end the fight. "We'll figure it out. I don't hate you."

The elevator doors slid open again. Figgy ran the back of her hand across her cheek and moved past them into the hallway. Alex followed behind. By the time they'd reached their room and Figgy stood back so Alex could swipe the key card, a plan had taken form. For the first time in a long time, he knew exactly what he needed to do. He'd take care of Figgy and the kids for the remaining days of the trip. He'd play the part of caretaker, big daddy, point man. He'd keep a close eye on Sylvie and schmear the bellboy and no one would know the difference. And the day they got home, he'd call Dr. Finkelstein.

Eleven

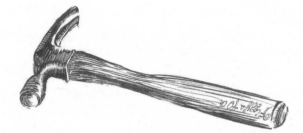

Aside from four square blocks of Santa Monica, most of Venice, and the noodle shops on Sawtelle, Alex couldn't stand the westside. As far as he was concerned, the westside was responsible for all the worst L.A. stereotypes—the Porsche-driving agents and insufferable spiritualists, the health-club megaplexes and whole industries devoted to Botox injecting, teeth whitening, and vagina rejuvenating. But even Alex had to accept that the westside had one thing the east just didn't: All the good doctors.

Which is why his whole day was wrecked because of a Thursday 4 p.m. consult with Dr. Lewis Finkelstein of Century City. He'd sent Rosa to get the kids from school and made a vague mention to Figgy about an errand that would take him most of the day. Now here he was, jerking through worsening traffic on the fringes of Koreatown. With each successive block west, he felt as if he was probing deeper into a hostile nation-state. "Proceed on the highlighted route," the GPS purred as he crossed over Doheny, in that silky, ever-confident way of hers, as if there was nothing at all alarming about the horror show unspooling out his windshield. Ten days in Hawaii had soured him on L.A.—he marveled at its deep and extravagant ugliness, its hot mess of poor planning.

Alex recognized a familiar black glass office tower looming on the horizon. The sight of it sent him scrambling for his cell.

"Huck," he said when the call connected. "Brotherman. Talk to me. I'm about to meet Finkelstein."

"The wizard?" Huck said.

"The very one," Alex said.

There was a silence, then: "Is Figgy making you?"

"No—she doesn't actually know. Keeping this on the DL."

"Sneaky," Huck said. "Props. Manning up."

There it was again—why'd everyone have to keeping using that phrase? He plowed on: "But I did a very bad thing. I got on Google last night. One guy—his testes blew up into bowling balls. This other guy got snipped and then *peed blood* every time he came."

Huck made a horrified croak.

"Am I gonna be that guy?" Alex continued. "I know I want to do this, it's the right decision... but I really *do not* want to be the guy who pees blood every time he comes."

"Calm yourself," Huck said. "Finkelstein's a pro—dude snips a dozen balls a day. Premium balls too—guy does half the Lakers. And I heard he just did the new state rep. Congressional balls!"

"I just need to know. Did you have any problems at all? I mean, after? You know—function? Sensation? *Operation?*"

"All good. I'm telling you, whole thing actually makes sex *sexier*. None of that meddlesome reproductive business getting in the way of you and the *pussay.*"

Finkelstein's office was now just a block away. Alex got into the right lane and slowed way down. "I think I'm going to throw up," he said. "I can't believe I'm voluntarily getting snipped."

"Wrong," Huck said. "You're getting *clipped*. He uses these tiny little titanium thingies—clamps 'em right down on your tube."

"Nice," Alex said. "I'm about to lose you in a garage—so listen, did you get the invite? For Figgy's thing?"

Alex had spent the last two weeks toggling between obsessing about his vasectomy and worrying about Figgy's birthday. Her fortieth was coming up on Saturday, and he'd left the party planning to the last minute. Figgy herself had been maddeningly vague about what she wanted—all she'd say is how much she hated that an arbitrary round number was forcing her to make a big deal... and that whatever they did should include a Hansen's cake with buttercream frosting. Alex understood that as the husband, he needed to plan something big, thoughtful—and expensive. The occasion, he knew, called for bling. But the prospect of buying her jewelry in their current circumstances made him intensely nervous. He'd be spending, after all, money he hadn't made. If he spent too much, she'd think he was a schmuck, wasteful and disrespectful of all she'd done to earn it. Not enough and she'd think he thought she wasn't worth it. He'd tried to explain the dilemma to Huck last week.

"Homes—relax," Huck had said. "Not a problem. You need to make some sort of gesture, obviously. But you don't necessarily need to spend *bank*. Remember the golden rule: free for those who can afford it. My boy Les has a whole guest room full of crap he gets in goody bags and luxury lounges. Coupons for African safaris, helicopter rides—they just sit there, piling up. I know he's got a few from jewelers. He keeps telling me to come take whatever I want."

Alex took this in. "So I can get birthday jewelry with... a coupon?"

"Not exactly. It's all non-transferrable—they don't hand out luxury goods to maids and assistants and whatever. They ask for your ID when you cash it in. Which is why I went down to Mac-

Arthur Park and got myself a fake ID with my picture and Lester Sychak's name on it."

Alex flashed on Huck idling his Audi wagon, slowing along the curb and signaling to a guy on the street that he'd trade cash for "mica." "So... you've got a driver's license that guys use for buying beer or working construction—for luxury-lounge coupons?"

"Genius, right? Wanna cash one in?"

It didn't sound exactly legal, but Alex figured there wasn't any harm in acquiring a celebrity freebie that would otherwise go unclaimed. Most importantly, Figgy would get her bling and he'd neatly sidestep the question of whose-money-it-was. The next day he and Huck paid a visit to the Beverly Hills jeweler Daniel Frick, who took one look at the coupon and handed over a chunky silver necklace with a single ruby. "It's part of our *celebrity* collection, Mr. Sychak," said the jeweler, his clipped British accent a tart mix of privilege and suspicion.

Beyond the bling, Alex knew he needed to arrange some sort of event. He'd had a meeting with a ginger-haired, pink-lipsticked party planner named Alice, and they'd traded an increasingly frustrating chain of emails. He'd considered, then rejected, an elegant dinner party (too conventional), a hot air balloon ride (Figgy got motion sickness), and a lavish blowout at home (parties made her anxious).

The truth was, Alex felt conflicted about any sort of grand gesture. It felt vulgar. His standard-issue liberal guilt was mixed with something else—was it hostility? Or resentment? Every time he checked in with Figgy at work, she was being fussed over, fetched for, and otherwise feted. Planning for her birthday made him feel like just another fawning attendant. Even sex had become a bizarre sort of combat. She claimed to be back on the pill, and Alex claimed to believe her, but he now made it a point to keep track of her ovulation schedule and pull out before the moment of truth.

"Just being tidy," he'd said last night.

She'd responded by turning onto her side and making a motion with her hand that looked suspiciously like a scoop and dip. Was she actually trying to inseminate herself with his spillover? Was she so committed to getting one past him?

All of which probably had something to do with why he'd gotten so excited when his mother came up with the idea for "a totally unique, unforgettable, socially conscious" surprise birthday party. It was risky—Figgy might very well hate it—but for sure she'd be surprised. And wasn't she always zigging when everyone else zagged? They'd keep it *real*. He signed off and got Alice the party planner going on the particulars. The invites had gone out yesterday.

"So we meet at your house at nine?" Huck said now.

"Yup—just don't dress up," Alex said. "Super casual."

"Fine—but you've got to help me out with something," he said. "Please do not invite Kate—the only way I can deal with this thing is if I can bring Sydney."

"Sydney?"

"The waitress at Interlingua?" Huck said. "With the calves and the blouses? It is *on*. I'm telling you, divorce—it's catnip, dude. I casually dropped a mention of the separation over coffee and she followed me home like a schnauzer in heat. And I'm telling you homes, these younger ones, they're *dirty*. Internet porn is a wonderful thing, my friend. I haven't had this much play since college."

Alex had run out of road and was descending into the parking garage. "Losing bars—gotta go," he said. "I'm going in. Wish me luck."

"Don't *even* stress this."

He hung up as he turned his keys over to the valet and headed for the lobby. The elevator was packed, and he had to wedge himself against the wall, keeping his head down to avoid the close cluster of faces. Everyone in the elevator, he sensed at once, knew exactly where he was going.

At the reception desk, he signed his name on a sheet of perforated stickers, pausing briefly at the box marked "reason for visit" and briefly considering "Snip?" or "Clip?" before settling on "Consult." As he eased into a padded chair with his clipboard and intake forms, he scanned the waiting room—just a nervous-looking guy in his forties clenching his hands hard on the armrests while a woman at his side ran her hand up and down his neck.

Alex tried to focus on the form, frowning a little as he spelled out the address on Sumter Court, and then making a long row of Xs in the NO column beside the shockingly long list of conditions: small stream, cloudy urine, dribbling, impotence, frequent voiding, stones. None, nope, not really, only sometimes, only when drunk, gross, super-gross, thanks for asking! Three pages in, on an insurance form so densely printed it looked like a solid block of gray, he wrote Figgy's name in the box marked "primary cardholder."

Somehow, he'd thought he could leave Figgy out of this whole business: Why'd *she* get to be primary cardholder? He knew keeping this business a secret was—how do you say?—wrong. But it also felt necessary, crucial even, not to mention *thrilling* in a way he couldn't quite explain, this throwing his feet up in the stirrups. He was a pioneering feminist, crossing state lines to exercise his rights. My body, my choice!

Alex finished the form and waited. It could've been ten minutes or an hour later, he had no idea—but finally, his name was called and he was ushered back into Finkelstein's office. The paneled walls were decorated with framed diplomas and a gallery of family portraits. Alex got close and examined the faces—mostly older, tanned, comfortable men with comely young women. In each photo, babies bounced on knees or slumped against shoulders.

"Ah yes—the Friends of Finkelstein."

Alex swiveled around and faced the doctor. Fiftyish and fit with small, wire-frame glasses and a big, crooked smile, he wore a loud paisley tie and a stethoscope slung jauntily around his neck. "My patients send me these pictures—I've helped bring over twenty-two hundred babies into the world, at last count."

"Isn't the general idea to *prevent* babies?" Alex asked.

"Vasectomies are simple—the lube job of urology, ha ha," he said. "Pure craft. Reversals, on the other hand—that's the art."

"Huh," Alex said, sitting down.

Finkelstein narrowed his eyes at Alex's chart. "So: thirty-eight, married, otherwise healthy, no prior urological issues. You've got—what? Two kids? All done? Positive you don't want any more?"

"Yup," Alex said. "Ready to hang up the spurs."

The doctor gave him a polite chuckle. "And Mrs. Sherman-Zicklin? Where's she on this?"

Alex flashed to Figgy at her office, glued to her laptop, gnawing on her nails, oblivious. "She couldn't get out of work today," he said. "But yeah—she's *great* with it."

A flicker of suspicion passed over Finkelstein's face as he leaned back in his chair. "I'm obliged to inform you that this is a one-way procedure. It can be extremely problematic to undo the work we do together. Of course down the line... if things change... as they so often do—especially among *my* patient population—you'll keep me in mind. I don't mind saying I have a tremendous success rate."

"I see," Alex said, gesturing over at the photos on the wall. "I think for now, I'm good with just the basic... lube job."

Finkelstein pushed a glossy brochure across the desk printed with huge block letters: CRYOPRESERVATION. Alex flipped it open and scanned pictures of men in lab coats, steaming metal vats, and happy couples walking toward bright horizons. "Are you up to speed on banking?" the doctor asked. "We collect a sample of your sperm before the procedure and store it—as long as you need it. There's no guarantee your swimmers will do the job once we thaw 'em out—frozen semen is not half as vigorous as fresh sperm. And then there's the cost of storage."

"No, thanks," said Alex, quickly deciding he'd rather not spend the next twenty years hiding monthly bills for the upkeep of a chunk of iced semen.

"Suit yourself," said Finkelstein with a smile. "My schedule's tight right now, but I'm sure Donna out front can find a place to squeeze you in. Recovery time is two days max—you'll want to stay off your feet and avoid any lifting or exercise. And you'll need someone to bring you in and take you home. The missus can get out of work for that?"

"Absolutely," Alex said. "No problem."

• • •

Figgy rolled in from the office at ten that night. Alex was sitting at the kitchen island working on a bottle of pinot that had arrived in a gift basket that afternoon. As she dumped her computer bag and plopped down on a barstool, he pulled the card out from a sparkling cluster of cellophane. "'We're thrilled to be in the Figgy Zicklin business. From all your fans at Streamz.'" He put the card down and gave Figgy a look. "That's Streamz with a 'z.' Sounds like some sort of porn thing. Or a dessert topping?"

Figgy cocked an eyebrow. "New Internet network. Run by some Cupertino guys looking for"—she air-quoted—"'content'. Nerds working on multi-platform, new-delivery-paradigm, what-ever-the-hell. I was spitballing in the room and mentioned *The Natashas* with Milla Jovovich attached. Seems they've got an *algorithm*—and when they fed Russian brides, Milla's cleavage, and the creator of *Tricks* into it, their computers all got hard-ons.

They want to go straight to series. No pilot—thirteen episodes."

"Seriously?"

"They're working on the deal now. It's kind of awesome."

"Jesus." Alex drained the remainder of the bottle into an empty glass and slid it across the island to Figgy. "Congratulations? I mean, this is a good thing, right?"

"I guess," she said, ignoring the glass. "Jess says we gotta strike while the iron's hot, but I don't know. I don't even know if there's an actual *show* there. I'm kind of hoping it goes away. They're talking about shooting Baltimore-for-Belarus in January. Some kind of tax boondoggle. Only upside is we got Franklin Sykes to co-star."

Franklin Sykes was a lanky, dreadlocked Caribbean-born singer-songwriter who'd recently started doing TV; his guest spots on a network police procedural never failed to elicit an audible groan of desire from Figgy. Alex distinctly remembered a post-coital game of theoretical hookups in which she named Sykes as one of two celebrities she'd get a free pass on. The other was Javier Bardem.

"That's just because he's Spanish," he'd said. "But what about that face? Those fish lips?"

"It's not any of that. He's so deliciously *rapey*. Don't you ever wanna, you know...?"

"What? *Rape* you?"

"Yeah."

"I don't know how I'd even *do* that," Alex had said.

They'd dropped it there. Alex knew Figgy didn't harbor actual rape fantasies, and there wasn't much chance of her ever encountering Bardem or any of her other theoretical celebrity hookups. But now, with a little maneuvering on her part, she'd put herself in a position to actually get up close and professional with Franklin Sykes.

"Hold on a second, now," Alex said, suddenly opposed to

everything to do with *The Natashas*. "What about *Tricks*? And the kids? And really, honey—*Baltimore*?"

She got up from the table and kissed him on the top of his head on her way to the fridge. "You know what they say—'television's a pie-eating contest—and the prize is more pie.'"

She sat back down with a big glass tumbler of chia-seed tea. "So—how was *your* day?"

He blinked hard. There wasn't anything to say about the book—he'd stalled out this morning after two hours at the typewriter, his glacially slow pace interrupted by a handyman who couldn't find the right part for a window shade. Scintillating. She'd have loved to hear about the creepy Friends of Finkelstein photos and the speech about frozen-versus-vigorous sperm, but that was definitely out. What was it he'd told Huck? Take it off the table. Ask forgiveness, not permission.

He should tell her about Wild Boar, the pop-up restaurant. Some hot-shit line cook was doing a nose-to-tail dinner for twenty-five with meats from Malcolm's; Miranda had sent him the invite. Their online exchange was getting increasingly flirtatious—it was still all food related, but it was way chummier than was probably appropriate. In any case, Figgy was almost certainly working that night, but the smart thing would be to ask if she wanted to join. But what if she said yes?

"Are you okay?" Figgy asked.

Alex realized he'd been babbling inaudibly for the last minute as all the things he couldn't talk about rolled around like a mouthful of marbles.

"So—what *did* you do today?" she said. "Just... hang out?"

"No," he said, a tad too defensively. He popped up from his chair and reached for a stack of papers beside the kitchen computer. He shuffled the stack. The warts on Sam's knee were back— were they okay with the dermatologist burning them with lasers? The painters were finished in the guest room, and the Deep Amber looked dark to Alex—was that really what she wanted? Katherine Pool had sent an invite to a Blue Man Preschool fundraiser featuring "original artwork by our sons and daughters"—were they *obligated* to bid on six-year-old Bingwen Pool's finger-paint masterpiece? And what about this crazy request from "Funbags," a breast cancer fundraiser that featured artful, neck-down portraits of the boobs of powerful Hollywood women. Did she want to pose?

Figgy frowned while Alex worked through the pile, offering terse verdicts on each item (no to the laser treatment, yes to the Deep Amber, $100 max for the Bingwen painting, *aw hell no* to Funbags). Then she laid her chin down on her arms.

"Is that it? I'm ready for beddy."

"That's it."

She slurped down the last of the chia seeds, then pinched the bridge of her nose. "You know what I hate?"

"What?"

"Forty," she said. "I'm ancient."

"Aw, honey," he said. "Forty's nothing. If you were a record, you'd be track one, side two. And look at everything you've got, right? All the pie?"

Figgy stretched her arms over her head and yawned. "I guess."

"You know what *I* hate?" he said.

"What?"

"I hate that I see you for twenty minutes a day and all we have time for is... logistics. I barely talk to anyone anymore who I don't write a check to. Except the kids. And they don't listen."

"I feel you," she said, rising up and heading for the stairs. "Just hearing about all this is exhausting. Thank you for dealing. See you in bed. I'm wiped."

• • •

In the days leading up to Figgy's birthday, Alex's phone rang every fifteen minutes. He heard a few times from the party planner, Alice. But mostly, the voice on the other end belonged to his mother, who'd determined that as the originator of such an utterly brilliant and original party idea, she had a special responsibility to direct a "festive, effective, *transformational* event."

"Let's make this a cell-phone-free space," she said. "We'll collect everyone's devices when they arrive. And I can do a handout on conflict minerals from the Congo—this could be a real teachable moment, right?"

Alex didn't discourage her, though he didn't even want to *think* about the carnage that would result if they tried to wrestle phones away from Figgy's twenty or so work friends. Instead, he did what he always did with his mother, which was to let her talk and then go ahead with whatever he wanted. In this case, that meant letting Alice the party planner handle the arrangements.

When the big day arrived, however, Alex quickly realized he should've maybe conferred a little less with Jane and a little more with Alice. She'd arranged for the guests to meet at the house and then travel together on a chartered bus. That seemed entirely sensible, until the moment came on the cloudless Saturday morning of the party and Figgy, the kids, Jane, Joan, Clive, and all the guests were gathered outside... and a forty-foot party bus with the words "Voodoo Lounge" printed on the side pulled up to the curb.

This wasn't right. At all.

Alex climbed the stairs and surveyed the interior. The walls were black lacquer and lined with mirrors. At the center of the bus was a dance floor of flashing colored squares arrayed around a copper floor-to-ceiling pole. *A stripper pole.*

Figgy grinned as she stretched out on a mahogany velour couch. "I hope we've got food for the drive—Vegas is four hours away."

"We're not going to Vegas."

"The roller rink?"

"No."

"Go-carting? Trampoline park? Disneyland?"

"No, no, no. Stop guessing."

The drive to the party was raucous, giggly, and, for Alex, increasingly tense. Everyone seemed to be having a blast. Mimosas were passed. Sam fired up the fog machine. Clive found a classic rock station on the stereo and cranked up Bob Seeger. Dani Dooling took a turn on the pole, swiveling around in comic gyrations. Alex had to physically restrain Sylvie from following her.

As the bus turned off the 10 freeway and downshifted into the densely packed streets east of downtown, Huck called Alex over. "Where *are* we?" he said, nodding toward a stray dog gnawing on the ripped upholstery of an abandoned lounge chair.

A block later, a small child in a saggy diaper stopped and stared as the bus pulled to a stop beside a chain-link fence.

"Okay, everyone, we're here!" Alex said cheerily, rising to his feet.

Behind the fence, the wood-stud framework of a half-built duplex was decorated with silver velvet ribbons and mylar balloons. In the dirt lot beside the building was a banquet table overflowing with flowers, purple "Figgy is 40" hard hats, and faux gold-plated hammers, one for each guest.

As the guests began to file out the door, led by Jane and her guitar, Figgy stayed put, pressing her nose against the window.

"Isn't it awesome?" Alex said, selling it. "That's not just any house over there—it's a *Happy Home*. You know—Happy Homes, the volunteer group? That builds houses?"

"So—we're *doing construction*?"

"And having lunch. After we build. You can drywall! Haven't you always wanted to drywall?"

Outside, the kids led a crowd of guests into the dirt lot, where

Jane was already perched on a pile of lumber playing her guitar and Alice was passing out glasses of pink lemonade.

"We're doing manual labor? For my birthday?"

"We're *giving back*," he said. "Come on—it's a party!"

She took another glance outside and frowned. "You sure we can't swing by Home Depot and just hire a few guys?"

"Come on," he said, trying to remember how Alice had put it: "'It's the most fabulous house-building party ever!'"

Figgy tilted her head dubiously and crossed her arms. For a second he wasn't sure if she'd even get off the bus. "We'll discuss this later," she said. Then she took a deep breath, collected herself, and headed out into the bright morning.

• • •

From the moment he stepped through the gate, it was clear that far from being cowed or chastened, Figgy's guests were tickled by the opportunity to play at hard labor. Or at least they weren't going to let the proximity to poverty get in the way of a good time. Laughter pealed across the worksite. The woman whose house they were helping to build circulated through the crowd, hugging everyone. Then she climbed aboard the party bus with her son and cranked up the ranchero. Figgy joined a crew of ladies and got busy drywalling a bathroom.

After spending an hour on the roof shingling, Alex made a circuit around the party. Figgy was holding forth in a pair of safety goggles, chatting happily with a group of moms from the Pines. He'd been counting on Mimi Feldenbaum, she of the high hair and strapless dresses, to make at least a small fuss about the dust or the roosters or the cholos drinking from bags on the porch next door. He'd imagined himself stepping in with an impassioned speech about how it was high time they pierced their privileged bubble and offered some real, tangible help to people in need—not a luncheon at the Beverly Wilshire or a half-page tribute ad or a tax-deductible donation to some annual bullshit appeal.

But he never got the chance—Mimi, like everyone else, was having a fine old time building and noshing and sloshing a roller around a paint tin. Looking around at the happy scene, he felt a pang of relief jolt through him, followed quickly by a backwash of guilt. How screwed up was it that he'd tried to sabotage his wife's birthday to make some passive-aggressive statement about economic inequality?

Figgy was crossing the worksite when Alex intercepted her, the wrapped and ribboned Daniel Frick jewelry box hidden behind his back. "Hey hon—how goes the hard labor?"

Figgy stopped and adjusted the strap on her hard hat. "Dusty."

"You still pissed at me?"

She turned back and moved in close. "This is fun. The nail gun is awesome. But I don't know, I was hoping for… maybe just a nice dinner? Or a hotel?"

Alex pulled out the jewelry box. "Open it."

She smiled and tore off the paper in one move.

Alex hadn't been sure how she'd respond to the necklace—she'd liked the few pieces of jewelry he'd given her in the past, but he hadn't had much choice in this one. As she held it up and dangled it in the light, he felt his chest tighten.

"Oh, baby," she said, holding it up to the light and dangling it from one end. "It's so pretty."

Pretty? That wasn't a word she used in relation to things she approved of. "You like it?"

She swiveled around so he could close the clasp. "It's the awards necklace, right? From the Globes? Helen Bamper has one just like it."

"Does she?" he said, panic welling up. "I got it from that place Daniel Frick—in Beverly Hills."

"Don't tell me you paid retail," she turned back to face him, one finger tracing the contour of the ruby's setting. "For the *awards* necklace?"

He made a quick mental calculation. What was worse, pretending to have paid full price or admitting that he'd gotten jewelry with a coupon? "Actually," he said carefully, "it was free. Huck hooked me up with one of Les Price's gift bags."

She took a moment and thought this through. "Thank God you didn't get taken by those fake-fancy English ponces. I just can't wear it around Helen, but that's fine. It's beautiful. Thank you."

Alex kissed her cheek and smiled. She liked it—more so because it was a bargain. He pulled her in for a hug. "Happy birthday, baby. Now get back to work—that drywall ain't going to hang itself."

He smacked her butt as she turned back to the scaffolding.

"Mr. A!" Clive called to him from the banquet table, where he was sitting in the shade, fanning himself with a straw fedora. Lunch was still a half hour away, but Clive had staked out a prime spot. He wore tortoise-shell sunglasses with green lenses and a linen, mandarin-collared shirt unbuttoned way down. The general impression was European Playboy at Moroccan Street Market. "The party—a triumph! What an absolute *gas.*"

"Glad you're enjoying," Alex said, plopping down next to him.

"Saw you up on the roof there. Impressive."

Alex shrugged. "I was just helping out—Jess is the real talent."

"Don't lay that modesty on me, Alex. Roofer, dad, event planner—you, Mr. A, are a man of many talents. I see what you do. Pulling off what you did with the house, getting this together, doing all you do with the kids—you're an *orchestrator.* Like me—I've spent my whole career behind the scenes. I appreciate the groundwork—don't think it goes unnoticed."

Alex shook his head and smiled. "Thank you Mr. C."

Clive looked up and down the empty table and dropped his voice a little. "Which is why I want to talk to you about something."

"Shoot."

"You know this show I've been developing? I've been going back and forth with the networks and syndicators, and I really think this thing is a game changer."

"The dog show?"

"Every year Americans spend $32 billion on *dogs*," he said, falling into his pitch. "More than video games, music, and *way* more than books, no offense. *Top Dog* taps right into that—no one has approached the animal space like this. That's not from me—that's straight from the VP at the Nature Channel. He flipped. Bought it in the room."

"That's great, Clive. So—you're starting when?"

"Depends," he said. "Lot of details to work out. Decisions to make. The dad is still giving me grief—can you believe it? I seem to have found the only guy in L.A. who doesn't want to do TV. We've got this incredible storefront for the new facility, perfect location. But I just keep thinking, why give this thing away? Why make someone else rich? The old broadcast model—last legs. I've seen this before, and if I go with this deal, I'm just another schlub on the death march."

Alex cupped his chin in his hand and leaned forward. He'd heard Clive talk shop a lot over the years—but this wasn't his usual name-droppy trip down memory lane. "What're you thinking?"

Clive scratched his beard and fixed Alex in a conspiratorial stare. "I ever tell you about Blake Ackerman?"

Alex shook his head.

"Blake Ackerman was a farm kid from Wyoming," Clive said grandly, settling in. "Comes to L.A. in seventy-one, gets a job as a PA on the *Dinah Shore Show*. Delivers videotape for me—nice kid. Three years in, he gets a promotion to cue card boy. *Cue card boy.* Fast track to nowhere. But he's got this idea for a show, keeps talking about it—*Laugh In* but with singing cowboys and dancing girls in cutoffs. I think he's full of it, but he gets money from his parents back home and shoots two episodes himself, after hours on the Shore set, gets some cowpoke singer drunk and sets him up on a hay bale, then shops this tape around to every podunk station from Sacramento to Saskatoon. You know what that show is called, Mr. A?"

"I do not."

Clive cleared his throat and paused for effect.

"*Cornpone.* Ran twenty-three years on 167 stations. Now Blake Ackerman lives on a macadamia farm on the north coast of Maui."

At the far end of the table, a burst of laughter erupted from a group of Figgy's work friends.

"So," Alex said. "You're gonna do it like he did? DIY?"

"That's the idea. The Nature Channel went crazy for it—they offered to finance the presentation one hundred percent, make a deal with one of their production companies. But—if we do this ourselves, we own it outright. It's presold—guaranteed on the air, pickup of twenty-five in the first season! We just need the equity on the front end, get us out of the gate."

Clive reached into a leather satchel at his feet, pulled out a manila envelope, and plopped it on the table. Alex gave it a curious poke.

"Here's the prospectus," Clive said. "Give it a look. I got plenty of guys to take this to, but I'd much rather keep it in the family. I could take it to Figgy, but you know how much she's got on her plate right now—and anyway, I think this could be great for you. It's right in your strike zone."

Alex pulled out a stack of bound, color-copied pages. The old man was working him, spinning him. But he couldn't help it; it felt good, to be approached like this, pitched as if he had something valuable to offer. He scanned the packet, past the clip-art cartoon of a dog with a curly-cue show logo emblazoned across the top, into the scanned spreadsheets and production budgets, and finally landed on a box marked TOTAL.

"Two hundred thirty—thousand?"

"Bare bones, right? Run and gun. Not a huge upfront cost, and normally I'd cover it myself, but we're a little upside down on the mortgage right now. All we need is a little help securing a lease on this amazing space on La Cienega—primary location. For the new facility."

"So you're shopping this around? Meeting with investors?"

"Investor," Clive said. "Singular. You."

Twelve

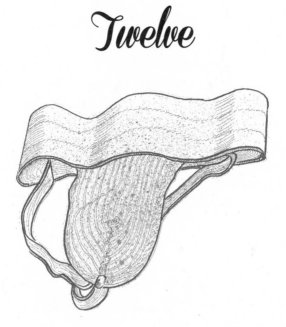

The night before his big procedure, Alex felt good, abnormally so, better than he had any right to. Figgy was staying late at work, or a work party, or just a party—who knew? She'd been out more nights than not lately—pulling all-nighters working on the first six episodes of *The Natashas*, doing panel discussions at the Writers Guild, meeting people for drinks at the Peninsula. Production represented a get-out-of-home-free card that could be cashed in at any time. Typically this meant Alex stayed home—because they would not be the kind of Hollywood family whose Salvadoran nanny fed the kids taquitos and let them watch TV all night while Mom and Dad gallivanted about.

Tonight, however, he was desperate for some gallivanting. After all, this was his last night as an unclipped, unsnipped, fully functional man. And it just so happened that tonight was Wild Boar, the pop-up dinner Miranda had been texting him about for the last week and a half. He hurried through baths, books, and bed, grabbed three bottles of wine, and bolted out, leaving Rosa to babysit. Now he was heading down Sunset with the sunroof open and the brassy shriek of a gypsy-funk marching band rattling the coins of the minivan's change tray.

He'd been looking forward to tonight, for the menu and also, he knew, for Miranda. Their text exchange had remained innocent so far, but her messages always left him feeling unclean, hot-faced, and a little dry-mouthed. Her similes were ridiculous; the corned lengua at Menudo Bites, she wrote, was "as tasteless as a bucket of dicks." Her own braised osso bucco, on the other hand, was "labial-fold tender."

Wild Boar had previously been held in an underground parking garage and a dentist's office; tonight, it was at a gallery on the eastern edge of Chinatown, near the freeway. Alex found a parking spot at the far end of a two-block walk street, the pavement slick from an afternoon drizzle.

Halfway to the gallery, he stopped at a wishing well set back from the path. It was a familiar spot, more a fountain than a well, mounds of dripped faux lava circled by a moat and wreathed with strands of plastic ivy. Perched along the ridge of the fountain was a row of metal Buddhas and a dozen or so miniature wooden signs, each printed with a prize for whoever landed a coin in the copper bowl embedded in the concrete nearby: WISDOM. LOVE. LONG LIFE. And at the very top of the fountain, set inside a miniature grotto above a bowl the size of a bud vase, was a sign for VACATION.

He'd laughed at that as a teenager, a lifetime ago. He'd hung out here one night after a show, having wandered over with Dotti and a few guys from a hardcore band from the Valley. (The Corruptible? The Corrupted?) He remembered leaning up against the gate and sucking on a tinfoil pipe, blowing blue marijuana smoke through the chain link. He'd had a long, drifting discussion about the pathetic soul who'd placed the VACATION bowl in the high-

est, most difficult-to-reach spot. "Fuck love!" he'd hooted, fling-
ing nickels. "Fuck wisdom! I wanna a week at Disney World!"

Then he'd looked down an alley behind Wong Seafood
and spotted, backlit by a yellow streetlight, three rangy coyotes
scrounging beside a dumpster. He remembered tilting his head
back and bellowing, then taking off up the alley, pulling out the
sides of his Army surplus overcoat, like the sails of a pirate ship,
the coyotes scattering as he approached, their tails whipping furiously as they skittered up the asphalt.

And then, just as quickly as it had formed, the memory broke
apart. That *was* him, wasn't it? Or was it Lloyd the bassist who'd
chased the coyotes? Could it have been Dotti? Had all that cheap
Mexican ditchweed fried his memory completely?

He reached in his pocket and tossed a quarter. It dinged the
edge of the WISDOM sign, ricocheted twice, and then rolled into
a bowl marked ADVENTURE.

No, he was sure of it: He'd chased those coyotes.

• • •

Miranda waved from across the candlelit gallery when Alex came
in. She was a whole different girl out of her chef's whites, her
wavy whitish hair loose and shimmery, hanging down over skin
so pale it seemed translucent. Alex headed toward her, but she
signaled for him to hang back then ducked into the back office
where the chef and his crew were scrambling, clearly in full crisis
mode. Tupac thumped on the stereo overhead. Alex found a pair
of empty seats beside a Cambodian girl from Pacoima and a pastry chef with two-inch plugs in his earlobes. After a quick mumbled introduction, the pair went back to surveying the room,
their expressions screwed tight with hipster standoffishness. Alex
opened one of his bottles and played with his phone, keeping
one eye on the passageway to the kitchen. The soup arrived forty

minutes and an entire bottle of pinot later.

"Shit show back there," Miranda said, at last pulling up a chair. "Gas line is clogged and they only just now got the burners going again. Is everyone starving?"

"We're primed," Alex shrugged. "It's like a rock show—any band that starts on time is never any good." He took a spoonful of oxtail soup. It had a deep mushroomy flavor, spiked with star anise. He let out a contented moan.

"Wait 'til you get up in the rib-eye," she said. "Dry aged. Absolutely bonkers. It's been in lockup sixty-five days. I'm telling you, Donnie's an artist of rot—his stuff is like battery acid on the tongue. In a good way."

They ate. Alex cracked a second bottle to go with the salted pork nougat with pickled radish and then moved on to a cab for the veal belly. Miranda knew everyone at their table, but she kept her shoulders squared toward him. Tipsy on the wine and meat, he launched into the full story of his upbringing, all the tawdry tales of his feral childhood in the mountains, his lesbian mom, and boarding-school punk adventures. It all tumbled out as practiced schtick, the mess of it repackaged into jokey patter. Usually, that was good for a sympathetic laugh, but Miranda just shook her head and shrugged.

"Oh, I can top that," she said. "My dad's trans."

"Your dad's—what?"

"Post-op, transgender. When I left for summer camp in seventh grade, he was Gerald, sad-sack insurance adjuster. When I came back, he was Geraldine, redhead ballroom dancer."

"For real?"

"He'd been doing the hormones for a while. Guess I was oblivious. Teenagers, right? It wasn't so bad, though. Going trans was the best thing he ever did. He's way happier now. And he's super comfortable as a woman—frumpy but adorable. Whole thing is *very* premium cable."

Alex took a slug of wine. "And your mom?"

"Still married—going on twenty-eight years. I mean, obviously there's no *sex* happening anymore, but that was never a real priority for them anyhow. She says it's beside the point. She swears she's found the secret to a good marriage: two wives."

Alex raised his glass. "Well then. Cheers to multiple moms."

Miranda touched it with hers, lingering for a moment. What was she—twenty-five? Twenty-six? Her top was sparkly, the color of butterscotch. What was she doing here, talking to him? What *was* this?

His face flushed; he was no longer just buzzed. How else to explain how fascinating he found her tale of worm composting or the particulars of her super-easy, super-delicious sauerkraut recipe? Why else would he volunteer out of nowhere his plans for the next day, unloading the full story about his crazy consult with Dr. Finkelstein and the cryo-preservation and the gallery of pictures of grateful second wives.

Miranda looked concerned. "So you're going in tomorrow? You're going to get cut open and… snipped?"

"No, no—they do it with clips now. Little titanium things. Same metal NASA uses for satellites and, like, space tools."

"But what actually *happens*? Can you still, you know, produce anything?"

"Oh, sure, absolutely! In fact, the clips just block the, um, swimmers from mixing with everything else. The sperm just sort of re-absorbs."

"Figgy must be thrilled."

So she knew about Figgy. How did she know about Figgy? He gave her a look.

"Doesn't she have another show coming up?" she said. "I saw the thing on *Deadline* yesterday. Something about Russian brides? Smart. Taking care of family planning before starting another project."

Alex felt his face go hot. Mention of the show was bad enough—he got a quick visual of Figgy and the Rasta actor Franklin Sykes lounging in a cast trailer. Even worse was the way Miranda had just assumed his vasectomy, which he'd come to think of as a brave, independent act, was all Figgy's doing—like she was sending him in for neutering. As if he wasn't neutered enough.

"Actually, *I'm* the one gearing up for work right now," he heard himself say. "This show I've been developing just got a pickup. We're about to go into production—"

"What? I didn't know—you're in TV too?"

"Afraid so. Fell into it—old colleague of mine asked if I'd EP this new syndicated show. Alternative programming. Reality. But not horrible. Really no one has approached the dog space like this before."

"The dog space? I *love* dogs."

"Who doesn't?" he said, rolling now. "I just don't know how I'm gonna get through the next few months. It's about to get so crazy—both of us in production. Figgy's just slammed—tomorrow I've gotta take a cab to my clippy thing. And I don't even know how I'm getting home."

She hooked a strand of hair over her ear and looked at him, her face lit up.

"I'm all open tomorrow."

• • •

Miranda made a move toward her handbag when the bill arrived, but Alex waved her off—"I got this," he said definitively, peeling off $180 in twenties and joking that this felt more like paying off a drug dealer than picking up a check. Outside, their voices echoed down the empty sidewalks. Her laugh erupted in a delicious burst. He was a crackup. She was a doll. They were flush with wine and food and lit up by the steely blue silhouettes of downtown. When they got to the minivan, she insisted he let her walk the last half block to her car. "I'm a big girl. Anyone comes at me'll be sorry—I know jujitsu."

"You do?"

"Oh sure."

"I should be careful then."

"You should be."

Alex pressed a button on his key fob and the side door of the minivan heaved open. The interior light switched on, illuminating carpet smudged with ground-up cereal and scattered with geometric building blocks and Sylvie's *Feline Sorcerer* books.

"Kids?"

"Two."

Miranda crossed her arms and smiled.

"Cute. I love kids."

Alex put his palms up and headed in for a quick goodbye embrace. Friendly, quick, nice. He saw a flash of her hand pass his face as her fingers glanced his cheek, then closed around the back of his neck. Warm clasp, pulling him close. Her lips touched his and then stopped, holding him there. He could feel the breath from her nose on his cheek, could taste the rib-eye and red wine on her lips. A small moan rose up from behind her teeth.

He reared back. "Okay then."

"Sherman, listen," she said. "You're busy, your life is crazy, I know. But whatever I can do that doesn't complicate things, I just want you to know, I'm available."

• • •

Alex woke up with a jolt the next morning, heart thumping. What was today? Thursday. V day. He'd tried rescheduling, but the only date he could get for his procedure was today, Figgy's last day in town. He sat upright and coughed. He felt panicked, scattered,

like he had a ticket for a flight leaving in an hour and hadn't begun to pack. Next to him, Figgy was curled around a body pillow, out cold. She was leaving tomorrow to start production on
The Natashas. Shit. The day's business rushed in on him. Get kids
up. Pack lunchboxes and backpacks. Make preemptive excuse to
Figgy about convalescence tonight. Drive kids to school. Come
up with plan to get $230,000 for dog show. Get clipped. Catch
ride home with hottie butcher. Shit shit shit.

It was insanity, all of it, but as he got up from bed, he moved
with an unfamiliar sureness of purpose, his concentration locked
on the tasks before him. Sam and Sylvie were roused, dressed, and
set in front of bowls of oatmeal. Figgy was kissed on the back of
the head and fed a story about a late-night food truck run with
Huck the night before. As he clutched his gut in feigned gastroin-
testinal distress, she murmured something about never trusting
a taco truck.

Alex had thumbed out an email the night before, sending a
two-word text to Clive: "I'M IN." Now today there was a text from
Clive with a long line of exclamation points, a smiley face emoti-
con, and two words of his own: "GOOD MAN."

It was as if he'd never had any doubts, as if he hadn't stashed
away and nearly forgotten the *Top Dog* packet the day of Figgy's
party. But now he felt like a seasoned producer, a guy with an
Aeron chair and a dry-erase board. What had seemed preposter-
ous before now felt inevitable—describing it for Miranda, *Top Dog*
became an incisive look at the immigrant experience in America.
"The dogs are just the hook—it's really about the people," he'd
told her, Clive's pitch re-forming in his own mouth. "This old-
world guy and his Americanized daughter, both grieving the loss
of the matriarch, bonding over these animals. And working all
this out in the pressure cooker of these competitions—it's great
drama." He reminded himself now to tease these themes out with
Clive. Working with him would be great—he needed partnership,

collaboration, the mentoring of an elder. And damn if Miranda didn't perk up when he talked about the show. The thought of her sent a twinge up his spine—that goodbye kiss? Tongues hadn't been deployed. So technically, it was really just a goodbye peck? A really prolonged, intense, super-hot peck?

Who was he kidding? He knew he'd crossed a threshold. The kiss might or might not technically count as cheating, but it definitely fell into the increasingly crowded category of things *not* to share with Figgy.

After dropping the kids at school, he immediately sat down with Clive's prospectus and a stack of statements from the bank. It shouldn't be hard to pull out two-hundred-some thousand in equity—during the renovations, he remembered Valerie mentioning something about home equity lines of credit. Because he was the sole officer of the blind trust, he probably wouldn't even need Figgy's signature to get it.

Of course he *should* talk it over with her first—but as this conversation played out in his imagination, he knew in an instant how it would go. He'd bring it up during one of their late-night logistics meetings, laying out Clive's folder on the kitchen island alongside the school forms and furniture catalogs. She'd think it was nuts. She'd tell him he shouldn't work with Clive. She'd shit all over it. And then what would he do? Insist he knew what he was doing? No. He was done playing the part of flaky middle manager to the decisive CEO of Figgy Inc.

By the time a cab arrived, Alex had downloaded a home equity loan application and made an appointment to meet with a manager at the bank. He'd tell Figgy about the show when the pilot was done and syndication was wrapped up. Maybe he'd make it a two-fer and tell her when he told her about the vasectomy. He pictured himself sitting down with Figgy as the autonomous, sterile, empowered, confident producer of a new TV show, negotiating his new place in the marriage from a solidified position of accomplishment.

The house was his as much as hers. But his balls—those were his and his alone. Time to start acting like he had some.

• • •

Alex had determined on the cab ride over that he was going to be utterly unembarrassed when Dr. Finkelstein cut a hole in his scrotum. He was going to be the steeliest, most resolute guy ever to don a paper robe and sling his feet into stirrups.

But now that he was here, naked from the waist down while Finkelstein finished up with another patient down the hall, he felt his resolve waver.

The setting was all wrong, for one thing. He'd been expecting something more like an OR, with a bank of swiveling lights and softly bleeping displays and at least one hovering resident in crisp blue scrubs. Instead, his transformational rite of passage was taking place... in an ordinary exam room with floral print wallpaper and a desktop radio on the counter tuned to an oldies station. The nurse, Diana, had teddy bears with party hats on her scrubs. He'd felt more seriousness at a teeth cleaning.

Alex shifted on the padded blue upholstery, his paper gown crinkling and warping, exquisitely attuned to updrafts from below the table. He kept his eyes fixed on a framed landscape of an Italian hill town. He flashed on Finkelstein in shorts and sandals at an art fair in Laguna Beach, picking this landscape off a wire grid display and sticking it in the trunk of his Acura.

"Hold still." The nurse held up a straight-edge razor. "Just a little prep before we get started."

Alex's heart hammered away. He pointed at the razor. "Haven't seen one of those in a while. So retro!"

She moved toward him without comment. He jerked up.

"Please hold still, Mr. Sherman-Zicklin."

He held his breath and she went in again. Shaving cream. It felt warm going on, the lather thick. He closed his eyes and sighed. When Huck had raved about getting his pubes professionally trimmed, Alex wrote the notion off as vain and vaguely pervy. But maybe there was something to be said for manscaping. This was very nice. A few slow deliberate swipes and she was done. Alex let out a quick breath, glad she'd stopped before the stirring in his groin had reached its full expression.

The nurse went back to her tray of supplies and then advanced again, this time with a roll of surgical tape. She ripped off three, four, five strips and then crisscrossed them against his penis, flattening it against his stomach, as if his now-tiny nubbin was a wild animal that might make a run for it. Then she mopped him down with a swab of cold fluid that filled the room with a coppery, vaguely vinegary odor.

The door swung open and in came Finkelstein, grinning and slapping his hands together like a headliner waltzing on stage after the warm-up act was through. "Okay Diana—all prepped here? Mr. Zicklin, you ready to go? You feeling okay?"

"Just dandy," he said, as casually as he could, trying and failing not to picture the view from the opposite side of his knees.

"Let's get the anesthetic going." Finkelstein knelt down and picked up a syringe. "You'll feel a slight sting." Alex swallowed hard. He flashed on Figgy in the delivery room with Sam, chin set against her chest, her expression locked in primal determination. Now here he was, a high, wheezy whimper escaping his mouth as the needle went in. The pain radiated into his abdomen and spread through his intestines.

Alex puffed out his cheeks and tried to keep quiet.

"All done. Just sit tight. You'll be numb in a second."

The pain flared and then eased, replaced with an odd tugging sensation, as if a massive weight was pulling his organs down toward his pelvis. He kept his eyes shut and head tilted to the side. Between his knees he was dimly aware of Finkelstein and the nurse working away.

"You catch the Ozzy roast last night? On Comedy Central?" The doctor shot a quizzical look over his taped-up member.

Alex opened his eyes a crack and looked down. "Sorry?"

"The Ozzy roast. Did you see it? You know he's one of the charter members of the Friends of Finkelstein. He's out there on the wall. His wife sent the picture in—such a doll. They've talked about me on the Stern show a few times—you must've heard that, right? You seem like a Howard guy."

Alex shook his head. "Must've missed it."

"I don't generally talk about my patients—but my patients generally don't talk about *me* on Howard Stern. So." He laughed. As he talked, his hands kept moving. From up here, he could've been shucking oysters.

"Everything... all right down there?"

Finkelstein went right on shucking. "For a guy who bites the heads off bats, you'd think Ozzy'd be okay with a routine proce-dure, wouldn't you? But oh no. Remember, Diana, what a wreck he was? Writhing around, shaking, crying? We had to give him a general."

"Wait—you can do that? I don't *have* to be awake right now?"

"Oh stop—you're fine. You're a champ. Almost done here." He turned to the nurse. "And how about that Lisa Lampanelli bit? The thing about how Sharon has to stick her arm up Ozzy's butt every time he talks? Did you see his face? Priceless."

Alex rocked forward. "Um, doc?"

"What I don't understand is how they get away with the lan-guage—I know it's cable, but I didn't think they could say *any-thing*. Did you hear that guy Jeff Ross call Ozzy a withered-up old cocksucker? It *was* after nine, but—"

Alex slapped a hand against the exam table. "Doc... maybe save the recap until after we're finished here?"

Finkelstein set something down in his tray, stood up and laid a hand on Alex's knee. "All done. No big whup, right? Don't forget the scrotal support and ice compress—normal to feel some discomfort. Avoid heavy lifting, give yourself a day to recuperate. I'll leave a prescription for the pain. Any serious swelling or discharge, let me know. Otherwise, see you in a few weeks."

"So that's it? Are we done?" He let out a long breath. As he was preparing to get up, Diana leaned in. With a single vicious motion, she ripped up all five pieces of tape at once, leaving behind a bright red crosshatch pattern across his belly and the underside of his dick.

"*Now* you're done," she said.

• • •

Alex still felt woozy after he got his clothes on and ventured into the reception area. "Vasovagal lightheadedness—totally normal," the nurse said, dropping Finkelstein's prescription into a plastic bag with a sheet of after-care instructions and a few squares of gauze. "There's a pharmacy in the lobby, if you want to pick up your scrotal support and medication right away. Ah, here's your wife now—"

Wife? Alex looked frantically around the waiting room. Miranda stood by the door, draped in a knit cardigan and plump leather purse.

Alex felt a jolt of giddiness as she came forward and took his arm. "Easy there, Sher. Let's get you home."

She'd come. She'd said she'd come and then she'd come. In the elevator, she asked how it had gone and then reached into her purse and pulled out a napkin-wrapped baked something. "Bacon scone?" she said. "Made it fresh this morning."

"Thanks—but I'm feeling a little rough."

"Suit yourself," she said, popping a piece into her mouth. She

checked her phone and followed him into the pharmacy, acting
for all the world like this was the most normal errand one could
be doing at one o'clock on a Tuesday, even when Alex got the
script filled, swallowed two Vicodin dry, and then asked for her
help comparing the various options when it came to scrotal support (finally settling on a basic-model jock strap with a protective
cup advertised as "padded for extra comfort!").

Maybe it was the empty stomach, but Alex felt the effect of
the pills almost immediately, his tongue going tingly and then a
warm molten sensation percolating up through his limbs. By the
time he was safely buckled in Miranda's car—a dented, plum-col-
ored Saab with a popsicle-stick-and-yarn craft dangling from the
rearview mirror—the wooziness in his chest was replaced by a
full-body tingle, like he'd just stepped out of a steam room.

Miranda rolled down the windows and turned on the stereo,
silvery ringlets flying loose against her face. Alex closed his eyes
and listened to the music. It was "Peace Warrior," an inoffensive
reggae ballad by Franklin Sykes, the singer who'd just signed onto
the cast of *The Natashas*. "Perfect," he said, his eyelids fluttering.
"Of course you love this guy. All women love this guy. Figgy has
such a crush on this guy...."

"He is pretty dreamy," she said.

They drove without talking for a while, Alex enjoying the
warm wind whipping around the car's interior, the shadows of
palm trees and billboards scrolling through the sunroof. He pictured what they looked like from the street, a guy of a certain age
in a Saab driven by a young, pale blonde. An attractive young
couple. It was such a beautiful city—so much prettier out of his
minivan, over here on the right, in the passenger seat. He never
didn't drive. When was the last time he didn't drive?

"Thank you for doing this—so sweet of you."

"It's fine. You needed a ride."

"I'm very grateful," he said, then paused to take her in. Her hair was flying all over, lit up from above. Every part of her was unfamiliar—the long, tapering neck, the spray of freckles on her arms. She flashed him a smile. She was attentive, nurturing. He thought about that kiss on the street, imagined what she looked like naked, a flush on her cheeks and a film of sweat on her forehead.

"I'm pretty looped," he said.

"So you are." She reached over and gave his knee a quick pat. "You've had a big day."

She parked on the curb outside the house and insisted that he wait for her to help him out. As he was fumbling for the seat-belt buckle, he spotted a stack of pages jammed between the parking brake and his seat. He had just enough time to pull it out and give it a look. It was a script. Miranda's name was at the bottom, with a date and WGA registration tag. GERALD & GERALDINE.

"What's this?" he said, getting out of the car.

"Oh that. Just something I've been working on. About my dad and the family and all that. It's a pilot."

"You're a writer? I didn't know you were a writer," he said.

"I didn't know you did reality TV. It's L.A.—what do you expect?"

• • •

Alex said goodbye to Miranda on the sidewalk, savoring the quick but close hug she gave him almost as much as the awestruck expression she directed down the leafy path toward the front door. "Some house," she said.

"Thanks. I can't believe—" he stopped midway through the line he used with everyone who came here for the first time: "I can't believe I get to live here." Not today. Not with her. For all she knew, there was no "get to"—this was all *his* doing. "What can I say? It's pretty ridiculous."

He promised to give her a tour some other time—right now the kids were home and he just needed to plop down on the couch. "Frozen peas!" She called to him as he went down the path. "The nurse said frozen peas! For the swelling!"

Alex walked in the door to find Sylvie camped in front of the kitchen TV and Sam at the computer. He dropped his keys and wallet on the counter. "Hey kiddos!" The kids grunted in response, eyes locked on their respective screens. Normally this is where he'd grab the TV remote and computer mouse and unilaterally shut down all media, demanding they speak to him—"Like a person!" he'd holler. He'd check their homework, maybe break out the Uno deck. But right now he was glad for the distraction. Rosa was on her way out, and he was on his own with the kids until Figgy got home.

Alex went to the bathroom, took a look at the contents of his underwear—swollen, discolored—and then put on his new jock strap and some sweats and returned to the kitchen. He plucked a bag of Trader Joe's soybeans from the freezer and headed for the couch. *Frozen edamame: the evolved man's choice for testicular swelling.* He plopped down next to Sylvie and unfolded a blanket hanging over the arm, stuffing the chilly bag down his pants and pulling the blanket around him in a tight cocoon. "Sylvie honey— we're not watching this," he said, wincing at the laugh track blasting from a Disney Channel sitcom. "Daddy veto."

"Fine," Sylvie said. "I've seen that episode like six times already. *King Chef*?"

Alex began scrolling through the DVR playlist, happy at the prospect of whiling away an hour or two with Sylvie as superhero chefs battled it out in the kitchen arena. But what about Sam? Besides the occasional fashion show, he couldn't be bothered with reality TV. After all that had gone on today, Alex had a sudden overwhelming desire to have both his kids cuddled up close. "Hey, Mr. Man," Alex called to Sam, an idea flashing before him.

"Get in here. I'm putting a movie on."

"A movie? Right now?" Sam said. "I haven't even done my vocab—"

"Vocab can wait." Alex furiously thumbed the keypad on the remote, splurging to download *For a Few Dollars More*. He'd watched the entire Sergio Leone oeuvre with his dad on late-night TV during one of his weekend visits after the divorce, as a sort of tonic for all the lady power he was fed at home.

"Get ready—this is only the best Western ever," he said, pulling them both close.

The kids made dubious groans—"This looks *old*," Sylvie said—but stayed put. The movie started and they all fell silent.

He'd forgotten how bloody it was—after the sixth body was riddled by bullets, Alex pressed pause, got up, popped another Vicodin, and checked that the kids were OK. Both of their eyes were wide and excited; they clearly had no objection to the violence.

"Who would you be?" Alex asked as he settled back in.

"What do you mean?" Sam asked.

"Which cowboy would you be? Clint Eastwood or Lee Van Cleef?"

"Which one is which?"

"Van Cleef's the older guy. The colonel. Clint's in the poncho—with the cigar? For me it's all about Van Cleef. That's who I'd be—I'd be right there, cracking safes and shooting bad guys from across the whole corral."

"You know how to shoot a *gun*?" Sylvie asked.

"Oh sure."

"That is *so* not true," Sam jumped in. "You can't shoot. And you're allergic to horses, remember? And dust. And also hay. You'd be all puffy and sneezy. The only guy in this movie you'd be is the man in the general store with the twitchy face and the ribbon tie. That's you, Dad."

Alex started to protest, then sighed. "Okay, fine. You're right. But I'd hire you as my right-hand man, to work with in the shop, okay? You'd hook me up with some Sammy's Salves? All these guys could use a skin-care regimen, am I right?"

"Seriously."

It was after dark and the movie was almost over when Figgy came through the door, lugging a pile of scripts and a bundle of mail. Alex started to get up, then thought better. "Hey!" he called across the room.

On the screen Clint had just tossed El Indio's body into a wagon overflowing with corpses. "What in God's name is this?" Figgy called.

"It's only the best Western ever," Sylvie said, squeezing Alex's shoulder.

Figgy dumped her stuff and then came over the couch, leaning down on the arm. "What's for dinner?"

Alex looked up at her blankly, the question of food not even occurring to him until now. "I dunno—what *is* for dinner? I can put some fish sticks in for the kids, and maybe we can just do soup or something?"

She rolled her eyes and sat down at the island. "Soup? Seriously? I'm exhausted and starving. And we need to talk. I've got news."

"Really?" Alex said, tugging the blanket up to his chin. "Can I just sit one more sec? I'm not feeling so hot. Those tacos last night ripped me up inside. I've barely gotten up from the couch all day."

Figgy looked annoyed. "That should be all cleared out by now, shouldn't it? Have you called the doctor?"

He crossed his arms under the blanket and held onto his sides. The tugging feeling in his groin was back, mingling with a narcotic bleariness. That last Vicodin was maybe not the best idea. She headed over to the fridge, swinging open the door and blocking her view—he had a quick window in which to somehow get rid of the now-soggy bag of soybeans jammed between his thighs. He got up quickly, tucked the bag under his shirt and headed for the bathroom.

Closing the door behind him, he splashed a handful of water on his face, then pulled out the bag and weighed his options. Stashing it here didn't seem wise. He had to dump it. He tore the bag open with his teeth and poured the contents into the toilet—the hard green pellets splashing as they hit the water, a good approximation of the sound that a man in his supposed condition should be making. Figgy had been home for two minutes and already here he was, a dope dealer ditching his goods when the cops came calling. He balled up the wet plastic and buried it in a wastebasket.

With that taken care of, he pulled down his pants and slid the jock strap down his legs to check himself. Everything looked fine—at least no bigger or more bruised than when he'd gotten home. Then he noticed it. Inside the front section, in the divot of the little pouch, were three irregularly shaped blots of brownish red.

His jock strap was bloody.

And all at once, he was back in Las Vegas on that thrifting holiday with Figgy, horrified by his gruesome bargain-bin discovery. He remembered holding up the bloody jock strap and inspecting it, baffled at what sort of circumstance could have produced such an atrocity.

Now he knew. He was the stranger his younger self could not even begin to contemplate.

He stepped out of the jock strap and sat down on the toilet seat, hanging his head and dangling the offending item from his index finger. He sat there for a while, elbows pressing down on his knees, head spinning. Outside the door, he could hear the TV back on, that same heinous sitcom laugh track booming through the house. Figgy was calling out to him—where was the shrimp curry she'd brought home the night before? Had he eaten it? A few more minutes passed. Why wasn't the printer working? Sam needed to print out hand-cream labels—why wasn't it working? Could he finish up in there already? She really needed to talk.

Alex sat very still, his eyes clenched closed. As long as he stayed put in here, he'd be okay. Let her sort out dinner and the printer. He'd just stay here until his head stopped spinning.

"What is that?"

He lifted his head. Figgy was in the doorway, eyes cast on the elastic in his hand.

"Can't you see I'm in here?"

"I do see that. What've you *got* there?"

Alex swiped his hand to the side, stashing the strap under his armpit. "Come on! *I* leave you alone when you're in the bathroom."

"*I* lock the door. *This* door is open. And you're sitting here *hiding* something. What are you hiding?"

Alex closed his eyes and took a moment. Then he pulled the strap from beneath his arm, looped one side around his thumb and flung it at her. She grabbed it out of the air and turned it over, her face a mix of horror and confusion.

The laugh track boomed from the TV.

"It's a jock strap," he said. "A bloody jock strap. Isn't that *hilarious*? Just like the one in Vegas! Except this one has *my* blood on it. How hilarious is that?"

Her eyes narrowed. "What—you got snipped? When?"

"Today. And it's clipped, not snipped. Little titanium clips—like NASA uses."

Her arms went slack at her sides. "You just... got a vasectomy? Without discussing it with me? And you were just going to keep it a... secret?"

"Yup." He bent backward, exposing his bare thighs and mottled abdomen. "Nothing to discuss. My body. My choice."

Her arms crossed and mouth fell open. He waited for the hollering, the screaming, the anger. Instead, she did what she never did: laughed, her shoulders heaving in deep convulsions. "Oh, you poor little shit."

"What? What's so funny?"

She reached into her pants pocket and pulled something out, then tossed it at him. He caught it in one hand. White plastic. Purple tip. Little window. Plus sign.

"Too late, daddy."

Thirteen

They didn't have it out right away, not with the shock of the strap-stick exchange still reverberating through the house like a blast of thermonuclear energy. Alex got into some pajama bottoms and managed to rustle up some dumplings and green beans for the kids while Figgy retreated to the bedroom to pack for her trip to Baltimore in the morning.

He got the kids down and headed to bed with a fresh bag of frozen vegetables. Corn this time. Much manlier. He lay atop the covers, starfished across the king bed. Figgy stepped in from the bathroom, a froth of white foam on her lips. She pulled a toothbrush out of her mouth and twirled it like a baton. She started to say something, stopped. Recalibrated. Started again.

"Seriously, what the fuck?" she said at last. "Who does this? Who goes sneaking around behind his wife's back to get a *vasectomy*?"

Alex propped up on his elbows. "I was being responsible," he said. "I don't know what happened with your pills—but at least I was being responsible. Some actual family planning? Accident prevention?"

She clamped her mouth down on the toothbrush. "Who said it was an accident?" she mumbled. "We've talked about it. Over and over. We never ruled it *out*."

"We never ruled it *in*. The last time all you said is you wanted to start trying. I never actually *agreed*. This is something you negotiate. You have good-faith negotiations."

Figgy wiped her mouth with her sleeve and rolled her eyes. "You want to talk about good-faith negotiating? I'm supposed to negotiate with a guy who just had... *secret ball surgery*?"

Alex plopped back down on the pillow and adjusted the bag. "You just haven't thought this through. Going from two kids to three—we're outnumbered! I can barely keep a man-to-man defense going—how are we supposed to go zone? Have you forgotten everything? The pumping, the screaming, the explosive doodies? I can't do it again. I just can't."

"I'm sorry—what *else* are you doing exactly?" she said. "I'm sorry if my pregnancy interferes with your punk-rock memoir."

A screech like a tea kettle sounded in Alex's head. "I told you, it's a *novel*. And yes, this *does* interfere. It does. It's bad enough that I'm trying to work with Rudolfo and Rosa and the FedEx man barging in every five minutes. Now what? I'm just supposed to put all that on hold?"

A droplet of toothpaste flew from her bottom lip. "I swear to God, Alex—you sure complain a lot for a guy with no job, a nanny, and a writer's studio in a solarium."

The tone in Alex's ears rose to a screech. "*You* wanted this house! And now—what? Another show, another baby, more and more and more! Are you *so* fucked up about turning forty that you think getting pregnant will make everything right?"

"So what am I supposed to do, exactly? Get an abortion? And

then go back to work so I can continue supporting the family I never see?"

She wheeled around and went back into the bathroom, kicking the door with her heel as she went.

Alex sat up and craned his neck toward the doorway. "Can't we at least talk about *options*? I mean, it's not like you've got *moral* objections."

He could hear her spit into the sink, crank on the water, and splash it on her face. "Not going to happen."

Alex flopped back on the bed. That was it—nothing more to be said on that subject. About all things related to Figgy's uterus, Alex was entirely, ideologically irrelevant.

She came back in, face flushed and T-shirt splattered. "You think I'm having *fun*? You think I *like* working all the hours I do and trying to be a halfway decent mom? You think I *like* missing Sylvie's recital and Sam's performance thing? How do you think I feel when these Pines moms call asking about play dates I have no idea about? You think I want to go schlep off to Baltimore just so we can afford to send our kids to that ridiculous school?"

Alex straightened out and tucked his legs under the covers. She walked over to her bedside table, squirted some skin cream on her hands, and began furiously kneading her arms and neck. "You're right—I'm forty," she said. "And this is my last shot. Bought two. Got one free. It doesn't matter how it happened. What matters is that I'm having it. I've got resources—I can handle it with or without you."

"What is that supposed to mean?"

Figgy wrapped herself up in the covers and turned her back. "I've got a plane to catch in the morning. I can't do this. We're done."

Alex closed his eyes and clenched his jaw, his chest roiling. *We're done?*

• • •

She was up just after six the next morning, Alex waking to the sound of the buzzer as she opened the back gate for her ride to the airport. He propped himself up on one elbow and watched her. She knelt at the side of the bed, yanking on the zipper of her suitcase. Her mouth was set in a hard line.

"Have you got Puffy?" he asked. Puffy was their name for the green, down-filled parka she complained made her look like a parade balloon. "It's freezing in Baltimore."

"Go back to sleep."

"I'm up. You want eggs? I'll make eggs. Like the husband in Fargo. Before Frances McDormand went out in the snowstorm?"

"Eggs—ugh." She heaved down her on her elbow, compressing the bag as she tugged at the zipper. "Not a good idea for me right now. I'll grab a yogurt at the airport."

He sat up and stretched, then reached over to touch her arm. "Fig, you don't have to go, do you? You hate production. Let Dani deal with it. You're always saying how great she is on set—you stay here. The timing couldn't be shittier."

"I can't not go. The studio's already annoyed I haven't been out for pre-production—I have to be on set. I can't run it from here. And maybe we need some time."

As she closed the bag and stood up, Alex's fingertips landed along the soft skin on the inside of her arm. The handle of her bag locked into place with a snap. She sighed and squeezed his hand, hair falling over her eyes. Her face was in shadow and featureless, impossibly distant. "It's three weeks. I'll get things running, set the tone. We can figure things out from there. I'll Skype with the kids at night. I left a list of appointments and phone numbers near the computer. Call Anne-Marie about plane tickets—I'll send for the kids in a week, when it calms down a little. Send them with Rosa."

Alex let go of her hand and squinted up at her, trying to catch up. "Send the kids... to Baltimore? With Rosa? What are you talking about?"

"The guy's waiting," she said. "I gotta go."

She swiveled around and headed out the door, the plastic wheels of her bag crackling against the hallway floor.

• • •

After a call to Rosa telling her she was on kid duty, Alex cut himself off from all contact with the outside world. With the drapes pulled tight and the house phone left off the hook, he slept for six hours, then roused to gobble another two Vicodins and a bag of mint Milanos. Before dozing off again, he summoned a gauzy image of Miranda backed up against his minivan, moving in close, the softness of her throat shadowed in the streetlight. They hadn't touched since that night, but he now imagined every inch of her, fixating on the curve of her neck and the divot at the base of her spine, a pang of shame registering in his chest as he tugged at himself, the stinging from his balls prohibiting any progress toward climax. He was curled into a ball humming an old TV jingle over and over again when he realized his cell phone had been buzzing on and off for the last hour or so. He rolled over, the soggy bag of corn thudding onto the floor, and picked up his phone. The caller ID read HUCK.

"Mhff," Alex said.

"You don't answer my calls anymore? I've left you like eight messages."

Alex put the phone on speaker and dropped it on his chest. "You remember that commercial for the Gap?"

"The Gap—what?"

Alex shut his eyes and sang out the melody that had been looping in his head all day. "Fall into the gap," he sang. When Huck didn't respond, he sang it again, his voice falling into a breathy croak on the long last note.

"Alex? You okay?"

"You remember that ad, don't you?"

Alex could remember the exact moment when he'd first seen that TV commercial. He'd been eleven, maybe twelve, alone in his red-checked flannel pajamas, sick with a viral infection. Much later, recounting the episode with a therapist, he blamed his inappropriately intense response on a 102-degree fever and anxiety over the whereabouts of his mom. He'd been running the same high fever for two straight days when the Gap ad had triggered something akin to a psychotic break. The images were horrendous enough, a big phallic cartoon needle-and-thread flying frantically through space, careening over undulating mountains of blue denim. Then there was the melody of the jingle itself, the way it plunged down, dropping into an impossibly low register—hearing it for the first time, he'd felt a flurry in the pit of his stomach that grew into a full-body quake. He was teetering over a void, an eternal darkness, an infinite chasm. When his mom came home after her weekend away, he was trembling in the corner of his room, dehydrated and delirious, face slick with tears.

"*Fall... in... to... the... Gap*," he sang again now, that same deep -down flurry overtaking him again. "How was that even an *ad*? Can you believe they sold jean shorts with that horror show?"

"Seriously, Alex? You get up right now and put on some clothes. No chinos either. I'll be outside in twenty minutes."

• • •

Huck ignored Alex's feeble protests and drove west to the Davies. After splitting with Katherine, he had practically moved into the club, partly for the emotional support of the boys at the bar but also to establish a claim on the club as *his* domain during the reshuffling of their marital assets, financial and otherwise.

"I shouldn't be out in public," Alex said as they saddled up to barstools under the gnarled branches of what looked like an old-growth olive tree. He felt greasy and rumpled. A few tables over, four guys in suits were swirling amber-colored alcohol in bulbous snifters.

"Come on, homes—it's a tequila tasting!" Huck said, raising two fingers to a passing hostess, who beelined past their table without a pause. "Small-batch shit from Jalisco. Infused with peppercorn and yopo plants—loaded with DMT, same stuff the Incas snort with bird bones. Mixed up in a cocktail called the Mystic Sombrero. Shit'll put a pretty golden halo on everything, make all your hurt go away. You need this."

Alex shrugged and squinted up at a string of white lights in a low-hanging branch overhead. He imagined what it took to get this tree up here, thirty stories up. He pictured a two-prop chopper hoisting the tree over the rooftops, the roots bunched in a bulging mesh sack, the trunk spinning in the wind, long, feathery leaves scattering on the sidewalks below.

Huck craned his head around the room, then ducked down and motioned for Alex to come close. "I tell you about my thing with Cruise?"

"*Cruise* Cruise?"

"He's between movies right now. Sits in the lounge, reads the paper, chugs smoothies. So last week I'm sitting right across from him and I figure—why not? He's a member, so am I, what the hell. So I lean over and I say, 'So Tom—I gotta ask: What's the *deal* with Scientology?'"

"You said that? Seriously?"

"Sure."

"What'd he do?"

"He looks me up and down, shakes his head and just goes, 'You're not ready.'"

"That's it?"

"That's it. *You're not ready.* Then he goes back to his paper."

"Wow."

"I know, right? What do you wanna bet Paul Haggis wrote him that line?"

Alex perked up as another waitress passed their table with a tray of cocktails. She reached the foursome of suits then went into a crouch. Alex zeroed in on a crease in her tweed miniskirt and watched it bunch up over a pair of sheer gray stockings.

"Figgy's gone," he said.

"What?"

"Flew out this morning. New show in Baltimore. Said she'll send for the kids in a week or so. Send for them—that's how she put it."

"And you're what—*bummed*? *You* wanna go to Baltimore? You're kid-free, wife-free—you should embrace that shit."

"I guess." He knew he *should* embrace that shit. But somehow, the thought of sending the kids with Rosa to visit Mommy on the set of her new TV show felt terrifying. It felt like a whole new reality. One in which Figgy's life kept right on going, busy as can be, all her responsibilities and needs attended to—while his life froze. Rosa would pick up the slack with the kids, Anne-Marie would help out with house duties, Zev would help Figgy work out her early-stage pregnancy hormones—and soon everything Alex contributed to the Sherman-Zicklin clan would be... *subcontracted.* She had the cards. She'd keep working, keep earning, keep being the same tough, anxious, hard-charging, powerhouse she was. But Alex? What became of the husband-of?

The waitress passed by again, this time giving Huck a quick shrug as she hustled by. Letting out an exasperated moan, he went over to the bar, reached over the counter, and returned to the table with a Mystic Sombrero in each hand.

"They better not be freezing me out," he said as he sat down. "I heard they're doing housekeeping on membership rolls—but it's only supposed to be agents and bankers and dweebs that get the boot. I'm a fucking creative!"

Alex took his glass and held it up to the light. "How much of this yoyo stuff are we talking here? Because I'm not really in the best shape to take a serious *trip*. I'm about two sips away from crumpling into your lap and weeping."

Huck shook his head, took a long draw on his glass, and leaned in close. "What is so wrong anyway?"

Alex explained as best he could, the events of the last few days tumbling out over one, then two more snifters. The kiss with Miranda. The strap. The stick. The feeling today that the fight last night was the big one, the one you never come back from.

When he was finished, Alex reached for his water glass and shut his eyes, woozy. When he looked up and across the table, Huck had his fist propped under his chin, regarding him like a clinician considering a chart. "What did she actually *say*?" he asked. "Did she formally, officially say the word 'separation'?"

"No—I don't know," Alex said, running the exchange back. "This morning when she left... she said something about us 'needing time'. But last night she did say we were 'done'."

"But no email, no note—nothing in writing?"

"No. Why?"

"Why? Come on. The clock is still running is why. There's been no formal notification, no official date of separation. How long 'til the anniversary?"

Alex felt his head swim. "Oh Jesus, Huck, this isn't about that."

"Come on. You can deny it all you like, but you both know what's really going on here. So when is it?"

"Next March. But it doesn't matter—she's pregnant, remember? She didn't get pregnant because she wants a divorce."

"Is that so?" Huck said. "Think about it. All the guys who take off on pregnant women—people don't talk about it, but come on, how many get *pushed*? A lot. Figgy got what she wanted. And now one phone call and she's got a nursery at the studio and twenty-four-hour childcare. You can come visit twice a week and then go home to your shitty Oakwood apartment and start dating bat-shit-crazy cocktail waitresses. Not a problem for her at all."

Alex straightened up on his barstool and put his face in his hands. The taste of the tequila was hot on his tongue. What Huck was saying—that was just Huck working out his own issues. His whole life had become a game of relational warfare—but he and Figgy weren't anywhere near that kind of hostile territory. But as soon as he'd had this thought, a jolt of doubt shot through him. Maybe Huck was right and Figgy was already far gone. Maybe like everything else in their lives, Figgy had figured out where they were going long before he'd had a chance to get acquainted with the new scenery.

"There wasn't enough Paxil in the world to get me to ten with Kate," Huck said. "But you—you can still squeak this out. I know you feel bad. You're wading around in the muck. But I'm telling you, shake that off. Quit this whole power mope. You can't believe how much better you're gonna feel when you stop living your life as a fucking *handbag*."

"What? How am I... a handbag?"

"You're an accessory, Sherman. A trinket. A coke spoon. A hood ornament. I've been there. It's crushing—you can't live like that."

Alex drained his tequila and motioned to the waitress for another.

"Look, just make nice," Huck said. "Let her know you're good with the pregnancy, sorry about everything. Get some sun. Relax. Go ahead and have some fun with that butcher girl of yours, but you keep that on lockdown. No matter how good it feels to have this sweet tattooed thing take off her apron for you—don't get sloppy. You go out tomorrow and get yourself one of those pre-paid SIM cards—and you pop that in whenever you and butcher girl trade recipes or whatever. You treat that second SIM with the care and respect you showed the rubber you smuggled around in your Velcro wallet in high school. Otherwise one day the wife is gonna pick up your phone, find a text from the butcher girl, and start typing away, pretending to be you. Next thing you know your wife and your girlfriend are sexting back and forth, having a grand old time—"

"Huck, stop." Alex waved his hand in front of him as if cutting through a cloud of noxious cigar smoke. "I'm not sexting with Miranda. And I'm not making nice with Figgy just so I can hit some magic ten. That's... deplorable."

"It's *sensible*, bro. Look, I didn't make ten, but I'm gonna be just fine. You, son, you need to worry. You're a bit part in a star vehicle. Unless you're careful, you'll get kicked off the movie before you join the union."

• • •

The particulars of the night out with Huck were lost to Alex the next day, blurred beneath the weight of a crushing hangover, the mix of Vicodin, tequila, and Inca hallucinogens producing a monster headache. He remembered running his hands over the olive tree while staring out at the silvery sci-fi city below. He remembered Huck clapping him on the shoulder in the elevator down. And he remembered going home in Huck's Audi wagon, the sunroof open, the radio up, his voice wailing into the night.

All the talk about the magic ten and the rest of it—when he thought about Huck's tutorial now, panic ricocheted around his chest. It wasn't so hard, not thinking about it. He had other concerns. Clive's show, his book, the kids—he was too busy living his life to worry about the ramifications of his anniversary or to plot any sort of settlement strategy.

Still, he couldn't help feeling like maybe Huck wasn't so full of shit. After drop-off at school the following Tuesday, he made a stop at a mini-mall electronics shop and asked the clerk to show him how to switch the SIM card in his phone. He practiced popping out one card and inserting the second one. In a few days he could do it in a single smooth gesture. He texted with Miranda while the kids were watching TV, shooting her a message about where she got beef cheeks. She said she'd order some at Malcolm's, then texted back with an offer to take him to a place in the San Gabriel Valley that did an amazing dessert made with mango and condensed milk.

During the week, after dropping the kids off at school, he had long pre-production meetings with Clive about *Top Dog*. As co-EP, Alex had imagined his role would be supervisory, even ceremonial. But Clive had other ideas. He tasked Alex with production budgets, casting sessions, and equipment rentals. Clive even asked him to negotiate the lease on the storefront for the Top Dog gym, a cavernous space occupied until recently by a Chinese restaurant with red leather booths and flocked wallpaper.

One night, after the kids were asleep, Alex found himself in the spare bedroom, naked save for a pair of rubber slippers. He powered up Mrs. Benjamin's tanning bed, heaved open its metal top, and inserted himself inside. The heat of the long bulbs radiated below his skin. He pictured his flesh turning toasty and hard, shellacking him like the crust of a crème brûlée. He couldn't believe how pleasant it turned out to be. Why had he never done this before? This, it occurred to him, is how people in his position get by. They harden their outsides, tenderize their innards, gather their strength. He pictured Figgy in her hotel suite, talking strategy with a divorce lawyer on her cell phone while Zev hovered nearby, feeding her triangles of Toblerone. No way was she not making the necessary preparations. Alex had to prepare as well. He'd remain still and calm and keep his eyes closed tight against the glare.

Fourteen

A lex had been holed up in the pantry of the new Top Dog training facility for six hours straight, eyes fixed on a bank of monitors. His butt hurt and the muscles in his lower back were knotted up. They were behind schedule on what was supposed to be the final day of shooting, and Clive had been AWOL since just after ten. "You got this," Clive had said on his way out to a progress meeting with an exec at the Nature Channel. He'd promised to bring back a deal memo; Alex had begun to worry a little about their supposedly rock solid commitment and looked forward to seeing some actual documentation. "Let Nancy deal with crew," Clive had told him. "You stay on story. Any problems, hit me on my Blackberry."

So far, Alex hadn't needed to call. He was handling it. That's what everyone kept saying—Nancy, a gum-snapping Aussie with a tight perm, couldn't stop raving about what a "natural" he was in the dynamics of "occu-soap," industry parlance for this particular genre of true-life workplace soap opera. It didn't seem that complicated to him; it was all about making sure the camera was pointed wherever interesting stuff was going on. Story sense, Nancy called it. This morning in the grooming parlor, for instance, as the dogs were being prepped for a competition that would serve as a climax of the pilot, he had to physically escort the second camera guy away from Maria, the Botoxed, bejeweled owner of a bichon frise. No, Alex said, steering the cameras back toward Al and Gina. Al, the heavy-browed, ox-like guy who technically owned the operation, had a way of clamming up when the cameras rolled. Alex had spent much of the morning jogging onto the set between takes to feed him encouragement. But there was something in his big, baleful eyes—a reluctance to play along with the big charade that made you love him. This morning he'd been fussing with a lumpy, lumbering shar-pei named Blossom, fitting her collar with a fat purple bow and muttering into her ear to calm her nerves. Gina was pacing behind him, her heels tapping percussively on the concrete floor.

"Dad, we can't enter Blossom. She's not ready. No way will she hold still during judging. And she looks like a hippo."

Al squeezed the dog's wrinkly neck and shrugged. "She's spunky," he said. "And I think she looks great."

"I know *you* like her, Pop, but this is America. People in this country don't want spunky—they want beautiful."

Al grimaced and took his daughter's face in his hands. "My gut is good, little dove," he said. "My gut says Blossom wins."

Gina made an exasperated huff and wriggled away. "We've only got one entry. If we go with Blossom, we lose. I'm getting the bichon ready."

Back in the pantry production booth, Nancy turned and high-fived Alex. "Gold!" she trumpeted. "We got stakes! Clive's gonna love this."

Alex half-smiled, half-shrugged, unsure whether he really

did have a natural talent for orchestrating reality TV or whether the bar for judging reality TV was as low as it seemed.

He was on his way outside to catch a little fresh air when his phone buzzed. He checked the caller ID: FIGGY CELL. His eyes narrowed. She'd been out of town for close to a month now, extending her trip after a production overrun and then barely talking with him when Rosa took the kids out for a long weekend. Since then their conversations had been brief, terse and mostly focused on the comings and goings of the kids. A conversation here would be tricky—he'd decided to put off telling her about the show until they got a firm air date—but since he'd already ignored two of her messages today, he ducked outside and took the call.

"Hey," she said. "Where've you been?"

"Here at the house."

"I called twice last night and three times this morning."

"Sorry," Alex said. "It's crazy here."

The line went silent. Alex closed his eyes and gripped his forehead. It physically hurt, lying like this. He wanted to tell her the truth, come clean about the show, his investment, all of it. But until they got the official pickup, she would just write it off as another one of her stepdad's crazy pipe dreams, this one made worse by his involvement. He needed to prove her wrong before she had a chance to object. By the time she got home he'd be a producer with a firm commitment from an actual network (and a suntan).

"We agreed you'd let me Skype with the kids before bedtime," she said. "That's why I called last night—to speak to my children."

My children?

The back door swung open and one of the PAs leaned out. "They're all set for the next scene. Clive's looking for you."

Alex put a hand over the mouthpiece and flashed a thumbs up.

"Clive?" Figgy asked. "What are you doing with *Clive*?"

"Nothing. I'm just here in the kitchen. That was just Rosa—she wants to know who's doing pickup at school today."

"You are, right?" she said, quickly changing gears. "They need their emergency kits—did you see that email from the principal? The one to 'delinquent parents'? About the bag of clothes and the family picture and some kind of recording? You were supposed to turn it in last Friday."

Alex sighed. "The bags are in the car. I'll swing them by the school later. I've just been really busy—"

"Oh, I know," she said drily. "It's not like you have swollen wrists and morning sickness and a director who takes two full days to finish a single goddamn scene."

Alex choked back a response. She was the one who'd gotten knocked up, left town, and then extended her trip by a week. She had no right to complain; her standing in the court of misery had been revoked.

"You still nauseous? What does the doctor say?" He knew from their online calendar that she'd had an appointment with an OB-GYN at Johns Hopkins.

"Green tea and wristbands," she said. "Utter bullshit. I've gotta scoot—talk later."

And that, apparently, was that. He'd wanted to ask about the sonogram. Had she found out the gender? It would be a boy, no doubt—she'd probably already chosen a name. Abraham—that's what she wanted to call Sam. Alex had nixed it because it was too Jewy. Back when he could nix things. Back before *my body, my choice.*

"Alex? Alex?" He was standing in the alley behind the gym, the phone dead at his side. The PA poked his shoulder. "Clive just showed up—you should get in here."

• • •

Alex walked into the gym to find Clive stationed against a back wall, keeping watch as Al and Gina lined up four dogs in a row for a pre-competition review. Gina was in a tizzy, the veins on her neck pulsing as she wagged an accusing finger at Al.

"They're gonna laugh us out of the show," she pleaded. "That dog is not competition ready. Never will be!"

"Let's just see," he said. Beside him, the shar-pei Blossom lowered herself to the floor and tucked her head down, jowls spilling over her paws. "She's different—the judges *like* different."

"No, Dad—they like beautiful. Why can't you get that through your skull!"

"Hold it!" The audio guy waved his arm back and forth over his head. "Sorry guys. Street sound. Truck went by—reset. Go again."

"For godsakes!" Gina threw up her hands and made a beeline to the makeup girl for a touch-up.

Alex went over to Clive and lifted his palms in a gesture of "what can you do?" Clive pulled a pocket square from his blazer and mopped his cheeks.

"It's like a Bikram class in here," he said. "We're gonna need to swap these incandescents with some LEDs. Less heat. Definitely worth it for the long haul. We'll get that in the budget for round two."

"Sounds good," Alex said.

"So—looking good? We making the day?"

Alex straightened up. "Sure. You're gonna love the Al-Gina stuff."

"Looks great." Clive put his arm around Alex's shoulder and pulled him in. "Having fun? Looking dynamite—color on your face, like a young George Hamilton over here. I knew you'd be great at this. We're all set for round two."

"Sorry?" Alex stiffened. "Round two?"

"Next round of financing. Get us through post, overages,

reshoots. It's all in the prospectus. Can't be more than another sixty thou—"

Alex pulled back. "What? I thought once we shot the presentation, the Nature Channel was stepping in—"

"About that." Clive mopped his brow with his hankie. "Talked that over at lunch today. They've made some changes over there. Big shakeup. New guy's frozen the whole development slate, says he wants to develop fresh properties. He's got some housekeeping deal with Magical Elves, and they're doing a doggie weight-loss show—as if anyone wants to see *that*."

Alex took a second to process. What Clive was saying—it couldn't be what it sounded like. "But the new guy—he'll come around, right? We've got a commitment, right?"

Clive shrugged. "We *had* a commitment," he said. "But our guy is out. And you know how it goes with these executive shuffles—the new regime won't touch the old guard's stuff. Politics."

Alex felt the air go out of his chest. "You said this was a done deal. You told me this was pre-sold."

Clive pulled him back into a half-embrace. "Did I say that? No—pretty sure I didn't say *that*. Anyhow, it's just a speed bump! We'll take it back out to market. Nat Geo and ABC Family passed, but I can take it to Nit-com in Cannes, or Reelz in D.C.—I can do like twenty meetings in a day over there, do the whole dog-and-pony show, lock down international rights."

Alex rubbed a knuckle against his temple. "So you're telling me we've just spent—that *I've* just spent—two hundred thirty thousand dollars on a show that has... no network, no home, no interest at all? We're all on our own? And now you want another sixty thousand?"

Clive straightened up and tugged at his beard. "It's gonna be fine, Alex. You'll see. We just can't lose our focus. You make your day here, then tomorrow you'll call Jess, maybe get us in touch with some people who can help. You and Jess are tight, right? I mean, thinking logistically here, if you talk to Jess, he's not gonna turn around and run to Figgy, would he? Because we don't need to loop her in until we're on firm footing, right? Anyhow, you just go back and cut us a check and we'll get started on round two...."

A bead of sweat slid down the bridge of Alex's nose and dripped into his eye. A siren rang out from the street outside, and the dogs began howling, their voices mingling into a single high-pitched wail. Clive was still talking, still pitching, still clapping Alex's shoulder and telling him it was all going to be fine. But of course it wasn't.

• • •

He stumbled out onto the sidewalk in a daze, blinking hard in the afternoon glare, dried sweat itching his neck. The crew was setting up for another shot inside. He needed to lie down. He needed a drink. He jammed his hands in his pockets and looked up and down at the neighboring storefronts, narrow boutiques and specialty shops crammed against the warehouse-size space with the new Top Dog sign above the door. Forget the show—a deluxe doggie gym in the middle of Hollywood was ridiculous enough. Even more ridiculous was that Alex's name was on the lease—Clive was still incorporating the production when Alex signed the papers. How was this *not* going to fail? What had he been thinking?

He got into the minivan and pulled into traffic. Automatically, he headed south to Koreatown. Miranda lived in a courtyard apartment south of Wilshire that had been graceful and desirable fifty years ago but was now occupied by sketchy old-timers, huge immigrant families, and the occasional slumming hipster. He followed an elderly lady through the front gate and went up the back stairs, squeezing past a man carrying a bouquet of inflatable toys.

Alex paused at her front door and ran a hand through his

hair. He flashed back to Miranda on the street, hand on his neck, voice in his ear: *Whatever I can do that doesn't complicate your life... I'm available.*

He pressed the button on her door, the dull clang like the bell on a kid's bicycle.

From inside came the intoxicating thump of bare feet on hardwood floors. Miranda swung open the door. "Sher?" Her blonde eyelashes cast pinkish shadows down her cheeks. She was in a tufty robe with a beige towel turbaned around her head. "What are you—?"

Alex moved past her. He took in her apartment. It was a one-room studio, with a little kitchenette in the corner and an unmade bed under the window. The walls were off-white and bare except for a pair of spidery line drawings. The whole space was tiny and bright and clean—like the inside of an egg. He reached the center of the room, and not seeing anywhere else to sit, plopped down on the bed.

"Aren't you shooting today? Is everything okay?"

He held his stomach and closed his eyes. "Sure—everything's fine." He looked up at her, his eyes wide and pleading, flashing for a second on Blossom the shar-pei crouched down beside Al.

"So—you're wrapped? All done?"

"*I'm* all done, yeah." He tried to smile.

"You don't look so good."

Alex dropped his elbows and leaned back on the mattress. "I fucked up," he said. The room was spinning. "All the startup money—gone. He told me it was pre-sold. He told me it was a done deal."

Miranda frowned and adjusted her robe, loosening the belt. "Let me get you some water." She rustled up a glass from the cabinet, filled it from the sink, and came and sat beside him.

"Two hundred thirty thousand. And that doesn't even include the rental. We're not *network* rich—that's real money." The floor rocked beneath him.

"You're hyperventilating," she said, reaching out. "Put your head here." She moved over and sat cross-legged against the head-rest, then took his head in two hands and placed it in her lap. "This is a panic attack. I used to get them all the time. You're going to be fine. Just tilt your head back and breathe slowly. Inhale through your nose. Exhale through the mouth. There."

Alex did as he was told, his breath following her whispered prompts. She rubbed his temples with her index fingers. "Now in... now out," she cooed. "Just relax. There you go."

He could feel the cushion of her calves under his head. A wave of calm washed over him. She smelled like licorice. He opened his eyes and looked up. Her face was reversed above him, the light from the window flaring behind the crown of her hair, her lips directly above his eyes. He felt swaddled, enfolded. He reached up and touched a pale freckle on her throat, then began tracing a line across the soft skin of her neck. She put her hand against his cheek. He held steady, holding her gaze. He was floating now, rising up and tilting his head to the side, his mouth pressing up against hers.

She returned the kiss, her hand pressing against his cheek and then down to the top button of his shirt. He reached up and slid his hand inside her robe, found the plush curve of her breast. Her nipple hardened under his fingertips.

"Oh Sher," she said, loosening his shirt. "There you are. Just lay still—let me."

She knelt beside him and in one motion hooked his pants with the arch of her foot and slid them down his legs. She ran her hand down his chest, over his stomach, under his belt. God, she was good at this. His penis popped free and she took hold of it, then slapped it playfully against his stomach.

"You're all good down here," she said. "Everything healed up nicely."

Alex's eyes shot open. "I... I can't believe I'm here."

"Just relax. Don't worry—let me."

"I just haven't—with anyone but—"

"Shhh." She kissed his neck and reached around and pressed down on his hipbone. "She's not here now. I am. No one has to know anything. She's far, far away. Baltimore is a long, long way away...."

He felt a jolt shoot through him. "Baltimore? How do you—"

Miranda loosened her grip. "I spoke with Anne-Marie yesterday—"

"Who? You mean *Figgy's* Anne-Marie?"

"Right—my pilot? It's on top of the pile. We're supposed to get an answer back next—"

Alex lurched backward, batting her away. "Wait, what? You're... doing a show? With Figgy?"

Miranda sat up, her robe draping off one shoulder. "Not official or anything—but... I thought maybe she'd told you. After you were so nice about the script—on the ride home from the doctor's? My agent sent *Gerald & Geraldine* over. I know Figgy's been busy, but Anne-Marie loves it and thinks we have a real shot—Figgy shepherding, me running the room. You know how big this could be for me...."

"So—what's *this* then?" Alex sputtered. "You really think Figgy's going to work with you after—*this*? You and me, we do this, and then you go off and make a show with my—my wife?"

Miranda took his hand in hers, leaned in, and kissed his fingertips. "*She* doesn't have to find out, dummy. She never has to find out. You're still nine months away from your tenth anniversary, right? *You're* not going to tell her—not now. And why would I? That would ruin my career."

A chill shot through Alex's chest. Miranda not only knew about the magic ten, she knew precisely how long he'd been married. All at once, Alex pictured himself at home, tangled up in his sweaty sheets, pathetically jerking off to visions of Miranda's milky white skin... and meanwhile, Miranda was perched on her bed with her laptop, methodically scanning Wikipedia and *Deadline* and Starhomes.com to piece together the particulars of his marriage, her career, the floor plan of his house. He tried to speak. All that came out of his mouth was a raspy stutter.

She pulled back and tilted her head. "Look, I like you, Alex. And I know you like me. This could work out for both of us."

Alex shut his eyes tight and coughed. "I know nothing."

"What?"

He scrambled backward and pulled apart his balled-up clothes. "I thought—I don't know—with the blog and the butcher shop and—I thought you were all about *food*."

Miranda stayed on the bed. "You know what a butcher makes an hour? It's ridiculous. I've gotta look after myself. I'm not like you—I didn't marry up."

He yanked up his jeans and took a wobbly step backward.

"Look, Alex—I'm sorry! I've just been trying to be *helpful*, you know? And don't you want to help me? With you and Figgy both in the business—we can all help each other. Isn't that what it's all about? *Relationships*?"

She reached over and touched his foot, her hand still warm. He said nothing. The silence was broken by a buzzing in Alex's pocket. He plucked out his phone.

It was a text from Figgy. "Emergency kits! School just called my office! Why haven't you taken care of this?"

"I'm sorry—I've gotta go," he said.

• • •

Alex drove across town in a daze, hands locked tight on the steering wheel, the usually soothing voice of the GPS faint and far away. He left Figgy's text unanswered. He resisted the temptation to call and tell her to get off his back, stop treating every dispatch from their proudly laid-back school as a matter of do-or-die urgency.

He arrived at the Pines just before dismissal and collected the emergency bags from the trunk. On the quad, a group of kids was clustered around a guy in a tank top finger-picking an acoustic guitar and a girl in short-shorts who looked to be about twenty-six but couldn't have been more than sixteen. She was scooping tiny colored pellets from an icebox painted with a sign that said "Dipping Dots for Darfur!"

He made his way to the administration office and plopped the bags on the counter. "Hi—I'm Sam and Sylvie's dad? I guess I'm a little delinquent with this—but can I turn it in now?"

A dark-skinned woman with a nose ring popped up from her desk. "Oh hi. I spoke to your wife. All here? Change of clothes, pictures, medications?"

He gave the bags a wan tap. "Yup—good to go."

"You're all set for the comfort recording?"

"Sorry?"

The receptionist flashed a tight smile. "The comfort recording. Part of our innovation initiative—you've been getting emails about it? Very exciting. Instead of traditional emergency letters, we're doing digital audio recordings. The studies show stress levels are dramatically reduced by the actual voice of loved ones in times of crisis."

Alex shook his head, a barrage of half-read e-mails now coming back to him. "I guess I'm a little unclear about the whole 'times of crisis' thing. What 'times of crisis' are we talking about here?"

"Earthquakes, obviously," she said. "But also flooding, gas leaks, shootings, police lockdowns, wildfires, urban uprisings—we need to be prepared for *all* contingencies, don't we? It's L.A., after all!"

She pulled open a drawer under the counter and produced a

handheld recorder. "Would you prefer recording a separate message to each child or would you rather address both children at once? We're absolutely amenable to shared messaging."

"Sorry—what?" Alex pinched his nose.

"Two recordings or one?"

"One is fine."

She handed him the recorder, nodding sagely. She stayed put, intent on ensuring that he properly completed the assigned task. He cleared his throat and looked around the room at the three or four other people working at their desks. No one paid him the slightest attention.

He clicked the red button and held the recorder to his mouth. "Hi Sylvie honey! And Sam—hey kiddo! Dad here. This is pretty weird, right? I guess something bad has happened? That's why you're hearing this? But it's going to be okay, okay? You're safe here at school with the teachers and the nice nose-ring lady and the kid who plays guitar on the quad? Sam, he's your buddy, right? Go get your sister and hang with him and I promise I'll be there as soon as I can, okay?"

He looked over at the receptionist and hunched his shoulders. She smiled and motioned for him to go on. He paused, not sure what else to say. He closed his eyes. At once, an image formed. Sam and Sylvie were crouched in a darkened classroom, faces smudged, strands of insulation hanging from the ceiling, electrical wires whipping overhead, flashlight beams cutting through the murk. And then he saw himself in his own kitchen at home, pinned against the floor in a pile of rubble, his voice calling out for help.

"But I may not be able to get to you," he was saying now, voice trailing out from the wreckage. "It's a time of crisis, right? I may be—I don't know, stuck under the fridge."

He kept going, voice trembling, the events of the day making the prospect of calamity entirely plausible. "The point is, shit *happens.* It just does. So if this really is the last time I get to say anything to you... God."

Alex coughed and looked up above the receptionist's desk at a square of sky through a high window. "Sam, honey. Are you gay? You're gay, right? You poor sweetie, that's gonna be hard. I always knew. You're so *mad* at me. Why are you so mad at me? I'm not mad at *you*—really I'm not. What other eleven-year-old has his own line of cosmetics? Do you know how incredible that is? You know *you* made more money than I did last year?"

The receptionist leaned forward with a look of concern. "Sir—maybe we should stop here and get some *tea*? Would you like some tea?"

He put up a finger and closed his eyes again. "Sylvie, honey. Oh God, Sylvie. You're such a princess. I've spoiled you rotten, I know. You're kind of a brat, aren't you? At least with Mom. That's my fault. The truth is that some sick part of me loves it when you ignore her and act rude to her—because when you do, *I'm* the favorite. You may not know it now, but that's some unhealthy vain shit right there."

"Sir, please," the receptionist said.

Alex took a single step back. He paused for a breath. "The point is, I'm sorry. I'm so sorry for not being a better dad—I've been so crazy, about Mom's show and the move and the rest of it. I've been checked out. But the truth is you guys are both so strong and funny and smart. I wish I could claim more credit, but everything that's good about you is yours alone—you came in fully loaded, and you'll have what's good about you long after I'm gone. So don't worry. You've got each other and you've got your mom—and she's the most loyal, ferocious lioness in the jungle. She'll keep you safe. She's a lot like you, Sylvie. And Sam, you too. What I'm trying to say, kids, is that being your dad is the best thing I've ever been even involved in. And you should know that I'm thinking about you even if my body has been cut in two by an industrial-grade refrigerator."

Alex clicked the stop button and put the recorder on the counter. The receptionist was silent, her eyes narrowed and expression blank. Behind her, the principal and a few others had come out of their offices and were standing around watching the show.

"All set then," he said, turning to the door. "See you at the gala."

Fifteen

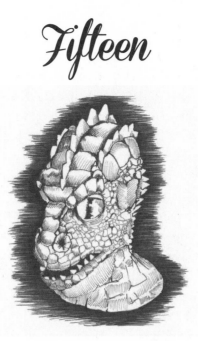

When he got home from school, Alex plopped the kids in front of the TV and ducked into the yard with an iPod, a bottle of Sancerre, and a bag of tortilla chips. He felt winded and lightheaded, a faint hum ringing in his ears. He sat on a bench on the far side of the lawn, shoveling back chips between slugs of wine. The Circle Jerks blasted in his earbuds as he picked through the wreckage of the day. The meltdown at school, the scene with Miranda, Clive's money grab—everything was collapsing around him. No, everything had already collapsed. He was just finally realizing it.

The encounter with Miranda—of all the day's humiliations, that had been the worst. How he'd gone limp on her bed, laid his head in her lap, arched his hips up as she slid his pants down, then scrambled away as she matter-of-factly explained her intentions—thinking of it now, his stomach tightened into a ball. Had he really been stupid enough to mistake her Hollywood hustle for actual attraction? Had there been anything real there at all? If she hadn't mentioned her script and the deal with Figgy, would he have gone through with it? Even though he hadn't technically consummated anything, he'd gone far enough. He'd cheated on his pregnant wife—what an asshole. Worse: what a cliché. And for what? For the sex? It would've been nice, amazing even—Miranda was so young and smelled so good, and he might never again get a chance to press up against a woman like that, to touch and taste and plunder all that freshness. And hadn't Figgy told him (in so many words, way back when) that as long as he kept quiet, he could do what he wanted? So why hadn't he gone ahead—why had he retreated like a prude the moment she'd mentioned Figgy? Now that he played the scene back, he knew. Sex was beside the point. The pull Miranda exerted, the force that drew him to her bed that afternoon—sex was just a flavor in the air, a hint of something else. He hadn't gone to Miranda to get laid; he'd gone because he was empty, defeated, wrecked. He'd ached for the way she made him feel when they talked and ate together. He'd gone to Miranda's apartment for the same reason he'd tried writing the punk rock book. He hadn't been horny—he'd been hungry.

What if Figgy found out? She might already know—that's part of why he loved her, her knowingness. It was miraculous. The idea of life without her flooded over him in a panic. The life they'd built together—their kids, their home, the whole mess of it—he had to protect that, get it back. All his plotting and score keeping and stupidity—none of it made sense now, it was all bound up in his fear of her leaving him, eclipsing him. And when she'd gone to Baltimore, it felt like he'd been ripped in two, like he might never get her back.

Then the sun was out of the sky and he was still sitting here, the bag empty and the bottle drained beside him. He needed to go inside and check in with the kids, see about dinner, corral them for baths, books, and bed. But he couldn't get up. Across the lawn, the dog appeared from behind an azalea bush and loped toward Alex, tongue lolling out of its mouth. He ruffled the fur around her neck and she plopped down at his feet. Alex brushed the crumbs off his shirt and stared up at the house. A face appeared in the façade, tufty bangs of rhododendron framing two top-floor windows, the patio doors below a crooked grimace. They'd lived here almost six months, and it still didn't feel like home. Would it ever? Regarding it from a distance like this, he felt a familiar mix of awe and discomfort. He might never shake the sense that this place, this whole life, wasn't *his*— this was Figgy's prize, her dream realized, her reward for a job that only got more punishing the better she did. He could enjoy the house, luxuriate in it even, but whatever pleasure he felt would forever be fogged by guilt... over what? His dependence? Her stress? The fact that he'd given up his livelihood to enjoy the spoils of her success? The fundamental fact that he was now a man who didn't provide, married to a woman who did?

And what the hell was *that*? The guilt, the anxiety, the teeth gnashing—was all that just symptomatic of some knuckle-dragging, hunter-gatherer, prideful *manliness* lodged in a deep cavity of his soft, gushy selfhood? No, never. That wasn't him. Marrying Figgy, having Sam and Sylvie—these were the most important things he'd ever done or would do. He was a caretaker, a householder. He was a new man. Making a life for his family didn't make him a mooch. And whether or not he ever felt like he deserved this life, he was here, in it. Somehow, whether through an accumulation of decisions or the inextricable pull of fate, he'd moved into the very house he'd peered into twenty years before, imagining an ideal imaginary future. The revolution had come. He'd landed in this life. It was time to stop agonizing over it and make some actual use of it.

He looked back up at the house. The face was gone, the thin

light of evening turning the garish pink of the house dusty and mild, all the bright colors muted in shadows. If he had any chance of repairing the damage he'd done, he had to start here, with the house. And in this moment anyway, in this half-light, he imagined the house becoming theirs, stripped of its power to impose and intimidate. If he could just find a way to *disinfect* it, to disempower it. Then they could all just relax and fill it with their messy, rowdy, twitchy, totally unfit selves and call it home once and for all.

Alex got up and headed inside, Albert trotting along beside him. The bag of mezuzahs was right where he'd left it, on the upper shelf of a broom closet right next to the hemp fabric bag his mom had left the day she'd come to visit. He brought both bags into the kitchen and spilled the contents onto the kitchen island, picking up a booklet and flipping to a page on "declaring your spiritual intentions." This was just the sort of language he normally dismissed as New Age twaddle. Now it was clear: The twaddlier the better.

Sam and Sylvie poked up their heads from the couch. "What's that?" Sylvie said.

"Magic stuff."

Sam wandered over and picked up a bundle of dried sage. "Stinky," he said, giving it a dubious whiff. "What're you supposed do with it?"

Alex flipped through the booklet. "The sage we burn. The water we drizzle. The mezuzahs go on the doorposts."

Sylvie gave a vial of holy water a shake. "Seriously?"

"Seriously. But before we do any of that—we all go outside and pee on the wall."

Sam and Sylvie looked at each other.

"You in?" Alex said.

"Absolutely," said Sylvie, already halfway out the door.

• • •

Alex had a week before Figgy returned home from Baltimore, time enough to get some portion of his shit together. He gave Rosa the week off and started packing lunches, catching up on house repairs, doing drop-off and pickup, and coordinating the ridiculous array of the kids' extracurriculars (Sam: weaving, improv, potpourri; Sylvie: soccer, ballet, glassblowing). He emailed Helen Bamper and offered to help with the school fundraising gala, which this year was being staged on the New York Street set of the Warners backlot. He made it a policy to say yes to everything, the volunteering and the schlepping and all the daily business of the domestic first responder. Days were spent doing errands and chasing the kids from class to appointment, after which he'd come home and prepare elaborate meals for three— paella, cumin-rubbed yakitori, five-spice fried chicken. Keeping busy with food and the kids meant not dealing with Figgy's pregnancy or Clive's production or the humiliation with Miranda or any of the rest of it. He ignored, for instance, the delinquent-payment notice that had recently arrived from the bank about the home equity line of credit. That was immediately stuffed deep into the pile, face down to hide the red band across the letterhead.

The kids, for their part, seemed only dimly aware of Daddy's domestic reengagement; Sylvie made no mention of her special bento-box lunches and managed only a confused thanks when he presented her with a crushed-velvet skating outfit he ordered off Amazon. And Sam just seemed embarrassed when Alex picked him up early from school one day for a trip to LACMA to see the Estée Lauder exhibit.

Communications with Figgy, meanwhile, were icy—he couldn't tell during their catch-up calls how she was doing beyond feeling nauseous and overworked. Their conversations were entirely focused on the kids, Alex hearing in her tone a tacit agreement that they should be face-to-face for the big talk. A few nights before she was set to come home, he tried to warm things up, telling her about the cleansing ritual and how they'd stunk up the house with sage smoke and how they'd made up special incantations for every room. (Alex was most proud of his blessing for the bathroom: "May this be a place of... release.")

"What a fun dad," she said, her voice plangent and impossibly far away. "Couldn't you have waited for me?"

Her plane was due to arrive in Burbank at noon on Saturday. The whole morning Alex was a wreck, skittering around the kitchen preparing a big shabu-shabu spread. As her arrival drew close, he grew more and more anxious, checking his phone over and over to see if her plane had landed and if she'd met the driver at baggage claim. Now that she was coming home, the avoidance, he knew, was over. The time had come to deal.

She finally came in the door just after two o'clock, keys clanging against the counter and bags thumping on the floor. She tumbled onto the couch and gathered up the kids in a big groaning hug. "Mama!" they cried, pawing and nuzzling. She looked great, her hair full and her cheeks soft and peachy.

He leaned into the squirming pile and landed a kiss on her cheek. She untangled herself from the kids, got up from the couch, and walked past Alex on her way to the fridge. Sam trailed behind her, one hand locked on the end of her shirt.

"Souvenirs?" Sam said, beaming up at her. "What'd you bring us?"

"Hold on, kiddo. We have any tea?" She smiled as the light from the inside of the fridge flooded over her face. "Oh God—all my food! My own kitchen! My own children!"

Alex got up behind her and draped an arm over her shoulder. "And your husband, too."

She looked over and gave him the briefest of smiles. "Yes— that too."

"So Mom Mom Mom," Sylvie said, joining them at the fridge, the three of them clustered around her in a tight knot. "Did you? Bring souvenirs?"

"Hang on, monkey," she said, pouring herself a glass of iced tea and lowering onto a stool at the kitchen island. "Just let me get settled. I'm all cramped from the plane. I think there's a yoga class at four—Alex, where's your phone? Mine's dead."

Sylvie rolled her eyes and made a beeline for Figgy's backpack, ripping open the top and reaching inside. "Where?"

"It's nothing, guys. Baltimore ain't exactly a retail bonanza. Little box is for Sylvie. Long one is Sam's." She took a long draw on her straw and cocked an eyebrow at Alex. "There's something in there for you too, Alex. Manila folder, near the top. But maybe not now. Open it later."

The kids tore off the wrapping on their presents—a charm bracelet for Sylvie and a silk necktie for Sam. "Pretty!" Sylvie said, motioning with her wrist up like a hand model. "Chic," Sam said, extending his chin as he double-looped a perfect Windsor knot.

As the kids began parading back and forth with their new accessories, Figgy picked up Alex's phone from the counter. "I need to check the class schedule," she said.

Alex took a few steps toward the backpack, suddenly overcome with a need to know the contents of the folder. "Can I?" he called over the heads of the kids. Figgy didn't respond. He opened the flap of the backpack and poked inside. Wedged between a pair of *Natashas* scripts was a manila folder with "ALEX" written in Sharpie on the tab. The folder was legal size. He could see documents spilling out from the edges. His heart stuttered.

"You want to do this now?" she asked. She was standing across the kitchen island, eyes cast down, fingers fiddling madly on the screen of his phone. "It's not really a present-present."

He swallowed hard, the packet trembling in his hands. He looked back up at Figgy, her attention locked on the screen. She wasn't nosing around his text messages, was she? He'd switched out his SIM card the week before, hadn't he? Or had he forgotten? The last text exchange he'd had with Miranda before the awfulness in her apartment had been a suggestive, not terribly clever riff on a story online about a restaurant in Shanghai that served fox vagina—she wouldn't stumble upon that, would she?

"Go on then," she said, not looking up. "Ten's a big one. We have to start planning."

Shit. Shit shit shit. Huck had been right all along. Figgy was no dummy. This was the official notification, just three months shy of the big anniversary. She'd spent her downtime in Baltimore meeting with lawyers, stashing money, and strategizing a clean split. And she was a few swipes away from discovering all the justification she'd ever need. His mouth went dry.

"Go on," she said.

He did. The type swam around his vision, smaller than it should be, with times and confirmation numbers. It was an itinerary. Five days in Napa Valley. A reservation at the French Laundry. Some kind of class at the Culinary Arts Institute.

"I know it doesn't make up for me being gone," she said. "But it'll be fun, right? We'll get my mom to stay with the kids? Take an early tenth-anniversary trip?"

Alex dropped the folder to the counter, his mouth dry.

"Look—I'm sorry I was so checked out while I was away," she said. "Things were so *bad* when I left. I want them to be better now."

"Me, too."

She gave him a sidelong look. "Are you crying?"

He coughed and swiped his cheek. "Maybe a little."

• • •

Figgy was still upstairs getting ready for yoga class when Alex's phone buzzed. Fuck—in his frantic preparation for Figgy's return, he'd forgotten to switch out his SIM card, and Miranda had chosen this precise moment to check in. He hadn't heard from her since that day in her apartment. "Hey stranger—How U?" He deleted the message, stuffed the phone in his pocket, and went to check on lunch. He'd just assumed that he and Miranda would never speak again—what else was there to say? A minute later, his phone buzzed again. After a solid fifteen seconds of resisting, he checked it.

"Just following up re script. Don't mean to pest, but I hear Figgy's back today and DYING to know. Has she read it? Super excited!"

Alex pursed his lips and blew out a long, toneless whistle. Was she serious? She was still working the connection, still trying to get her pilot read. He took a deep breath and thumbed out a response: "Hi. Figgy read your script. Told me to tell you: It's a pass. Sorry!"

That closed the loop, didn't it? He made a mental note to circle back with Anne-Marie, find some natural way to confirm that *Gerald & Geraldine* was indeed just where he thought it was: deep in a pile of unread submissions that had about as much a chance of getting made as Alex did of finishing his punk rock novel. He headed up the stairs, through the bedroom, and down the hall toward Figgy's closet. He stopped at the closed door.

"Hon?" He shouldn't let this drag out. "We have to talk."

"Hang on a sec." Her voice was muffled by the floor-to-ceiling racks of clothes. "I can't find my good stretchy pants—"

"No, seriously—we need to talk."

"Can it wait? I'm kind of—"

Alex rested his head against the door. "I need to catch you up on some stuff."

"Stuff?" He could hear a drawer close, then another. "What stuff?"

"The trip you planned? That's so nice, so great—and a big

surprise. A really big surprise. It's just… when I saw that pack-et—I thought it was something different."

"Did you want a new barbecue? Because we can still—"

"No. Not a barbecue. I thought you were serving me. Like, with papers. With our anniversary coming up, I thought you were going to end it. I thought maybe you and that guy Franklin Sykes, or maybe Zev the DP—"

"Franklin Sykes? Please. The guy barely bathes, and I'm pretty sure he's got TB. And Zev? He's dating a twenty-four-year-old from Anaheim."

"I was afraid you were trading up. For a newer model. Be-cause of the ten-year thing. You know that, right?"

Alex waited for a response from inside the closet. None came. He plowed on. "I'm really glad that envelope wasn't what I thought it was, but look—I need you to know. While you were away—I did a bad thing. You were gone. I just got into this really fucked-up place. I felt like, how come *she* gets to go off and make her show while I deal with the house and kids and everything—which is crazy, I know. I mean, you've got a *job* and so do I, right? I run the business of the family, and you run an actual *business*. But you actually make something, you're out in the actual *world,* and what do I have to complain about? Anyway, I haven't been able to tell you because I've been afraid what you'll say."

It was quiet behind the closet door. Then Figgy said, "What did you do?"

"I'm just warning you—it's bad," he said.

"How bad?"

"Bad bad."

Silence. He took a big breath. "I got involved… in a *reality* show. Clive's reality show. I started working on it."

There was a beat, then: "The dog show?"

"Yes, the dog show." Alex paused. "But really it's a show about people—"

"Oh, don't start. He's been shopping that around forever. You know he hit me up a year ago. Why? What did you do?"

Alex's heart pounded. "It was at your party—Clive approached me about coming aboard as EP. I thought it sounded nuts, but then I wrote him a check and before I knew it, I was all in." He leaned his head against the closed door and waited a beat. "So what I'm saying is, I've been so crazy and I've had all these secrets and I totally understand if… if you *do* want to file papers… before the anniversary. If you want out, I won't fight or try to take the money you made—it's yours."

The closet door swung open. Figgy was standing still in the center of the closet, one hand on her stomach. Her face was white.

Alex grimaced and took a step forward, bracing himself for her response. "So—what do you think?"

"Call Dr. Hudson," she said. "I'm bleeding."

• • •

By the time they got across town, Alex was dizzy. He'd managed to get from the east side to Beverly Hills in twenty-five minutes, which he knew must count as some sort of record but which involved two illegal left turns and a maybe-yellow-probably-red light on San Vicente that would undoubtedly result in a $550 fine stapled to an official notice with one of those grainy automated pictures of himself silently mouthing the word "shit." He kept his eyes forward the whole way, unable to look beside him, where he knew Figgy was hemorrhaging their unborn baby all over the minivan passenger seat.

As he pulled into the underground garage, he worked up the courage to face her. She was calm, her hand resting serenely on her stomach. Okay, so maybe she wasn't bleeding out. She put a hand on his thigh. "Calm down," she said. "It's all going to be okay. *You* know all about spotting, don't you Mr. Bloody Jock Strap? It's nothing. This is just a precaution."

"Just sit tight," he said, jumping out of the minivan and hurrying around to help her. By the time he got around to her door, she was already sashaying across the parking lot as if heading in for a routine checkup.

"Slow down—no jostling!" he called, chasing her toward the elevators.

Dr. Hudson's office was crowded, the overstuffed shabby-chic sofas in the waiting room occupied by women in various stages of pregnancy, a few couples, and new moms with their infants swaddled tight against their engorged new-mom bosoms. Alex summoned a nurse, who thankfully ushered them straight into an exam room. After a brief wait, which Figgy passed flipping through a copy of *Us Weekly*, Dr. Hudson glided through the door, her clogs making a pleasant wooden thonk on the linoleum. Her strawberry blonde hair was tied back in a complicated bun, framing her soft features. "How you doing, Fig honey?" she said. "Why don't you just hop up on the table here and let's see what we got."

"Hi, Janie," Figgy said, an easy familiarity instantly taking over, Dr. Hudson having delivered both of their babies, in each case maintaining a cheerful calm during what Alex could only describe as a violent assault. She snapped on a pair of rubber gloves and wheeled over an ultrasound machine. Alex stayed in the corner, arms crossed tightly across his chest, as Dr. Hudson fitted Figgy's feet into the stirrups and ducked between her knees, a concert harpist approaching her instrument. She was simultaneously elegant and professional, Alex thought, the sort of doctor who'd never even think of interrupting a pelvic exam to, say, chat about a Comedy Central roast.

"I see some blood—it looks dark," she said.

Dark blood? A chill rolled through Alex's chest. The baby was dead inside her. And it was his fault—he'd tried to prevent the pregnancy, then betrayed her in more ways than he could even process right now. If he'd just been more supportive, kept Figgy home, forced her to rest. He flashed on the dewy face of Helen Bamper, that night in Hawaii: *"I just want things to be easy for him."* He hadn't made *anything* easy.

Dr. Hudson pulled off her gloves and adjusted a knob. "Dark is good—means the bleeding's not ongoing. You're not passing any tissue, and your cervix looks great. Really, *gorgeous*. But there's still the possibility of something sub-chorionic. Let's check the sonogram."

Figgy pulled up her shirt and Dr. Hudson flipped off the lights, then squirted her stomach with a strand of clear jelly and pressed down with a plastic knobbed wand. Alex kept his eyes locked on the monitor as the ghostly image wobbled with static. After a moment, the blur of white formed into something Alex was sure was a head, bobbing over the rounded curve of a spine. One second it was just pixelated fuzz and the next it was something entirely different: an unmistakable shape. A body. A little life. A baby.

Time seemed to slow, then stop. "Well hello there," he heard himself say.

"Strong heartbeat," the doctor said. "Looks like there may be a small clot here, but nothing to worry about."

Alex unballed his fists as the doctor clicked the lights back on and pulled off a glove. "My guess is this is just some attachment bleeding."

"Attachment bleeding?"

"Common in early pregnancy," she said. "Happens when the embryo attaches to the placenta. It's no longer just a mass of dividing cells—it's latching on, getting comfy. Which doesn't guarantee this can't still proceed to miscarriage, so I want you to take it easy for at least a few days. Pelvic rest—no sex, no douching. Take your time getting dressed—and I'll see you for your regular exam in two weeks. Okay?"

And with that, Dr. Hudson winked at Alex and headed out the door. Alex left his place in the corner and pushed a strand of Figgy's hair away from her face. At his touch, her eyes went glassy and her brow screwed up into hard knot. "Oh my God," she said, her voice froggy with emotion. "Oh my fucking God."

"Didn't you hear? You're fine. The baby's fine!"

Figgy sat upright and began sobbing. "It's *attached*," she cried. "I don't know what I thought—maybe I thought it was coming out today? Then I wouldn't have to go through all this. How am I going to have a baby, with two shows and the kids and *you* coming apart?"

"Oh, honey," Alex said, conviction clicking into place. "Of *course* it's a good thing. You saw the ultrasound, right? I know it's early, but I'm pretty sure I saw a little something between the legs. A little brother for Sam and Sylvie—you'll finally get your Abe!"

She looked up at him and blinked, a fat tear trailing down her cheek.

He went on: "The vasectomy, I never should've done that without telling you. I'm sorry."

She sniffed. "Well, I guess I'm sorry for getting knocked up without really talking it over."

Alex shook his head and laughed. Her eyes were bright and moist behind her glasses, her cheeks slick with tears. "You really thought I was filing papers on you?"

"I did, yeah."

"Stupid man. You're stuck with me. Get that through your skull, will you?" A droplet trailed down her cheek.

Here they were again, she collapsing just as he came together—their same old dance. Their insanities moved in tandem, magnetic poles held together by some invisible force. He flashed on a memory from two summers ago—they'd taken a family trip to the mountains near Arrowhead, renting a cabin with wood-paneled walls. On their first night he and Figgy had made love in the narrow bed, the firelight and the thin, pine-scented air giving their usual dance a hot, dreamy urgency. In one particularly intense moment, Alex grunting, Figgy moaning, and the headboard thumping against the wall, a voice called out from the adjoining room: "Daaad? Mooom? Are you okay?"

Alex froze. How was Sam still awake? "We're fine honey," he called. "Go back to sleep."

He and Figgy giggled and held each other close, whispering worries about what sort of mutual torture their eight-year-old son had imagined. The next morning over oatmeal, Alex decided he better have a little father-son talk. Maybe this was a teachable moment. "So I guess you heard some noise from our room last night?"

"Mm hmm," he said, spooning a mound of oatmeal.

"Do you want to talk about it at all?"

Sam rolled his eyes.

"Are you sure? It's okay. I mean, do you know what was going on?"

Sam swallowed and looked into his lap. "You were struggling," he declared. "But not bad. It was the good struggle."

Alex had left the conversation there, happily reporting back to Figgy that Sam was fine. The boy had gotten it exactly right. Alex thought of those words now—struggling, but not bad: the good struggle—and looked at Figgy collecting herself on the exam stable, his chest swelling, her pregnancy in this moment becoming real and even inevitable. Of course they would have a third child. That had always been the plan. They'd have a big life, a big family—it would be impossible, and they'd make mistakes, but they'd struggle through.

"It's good, Fig—it's really good," he said. "All this puts everything in perspective. New life. Dwarfs everything. Even the money—it's all just a side issue, right?"

Figgy buttoned up her shirt and shot him a look. "*What* money?"

"The two hundred thousand," he said. "Two hundred thirty, really. The investment in Clive's show. That's what I was telling you in the closet."

Figgy jammed a foot into a sneaker and shook her head. "Two hundred thirty thousand—you gave Clive two hundred thirty thousand dollars? For his *dog* show?"

"It wasn't about the dogs—" he began, then thought better and stopped. "He wanted a lot more—that's when I got out. He wanted another sixty."

Figgy pulled on her other shoe and stood up, her expression consumed with calculations. "Two hundred thirty thousand—after taxes," she repeated. "This isn't fucking play money, do you know that? Do you have any idea how many scripts that is? How much work I've got to do to make up for that?"

Alex kept quiet. He had no idea.

"And besides, do you realize that all the work I'm doing could stop tomorrow? That's how my work is. It comes—and then one day, boom, it stops coming!"

He winced and sat down on the exam table. "I get it. But this was an investment. You don't know anyone who's made a bad investment?"

"Maybe—but not like this, not in *secret*." Her voice was loud. "Tell me, you've been keeping this to yourself how long?"

"Just a few weeks. Since you were away."

She got up and went for the door, then swiveled around and faced him, her nose a few inches from his face. "I'm going up to the nurse's station to make my appointment, but I need to know right now—is there anything *else* you want to tell me, now that we're sharing?"

Alex held up his hands defensively. "No... no! Absolutely not," he said. "That's it. Let's go home."

Figgy turned toward the door. "I fucking hope so."

• • •

Alex knew he owed nothing to Clive and would be better off avoiding him entirely, but in the two weeks since he'd walked off the set of *Top Dog*, he'd come to accept that he couldn't duck him forever. So when Clive called suggesting they meet at the Top Dog storefront for a progress report, he agreed, setting the time for 3:30 on a Tuesday, after pickup at the Pines. Showing up for their meeting with kids, Alex thought, would send a clear message: Sam and Sylvie were now his priority.

"Look kids—a dolly!" Alex said, ushering them through the door and pointing toward a wheeled cart in the corner. "Doesn't that look fun?"

Clive stepped forward and flashed his palms up in a feeble attempt to ward them off. "Please, kids! Careful! That's rental equipment! I've got a security deposit!"

The kids charged past him, Sam grabbing the handle of the cart and shoving Sylvie across the empty floor. The ramps, the hurdles, the tunnels, the cones—everything from the agility course was gone. All that remained were the lights, the cables, and the carts loaded with sound and camera equipment. Alex turned and wrinkled his nose at Clive. "So—the business, not happening? What happened to the Barsaghians?"

"They lost at regionals," Clive said. "Fiasco. Gina was right— the shar-pei actually peed on one of the judges. Gina went nuts. Which would've been great, but the cameras missed it all. So we lost our third act. Then the dad came in and said they've reconsidered the whole thing. Their relationship is too important, he says—they want to close the new place and get off the show."

"So the show's done then? What's all this stuff still doing here?"

"That's what I wanted to talk to you about," Clive said, his voice dropping into a conspiratorial whisper. "I want to extend an offer. I know everything didn't work out quite how we'd planned in phase one, but really Alex, you were so great. You could have just capitalized and dematerialized, but you didn't. You showed up, got your hands dirty. You showed real creativity, real enterprise."

Alex shook his head and frowned. "Thank you Mr. C," he said, wanting very much not to feel flattered but feeling flattered nonetheless. Clive had worked him over, played on his vanity, fleeced him—but being back here, he was reminded that Clive was right about one thing: He'd actually done his job pretty well. And he'd liked doing it, working with him, doing stuff in the world. As he ducked his head into the darkened kitchen area, Sylvie toppled off the dolly and landed sideways against a coil of cable, her screech echoing across the room.

"I'm okay!" she called, already on her feet and charging at Sam.

Clive motioned at the kids. "Maybe you could've left the kids at home? I thought this was going to be more of a *business* meeting."

"There's no real *business* here from what I can see," Alex said. "Besides, as long as the kids are free to run around, we can talk all we like."

Clive took him by the elbow. "So, look, I know you have a nice thing with Al—talk to him, get him back on board. Then we reshoot the pilot, do it right. We just need to get going on round two. All that's missing is capitalization."

And there it was again. The ask.

Alex stepped back and motioned around the room. "Would you look around, Clive? You really want to drag that poor guy back into the mess we made? Let Al and Gina stay in their shop with their dogs. Let them be. Besides, I can't just keep *sneaking* money—from my wife, remember? Your stepdaughter?"

"It's yours just as much as hers. You're married, remember? I'm just saying, I know that girl, and I know she doesn't need to be bothered with this now—she's got enough on her plate."

"No. She doesn't need to be bothered with it now because you already bothered her with it *a year ago*. And she turned you down—not because she had a lot on her plate but because she knows you better than I do. Look Mr. C., I loved working with you, I really did. And maybe you can salvage this thing—you've got enough footage for a pretty decent pilot. Cut it together right and you might really have something. Maybe it'll be the next *Cornpone*, and we'll all come visit you on the macadamia nut farm. But I can't keep going."

Clive stiffened and puffed out his chest. "I get it. Not everyone has the stomach for show business. But hey: I've got other investors. I'll get the Barsaghians back in here, get up and running again. I've still got a two-year lease on this place."

Just then Sylvie ran the dolly into a six-foot high lighting rig. It went toppling to the floor, the sound of crashing metal and glass exploding into the room. She froze in place, then turned to the two of them with an apologetic grimace.

"For godsakes, Sylvie," Clive exploded, his face now deep red. "I told you to be careful!"

Alex started across the room to help, then stopped short and swiveled around to Clive. "Wait a minute—you know what? *You* don't have a two-year lease on this place. I do. And I think you better get all this stuff out of here."

• • •

Over the next two weeks, Alex and Figgy fell into an unfamiliar routine. She worked from home, and he eased off on the good-dad campaign, enlisting Rosa to help with shopping and carpool. Figgy propped her laptop on a pile of pillows on the sofa while Alex churned out meals in the kitchen and scribbled notes in a pocket-size Moleskine. They let the phone ring and shut off the

WiFi, limiting their media exposure to a stack of Hayao Miyazaki DVDs they put on when the kids came home from school. They didn't talk about the pregnancy or work or *Top Dog*—it was as if they were hunkered down against a storm, and they'd all resolved to stay safe inside until they got the all clear. Figgy was pleasant enough despite being almost completely silent. She's processing, Alex thought. She's still pissed about the money, wiped out from Baltimore, and scared about the baby. Give her time.

The kids greeted the news of the pregnancy with wild enthusiasm, Sylvie especially. She burrowed her face in Figgy's belly, closely examining the still-tiny bulge and announcing that she and her new baby sister would be best friends forever and ever. Sam begged to differ, telling her she should stop pawing at Mom and let their little brother alone.

With each day, Figgy seemed to soften just a little. He'd bring her a blanket or a bowl of soup, and he'd see in her face an old, familiar fondness. It wasn't the happily unhinged look she used to get when she'd pull him close to inhale his smell. It was more like the warmth he felt from her in those foggy, disoriented years when the kids were small. She used to say that that's when she really fell in love with him, when she saw him with their babies. Now that another was on the way, he could sense the recommencement of an old rhythm between them, steady and equal, each beat animated by their combined love. It was true what she'd said that night when he'd decided to quit his job, for her anyway: Caretaking was hot.

By the time the big Pines fundraiser rolled around, Alex was antsy, ready for reentry to the world. He rallied Figgy to get up, get dressed, and join him. He'd done all the menu prep with the caterer and had promised Helen Bamper he'd help coordinate— and anyway, he said, "it'll be fun. There's a fortune teller!" Figgy groaned but reluctantly agreed.

As the two of them were heading upstairs to get ready, Alex

looked over at Sam, who'd been strenuously ignoring Alex's pleas to go outside and play all afternoon. He was now splayed out on the couch with a copy of *Elle Decor*. "Hey kiddo," he called across the room. "Come upstairs to the bathroom? Just for a sec."

Alex hurried ahead and found what he was looking for under the bathroom sink. "Okay—let's try this," he said, pulling a bee-pollen moisturizer from an assortment of Sammy's Salves. "Could you maybe, I don't know—moisturize me?"

Sam crossed his arms and gave Alex an appraising look. "You're joking."

"I'm not. I'm all yours. This is a big-deal party and my skin is—I don't know—chapped? Dried up?"

"It's *dire*, Dad," he said. "You're like Lee Van Cleef." Sam moved to the counter and picked up a bottle. "But we're better off with a mint-cucumber mask—that ought to bring some life back."

Alex spent the next half hour submitting to Sam's treatment—which was, he quickly discovered, entirely lovely. As Sam applied a warm washcloth to his face and the layer of hardened lotion cracked and began to melt away, he let out a long, contented groan. Figgy rummaged through her closet, trying on various dresses and modeling them for her boys. After Sam had signed off on a bright green cocktail dress for Figgy and a three-button suit for Alex, the two of them kissed the kids and headed for the door. On their way out, Figgy told Alex she wasn't bringing a wallet or keys. "You got me, Big Daddy?"

"I do."

On the freeway, Alex looked over at her applying a fresh coat of lipstick. "Look—no traffic," he said. "Five clear lanes on a Friday—at rush hour. How lucky is that?"

She snapped on the lipstick cap. "Would you be quiet? Say that out loud and you'll jinx it."

He rolled his eyes and poked his head out the car window, looking toward the dusky sky. "You really think the traffic gods are listening right now? You *know* we don't actually control the traffic with our words, right?"

"Just keep quiet, will you?" She tugged at her bra strap and asked, "Why are we going to this thing again?"

"It's important. The school is raising money for a sister school in Pico Union—they're getting iPads for all the fifth graders. It's the least we can do."

"Can't we just write a check?"

"We could, sure—but I feel like we need to show up." A moment passed, the hum of tires on pavement rushing through his open window. Was this how people in their position made peace with themselves, by overpaying for fancy parties where they bid on things they didn't need and socialized with people they never saw otherwise? He pushed his head back into his leather seat and tugged at his necktie. "Doesn't it bother you?" he said slowly. "How lucky we are? We have it so good—it's incredibly unfair."

"Hey—I earned what I have. Do you have any idea how hard I've worked? How much shit I've had to shovel?"

"I didn't mean that—absolutely you deserve it," he said. "I'm just not sure *I* do."

"Sure you do," Figgy said, smiling. "You were clever enough to marry me, weren't you?"

Alex leaned forward in his seat and slapped the steering wheel. "It's just—I've been a bit of a Federline, you know? I'm not blaming you, but it's just *hard*, being married to someone like you."

"What do you mean, 'someone like you'? Like me, how?"

"You know—queen bee. Bacon bringer. Power Jewess. All that. I guess I just have this deep down *thing* that wants to be at the top of a mountain with you kneeling next to me in a bikini. I'm not sure I can ever just look after you and the kids and have that be *it* for me—I can't *not* do anything else."

"Okay—so what? What else can't you *not* do?"

Alex took a long breath. "Hear me out," he said. "The storefront where we did the dog show—it's three thousand square feet, great location, twenty-space lot in back. The other day, when I was there with Clive—the kids were running around and I just kind of saw it. Tables around the perimeter, all the adults eating and talking, all the kids climbing around one of those cool sculptural play structures in a sunken play area in the middle, visible from everywhere. Good food, too—no chicken strips. I've got a whole menu—Hawaiian barbecue, yakitori, plus some fun stuff like frozen yogurt balls, glow-in-the-dark lollipops! A family restaurant—but for real foodies. Call it Familia? Or maybe Brat Haus? Or if we want to get really punny, Time Haute?"

Figgy took it all in, wheels turning. She said nothing.

He went on: "I know I've got to figure out staffing and table turnover and insurance, and building out a kitchen can be expensive, and permitting can be a nightmare—"

"Where are you getting startup money?" she said. "With the house loan and your little adventure with Clive, we're not exactly in a position to underwrite a whole new—"

"I'll raise it. I'll put together a plan and go out and sell it—I know how to do that, remember? My dad can help. He's been wanting to. It's about time I called in that chit. Anyway, I'll have to juggle—but I'll keep the days free for you and the kids and work nights. Maybe it's my turn to hustle a little."

Figgy pushed a button on the car door and let in a blast of air. She checked her face in the rearview mirror and smacked her lips together. "You sure you're not running off on another one of your adventures? Remember the book? Or how excited you were about being a full-time—what? Domestic first responder? I have a hard enough time handling success—but seems like you *really* can't handle it."

Alex started to protest, then stopped. "It's just aggravating is all, being home, chasing after the kids, when all anyone is really interested in is what *you're* doing, how you're getting on. I get lonely, aggravated. It's making me into a boring person! You've got people at work, the whole operation at your fingertips, everyone counting on you—I just sometimes wish it was the other way, that we could trade places."

She stretched her legs and leaned back, her posture suddenly exhausted. "So do I."

Wind from outside roared around the interior of the car. Would they ever be done playing the Misery Olympics?

"Don't you see?" she said. "I can't do what I do without you. You make it possible."

Alex got off the freeway and started working his way down Lankershim. The silence in the car deepened. "Thank you," he said. "I like being at home. But I also feel like this restaurant thing might really be what I need. I've been so busy trying to self-actualize that I missed it. Cooking and kids and a big operation with a lot of moving parts—these are the things I'm good at."

He stopped short, suddenly self-conscious of the sales job he was doing. Figgy stayed silent.

"So," he ventured. "What do you think?"

"I think I'm giving up *The Natashas*."

"What? Why?"

"The only way your thing works is if I'm at home more," she said. "I think it's what I've wanted all along. I'm having a *baby* and I've been pretending like nothing would change—but it *has* to. I can still go back to *Tricks* next season, but running a second show is just crazy. I'm tired. It's no way to live. Just 'cause Shonda Rimes does it doesn't mean *I* have to. Fuck it—I'd rather just supervise, let someone else run it, and take Sylvie for a mani-pedi."

She reached over and squeezed his hand. "You're right, Alex— you hustle a little more, I'll hustle a little less. We trade off a little."

Alex looked over at her from over his sunglasses and smiled. He'd been so nervous about announcing his plans, worried that she'd need coaxing and convincing before she got used to the idea. But yet again she was three steps ahead, already working out particulars and determining her own role within it.

After a long silence, she let go of his hand and looked idly out the window. "Just don't call it Familia—pretentious. That lowered play area in the middle? Riff on that. Call it the Pit," she said.

"The Pit?" he said, pulling into the Warner Brothers parking lot, a picture of a wooden sign with THE PIT in bold capital letters forming in his mind's eye. She couldn't help herself; she had to top it. "That's good. The Pit it is."

• • •

While waiting at the registration table, Alex scanned the crowd as the guests milled around the faux New York stoops and sidewalks. Over by the soda fountain, he spotted Huck shoveling a forkful of papaya salad into the mouth of an older woman he vaguely recognized from Pines pickup. Dating in the Pines mommy pool? That would kill Kate—which was probably the point, Alex having heard that divorce proceedings had turned ugly. Nearby, Helen Bamper was restocking the cheese spread with cubes of sweaty cheddar, a walkie-talkie clipped to the waist of her cinched gown.

"Name?"

Alex looked down at a woman with a salt-and-pepper bob, chunky ceramic earrings, and frameless glasses. She tapped a sheet of computer printouts.

"Sherman," he said. Seeing her run her pen up and down the list a few times, he added, "Or it could be under Zicklin? We trade off."

"Oh, of course—Mr. Sherman-Zicklin—hello!" said the woman behind the table, tugging at her nametag. "It's me—Daria? Principal at the Pines. We met when you came in for your comfort recording."

Alex shifted uncomfortably and reached out to shake hands. "Of course—good to see you."

Daria handed over their nametags and then did a fast and breathless breakdown of the evening program—"Inner-city hip hop dancers at nine, flip-book booth open until eleven, tarot and palm readers at the tables in back"—then gave them each an anonymous bidding number for the silent auction. As they were turning to go, Daria stood up and reached across the table and held Alex's forearm.

"I just have to tell you—the recording you did? *Incredible*, really."

"Thanks," he said, the memory of it triggering a cramp in his gut.

He started to pull away, but Figgy stopped short. "What recording?"

"Didn't he *tell* you?" Daria said. "Not to toot my own horn, but the comfort recording *was* my initiative—I'd always hoped a few parents might really *grow* and *learn* from the experience. But your husband—wow! Beyond anything I could've dreamed of. Just transformational. I have to tell you, we've been using it in staff seminars—with your blessing, I'd love to devote a whole breakout session to it at the staff retreat. It's helped us reconnect with what's really *happening* with our Pines fathers. Honestly, I wish my husband was half as reflective and honest as this man here—you're a lucky woman, Mrs. Sherman."

Figgy pursed her lips, her face a mix of pride and confusion. "Thanks?" she said. "But I'm afraid I don't—"

Before she could continue, Helen Bamper burst through the crowd, latched on to Alex's arm and began pulling him toward the buffet tables. "Oh *thank God* you're finally here," she said. "The people from the Test Kitchen are driving me nuts. They say we're out of bruschetta and gluten-free cookies and no one seems to know who's in charge—"

Alex stopped and turned back to Figgy. "You okay without me for a bit?"

"Sure," she said. "I'm fine. Go do your thing."

He squeezed her hand and felt a tingle up his arm. As he followed Helen into the party, he felt an unhealthy charge—not minding at all the feeling of being tugged away from his wife by the impossibly fit Helen Bamper. He followed her through clusters of chatting parents and teachers and into the volunteer and staff area.

The bruschetta situation was quickly worked out, and he'd soon located the missing trays of baked goods and assigned two additional staffers to restock the buffet table. Helen stayed at his side, her panic abating as he quickly extinguished the fires she'd only managed to flap her arms at.

"Thank you, Alex," she said, grabbing a flute of champagne. "I can handle things from here. Go mingle—I'll hunt you down if things get crazy again."

Alex ducked back into the crowd, spotting Figgy huddled with Richard Bamper by the portapotties. He headed in their direction but took a detour to check out the silent auction table, surveying the items up for grabs. Three complete Botox sessions. A body-fat consultation. Two tickets to Vegas to see Celine Dion. So that's why the auction numbers were anonymous.

Close to the far end of the row, he stopped at a clear plexiglass box containing a mounted sculptural head. It was orange-skinned and bug-eyed, pebbled with misshapen warts and softened by a downy coat of silvery fur. A sticker identified it as part of a lizard monster costume used in the remake of a cult sci-fi TV show. Hundreds of bids were being made for the Spectacular Sushi Soiree, the Aspen ski weekend, and the walk-on part on *Mad Men*, but the bid sheet for the monster head was entirely blank.

It was hideous and glorious and totally out of place. Alex knew they had to have it. He pictured it in the living room of the house on Sumter Court, staring down at them from one of the oak bookshelves. He wrote down his number, then moved a nearby basket of Kiehl's to obscure the monster head from view.

He made his way over to the winery tables and drained a cup. As he was standing in line for a plate of chicken satay, he caught sight of Huck. It had been a few weeks since they'd seen each other, and Huck made a fuss, pulling him in for an extended, four-slap man hug. Huck had on a caramel-colored suede coat, pinstripe pants, and a loose linen shirt, his Euro-'74 jet-set vibe undercut only by the giant leather purse he was failing to hide behind his back.

"Nice bag," Alex said.

"Sandra just asked me to hold it while she went to pee."

"Sandra? That her over there?" Alex said, nodding toward a fiftyish woman with kinky hair and a Harari pantsuit, chatting with a group of other women by the dessert table. "What happened to the amazing Sydney?"

"Got old." Huck sighed. "No more spinning instructors or waitresses for me—Sandra's VP of business affairs at Touchstone. Total package. Kid's a senior at the high school—off to Brandeis in the fall. Seriously—I think this one's for good."

"For good, for good?"

"She keeps talking about popping off to Vegas for a quickie ceremony, but I'm in no rush. I've got three more years of alimony coming from Kate. Gotta keep the balance, right?"

Alex smiled and took a slug of wine, trying to reckon what constituted Huck's idea of balance. As long as he kept getting alimony from Katherine, he could remain Sandra's equal partner? He flashed on that night at the Emmys, when Huck had come to his rescue with the roll of gaffer tape. He'd seemed to know everything then, to possess knowledge of the world Alex could never hope to glean.

"Seriously, Huck?" he said. "That's kind of despicable, you

know that?"

Huck just laughed. "You are in no position to judge, friend. How *you* doing anyway? Big anniversary coming up. You keeping your head down?"

Alex shrugged and craned his head over Huck's shoulder, suddenly anxious to extricate himself. "Something like that," he said. "Listen, I better go catch up with the lady."

"We should hang next week," Huck said. "Hit the Gem spa? Hang some dong?"

Alex turned to go. "Pretty crazy right now. Got a lot on my plate. But I'll call you."

He did a circuit around the crowd and ended up back at the silent auction area. The monster head was still hidden behind the gift bag, but on the sign-in sheet he found that another bidder had taken an interest. Number eleven. He frowned, grabbed a pen, and doubled his bid.

He thought he might find Figgy at the tarot card tables and headed over in that direction. Twenty minutes and two more plates of baked goods later, he was back at the monster head. It had happened again. Number eleven wasn't backing down.

He upped his bid again and worked his way back to the wine table, getting ever more tipsy and ever more determined to beat out the mysterious bidder for the thing no one else at the party seemed to want. The fourth time he returned to find a bid from number eleven, just five minutes remained in the auction. He decided to dig in and stand guard. He'd stop the one-upsmanship and face number eleven in person.

Then she appeared, charging forward with a ballpoint pen like a dagger. "Oh God, Alex, you'll never believe what I found!"

"I know," he said.

Then Alex leaned forward and kissed his wife. And took away her pen.

Acknowledgments

My deepest thanks to the friends who read early drafts and offered suggestions: Ali Rushfield, Rick Marin, Jill Soloway, Matt Weiner, Linda Brettler, Joel Stein, Dave Jargowsky, Peter Micelli, Dana Reinhardt, Rhona and John Conte, Dave Jargowsky, Micha Fitzerman-Blue, Jamie Dembo, John Ross-Bowie, Laura Slovin, Tracy Miller, and Bob Schmidt. Nasrin Aboulhosn helped me work out plot and dialogue.

A special thank you to all the experts who schooled me in aspects of the story: Mitch Kamin for sharing his experience in the LA punk scene; Douglas Wilson for an inside look on reality show production; Nate McCall for letting me pick up a shift at McCall's Meat & Fish; Josh Weltman for advice on the business of marketing; Audra Lehman for the tutorial on obstetrics; Renee Mochkatel for her consult on California divorce law; Patti Ruben for the real estate expertise; Mary Yanish for feedback on illustrations; and Robert Russell for the cover design.

A special plus one thank you to Bruce Gilbert, Pete Weiss, Gareth Kanter, Charlie Mars, and John Huck for their coffee-klatch gabbing on mornings when I should've been working. And to all the relatives who read and offered feedback: Jenji Kohan, Rhea Kohan, Buz Kohan, Marti Noxon, Nick & Nicky Noxon, Mary Worthington, and Pam Gruber.

Huge thanks to my agent, Betsy Amster, for her tireless support and expert edit. And to Colleen and Patty at Prospect Park—thank you for your enthusiasm, creativity, and resourcefulness.